I0538961

BOSTON CORPSE

WOL-VRIEY

Burning Bulb

PUBLISHING

Other Books By Wol-vriey:

The Bizarro Story of I

Meat Suitcase

Chainsaw Cop Corpse

Vegan Zombie Apocalypse

Boston Posh (Bud Malone #1)

Vegan Vampire Vaginas

Vagina Mundi

Melanie Nemesis Catchpole

Bizarro 101: A Basic Primer

Novellas and Short Stories By Wol-vriey:

Big Trouble in Little Ass
A novella featured in
Westward Hoes

Forever Ago Sunshine
A short story featured in
The Big Book of Bizarro

BOSTON CORPSE

BUD
MALONE
2

WOL-VRIEY

Burning Bulb
PUBLISHING

Boston Corpse
By **Wol-vriey**

Burning Bulb Publishing
P.O. Box 4721
Bridgeport, WV 26330-4721
United States of America
www.BurningBulbPublishing.com

PUBLISHER'S NOTE: This book is a work of fiction. Names, characters, places, and incidents are either the product of the author's imagination or are used fictitiously, and any resemblance to actual persons, living or dead, events, or locales is purely coincidental.

Copyright © 2015 Burning Bulb Publishing.
All rights reserved.

Cover designed by Gary Lee Vincent.
Author Photo: Lolade Akinsowon © 2014

First Edition.

Paperback Edition ISBN: 978-0692462140

Printed in the United States of America

DEDICATION

To everyone who likes weird fiction.

ACKNOWLEDGMENTS

Thanks to Gary and Rich at Burning Bulb Publishing, Gary's wife Carla (for her input concerning the cover), my wife Victoria (for her input on me), and everyone else everywhere who's ever supported my writing.

Peace, Everyone!
Wol-vriey.
6/4/2015

PRELUDE: 2036 A.D.

Sara Fischer was now President of the USA.

The Forks—the cutlery kitchen gods who'd reduced the Earth to ruins—considering Sara the closest link to the last elected US president Jefferson Lincoln (being his childhood sweetheart), had spirited her away to Washington D.C. and installed her in the new White House . . . one constructed from human bones.

To everyone's immense relief, the Forks had taken the dragons with them to D.C.

All the dragons, including Bud Malone's girlfriend, Posh Lane.

It had been a sad parting between Posh and Malone, but one both agreed was for the best.

For one thing, it gave Posh a career in politics. Posh—still a porcelain dragon—was now US Secretary of State.

On assurance from the Forks that the dragons wouldn't return, the Boston Grid had been dismantled.

Life had returned to a surreal, uneasy normal.

There were no longer dinosaurs in the city either. (For the most part, the one-time Jurassic terrors had now learned to fear man again.) The T-Rexs and apatosaurs and raptors had all migrated west, deep into the Massachusetts forests.

The Beetles too. It was a common occurrence to find one laying a skyscraper out towards Mount Greylock.

***

In the greatest display of their power anyone on Earth had yet seen (and one which set the seal on a worldwide policy of 'cooperative/collaborative non-resistance with Ferramenta Sapiens') the Forks had repaired/reversed a lot of the damage they'd done, effortlessly restoring most dragon-ravaged human towns and cities back to their pre-takeover condition, even rebuilding collapsed skyscrapers in the blinking of an eye.

Needless to say, after this, no one planned on messing with them anymore.

What the Kitchen Gods wanted? No one really knew. There was a school of thought which believed that the Forks themselves had no idea what they wanted, that they simply *were* and *did*, because after having somehow attained divinity, their unbelievable powers demanded of them that they be exercised.

So the Forks fixed most things that wouldn't someday become a nuisance to them.

(Now there were lots of empty houses around the country, many occupied by creatures better left to the imagination.)

And life went on. The population of the USA, for instance, was still only a thirtieth of what it had been before the Forks fucked existence up, but life went on.

But the ODs—the Otherworld Doors—were still everywhere. These space-time portals had already let a lot of weird stuff into Boston and were pumping yet more in everyday.

And then there was the big matter of the Forks opening up The Groad.

The Groad was part of Hell. The Bizarro-fucked-up, completely incredibly warped part of Hell. And one of The Groad's primary access ways (and some believed a large chunk of the infernal warpspace as well) lay right under Boston, MA.

***

It was against this background that Lucy Tang arrived back in Boston.

Lucy, once casino owner Sookie Ling's most gorgeous drag queen, now had a vendetta with her former employer—a debt that could only be settled in blood. Sookie's blood.

There was also the issue of who controlled Boston's lucrative dragonreich trade to resolve between the two women.

Thus the stage was set for bloodshed and carnage.

2

CHAPTER 1

Malone

A warm mid-June morning.

Bud Malone rifled through the files spread out over his desk. He selected one and began reading it. It wasn't as interesting as he remembered. He dropped it and picked up another.

With nothing doing at the moment, Malone was reviewing old cases to kill time.

While reading the current file, Malone whistled with memory. The file concerned Thomas Palmer, a USAcme (previously Grid-Omni) salesman who, two years ago, had mysteriously vanished. Nothing really strange about that (back then the dinos and dragons had routinely eaten loads of people), but Tom Palmer had been charged with marketing an experimental vacuum cleaner prototype.

Though according to his bosses he'd not been in the know, the vacuum cleaner Tom had been told to sell door-to-door (while supposedly for cleaning up rat droppings for rich housewives) was actually a protective device being beta-tested to combat the dinosaur menace. Once placed in a house, the device broadcast sonic waves on a frequency dinos (particularly raptors and pterodactyls, both of which were notorious for breaking into residences and eating their inhabitants) found extremely uncomfortable.

It would have been an almost perfect deterrent. But then, Tom, carrying the first batch, had gone missing . . .

Malone stopped reading for a moment. Leaning back in his office chair while fanning himself with the sheaf of papers, he regarded the world outside his sixth-floor Milk Street office window. The colors of Boston evening; the sky streaks of morbid gray across an orange background as (invisible to his right) the sun fell out of view. The little blue that remained grayed as he watched.

The atmosphere of daylight being ostracized affected Malone. He dropped the Palmer case file, rose, and crossed to the window. Fingertips on the cold glass, he regarded downtown.

The most obvious difference now was the lack of The Grid, and the people everywhere walking about heedless of the darkening sky, their blithe unconcern inconceivable in the recent past.

Now that the dragons had left Boston, the wiven shield that once protected the city's lower levels from their aerial attack was being recycled to make antigravity cars. Malone watched several of the new wheelless vehicles float left and right between normal cars.

He grinned; it was great to not fear being outside one's house again. Okay, so it was different—occasionally he missed the excitement of those days, the adrenalin rush of moment-to-moment uncertainty—but there were new dangers to be wary of, new alleys of horror to navigate with caution. New investigations for a mystery-addicted private eye . . .

Eyes still watching the city, his mind returned to the Palmer case. USAcme had suspected industrial espionage, that Tom had either been abducted by a competitor, or, on somehow discovering what he'd actually been charged with selling, had absconded with the devices. Both worries were realistic ones.

USAcme had paid Malone a lot of money to find Tom.

His investigation ended abruptly two days later: A tip gleaned from Mei Ling, a waitress at his local watering hole, had ironically led Malone back here to Milk Street, where Mrs. Finley, a neighbor of his, had described seeing Tom's gunmetal-gray Ford Camaro vanish through a thick cloud of green smoke that had suddenly appeared in the middle of the road.

That was that then. Case closed. One more person lost to the ODs—the Otherworld Doors.

Malone sighed. Lots of people had vanished that way back then—by being in the wrong place at the wrong time. Lots of people still went missing that way—opened the wrong door or touched the wrong wall . . . and were never heard from again. He'd himself lost several close friends . . .

Feeling like he'd shortly fall depressed, he returned his attentions outside of his mind.

The sky was a bright orange now, with, far off to the west, the vanished sun glowing like dimmed movie lighting. Utterly resplendent. Directly facing him south gleamed the mirror-walled towers and golden domes of the Golden Dragon Casino. Left/east of the casino rippled the blue waters of the Fort Point Channel.

Watching light dance across the casino buildings, Malone laughed. Ah, Sookie Ling had made a genius investment there, what with Las Vegas still out of commission. *Not for me such places, though,* he thought. *I haven't worked my ass off for a decade as a PI—getting shot up, blown up, gutted and eaten—just to lose everything I earned in ten minutes betting on a roulette wheel. Now that'd really be playing Russian roulette—death wish without the bullets. The idle rich can have their high-stakes games.*

After slaving for ages, Malone was comfortable now. He had enough money banked to live well for the foreseeable future; several good investments too. He felt lucky—his financial security had come just as the country was becoming settled again (and fortunately, just as his youthful energies were fading). His financial advisers assured him things would only get better.

Now Malone only played detective intermittently, when the case either interested him, or the client was paying enough to make it interest him.

Oops. Malone suddenly recalled he had a date this evening at *Umbria* (an Italian seafood place on Franklin Street) with Ann Calloway, a pretty USAcme receptionist.

Their date was for seven. He checked his watch: six-fifteen.

Malone's apartment was on the floor above, directly over his office. He climbed the connecting stairs to have a piss and freshen up.

***

After washing his hands and splashing his face with water, Malone regarded himself in the mirror. It was odd: though he saw himself this way every day, he many times still had difficulty recognizing his fortyish reflection—the dark hair and eyes, the lined but still handsome face, the calm mouth—all seemed part of someone he had a future appointment to become, a person he wasn't yet ready to be. *I'm getting old,* he thought. *I look way older than I should—this damn PI job's caught up with me.*

He wasn't fat, showed not even the ghost of double chin or paunch. He was very pleased about that; was still in good physical condition too. He felt one of his arms. No flab at all, all was muscle. He wasn't a slob—he knew women appreciated that he took care of himself.

He ran his right hand through his hair, then examined it, turning it around and studying it as if in disbelief. *Flesh and blood.* He felt embarrassed to be excited by something so mundane. *Screw that— I'm normal again.* After living for seven years with a body altered by the Forks, now he *was* normal. It felt good to be ordinary.

He recalled his last discussion with the Forks before they'd all departed for Washington D.C.:

"Hey!—I thought you said you couldn't fix me? You said I'd be stuck like this."

"We worked out how," came the amused tinkling reply.

Next, he'd yowled. It had felt like a million pinpricks all over his body, and his strange red right arm (which the Forks had always claimed was formed from his blood) had shrunk back into his shoulder, after which a normal arm had grown out in its place. The whole transformation took three minutes. The Forks had next vanished, along with the past.

The past really is just a dream, Malone thought, combing his hair. He grinned at his reflection. *Looking at me now, who'd ever believe I once had a porcelain dragon for a girlfriend? Hell, even I hardly believe it!*

The memory sobered him. Yes, Posh had been gone a year now. In the interim period he'd met some really nice women and had some bedroom fun—several one-night-stands and a couple of longer relationships. But nothing had lasted, he'd never emotionally clicked with anyone.

Maybe it was because he was getting older, but Malone felt it was really time for a serious relationship again. One that would keep. He felt the emotional void growing like it sought to consume him in loneliness. No doubt about it—he needed a woman to love.

He grinned. Maybe, just maybe . . . Ann, his date of this evening, would prove the one. She was cute, built just the way he liked his women. Fingers crossed on this one then.

He checked his watch again. Six-thirty. Time to get a move on. He strapped on his blaster and left the apartment.

CHAPTER 2

Sookie

A quarter-mile south of Malone, in the penthouse suite of the Golden Dragon Hotel (a forty-story high rise she preferred to called her 'High Tower'), Sookie Ling, Queenpin of the Boston criminal underworld, sat with legs crossed, staring dreamily out of her wide floor-to-ceiling penthouse window at the darkening sky.

Her gaze rolled slowly over the complexes that formed her Golden Dragon Casino, the hub of her empire. (And Sookie fancied herself an empress, like the grand dowagers of ancient China.) Her green eyes crawled up each building like lizards, focused on their glittering glass walls and windows like each was a mirror reflecting her. And in a way they did—each building reflected her success.

(Situated right opposite Chinatown Park, and occupying most of the former Leather District, the Golden Dragon Casino filled the rectangle enclosed by Essex and Kneeland Streets north and south respectively, Purchase Street to the west, and Atlantic Avenue on the east. The casino's being adjacent to South Station was great for those gamblers who didn't wish to fly into Boston.)

Sookie Ling smiled. She could afford to smile. From humble beginnings as a prostitute when she'd first arrived in America, she'd come a long, long way.

"I come very long way," she said softly into the apartment's incense-perfumed air. (In the fifteen years she'd lived in Boston, Sookie's English had never gotten off the ground. She'd never given it a chance to: Initially she'd been too busy giving cheap blowjobs to make ends meet [her mouth too regularly full of American penises to practice correct speaking], then, when she'd become a madam with her own thriving brothel, she'd discovered her clients liked the exotic erotic delights her Chinglish seemingly promised them, at which point she'd decided "hell with learn speak well" and taken pride thenceforth in her mangling of the English tongue.)

Sookie was middle-aged. She was smallish, with long hair and a thin hawkish face. Her lips, however, were plump like they'd been inflated with collagen. Her eyes . . .

Due to Sookie's addiction to the drug dragonreich, her eyes were completely green, fluorescent ovals with no whites at all, nor pupils. (Except when with close friends or if she felt like creeping someone out, she kept them hidden behind shades.)

Sookie picked up a vial of the drug—iridescent sprinkles— rotated it in the light. The crystals glittered like dragonfly wings. (Her glossy six-inch-long 'dragon lady' fingernails formed an emerald kaleidoscope with the reich.) Dragonreich did weird things to its users—every addict's body altered after a time. Some alterations were subtle, other not so. Some users grew tails; some developed superpowers.

Sookie opened her kimono and examined her breasts and belly. Both were now completely covered with patterned yellow scales like a snake's.

Am I become dragon someday? she wondered, then decided it didn't matter. What did was how she felt great. Better than ever.

She spilled a large heap of 'reich' into her palm and snorted it. She sat back in her armchair, delighting as the rush hit her like a boxer's punches, like the best orgasm ever (ironic, as the drug had completely killed her libido—she'd not come once in ten years). She luxuriated in the feeling, knowing her already fluorescent eyes now glowed like lamps.

The initial surge of transcendent feeling waned. Sookie staggered up out of her chair, shrugged off her kimono, walked nude to the window. Between her swaying fleshly buttocks, brown tentacles waved—another reich side effect.

***

Sookie stared southward across the labyrinthine sprawl of gambling halls. Beyond them, its view blocked off by the restaurant complex, was an estate of rental cottages for those casino clients who wanted seclusion, accommodations for rich patrons who desired more privacy than even a luxury suite offered.

A big dragonreich deal was going down right about now in one of those secluded cottages. A group of anonymous buyers from Springfield had ordered a massive reich shipment—uncut. They'd be paying cash too, trucking twenty million dollars in-town.

Sookie laughed. Oh, this modern world was resplendent with ironies. She owned a casino (the perfect money laundering front) but for possibly the first time in US history, there was no need to clean up or hide her illegal earnings—there was no longer any IRS to hide her profits from! To make matters worse/better, it wasn't even illegal to sell dragonreich! She laughed louder, then frowned. *Not yet least; hope not long while! Old Sara Fischer have too much work do in White House. Human bones haunt evenings. Angry ghosts haunt cabinet! At least another year, then President remember harass innocent drug dealer.* Then the dragonreich in her system drowned such minor ill humor. Giggling, she made her way across to her desk, picked up her cell phone. Dialed.

"Hey, Stan? Boss Sookie here. . . . How going? . . . They arriving now? . . . Good. . . . Cash front or nothing, dig?"

Satisfied, Sookie hung up the phone. Twenty million additional dollars would shortly be hers. She stared once more out of the window, then retrieved her kimono from the floor. It looked to be a good evening. She'd have some dinner then head for the Casino; there were always friends to meet; girls/guys to arrange for the high rollers. May even some kinky fun for herself. It had been a while since she'd seen a flesh show.

True, Sookie Ling didn't fuck anymore, but she still enjoyed watching others do it.

CHAPTER 3

Stan

The huge drug deal was going down in private Chalet 19.

As well as being out of view of Sookie's penthouse, the cottage was obscured by elms, making it the perfect rendezvous point. On this street there were six cottages, each one deeply recessed off from the access road; ships of seclusion adrift on oceans of privacy.

Two cars were parked in Chalet 19's driveway. In one sat a darkly handsome, mustached young man, Bruce Reed. Close scrutiny of his face revealed a slight nervousness.

An older, Chinese man in a long black coat guarded the front door. Li Hu's eyes were alert as a startled snakes, flicking to every motion of tree shadows, leaping over the fence as a solitary car drove past the house. His finger rested steady on the trigger of the machine pistol under his coat. No one was getting inside the chalet. No one except those now transacting business inside it and the pretty Chinese maid who'd earlier cleaned it.

Inside Chalet 19, five men faced themselves across the living room coffee table. An air conditioner kept the evening temperature down.

The Harris Boys were the buyers. Mark and Jesse Harris weren't related in any way—they just shared the same surname. Mark was tall, dark, and skinny; Jesse, blonde and stocky. Neither man was handsome; both had cold eyes that marked them as killers. Both wore expensive three piece suits. Beside each of the Harrises stood a massive wheeled suitcase stuffed full of money.

Opposite the pair sat Sookie's men, led by Stan McCaulkin. Stan was big—six-feet-four and rippling with muscle. A onetime NFL linebacker. He was in his fifties and good-looking, with sky-blue eyes. In contrast to the Harris's formal dressing, Stan looked like a biker—denim pants, leather jacket, bandanna, metal-tipped boots. Thick graying beard; long hair done up in a ponytail. Designer shades hung from a jacket pocket.

Stan was Sookie's right-hand man . . . and her number one enforcer. Loyal to the core of his black soul. Absolutely *no one* fucked with him. (By Stan's legs stood a smaller rollalong suitcase; this one contained twenty million dollars' worth of uncut dragonreich.)

Stan's companions were Roddy and Wu Jun, reliable foot soldiers here for backup, and to move the money afterwards. Each man carried a riot shotgun, sat well back from their boss, and kept a poker face.

Stan and the Harris Boys sized each other up for a while. The atmosphere in the living room was tense, but not overmuch so. It was a new connection, with the usual suspicion. So far, however, the Harris Boys seemed legit. And when someone bought twenty million worth of reich from you for starts, there was certainly more big dealing where that came from. So . . .

"So, guys, welcome to Dr. Sookie's clinic," Stan said finally, a cold grin on his handsome old face. He spoke with a slight southern drawl. "You got our money, we got your medicine. Let's deal."

"Lovely joint this is," Mark Harris replied. "If I was rich, I'd enjoy losing my hard-earned cash here too."

"We try to please, gentlemen."

Jesse said, "You should fire your interior decorator, though. The bitch or her son has no taste at all. What sort of horrid pink paint is that on the ceiling?"

Stan looked up, then winced. "Yeah," he agreed with distaste. "Looks like total shite." Then he grinned afresh. "What can I say? Hey, the boss lady's Asian—she likes 'temple vibe' stuff." He tapped the drug suitcase. "Guys, the night's young. Let's hurry this over with—it's a straight count-out and we're done here." He gestured back at his companions. "Then the boys will stay here keeping the dope safe while I give you two a guided tour of the complex. Sookie's laying it on big for you fellas tonight— everything on the house. And I mean fucking everything." He leered through his beard. "If you like *fucking* that is. We've got us some ladies of the night like you'd not believe. Elite ten-thousand-bucks-a-night pussy! Believe me, it ain't just the gambling that keeps bringing those rich cats to Boston."

The Harris Boys laughed. Jesse pulled his suitcase towards him. "Better count mine fir—"

Stan interrupted him with a raised hand. "Wait."

Jesses stared a question at him.

"Something's wrong," Stan said. "Something's definitely wrong here. Gotta put my finger on it."

At those words, his companions rose from their seats and pointed their shotguns at the Harrises.

Stan waved them off. "Nah, put the damn guns down, you idiots. It ain't them. They're here to deal, right? We've seen the money in their cases, we just need to count it—you know how anal Sookie is about fucking accounting."

"You worried 'bout Robopol?" Mark asked, looking worried himself. "Madam Sookie assured us that . . ."

Stan, face creased up in concentration, waved the statement off. "Forget the damn cops. They don't come here—"

"We saw some when we passed the casino."

"Forget 'em. Those robos are there to make the clients feel safe, remember some of them are carrying millions of bucks. So having a robot cop or two on the premises dissuades thieves. But reich dealing? Nada. Golden Dragon Casino brings more money into Boston than anything else does. Even the dino-meat exporters don't run close. Sookie also pays forty percent of profits as taxes—she's mega smart like that—so the city won't fuck with her operation for anything. And remember, it ain't illegal to sell reich. No, the cops won't come over this way even if there's a gunfight." He scratched his gray-streaked beard. "Yeah, something's wrong; but I can't put my . . ." He froze like a rabbit that smelled danger, looked back over his shoulder. "Roddy, where'd the maid go?"

"Which maid?"

"The one Joyce sent over to clean this place up. I saw her here earlier—tall Chinese girl, pretty, with big breasts."

"She must've left."

Stan got out of his seat. "Where? How? She *can't* have left. We arrived half an hour after she did."

"Shit!" Roddy said. "You think . . . ?"

"I don't know," Stan said with deadly calm. "Hold on a bit." He pulled out his cellphone, made a call. "Joyce, it's Stan. . . . The girl you sent to clean '19,' she reported back yet? . . . No?"

He hung up, stared at the Harris Boys. "I'm not liking this." He gestured to Roddy. "You and Wu, check the house."

The pair departed in haste out the living room doors.

Mark Harris said, "I don't get it. You say yourself it's a secure operation; what harm can one missing girl do?"

Before replying, Stan glanced up at the pink ceiling like he was praying. He winced. Considered alongside the living room's lemon walls, it was an utterly atrocious color. Sookie must have handpicked it.

Then, whispering like they might be overheard, he said, "There's a rival gang in town who keep trying to muscle in on Sookie's biz."

"Jacobi?"

Stan nodded. "Yeah. Jacobi's a persistent asshole, doesn't know when he's good and beat. Sookie could easily run him out of town, but she doesn't. She likes their cat-and-mouse game, says it keeps her instincts sharp." He winced. "Me? I fucking hate it. Even my ulcers are getting ulcers now."

Mark and Jesse nodded grimly. Mark scratched his nose. "You think the cleaner was a spy, then?"

"Right. I'm bothered they might try to ambush us. The cops won't come this way even if World War IV starts—damn robots completely lack initiative—"

"She ain't here," Roddy said, bursting back into the room.

"We found her clothes," Wu added, holding up a cleaner's uniform and sneakers. "But all the doors are locked." Both underlings looked perplexed.

Stan turned back to the Harris Boys. "Like I suspected: the bitch was spying for Jacobi. She's long gone now."

Mark and Jesse frowned, their mouths unpleasant slits in their ugly faces. "We call off the deal then? Come back later? Guys back home won't like that though; we wanna monopolize the corridor west to Ohio before someone else gets the idea."

Stan guffawed. "Call it off? For a minor inconvenience like that Jacobi punk? Fuck 'im. You're already here—we're still dealing. Besides, it'll be a hell of a long ride back to Springfield for you guys now Jacobi knows you've twenty million bucks in the trunk of your car. We don't panic. Once we're done here counting the cash, I'll have more guys sent over to keep your stuff safe. Matter of fact I'd best do it now." He raised his phone to dial again.

"Wait."

Stan paused, hairy index finger hovering over the '4' on the touchscreen. "Yeah?" Behind him, Roddy and Wu Jun stood like statues, like they'd been paused too.

"The cleaner hasn't left the building," Mark Harris said softly. "She's still in here."

Stan gaped at them. "What you guys talking 'bout?" Unease surged through him, however, on seeing both his visitors grinning as at a private joke. "Oh shit—you're making Elvis gags?"

"He's right," Jesse Harris said. "You've nothing to fear from Dave Jacobi."

"Guys," Stan said softly, dropping his Nokia on his chair and sweeping the hand down to his waist for his gun. "Can you please explain better?"

Laughing, both Harrises pointed up at the pink ceiling. "Behold the cleaning woman!"

***

Stan gaped upward. The ceiling was rippling in pink waves, like it was covered with unhappy skin.

He looked back down at the Harris Boys. Both grinned back at him. Stan's blue eyes were scared now. His gun shifted back and forth, first pointing at one ugly amused face then the other. "What the hell is this shit?" His raspy voice was tight, fear warring with his courage. Above them all, the ceiling now undulated in furious waves.

"We just told you," Jesse Harris said, laughing. "It's the missing chambermaid."

Stan got ahold of his nerves again. Whatever lived could die. He looked around at Roddy and Wu Jun, both of whom stood with their guns pointed at the ceiling. "What the fuck are you sons-a-bitches dallying over? Shoot the damn thing!"

Neither Roddy nor Wu got off shots, however. Both Harris Boys suddenly burst into motion, dashing past Stan at ridiculous, impossible speeds. Next thing, loud screams and horrible slobbering and splashing sounds issued from behind him.

Stan spun around, poised to shoot. His finger froze on the trigger in disbelief. He felt like someone had dripped him in liquid nitrogen. The Harris Boys had vanished. In their place, two monsters—mutants—stood ripping Roddy and Wu to bits. Both men had already been decapitated—their severed heads rolled across the bloodied rug—with blood spurting everywhere.

The monsters that had killed them were identical—wet pink masses that flopped with tentacles. Each had a bulbous head with a single purple eye over a huge bloody mouth. The monster on Stan's left had Roddy's headless neck completely in its mouth and was drinking from it, making horrid swallowing sounds as it drained him like a cup.

The other monster was pulling Wu's limbs off and flinging them everywhere.

A severed leg whizzed towards Stan. Cursing, he flung himself to the floor, then quickly rolled over. Lying on his back, he was staring up at the rippling ceiling. He almost wet himself in fear— the damn thing was blinking down at him with brown eyes the size of basketballs. The creature itself looked like a pink sheet with glass shards stuck in it. It now practically hung all the way off the ceiling, its wet pink flesh looped in shivering ruffles.

Stan got a grip of himself. *That thing fucking looks about to drop; what's it waiting for?*

A chunk of bloody meat flew over him. He spat. Down there on the rug (he was between coffee table and armchair), most of his view of the monsters eating his men was blocked. He looked under the chair, saw Roddy's legs dangling as the monster kept drinking the blood out of him; saw Wu's limbless torso with a slimy mass of tentacles slobbering over it; saw the blood-soaked carpet. He shivered like he had a fever. He regarded his gun, considered shooting the creatures through the chair, then abandoned the thought as suicidal. *The ex-Harris-monsters seem happy enough with Roddy and Wu's corpses, why the fuck should I remind them I'm here too? Best I get the hell out of here while I can. And I'd better alert Sookie to send over the cavalry. Now where the fuck is my phone?*

He remembered he'd dropped it on his chair. About reaching up for it, he noticed the sheet-creature on the ceiling freeze its motion. It took him a few moments to work out what was going on: with him down here like this, wedged between the furniture, the pink sheet wouldn't be able to smother him if it dropped like he guessed was its intent. But if he lifted part of his body out of concealment...

Shit! Stan thought, sweating bullets. *I'm fucking trapped down here. How the hell am I gonna get out of this?* Conscious of time fast running out—at any moment, the Harris-monsters could tire of the corpses and attack him—he looked across the room for an escape route.

Above him, the monster on the ceiling had opened a mouth full of glassy teeth and was dripping thick saliva down on him.

The front door was well to his right; he'd have to pass the monsters.

Facing his feet was a corridor. Reaching it, however, meant coming out of concealment for two yards, more than enough distance for the ceiling monster to snare him.

Noticing the direction of his gaze (and clearly anticipating him to try and escape that way) the creature now opened another mouth (one even larger than the first) just over that exit.

Stan winced; then he winced again. The slobbering feeding sounds coming from the two monsters had abruptly stopped. Next, he heard wet, squishy footsteps heading his way.

Oh shit! he realized. *They're coming for me!*

There was a horrible moment when the monsters stood beside the chairs staring down at Stan, while he got his first proper look at them. Covered in blood, both creatures looked even more disgusting than before.

"Sorry, man," one of the Harris-monsters grunted in an approximation of a human voice, "but you fucking die too now." Stan saw it had no arms, just sixteen fat tentacles depending from its torso. Blood ran off the tentacles, the crimson mingling with its slime, pooling on the floor. Like it agreed with the prophecy of Stan's death, the dangling ceiling creature rippled like a sail billowed by wind.

The other monster swiped a tentacle over its bloodstained head, blinked its huge violet eye. "Jesse's right. We think you're cool, but business is bus—"

"Screw you two ugly motherfuckers!" Stan raised his gun, ready to go out fighting.

The monsters bent towards him. He wondered how he wasn't shitting himself. He aimed for the nearer monster's eye; that should stop the bastard . . .

Then the front door opened and Li Hu, the sentry, peered in.

"Hey, Stan, you guys okay? Sounded quiet in here. I went to have a piss round the side of the house and . . . Hey! What the—"

Before he completed the question, the Harris-monsters had swarmed over him.

Stan paid no attention to either Li Hu's horrible cries or the slobbering feeding and drinking sounds that accompanied them. He'd noticed that the creature on the ceiling was no longer watching him; its gaze had swiveled to regard the new arrival.

He leapt up and dashed for the hallway door. Almost there, he saw the pink sheet falling towards him, a gaping maw of teeth yawning at him. He dove under it, losing his gun in the process when his hand slammed hard against the door frame.

He forgot the weapon, leapt to his feet and ran.

The rear door was locked. *Oh fuck, where's the fucking key?*

No key though. Stan dashed back down the hallway and ducked through the nearest door. Realizing its key was on the outside, he reached out, pulled it from the keyhole, locked the door from the inside, then looked around.

Shit, I've locked myself in the storeroom! If they come looking!

He calmed somewhat, felt around in the dimness till his hands touched loose wood. It was an axe, big and sharp. Well, if he couldn't escape, he had something to fight with. He'd take at least one of those Harris bastards along with him before dying.

Okay, now calm down. First things first. I gotta alert Sookie that . . . Shit—my phone's out there. She-it! That's twenty million bucks gone!

He waited for someone to break down the door, so he could bury his ax in the motherfucker's head. And while waiting, his graying ponytail caked with cobwebs, he pondered worriedly:

Okay, now mutants I've seen before, but what the hell was that fucking thing on the ceiling?

***

In the living room, the sheet of pink flesh that had dropped from the ceiling slowly slid sideways off the furniture onto the floor and compacted itself into the form of a naked, beautiful Chinese transsexual woman.

"Damn, this feels good," Lucy Tang said, once in human form again. "I've waited forever for this moment when I'd be able to stick it to Sookie."

Mark Harris (also in human form again though his clothes were in shreds) peered in through the hallway door.

"Stan's locked himself in the broom closet, want me to shoot his ass through the door?"

Lucy caressed her breasts. "Leave him. His phone's here so he can't alert anyone. And I doubt he's stupid enough to come out of there." She pointed down at her penis, which was stiffening. "Get Bruce in here. I need a blowjob."

Jesse Harris, also now his ugly human self again, shook his head. "Uh uh, mamasan; not here and now. We take the money and scram."

Mark nodded, "Jesse's right, Lucy. We ain't got time for that." He gestured at the mess they'd made of Sookie's three men. "We're lucky we got them all before they could shoot, but we need to get the hell out of here before someone comes checking." He pointed to Stan's phone. "Or before Sookie calls."

Lucy Tang scowled, then tapped her semi-erect member. "Oh alright, but you know how reich gets me all horny." She frowned. "Get Bruce in here anyway. You guys load up the car again; I've got to write a note."

While the Harris Boys and her boyfriend moved the cash and drugs out into their car, Lucy Tang composed her note. She took her time doing it, occasionally stroking her erection as if it was her copy editor.

Once done writing, she walked out to the broom closet where Stan was hiding, and tapped on the door.

"Hey, asshole! I fucking know you're in there, okay, so no need to pretend. Now listen. I'm pinning a note to this fucking door. You give it to Sookie for me. Tell her Lucy Tang's back in town, and I'm out for her blood. Okay? Rap on this door thrice if you understand me. If you don't, I'll get a shotgun and educate you better."

She waited. Three loud raps came from Stan's side of the door.

Lucy Tang smiled coldly. She pinned the note to the closet door, and walked off, buttocks swaying, planning what she'd do to Bruce once she got his ass in bed tonight. Her stiff penis poked the air ahead of her like a compass needle showing her the way.

CHAPTER 4

Malone

Malone smiled across the dinner table at *Umbria*.

Hiding a blush, Ann Calloway smiled back.

Ann Calloway was a small, polished brunette. Red lips, blue eye shadow. She oozed sophistication as she sipped her wine. Her blue dress emphasized her curves. In the subdued restaurant lighting, Malone found her breathtaking.

Malone was pleased; so far the night was shaping up very nicely. Ann was proving everything he'd hoped she'd be when their eyes had first locked across her office desk: a calm, cool, and collected confident career woman. Best of all, she seemed as interested in him as vice versa, kept giving him coy suggestive glances.

Ann lowered her empty wineglass. "I moved up here three months ago," she said. "I used to live down in Arizona." Her voice was soft, like a sad sprite in the restaurant candlelight.

Malone grinned. "For real? You don't have even the ghost of a southern accent. If anything, you sound more urban than me."

She laughed, flashing pearly teeth. "That's because I grew up in NYC; lived there for twenty-two years. My sister and I fled south when the dragon and dinosaur trouble started. Our Uncle Jackson owned a ranch near the Phoenix Sonoran Desert Preserve, right by Skunk Creek—safest place we knew to go." She giggled demurely. "Only place we knew to go."

"What was it like—living there during the crisis?"

She pursed her pretty lips a moment before replying. "Weird, is the only correct way to describe it. I mean, we hardly ever saw any dragons. The ranch was appropriately named the 'Happy Hidden.' When we did see dragons, they were mere specks in the distant sky, like floating diamonds—Uncle Jackson said they were headed east to Florida—and Claire and I never saw a single dinosaur at all in all the time we spent on the ranch. So it was really odd, you know, hearing from people fleeing New Mexico or Texas for instance, the horror stories that everything was utter carnage back there."

She paused again. Malone refilled her glass. The splash and tinkle of the straw-yellow Critone as it filled the glass was echoed by similar liquid sounds across the dining room, blending in with its ambience—soft background music, the clatter of forks, spoons, and knives on expensive china, the laughter of other diners, a woman gasping in surprise, a waiter's explanation . . .

"What I was about saying," Ann went on, "is that, even though we'd both seen the dinosaurs eating everyone here up north, once we'd been living on the ranch awhile, everything that had previously happened now seemed like a dream to us. It was even possible to convince ourselves that the occasional passing dragon was some kind of transparent airplane. It was only when people passed through—the West Carefree Highway ran right by our place—that we had reminders of what the rest of the USA was like." She raised her glass. "A toast . . . to survival."

Malone raised his glass. "Oh, lady, I'll drink to that."

They drank silently awhile, playing eye games with each other, studying one another. Around them the dining room buzzed.

Malone checked his watch. "I wonder what's happened to our dinner? It shouldn't take them this long to prepare lobster, even if they have to go fish for it."

A giggle. "Don't worry, I'm enjoying the wait." She reached across the table, stroked his hand with soft fingers.

Malone hid a smile. *Yes, she's definitely the woman I want! After all this time—*

"Hello," a low male voice interrupted his thoughts. "Ann? It is Ann, isn't it? Ann Calloway?"

The voice had come from behind Malone. Looking up to see who'd spoken, his eyes caught the flicker of delight in Ann's eyes as her startled confusion became recognition. *Damn!* he thought. *She's not looked at me like that all evening.*

"Bobby? Bobby Richman? Oh, my God! Oh, my God! Oh, my God! Oh, my God! Oh, my God!!!" With cheerleader-like agility, Ann Calloway leapt out of her seat and into the man's arms.

Malone pushed his chair back from the table and watched. He couldn't believe what was happening.

Bobby Richman was youngish, tall, dark, and handsome. He looked rich, rich, rich. That in itself wouldn't have been so bad, but Ann—Malone's date—was kissing Bobby! She had him in a tight liplock like she'd suffocate him, like she wanted him to realize she was the air he needed to breathe. And Bobby . . . Bobby was kissing her back with equal fervency.

Oops, Malone thought. *Life just screwed me over again.*

The kissing couple came up for air. Bobby held Ann at arm's length. Seeing the adoring look in Ann's eyes, Malone felt like he'd been punched in the gut. A deadened feeling spread through his limbs. It was all there in Ann's eyes, all the love he was planning to get from her, and it was directed at someone else.

"Oh Bobby," Ann was saying, tears on her cheeks. "I've missed you so, so, so, so, so, so much. I never thought I'd ever see you again!"

Bobby Richman pulled her close to his breast. "Darling, I looked all over New York for you, then Angie . . . Angie Davies said you and Claire had travelled south; only she wasn't sure where. I called and called and called."

"We lost our phones that very first day. It was Claire's damn fault. She forgot them on—"

"Then the phones stopped working anyway."

"Oh, honey! I can't believe it's you!"

They began kissing again.

Malone was aware that other diners in *Umbria* were staring at him curiously. Some of the women had looks of intense pity on their faces. Still, Malone couldn't help but be impressed: Ann and Bobby were so engrossed in each other that they'd clearly forgotten his presence. He coughed politely, then louder. They still ignored him.

He got up, tapped Bobby on the shoulder. Once, twice . . . then a very hard third time.

Bobby finally separated from Ann. He looked at Malone, really noticing him for the first time. A hint of anger clouded his handsome face. "What's your bug, man? I'm just seeing my baby for the first time in ten years. I thought she was dead."

Ann nodded fervently at Malone, her face flushed like she wanted Bobby to start making love to her there and then on the floor. "It was just two weeks to our wedding when the dragons struck. I'd gone to Jersey with my sister to get my gown refitted, and I never saw him again. Oh, I just never imagined . . ."

Malone felt sickened by Ann's wet-vagina voice. He filtered her noise out, stared coldly at Bobby's face. Then suddenly, he deflated, his anger leaking away like pus from a septic wound.

Bobby was swelling in his dinner jacket, like he didn't mind fighting Malone. Malone was immensely amused. Despite Bobby being several inches taller than himself, the kid was no match whatsoever. Okay, except in Ann's besotted mind. Malone knew he'd kick Bobby's ass halfway down to the Panama Canal and back again.

"Yeah, man, what can I do for you?" Bobby repeated, his voice now holding a warning blend of machismo and anger. The look in his eyes clearly said he felt his territorial integrity was being compromised here. A fistfight over Ann wasn't too far off.

Malone smiled benignly at Bobby, pointed to his vacated chair. "I just thought you might like to sit down. You two sound like you've a lot of catching up to do." He grinned. "No need to worry about me—Ann and I will finish our business discussion some other time."

He nodded to the elated Ann, gestured to her seat, "You too, dear," then looked at Bobby again. "We ordered lobster; I hope that's fine with you."

Bobby nodded slowly, clearly unsure what to make of the situation. Malone winked at a man at the next table who sat drinking with a busty redhead barely out of her teens. The man smirked back. His gaze said it all—he wasn't fooled; he knew Malone had just gotten the big brush-off in favor of a younger, more virile model.

Malone shrugged. He didn't feel too good himself. Now he almost wished Bobby would insist on making an asshole of himself so he could put his lights out.

Bobby, however, didn't. He'd suddenly worked out what the deal was here. His expression remained defiant, though. He didn't care that Malone was being made to look foolish.

Malone understood the kid's feelings: You don't search for the woman you love for ten years, then let her date get in the way of your reunion.

Malone picked up his glass of wine and drained it. He looked at Ann, who, now sobering down from her euphoria, stared rather shamefacedly back at him.

He smiled, put the empty glass down. He felt confused; it seemed wrong to leave Ann, and yet it was humiliating to stay, and would only grow more so.

Finally, helped in part by the approach of the waiter with the dinner he'd ordered, he pulled himself together.

"Make sure to invite me to the wedding," he told Bobby. "Or else . . ."

Bobby nodded cautiously. "Whatever you say, man."

Ann tittered nervously. "You'll be the kid's godfather." Malone felt sick again. It was disgusting what love did to people. Here was a woman who'd been cool and calm (and planning on fucking him) just ten minutes ago, now looking more emotionally disheveled than a horny teenager. And planning to fuck someone else even more passionately than she'd have fucked him.

The waiter began laying out the dishes of seafood. Looking coldly around him, Malone stalked away towards the exit.

"Who was that guy?" Bobby asked loudly as Malone left. "Dude's real cool to give up his table like that."

"Just my Uncle Mal," Ann replied even louder. "He's our family lawyer. Some damn inheritance papers I have to sign about a ranch down in Arizona."

Both their voices were clearly raised for the benefit of the other restaurant patrons. There was some knowing laughter, some snickering.

Despite wishing the ground would open up under him, Malone had to laugh as he stepped out into the night.

***

Driving home, Malone shuddered at the memory of what had just transpired. *Women! Damn Ann Calloway! The horrible bitch! Fuck! How could she do that!?* Forced into leaving *Umbria* like that, he felt like a man who'd cornered a burglar in his house, only, instead of the law taking its normal course, the burglar had had him, the homeowner, arrested for breaking and entry.

He felt depressed—there were no words to convey the emotional shading of his psyche.

He drove past two Robopol officers standing by a parked antigravity car. Their cop car, an armored SUV, hovered several meters behind. Malone was uncertain what the robots, white faces and hands glinting against their black suits and felt hats, were up to. The antigrav car's driver, a large woman in a bright yellow dress, gesticulated furiously at the police machines, shaking her driver's license at them. The plastic strip flickered like an opened compact. Her vehicle bobbed up and down over the blacktop like her weight made it unstable.

Malone left the arguing trio behind, their voices and colors swallowed up in slipstream. He turned onto Milk Street. His mind dropped back to his romantic concerns. As vehicles and houses flowed past him, he felt disoriented, a drifting part of the night, something unstable that could at any moment fracture and be lost.

Then he rallied, reflecting that in its own awful way, the restaurant scene was funny. Tragicomic—the older guy's new woman being knocked off her feet by a young romantic blast from the past.

Malone drew himself from the well of self-pity. He shrugged Ann Calloway off like a dirty shirt, consigned her face to the vaults of dusty memory. There were lots of other nice women in the world. He'd met some of them before, would yet meet others.

He turned into his driveway, his mouth less bitter than before.

CHAPTER 5

Sookie / Stan

Sookie Ling paced her penthouse suite like a caged Xiamen tiger. "How dare she! Bitch! Shemale cunt! I-I-I—" Her face was white with rage, her monochrome green eyes flashed like high-wattage light bulbs. She froze a moment, hands on the floor-to-ceiling window, looking toward the cottages, then whirled around. She crossed to Stan, the folds of her green kimono flapping open like wings.

Stan sat quietly on a leather sofa. He still shaken over what he'd seen, and didn't want to talk at all. But they had to discuss this. (He'd made a cellphone video of the carnage for Sookie to view. Sookie, however, had been too angered over being played for a fool to feel nausea over the horrible scenes recorded on the phone. Not so Stan. While cooped up in the broom closet, he'd puked several times from the memory of how the transformed Harris Boys had ripped his men apart and frolicked in their blood. He felt like puking right now, in fact.)

Sookie grabbed Lucy Tang's note up from the coffee table, and shook it at Stan.

He avoided her gaze. He knew what the note—inscribed in beautiful feminine cursive script read:

Hello, darling Sookie,
Remember me? I'm back in town and I think it's time I have my revenge. I see you've been doing so well in my absence.
Now read this and read it good, you murdering bitch. I'm going to shove my penis so far up your withered Shanghai anus, it'll come out your mouth—you'll think you've been constipated for a year.

I've never forgotten what you did to my darling Emil. And I'll never, ever, forgive you. Okay, now it's time for payback . . . Prepare to fucking die.

Oh, mamasan bitch, and thanks too for the twenty mil worth of dragonreich, I needed some gambling money,

Lots of hate, cunt!

Lucy Tang.

Sookie ceased her glaring at Stan. She read through the poison pen letter again, large lips curling in amusement as her glowing eyes descended the page. At length, she laughed and dropped the note back onto the coffee table, then sat opposite Stan.

"What's so funny?" he asked.

Sookie grinned evilly. "Stupid Lucy funny. Bitch imagine smart; but Sookie mistress of game." She made an expansive gesture. "Why else I own casino?" She looked pointedly at Stan. "We plan now."

Stroking his beard, he nodded cautiously. "We need to get the drugs back. Twenty mil's a—"

"Forget drug. Plenty more available. We plan fuck Lucy's butthole. Tear anus so big whole of Tibet fit inside. Okay?"

Stan nodded. "Whatever you say, Boss. How'd you want to go about it?

Sookie crossed her thin legs. Her kimono was loosely tied; Stan caught a flash of scaly yellow thigh. "What think, Stan? Brains also why I employ you."

He grinned at the flattery. *Yeah, and also to get my old ass killed.* "Well . . . we set a trap . . . another reich deal, one so big Lucy Tang will find it impossible to resist."

Sookie frowned. "Use head. Lucy not buy from us. Not again. Know we set up."

Stan nodded. "I'm considering that. Joe Collins has been hounding us for months for a big shipment for his Texas clients, right? So we sell to him now, only it's really a trap: we leak the news over the grapevine that the deal's going down—"

"Add fake news that casino lose money like diarrhea. Big Boss Sookie need sell huge drugs to raise cash. Without sell, Jacobi gangs take casino." She scowled. "Lucy want humiliate me bad— this attract her good."

"Jacobi's nowhere near strong enough to take you on; she knows that."

Sookie spat, slashed the air with her six-inch-long green fingernails. "Fuck her little prick knows! Say so!"

Stan raised hands to placate his angry female boss. "Cool. I'll add too that the NYC Mafia guys—the Big Apple Mob—are into you for half a billion you borrowed to build the casino. They're just waiting for an opportunity to screw you over. How's that?"

Sookie pursed her lips. "That good too; but keep low profile information. Too many people believe debt rumor, I lose big-time face in Chinatown."

He nodded. Behind Sookie, moonlight reflected off the windows, a breeze rustled the white lace curtains. Sookie stood up, walked over to the penthouse's corner bar, and poured two glasses of red wine. She returned, handed one to her companion.

He thanked her and sipped. "You know," he said, "We've another option to trap Lucy."

Sookie, now sitting on the arm of his sofa, raised eyebrows. "Tell me."

"Malone. He'll find her for you. Likely be cheaper too."

Sookie sipped her wine, her luminous eyes like magnified fireflies. With the fingernails of her other hand, she scratched the sofa. Stan thought she looked like an angry cat. "No. Malone best in Boston, but . . . long time ago, Lucy not kill him. Maybe he grateful, warn her off."

Stan raised an eyebrow. "When was that?"

"Long before employ you. Ancient history—maybe tell someday." She finished her drink, collected his glass, rose to refill both. Her feet padded lightly across the plush rug. Her toenails were painted a dark green that was almost black, long, but not overlong. "Malone last option. For now, trap you suggest best: We use Collins decoy, ambush Lucy with heavy artillery."

Stan accepted his refilled glass from her. "Whatever you say, boss." He felt a lot more relaxed now they had a plan. Images of Roddy's, Li Hu's, and Wu Jun's shredded corpses in the blood-splashed cottage living room still floated through his mind (*Oh fuck, I have to delete that damn video from my phone!*), but the wine—Sookie always had the best vintage stuff; real dry too, no wimpy sweet alcohol percentages—was shaving the edges off the horror. Yeah, the wine *was* helping. It was almost possible to forget the cleanup crew now busy scraping three men's remains off the walls down there.

Sookie laughed suddenly. "So tell me good: Lucy is pink bed sheet drop from up? Many glass teeth? Ah, no wonder she angry now—looks all faded; macho men not like any more." She laughed louder. "Or tranny anus slack now. Lucy fuck too much—overworked asshole. No friction for penis anymore."

Stan tried, but couldn't share her mirth. "It ain't funny, Sookie; you need to have been there. I ain't never seen anything like it. It was—"

"Always first time person enter nightmare. Pull worried mind together, Stanley. Go find tight pussy; fuck very hard; feel alright afterwards with empty balls."

***

Once Stan had left, Sookie entered her bedroom to dress for the night. It was time to visit the casino, mingle with the gamblers. While slipping into a clinging green cheongsam she post-mortemed the evening's events in a mental morgue.

So Lucy Tang back, eh? After eight years. I think slut dead. But not . . . True Chinese woman anyways—have kung-fu film memory, must revenge . . .

Sookie smiled coldly. Fuck the stolen reich, this was way more personal that some woman murdering her men and robbing her. Eight years ago, Lucy Tang had killed Sookie's niece Gorgeous Wong. But the feud went back before that even—Sookie had first killed Lucy's boyfriend Emil.

Sookie smirked. *That Lucy fault—stupid lovers steal reich, plan kill, overthrow me. Ah . . . but very sad Gorgeous die when hunting Lucy!*

Their history went back way further than blood and death, however: after emigrating to the US from Hong Kong, Lucy Tang—gorgeous beyond belief in makeup—had performed drag shows in Sookie's brothel.

Sookie was quite the fatalist. She felt this feud between herself and Lucy Tang was meant to be. Similarly, she only saw one resolution to their conflict—death for Lucy. Or maybe the death

Sookie saw was hers. Whichever it was, however, Boston, no the entire USA, the fucking planet even, wasn't large enough for both of them.

So, Lucy, bring it on, hah! You tasty dog meat—I fry and eat up, digest completely, shit out.

Sookie zipped up, examined herself in the mirror. She pinned up her black hair, sat at her vanity, began applying her makeup. This was simple—silver eye shadow, purple lipstick, some blush. It had to be simple—her extra-long nails made handling the pencils and tubes awkward.

Done, she reviewed herself critically. *Still looking good, Sookie baby. True, eyes very scary, but . . .*

As if scared of scaring herself, she put on her shades then examined herself again. She stood up, pirouetted. *Oh yes, I hot bitch. Okay, aging hot bitch. What important is I hot.*

She giggled, forgot her appearance, let her mind return to her returned nemesis. Suddenly she laughed, her blood racing with childlike excitement. This would be fun; it had been ages since she'd had a tough opponent to pit her mettle against. She currently had Dave Jacobi, her sole Boston crimeland competitor, under her thumb. Indeed Jacobi was so cowed—at least in Sookie's opinion—that she imagined if she handed him a cup of her excrement and a spoon and informed him it was ice cream, he'd gladly eat it.

She grinned. Having Lucy back would be good for her health. For a little while at least. But the matter must be resolved quickly. A deep wound could be borne and suffered through, gloried in even, so long as it healed fast. There was nothing worse, however, than a niggling ache that refused to heal; a pain that continued year after year after year. Sookie realized that if she didn't finish off Lucy before she got her 'legs firmly beneath herself' the other woman could become a major thorn in her side.

No, I not let Lucy become pain in ass. Anus already itchy from tentacles.

It was all set up then. Yes, they'd do the Collins decoy. But . . .

Staring at her huge double bed, Sookie suddenly reached a decision. She picked up her iPhone, entered 'Contacts,' and scrolled down the list of names till she found a particular number. She dialed.

"Hello, Soledad? Boss Sookie speaking. . . . Fine, thank you. . . . We need see. . . . Very, fantastic important. . . . Ah, you busy tonight? . . . Early morning good. Yes, very good, I waiting. . . . See you too."

Sookie hung up smiling. She noted the phone time. *Almost eleven. Must rush; fat-wallet customers wondering what up?*

She grabbed up her purse and hurried from the penthouse.

***

Sookie always preferred to ride down in the High Tower's external elevator. From this vantage point, the harbor view was just gorgeous, particularly on brightly moonlit nights like this. Now, she feasted her eyes on the shimmering gray waters as they rippled with trails of light, giggling at the black question-marks floating across the harbor surfaces—the necks of apatosauruses and ichthyosaurs. *Ah, dinosaur also like sweet moon! Play like child in candy store.*

A cloud shadowed the moon; a cloud shadowed Sookie's mind. Not Lucy Tang now, though her nemesis was the catalyst to her thoughts going awry. Sookie's thoughts skewed on tangents through the maze of her sentiments and reasons, knocking aside business deals, friends and family, and a myriad of other little things, important and less so, till finally the runaway train of thought parked at a very out-of-the-way mental station.

A name: Rick Rogers.

Rick Rogers owed Sookie two hundred thousand dollars in gambling debts. It was an old debt (Rick was an old friend of hers), and a bad one (Rick was quite incapable of paying). For all practical purposes, Sookie had written the money off. But now, reviewing the buried matter of Rick's indebtedness through the morbid filter of the evening's events, Sookie was suddenly possessed by the violent desire to have her money back. At whatever cost.

Ah, not good so. Not careful, soon everyone take boss lady for granted, think me easy pickings. I become laughing stock—trade on entertainment stock exchange. Sookie value drop badly. Yes, I soft too much. Friend Rick cough up money fast, or die trying.

The clouds cleared off the face of the moon. Sookie's face remained dark, however, as she reached the ground floor plaza. She exited the elevator. Her retinue of mobsters, retainers, and sycophants swamped her.

"Ah, Boss Sookie," a man simpered, "you look totally ravishing."

"Just fantastic," another added.

"Sookie always fantastic," she retorted, slipping easily into her role of casino owner, "it vital necessity." She looked around at the adoring faces. "Okay, we go now, guys. Time start gambling party properly. Otherwise, how big-time rollers have good bad luck, lose enough money so I pay all of you obese salary?"

Everyone laughed. Sookie led the way to the gambling halls.

CHAPTER 6

Stan / Rick

61 Joy Street, Beacon Hill. Two Mornings Later.

"Noo, don't . . . fuck!"

Rick Rogers reeled back across his living room, slamming into the rear of a ratty blue armchair. Stan's punch had almost lifted him off his feet. He spat blood, felt his lips for cuts, his mouth for broken teeth.

"B-b-b-but . . ." he finally managed to sputter, "S-S-Sookie's a friend of mine!"

Stan strode towards Rick. The big man rubbed his fist in his palm, and shrugged. "Look at it this way: the boss is having a bad week. We've been taking a heavy beating at the casino—some Kansan S.O.B. is playing a new system to beat the odds. So she's pissed off; needs the money."

(Stan was delighted to have some action this morning; it made him feel manly again, not like yesterday night when he'd been almost shitting himself in a broom closet, hoping the bogeymen wouldn't come get him. He laughed to himself; punks like this nerdy Rick Rogers here—wannabe big shots—he could handle, eat the little shits for breakfast with Starbucks coffee, no cream. Rick was just unfortunate, that was all—a moose caught in the crossfire of Stan's need to reaffirm his manhood. This morning, Stan wasn't taking any prisoners. No sir, he wasn't.)

Stan feinted like he'd throw his right hand, then hit Rick with a left hook that practically knocked the brain out of his head.

The blow upended Rick over the old armchair. He wound up with his back on the seat, legs draped up over the rear of the chair, waiting for the cotton to clear from his vision. Rick, gray eyes scarcely able to focus, was conscious of Stan tramping around the

34

armchair, then of the old guy staring down at him, his thick ashy beard and black shades making him seem a jacked-up biker version of Karl Marx. Rick remained where he was. "Man, please don't hit me again."

"Now look, dude," Stan said coldly, clearly enjoying Rick's pain, "Sookie's laying down the law here, okay? I'm just the messenger." He frowned, said as if to himself, "Even though it's way, way below me to run this kind of garbageman errand." Then, like he'd remembered Rick again, he continued: "It's no biz of mine if you live or die? Dig?"

Rick nodded glumly.

Stan stroked his beard. "All I've done now is simply give you a taste of what to expect if the Boss's cash ain't ready by six p.m. Friday . . . okay?"

"Friday? Friday!!?" Rick made to rise, his visitor shook a meaty fist in his face. Rick took the hint, subsided again.

"I ain't done talking," Stan said. "I was about sayin'—"

"But I don't have the money," Rick protested. "I don't have a cent!" He gestured around the rundown apartment with its stink of roaches and rats. "You can see how I'm living!"

Stan frowned. "Yeah, I guess you are broke, living in this shithole. Still it doesn't matter. Like I said, I'm just delivering Sookie's message." He rolled Rick's legs off the rear of the armchair. Rick's head followed his legs and torso, he crashed onto the floor. A moment later, he was yanked upright and staring at Stan's face.

"Have half a heart, Stan. This is Wednesday. How am I supposed to find two hundred grand before Friday?"

Stan grinned discolored teeth. "Dunno. Try magic, sell your soul to the Devil. Have a winning streak in some other casino. We *don't care* how you get the fucking money—just have it ready by Friday nightfall. Or else . . ." Both their gazes moved to the machete Stan had left standing in the angle of the front door. "Or else, you're gonna need a wheelchair forever after. I mean what I'm saying, man: Sookie Ling ain't playing games with ya no more. You don't have her money next time I see you—I'm chopping off both your legs for real. You do the math—that's a hundred grand per walker."

He crossed the eroded blue carpet to the front door, dragging a protesting Rick after him. "Am I getting through to you? Am I?"

"I'll try," Rick said. "I-I-I'll do my best to raise—"

He stopped explaining, tried to duck the punch floating towards him. No use. He was either too slow or it was too fast. Stan's fist hit him full on the left cheek. It felt to Rick like the blow was crumpling his face: he could feel his head flattening, and the world going white. His legs buckled. He only remained upright because Stan had a firm grip on his collar.

"I asked: do you fucking understand?"

The question sounded like it came from out of town. Rick, only able to see a giant biker-like ghost holding him up, wondered why Stan was going so badass on him. He felt warm blood running down his cheek from a cut.

Then his face began ringing with slaps. *Thwap! Thwap! Thwap!*

"Fucking wake up, you loser punk!"

Rick's vision cleared up fast. To the roaring pain in his head was now added burning across his face like it was being ironed.

"Stop hitting me, man. Please."

Thwap! "Only when you say you'll *find* Sookie's money, not *try to* find it."

"Okay, I'll try . . . no, no no!" Rick cringed before the cocked fist. "I'll find the damn money! I'll get her money!"

"Son-of-a-bitch." Stan let go of Rick, who, with a grateful groan, crumpled to the floor. He sat there, holding his head in his hands, trying to shake himself together, wondering why he couldn't coordinate his limbs. Crimson dribbled from his cheek and lips.

Stan cracked his bloody knuckles, toe-poked Rick with his right boot. Rick looked up dully. Stan grinned down at him, liking what he saw. Yeah, the punk had gotten the point, alright. He picked up the shiny machete, slapped its flat side against his palm.

"Okay, so I'll be going now. Remember: Friday evening, or both your legs walk off into the sunset without you." His expression hardened momentarily. "And I know you ain't dumb enough to try and leave town. Or are you?"

Rick shook his head. "No, Stan. My ass stays in Boston."

Stan grinned broadly and stepped out into the hallway.

Watching the front door swing to, Rick Rogers felt like his whole life was a hammer falling down to crush him.

***

Icepacks pressed to both sides of his head, Rick Rogers lay back across his ratty sofa and pondered his future. It seemed he didn't have one.

Friday, the old bully said. Where the fuck am I gonna find two hundred grand before then? Memory of Stan's shiny machete and the man's hanging threat drilled through the pain in his head. *He's coming to cut off both my legs? Fuck.* Like he needed to reassure himself that his legs were still attached, Rick leapt to his feet, dropped the icepacks on a dusty stool, and paced. Inside his head, his mind raced furiously, darting left and right like the gaze of a terrified rat seeking impossible deliverance even as the jaws of the trap came together on its neck.

The question hung over him: *Shit! I've only two days! What am I gonna do?*

Physical resistance was out of the question. Rick Rogers wasn't a fighter. He'd always been too undisciplined to learn any unarmed combat skills. His body type too was wrong: though tall, he was lanky, with no worthwhile muscle on his bones. Besides, Rick was completely scared of any kind of pain or discomfort. He even disliked shaving for fear of nicking himself.

Rick had always relied on his charm and glib tongue to talk his way out of trouble. His youthful passably good looks—short brown hair, sunny gray eyes, thin face, sensual mouth with a ready smile—made him a minor hit with the girls.

Remembering the girls, he winced through the fog of pain disorienting him. *Thank heavens Stan didn't break my nose!* Then he sighed (which caused pain to zig-zag through his brain like a lightning bolt) and wondered why he was worried about female opinion of his looks. Since he'd lost his luck—yeah, and two hundred grand was a lot of luck to lose—there hadn't been any women. Not after a while. At first, a few of the hostesses and female croupiers from the casino had still hung around Rick, thinking he was just having a slump—it happened occasionally that a gambler had a bad patch—but Rick's slump showed no sign of easing up, and the ladies deserted him like fickle fleas fleeing a drowning dog.

Rick's lips pursed tight at their betrayal. Greedy bitches they all were, only with his ass for a good time. Once his money ran out, so did they . . . out the goddam door, never to be seen again. Then, looking around his apartment with its ripped wallpaper and flyspecked surfaces, he laughed bitterly. *Yeah, dickhead, so you expect those classy honeys to hang around this dump? Get a grip on yourself, Rick. You hate this place yourself—it ain't the ladies' fault! A man needs cash, cash, cash to live!*

This last thought sobered him. It was true: he literally did need cash to live. Rick tried to imagine himself as a double amputee in a wheelchair. He got the vision down pat—his body just angry itchy stumps from the thighs down, drunk and dirty, panhandling on a sidewalk with a 'help me' sign; or if he was luckier, being pushed around in a rusty wheelchair by some old wino bitch who hated him but needed him as a cure for her own loneliness.

He jerked himself out of the vision, found he was shaking from its intensity. His heart was beating fast and furious.

Hell no! he swore, cold sweat running down his face. *That isn't me! That'll never be me! Oh no—it's not happening! I'd rather kill myself, blow my brains out.*

Rick was serious about killing himself if he lost his legs. His frail ego couldn't cope with being crippled. But how? He couldn't imagine sticking a gun in his mouth and pulling the trigger, though he'd heard that doing it that way didn't hurt much. Then there was the added fear that all suicides supposedly went to Hell. Rick remembered burning his hand on the gas ring last week—the agony. *Hell no, I ain't going down there!*

He forced his thoughts back to the now, sat in his armchair again to think. The specter of the gleaming machete hung like the Sword of Damocles over his head. *There has to be a way I can raise the money, but how? How? How? Forget borrowing it, my credit's a joke . . . no one'll lend me a dime.*

Rick's thoughts leapt divergent tangents through his worried mind, hopping like startled monkeys from one deductive neuron to the next, till finally they converged on a single point.

One of Stan's wisecracks: "Dunno. Try magic . . ."

Rick rose from his chair and paced again. He found no alternatives. He couldn't even steal the money. (He didn't *mind* stealing it; he just had no idea where to steal it from.)

So, magic it would have to be then. Not something he'd have normally considered, but . . . in desperate times, desperate men did desperate things.

Rick Rogers was no magic adept—he couldn't cast a spell to save his life. But he knew a woman who could. Oh, most definitely. A bona-fide witch.

An old friend of his: Soledad Bathory.

Feeling somewhat better, Rick rushed into his bedroom, grabbed up his cellphone and called her.

"Hello, darling," Soledad's husky voice came over the line, "I'm not available right now; but please leave a message when the black cat hisses." She laughed throatily. "It really is black, you know, though you can't see it."

"Soledad," Rick growled after the cat hissed, "it's Rick . . . Rick Rogers. I'm in serious trouble and I need to see you. My legs depend on it. Call me back fast, please."

Rick settled down to wait. Then, when Soledad still hadn't called him back two hours later, he put on his coat and went out to look for her.

It was drizzling outside, the weather for once perfectly in sympathy with Rick's emotions.

CHAPTER 7

Malone / Steelberg

"I need some human brain juice feedback," Robopol detective Lieutenant Steelberg told Malone. "Strangest case I've ever seen."

Malone nodded back. "Shoot, I'm listening."

It was noon. The pair were in Malone's office. Steelberg, a mandroid—a human-shaped robot—sat across the desk from Malone.

Malone regarded Steelberg with some amusement. The white robot wore a rumpled black suit and a crumpled hat, its clothes damp because it hadn't thought to use an umbrella. That was the sort of things robots did, what separated them from mankind.

Steelberg—the robot's name was a pseudo-anagram of its serial number 5-T-337-63R9—was one of the first group of mechanical police officers dispatched into Boston service as part of a joint City Council/USAcme crime control initiative.

The robots, built locally on a New Korea license, were fast, efficient and impartial. You couldn't bribe them, they didn't fuck up. There weren't yet enough of them, though; cost of manufacture was still being weighed against demand, with Boston being viewed by the rest of the country as a test case. If the Boston Robopol experiment worked, USAcme would be dancing all the way to the bank.

Lt. Steelberg was a prime example of the Robopol COP (Criminal Offensive Pacification) unit. It was six feet tall, a gleaming white metal/plastic sentinel. An almost indestructible body (you'd need a rocket launcher to dent it), slim limbs that moved like poetry, slender hands that could thread needles or punch holes through walls. It had two guns, both shotgun-like tubes built onto its forearms. The left was a blaster, the right fired

40

projectiles; both weapons were automatically reloaded from magazines inside its body.

Steelberg's head was a smooth white egg dotted with two red eyes and a speech slot. It recorded everything it saw, backed it up to triple memory drives for use as evidence. In short, the Robopol COP unit (in this case 5-T-337-63R9), seemed the perfect police officer.

However, despite their many advantages, all Robopol units had one basic flaw.

While the mandroids were fantastic at extrapolation, building jail cells in the sky by connecting different criminal dots, they lacked both creativity and its offspring—those intuitive leaps of illogic so common to mankind, those random associations of concepts that resulted from a flesh brain's neurons firing out of a pre-ordained sequence.

This meant that robots lacked 'randomized deductive capacity'—they couldn't see beyond their noses. Once a puzzle proved illogical—outside the stiff grid of their programming—they were stumped.

Robots *could* empathize (one simply programmed an exhaustive list of rights and wrongs into them), but they could not build a concept from scratch—they lacked originality of any sort.

It was because of this that Steelberg was currently visiting Malone. Each Robopol detective had a human consultant it worked with on 'illogical' cases.

Malone finished his appraisal of his metal colleague. He glanced outside at the rain. It made him strangely maudlin. His memory hopped two days back, to the embarrassing restaurant scene with Ann Calloway. He smiled sadly. *Hope she's happy with Bobby.*

He returned his attentions to the robot seated opposite him. "You really should carry an umbrella, Metal Guy."

"Why? I'm waterproof," Steelberg replied in its drawl like a detuned synthesizer.

"Your clothes aren't."

"They'll dry—they won't die."

Malone laughed. He had no idea if the robot was joking or not. He wasn't sure if robots could joke. "Okay, I'm listening. So what's this strange case?"

The robot cop lifted a white hand like it was stopping traffic. "Yesterday about noon, I got a call out to Danny Cho's. It's a Chinese-owned business on High Street."

"I know it," Malone said. "Cho supplies temps to other businesses. Security guards, secretaries, teachers, chefs—they're a one-stopper for whatever you need."

"Yeah, that's the one. Hey, Malone, why don't *you* have a secretary?"

"They cost too much. Go on."

Steelberg said, "Alright, so yesterday noon we get this call at HQ. Sounds like I'm being pranked, but I drive over there anyway."

"And?"

"They've got this man there, young chap about twenty, not Chinese, who's claiming to be Jenny Yang, a female employee of theirs."

"A psycho," Malone said. "They should have dumped him out on his ass." He had a certainty, however, that he was very wrong. There were bins for loons; Steelberg wouldn't be here if the kid was just nuts.

Steelberg nodded. "Everyone at Cho's first thought the same as you. But . . ." the robot tapped the desk for emphasis, "but then, the young man—his ID shows his name as Scott Parker—began telling everyone things that only Miss Yang could possibly know. Long story short, finally everyone at Cho's is convinced it is Miss Yang, apparently stuck in a man's body. So they call 911."

Malone felt chilled. Now here was something new. "Did Miss Yang—assuming Parker's not simply a great faker—say how it happened?"

Steelberg nodded again. "She was on her way to work that morning. She'd just gotten off the Red Line at South Station, when she felt someone touch her. And it's suddenly hotter than normal. Next thing she knows she felt something shift her—she said it felt like she was swept up in a rush of wind—and she's in Parker's body. Horrified, she turns and watches her own body walking away from her."

"Did she follow . . . *herself?* I mean, see where she went?"

"An odd way to put it. But yes, she did. But, remember Miss Yang was understandably traumatized, very confused as to what to do. After a while she became so disoriented she fainted. When she came to, her body had disappeared."

Malone whistled. "That's quite a tale, Metal Guy. So let's clarify this: you're currently searching for Jenny Yang's body, and when you find—"

"We've *already* found Miss Yang's body," Steelberg interrupted. "Two hours ago. There's a problem, however."

"How to switch her back into her own body? Yes, that's . . ." Then, something about the way the robot sat in its crumpled suit, its confused poise, warned Malone there was more coming. But what could possibly be weirder than a seemingly random body transference?

He looked pointedly at the Robopol officer. "There's something else, right?"

Steelberg said, "Plug me into your laptop and I'll show you."

***

Malone gaped at the scene on the laptop screen. It showed a young woman, a pretty but completely disheveled Chinese girl, dashing about on all fours along a street, while two human medics (one of them holding a straitjacket), tried to restrain her.

Jenny Yang (it *was* her body at least) leapt atop a trash can. The medics cornered her there. She fiercely scratched the face of one man, leapt over the head of the other, and then, showing astonishing agility, scrambled up a nearby maple tree. There, she balanced on a thick branch, baring her teeth (she was missing several) and hissing at the two men. Blood trickled down the face of the one she'd savaged.

"A few inches higher and she'd have gouged his eye out," Steelberg said emotionlessly.

Malone didn't reply. He watched as Jenny Yang was finally subdued by tranquilizer dart, fell out of the tree, then was straight-jacketed and stretchered off into a medical van. The video froze as the departing van turned a corner.

"That's as much footage as I recorded. Want me to replay it for you?"

Malone looked at Steelberg. "No. Just leave a copy on the hard drive in case I need to review it later." He waited while the robot disconnected itself from the PC's USB port. He was chilled by what he'd just witnessed. Now he understood why Steelberg was consulting him: what they'd watched made very little sense to him, and he was human. He could imagine how confused the robot must be.

"Where'd this happen?" he asked.

"Beacon Hill—at the river end of Revere Street. Just as a note, Miss Yang lives over there, on Phillips Street; say two hundred meters from where we picked her body up."

Malone reflected on that a moment. It made a sort of sense: the MBTA's Charles Street station was close by. The Red Line train would be the simplest transit connection to get Jenny Yang to work and back. So viewed in that light, 'her' coming home made convoluted sense; just not her—

"What I don't understand," Steelberg interrupted his thoughts, "is why Miss Yang's body is behaving like a cat."

"Yes . . . a cat," Malone said. Hearing his personal impressions spoken aloud made the puzzle that much more concrete.

"A cat," Steelberg repeated. "It's completely illogical. Remember what I told you: Miss Yang said she was touched by a *person*, and ended up in that person's body. And then that person in *her* body walked away, not *crawled* away . . ."

The robot's voice creaked, it sounded close to breakdown. Malone sympathized. He frowned. "Okay, Metal Guy, quite a problem you've brought me this time—a real doozy. Yeah, why the hell is there a cat in Miss Yang's body, and not Scott Parker? Where the hell is Scott Parker now? In a damn cat? Or is that actually Scott Parker in her, only he's now deranged and thinks he's a cat?"

"I don't know, Malone," the police robot replied, "that's why I'm here. What to do now?"

Malone considered. "Thankfully, I know a lady who might be able to help us." He got out his cell phone. "One Soledad Bathory. She's a witch—stuff like this is right up her main street."

CHAPTER 8

Rick / Soledad

While still calling her phone over and over again to no avail, Rick headed over to Soledad's house. Thankfully, the rain had stopped now.

Soledad lived up in North End, in a secluded mansion on Salem Street. A very old place. Three impressive stories shut off by high stone walls.

Rick pushed the wrought iron gate open, walked into shadows cast by massive oak trees. The yard was cool, cold even, in the midday sun. Strange breezes fluttered through the trees.

Feeling an almost preternatural chill, Rick ran his eyes over the house's frontage—the massive double doors of carved ebony, the arched windows with their panels of stained glass, the ultra-realistic gargoyles perched on each ledge, their stone eyes regarding eternity.

A fabulously gothic building. But then, a witch lived here.

Rick suddenly felt like the gargoyles were watching him. He crossed quickly to the mansion, climbed the steps, rang the front doorbell. It was an odd doorbell, shaped like the old pirate's emblem of skull and crossbones; only this skull had vampire fangs. Rick shuddered.

The ghoulish ambience of his surroundings was getting to him now; he questioned the wisdom of his coming over. But the woman who lived here was possibly the only person able to deliver him from his current straits.

There was no reply to his first buzzing, so he did it again. He was prepared to wait; keeping his legs depended on it.

The door opened. Soledad Bathory stood there in a black robe, regal as ever. She stared at him perplexed for a moment, taking in his battered face, then said, "Rick? What happened to you?"

"I just got the beating of my life," he groaned. "I've been calling your cellphone for hours; kept getting voicemail."

"I was casting a spell and put it off," she said. "Demons hate my ringtone. And I thought they'd love Metallica."

Rick's mind formed the obvious question: *Why not just change the ringtone?*

He looked Soledad over: it had been a while since he'd seen her last.

Soledad Bathory was tall, with silky blonde hair braided in a pigtail that hung forward over her left shoulder, its end falling to her navel. Her eyes were a soft blue, and seemed much deeper than their surface, like they held stores of mystery. Her nose was a trifle large for her face, but wide sensual lips, high cheekbones and a perfectly shaped chin confirmed her as a classic beauty. There was a suggestion of possible cruelty to her mouth, but not malice.

Her black silk robe, its edges trimmed with crimson satin, both caressed and showed off her figure. (Rick could see she was nude beneath it.) She was well-built, shapely with small firm breasts and a nice backside. Delicate arms, toned legs, small hands and feet.

She frowned at Rick. "Come inside." She led the way into the mansion. Rick followed.

***

After Rick hung up his coat, Soledad led him to a living room on the second floor. She opened the drapes to let daylight in, poured Rick some brandy. Then she sat opposite him, legs crossed, and listened to his tale of woe.

"It's a really bad case," she said when he was done.

"Can I get my luck back?" Rick asked quickly.

She squeezed up her face in thought, laced her fingers together over her right knee. "No and yes. The *no?* Your old luck's gone for good."

"And the *yes?*"

"I can get you some fresh luck. It's easy enough. Lots of people die without using theirs up, then they take it to the grave with them." She frowned in concentration. "But . . . you're a gambler, you need a high roller's luck." She stood and paced the beige carpet, then regarded him coolly, her blue eyes duplicate oceans. "You know of any high rollers who died recently?"

Rick shook his head in disgust. "Nah. I'm bad news now—they don't let me into the gambling halls anymore."

"No problem, I can find out. It's best if it's someone who's just gone, then we'll just attend their funeral. If a guy's been dead awhile, their good fortune might wear out down there in the grave."

"How long'll this take? I've only got till this Friday evening."

Soledad sat and crossed her legs again. "Yeah, I'd forgotten that. Two days is way too short to work it. We'll have to postpone getting you some luck; the ritual takes almost a week to set up right."

"A week?! Soledad, I don't have a fucking week!"

"Calm down and let me think up a solution for you. This mess is your fault, not mine."

Rick began running nervous fingers through his hair. "Yeah, yeah, you're right of course. Just get me out of this damn fix. Please, I'm begging you."

***

Finally, Soledad led Rick downstairs into her mansion's basement—her witch's chamber of horrors.

The cavernous space stank of horror and despair, of the sweat of fear, of copious bloodshed. Of despairing life, of triumphant death. Its walls, floor, and ceiling were painted with runic letters and cabalistic symbols (drawn in blood, fat, and bone-ash) and were fixed with shelves holding bottles of preserved human organs alongside dried fetuses and animals.

These were mere routine oddities. All the way across Soledad Bathory's basement, between the packed shelves, stood many shimmering ovals like massive mirrors stuck on the wall.

Rick knew these 'mirrors' were ODs—Otherworld Doors—space-time portals that the witch, through her magic, had somehow shunted into her basement. He wondered at their present profusion, they'd been much fewer last time he'd visited.

He didn't comment though; his mind was brimming over with worry. *I don't even know what the hell is this I'm about doing. And even when she tells me what to do and I hate it, I've no choice but to go along with whatever she suggests.*

Soledad Bathory left Rick with his thoughts and padded off somewhere out of sight. Rick looked around, his apprehension growing.

Four immense carvings (grotesque otherworldly idols that seemed neither god nor demon to Rick's mind) stood one in each of the basement's corners. Between the support pillars were arranged metal tables bearing moldy corpses.

He gave a start: the table to his right bore the body of a teenage girl. The kid had been y-sectioned open, her skinny torso scooped empty of organs. He sighed. He knew Soledad hadn't killed the teen—she'd just exhumed her grave. *But why, why the fuck can't she stick to everyday magic?*

Soledad returned then, sat opposite Rick. About to speak, the ring of her cellphone—Metallica's *Enter Sandman*—cut her off.

"Hello," Soledad said, then: "No, Sookie, not yet, but don't worry . . ." She laughed. "Don't be impatient; it's *guaranteed* to work. . . . No, I can't say how soon, but it will. . . . Okay, later, Boss Lady."

She looked at Rick, who'd begun trembling. "Your creditor of course."

He nodded. "What was that about?"

"Don't worry. She's not looking for you." She grinned evilly. "Not yet, anyway."

Rick stared pleadingly at her. "My legs?"

Her grin broadened. "We'll save them yet."

"How? When? I'm just sitting here watching you."

"Calm down. It'll be fine. I was just about explaining—"

Rock guitars blared again from Soledad's cellphone. Rick decided he hated James Hetfield.

"Hello? . . . Malone? . . . How are you? . . . A case?" She glanced at Rick. "No, I'm busy at the moment, can't see you now. . . . . Nah, the whole day's booked; once I'm done here I need to rush over to Logan Airport and pick up my cousin Josephine, she's flying in from Frisco. . . . But, hey, how about tonight, at Sookie's? . . . Yeah sure, the Rosebud Bar's cool. . . . Say about seven? . . .

That's great . . . I'll bring Josephine to meet you too. . . . Okay, ciao."

She hung up, stared at Rick. "Malone's got some weird case he's working on, wants my advice."

Rick knew Malone. Tough PI, the sort you hired if you fell in deep shit. *Okay, by that definition I qualify for his help. But . . . but Malone's a tight friend of Sookie's. Shit!*

He nodded at Soledad's phone. "Josephine's coming back to town?"

Soledad nodded wearily. "You know what she's like. She says the scene in San Francisco's doing her head in."

"Wasn't it a similar reason she gave for leaving here?"

"Yep, that's my cousin. It's her excuse for wanderlust."

"She still into her S and M trip?"

"You ever hear of a vampire changing its diet? Josephine's even more freaky now, a whole lot so. I really don't know what I'm gonna do with her. I mean, she's welcome to stay here forever, but I need to find her someone to use up her time or she's going to waste mine." Soledad frowned. "Forget Josephine for the moment, let's take care of this problem of yours. For one thing, no more interruptions . . ." She snapped her fingers twice, her cell phone disappeared. "I can't hear it ring upstairs." She uncrossed her legs and leaned forward, elbows on her knees, fingertips steepled in front of her lips.

"Okay, down to business. Like I said, I'll fix your luck, but that won't be till we find a really lucky gambler who's about to be buried. But as far as that two hundred thousand goes, at the moment there's only one thing for it—you'll have to take a trip down into The Groad."

Rick's face instantly fell. "The Groad? Shit. Soledad, The Groad is part of Hell."

She nodded back. "Yes it is, but don't worry about it; The Groad is the *cool* part of Hell. Besides, I got your back." Soledad Bathory pointed to the fourth space-time portal to their right. "It's a simple trip in and out. Also, the lady you're going to see lives far away from the fiery furnace."

"Lady?"

"Yeah, sort of. Her name's Anastasia Wormwood."

CHAPTER 9

Lucy Tang and the Gang

Bruce Reed was giving Lucy Tang a blowjob on the living room sofa in their hideout when, all excited, the Harris Boys burst in.

(The four of them were rooming/hiding in the disused Boston Harbor Hotel on Atlantic Avenue. The Harris Boys kept protesting their hideout being so dangerously close to the enemy (it was a mere half-mile from the Boston Harbor Hotel to the Golden Dragon Casino), but Lucy overrode their fears. She'd selected the hotel for that very reason: to be near Sookie. She liked being able to almost reach out and touch the woman she hated so much, liked to peer from her south wing suite down at the casino and visualize herself reducing it to ashes and ruins.)

Startled by the Harrises unannounced entrance, Bruce looked up, his mouth slurping loudly off Lucy's penis. Mustache like a wet brush, he stared at the two ugly men, one short, one tall. "What's happen—?"

"You'll find out later," Lucy Tang interrupted. She lay draped over the seat with her skirt up around her waist and her breasts out, her nipples a stiff brown. Gently but firmly, she pushed Bruce's head back down onto her wet erection. "Or even right now—we listen with our ears, not our mouths, dear. Just keep sucking me: I'm almost here."

Lucy groaned as he resumed fellating her, each stroke of his soft lips on her member resonating up into her breasts, making her nipples tingle. She waved to Mark and Jesse. "Hi, guys. What's got you both so excited?"

The Harris's had now realized they'd interrupted something.

"Shit, not again!" Jesse groaned as they sat. "Can't you two keep it in the bedroom?"

"Or lock the damn door," Mark added, wincing. "We could've been someone else."

Lucy wagged a finger at their reproof. "And you two could have knocked. And stop acting like you've never seen a woman having her penis sucked before. Besides, no one knows we're here. This hotel's been abandoned for only God knows how long." She groaned as Bruce stuck a finger up her anus and tickled her prostate while tightening his lips around the crown of her penis. She gave a start, her eyes spreading wide. "Hold the switchboard, Operator, I'm coming! Shiiittt!"

She gripped Bruce's head tight, emptied what felt like both her legs into his mouth. Bruce kept fingering her anus, kept sucking her till she was drained.

Then, almost like her orgasm had imploded her, Lucy's entire upper body—head, shoulders and arms, breasts and belly—flattened out against the sofa. She looked like pink rolled-out dough.

Bruce pulled his mouth off Lucy's penis, waved to the Harris's. "Hi, guys."

Mark nodded back; Jesse regarded Bruce with thinly veiled disgust. (Watching a man suck on another man's . . . okay, a woman's . . . penis made Jesse Harris feel queasy, like his balls were shrinking up into his belly.)

Bruce didn't notice the other's scorn. He licked a white smear of semen off his lips, wiped his mouth dry with a hanky, and sat back smiling.

The three of them waited for Lucy's flat-as-a-sheet upper half to reform itself back to normal inside her top.

When she was once again her gorgeous self, Lucy Tang tucked her limp penis away under her skirt.

She nodded coolly to the Harris's. "Sorry, boys; I can't help it—dragonreich always gets me super horny." She stroked her boyfriend's thigh. 'I'm just lucky to have Brucie here; otherwise I'd have to masturbate all the time." Then her expression turned cold and serious. Her slanted eyes thinned, flicked like a snake's over the two men. Playtime was over. "You were both all excited when you burst in just now. What's the big deal? You discover something to make my day?"

"Oh, you could definitely call it that," Jesse said. Mark nodded assent.

"I'm listening."

Jesse ran thick fingers through his blond hair. "We've just found out how to put Sookie Ling permanently out of business."

"And we mean *permanently*," Mark added, a wolfish grin on his skeletal face. He formed his left hand into a tentacle, trailed it playfully across the carpet separating them. "You ready for this, Lucy baby?"

Lucy leaned forward, her beautiful Chinese face intent, her long black hair flowing over her shoulders. "Talk! Stop this damned suspense."

Seeing she was getting angry, Mark shook his tentacle in a pacifying gesture. "Sorry, just kidding with ya, Lucy."

"About finishing off Sookie? Mark, if you are, just get the fuck out of here already."

He shook his head. "No, this is seriously for real. Sookie Ling is in deep financial shit. From what we just heard, she got the money to build the Golden Dragon from the Big Apple Mob."

"Oops," Lucy said with a glimmer of malicious pleasure. Then her expression sobered. "So? That's normal practice. Mobs loan out cash, don't they?"

"Not half a billion."

Lucy mused on that. "It's a lot, true; but it's still just a loan."

Bruce nodded. "So fucking what, man? The casino makes loads of money. We all know that."

After give Bruce a cold stare that said "Reserve your damn mouth for sucking Lucy's penis," Jesse took over the narration: "That's where you're wrong, see? Apparently the Golden Dragon Casino's been losing money like a breached damn. So much so that Sookie, to forestall the Big Apple Mob staging a hostile takeover, has desperately set up the biggest drug deal in US history."

Lucy looked coldly from one Harris to the other. "Is this on the level?"

Both nodded back. Mark said, "Oh, it's on the level alright. A friend who works in the Casino's accounts department told me; another confirmed it. Sookie needs cash desperately." He draped his tentacle-arm across his left knee. "And . . . . she's worked out how to get it. Joe Collins—the Texan runner—has been after her for ages to up his reich quota so he can control the supply down south. Sookie's been resisting every offer Joe's presented her with. No matter how lucrative it's seemed, she's always been scared of biting off more than she can chew—if the market opens up down there and she can't meet demand, she leaves the door open for competitors to step in." He grinned. "But now—"

"Spare me the long lecture," Lucy growled. "How much is Collins buying and when?"

"Three hundred million dollars' worth of uncut reich," Jesse Harris said. "Collins has confirmed that he's raised the money. Sookie's confirmed that the drugs are ready."

Bruce sniffed. "Unrealistic. That's a hell of a lot of money."

Jesse smirked at him. "So what? It's coming in an armored van. Some thousand buck notes to keep the bulk down. Once the money's here, it vanishes into the casino; the mob's none the wiser."

Lucy patted Bruce's thigh. "Besides, baby, the reich's much smaller; easier to transport back down south. They could even ship it . . ." She focused her gaze on Jesse, her dark eyes piercing as drills. "You're right—we screw this up for Sookie and she's finished. "Okay, where's the exchange happening? And when?"

Mark tapped his tentacle on the floor. "That's why we rushed back. The deal goes down eleven p.m. tonight at the Beacon Hill Hotel and Bistro."

"Tonight?" Bruce said. "That's way too soon."

Jesse gave him a pained expression. Mark formed the tip of his tentacle into a hook, and pointed it at Bruce. Bruce ignored them both, looked at Lucy. "Isn't it, Lucy?"

"No it isn't, darling," Lucy chided him gently. "Oh, I've waited eight long years for this moment. We just need the right plan and Sookie Ling will shortly be one very suicidal woman." An expression of intense glee spread across her features; she grinned at the Harris Boys. "I mean, anyone would be after losing three hundred million dollars, wouldn't they?"

"Six hundred," Bruce corrected. "Sookie's guys will have the drugs."

"I forgot. Yes, six hundred million." She frowned, then shrugged. "It means we'll have to kill Joe Collins too. We can't leave witnesses, not unless we want the mob after us."

"And no," Mark grinned, "we don't want that, do we?"

They all laughed. After a while, Bruce shook off his apprehension and joined in the mirth. "Okay, you guys, whatever you say. The heist is on. But remember: I'm only driving the getaway car."

"And sucking Lucy," Jesse said. "Make sure you don't forget that other duty of yours."

Bruce gave Jesse the finger. Lucy and Mark laughed.

After a while the laughter subsided and the planning began.

CHAPTER 10

Malone / Soledad / Slave

Malone arrived at the Golden Dragon at five-to-eight. After parking his black BMW, he walked briskly across the brightly lit lot toward the Rosebud Bar.

The bar was one of eight long all-glass cottages that, in an arrangement like an octopus's limbs, jutted from the west side of the main casino complex. Its coating of glass was all one-way: you could only see out, not in.

Malone reached the Rosebud. Nodding to a couple of security men who knew him, he climbed the steps and entered.

He was instantly wrapped in a welcoming ambience of people talking, glasses clinking, and much laughter.

The tinkling glassware reminded Malone of Ann Calloway again. He sighed. Trying for a new relationship was much like a drowning man trying to save himself: there was no way to tell beforehand if you were clutching at steel or straw . . .

It was with relief that he spotted Soledad Bathory waving to him from a booth.

The woman with her (seated farther inside the booth near the window) had to be the cousin she'd mentioned on the phone. Back from San Francisco. What was her name again? Jessica? Jennifer?

He crossed the bar to their booth, slid in opposite them. The pair were drinking sherries. Outside the see-thru walls, the night was like ink.

"Hiya," Soledad Bathory grinned. She wore a long-sleeved green dress trimmed with gold lace; green eye shadow. "I'd like you to meet my cousin Josephine . . . Josephine Bailey."

Malone smiled nicely at Soledad's cousin, then froze in surprise at how beautiful she was. She was absolutely gorgeous. Dressed in red leather, she was slim yet bosomy, with an almost perfect face framed by long curly brown hair that spilled down over her forehead into her eyes. Large brown eyes, a nice nose, lovely large lips smeared a shocking pink.

"Nice to meet you, Josephine."

She shook his extended hand. Her eyes danced, coolly amused with him. Her slim fingers felt electric in his grasp. "Call me *Slave*," she said.

"Slave?" Malone was taken aback.

"Josephine," Soledad said sharply, "don't start that here, this is business."

"Slave," she repeated. Keeping her dark eyes fixed on Malone's, she flicked her curls off her forehead. "My name is *Slave*."

He barely concealed his shock. Either cut or burnt into Soledad's cousin's forehead was the word 'SLAVE.' The pink scars stood out in bas-relief on her skin, the way a brand would on a—his mind quailed before the words—a *slave*.

He looked down, locked eyes with her. She stared back brazenly. Malone realized she was waiting for his acknowledgment of her difference, insistent on his taking her at face value. Flustered by her, he nodded. "Slave it is."

She smiled smugly, let her hair bounce back into place.

Soledad was watching her cousin with clear anger on her face; the 'I now regret bringing you along' look. Malone looked around for a waiter. He really needed a drink—what he'd just seen had unsettled him. He caught a waiter's eyes. The man came, took his order for a brandy.

Malone returned his attention to Soledad and . . . Slave. Two beautiful women, scions of the same family tree; both odd in different ways.

Malone considered: Judged by looks alone, the familial relationship between both women seemed tenuous at best. But then, he reasoned, like the difference between the head and tail ends of a snake, there'd clearly been quite a bit of gene splicing in between.

Malone jerked out of his thoughts, saw Slave's beautiful lips moving, realized she was speaking to him. "Huh?"

The brunette laughed. "You're wondering which of us is odder, right?"

Soledad rolled her eyes at the question. Malone imagined that, usually the center of attention herself, the witch disliked being upstaged by her cousin. Then he caught his thoughts. *Upstaged? Do I look that distracted? But I've never met a woman with words scarred into her forehead before. And intentionally at that.*

He smiled politely. "It's a hard choice between a witch and. . ."

"A *slave* . . . I'm a practicing masochist. You know, sexual pleasure through pain and being dominated, that kind of thing?"

It wasn't what she was saying, as much as her seeming lack of lunacy that bothered him. She spoke simply, very matter-of-fact. Like the girl next door would. It was quite disarming. *Somehow, I'm sitting opposite this gorgeous woman who likes being beaten. And she's not a crazy? And why . . . why is she staring at me like a vulture does at a corpse?*

"Masochism isn't insane; people just think it is."

Malone nodded. "Maybe you're right. I've too little knowledge of the BDSM scene to judge. No firsthand experience."

"I can always educate you." The words were soft, but with no hint of a joke. She licked her lips. "Wouldn't you like to spank me sometime?"

Malone looked sharply at Soledad; she still looked pissed off. He suddenly felt disoriented, a mental boat adrift on the bar's many sounds.

He looked back at Slave, shook his head. "You're too beautiful to hit."

"Oh, you only beat up *ugly* woman?" Her voice and eyes both mocked him.

She'd angered him now. "I'm not spanking you," he said curtly. He winced; she *was* just another kook. He wondered where all the nice, sane women were, the kind that didn't drive a man crazy. Did they even exist?

Slave was unbothered by the brushoff. She relaxed back into the leather seat and sipped her sherry, a knowing smile on her face. Malone's gaze floated left from her to her cousin; the blonde witch's eyes were distracted. Soledad appeared deep in some emotional turmoil. *Oh, yeah,* he decided, *there's definitely something genetically skewed about their family. Well, I'm here on city business; the sooner I get this over with—have something for Steelberg—the sooner I can bid them both a cordial goodbye.*

"Your drink, sir."

"Oops, saved by alcohol," Slave whispered to her glass.

Malone turned to the waiter. He took the brandy, downed half of it in one gulp, and ordered another: "A double this time."

The waiter left.

"Okay, to business," Soledad Bathory said, surfacing like a shark from whatever dark emotional waters she'd been under. "What's Boston's big emergency?"

Taking care to not meet Slave's 'interested' gaze at him, Malone explained.

***

"Steelberg's an alarmist," Soledad said with a smile when Malone had finished. "Machines think everything illogical is a crisis."

Malone nodded. "Then you don't think . . ."

She shook her head. "No. It's a simple case of mind transfer."

Slave spoke up: "What's simple about mind transfer?"

"Okay, not so simple; but then neither of you are magic adepts. What I mean by simple is this: we've two people now stuck in each other's bodies."

"Malone said Jenny Yang's body was behaving like a cat when they found it; not like you'd expect that man Parker would. Okay, so why's that?"

Soledad sighed. "I need to be clearer. Okay, consider this: the only likely way the pair could have switched bodies would be through an OD, right?"

Malone and Slave nodded. Malone said, "You mean a tiny floating one?"

"Yes. They're rare, but do occur. Some appear for mere seconds." She laughed. "But then, Malone, who am I to educate *you* about ODs, right? You possibly know more about the portals than anyone in Massachusetts."

He laughed. "Basic knowledge, mostly gleaned from falling through them."

"What I'm getting at is that you understand how they work. There's no guarantee that you stay normal afterwards." She frowned. "Jenny Yang was lucky—she kept her wits; Scott Parker wasn't—he slowly spiraled down into madness. And now . . ." She spread her hands.

"Makes sense," Malone said as the waiter served his fresh drink.

"Nah, sounds too pat," Slave said.

Soledad turned to stare sharply at her cousin. "And what do *you* know about mind transfers?"

Slave was unperturbed by her angry gaze. "Very little, I'll readily admit. I'd happily go along with your explanation, But . . . something about it doesn't ring true. I'm still trying to put my finger on *what*." She smiled across at Malone. "We're trying to help out your handsome PI friend here; I think we need to consider alternatives."

Soledad sat back. "What alternatives?"

"I'm not sure . . . Like I said, the idea of that floating OD and Parker's subsequent descent into madness strikes me as too routine."

"Nothing wrong with routine if it resolves things," Malone said coolly. "You'd be surprised at how many cases I've tied up by following a hunch based on the simplest explanation."

"Not in this case," Slave said. "Trust me, something's weird here."

"What now?" Soledad said acidly. "You don't just want him to spank you anymore? You now want a job too?" She turned hooded eyes on Malone. "If you are hiring, she comes highly recommended: IQ of 175; postgrad degrees in computer technology from MIT and Harvard. She used to be Systems Manager with—"

Slave slapped Soledad's arm. "Stop it!" She was blushing with embarrassment.

Malone watched the interplay between the two women with keen interest. Slave was that smart? Malone's own IQ was 116. (He tended to resolve most cases, not by intuitive understanding/insight, but rather by a dogged hacking away at them.) He put questions of mental superiority aside for the moment. While he'd been about going with Soledad's simple explanation, he now agreed with Slave: Something wasn't right. And that *something* was Soledad's behavior; both when she'd been explaining, and now, how pissed off she was acting towards her cousin. He had the clear feeling she was hiding something from them both.

He didn't mention this, however. Instead he said, "You know, Soledad, she might be right—maybe there is another explanation."

"There isn't," Soledad said with finality, an Artic coldness creeping into her blue eyes.

"I've got it!" Slave yelped beside her.

"Got what?" Malone asked.

"What's flawed in the family witch's 'simple switch' explanation is the time lag."

Soledad instantly looked deflated. "What are you talking about?"

Slave leaned forward, brown eyes glimmering. "It's simple . . . Okay, let's revisit Malone's telling of the case. After Jenny Yang gets transferred into Parker's body, she's disoriented, right? She watches her own body walk off and tries to follow it?"

She paused.

"I don't see what the hell you're driving at," Soledad said.

"Go on," Malone said, suddenly alert.

"Okay," Slave said, brushing chocolate curls out of her eyes then fiddling with the zip of her red jacket. "What we've so far been overlooking is Parker's reaction. No one questioned him, true, but Jenny Yang said he just walked off. Doesn't that strike you guys as odd?"

"I don't see why," Soledad said.

"I think I see what you're getting at," Malone said. "Parker doesn't show the same sort of disorientation as Jenny."

Slave nodded fiercely, giving her cousin a look of triumph before continuing: "And he should have: he's just been transferred into a *woman's* body—that would be incredibly disorienting for any man. But no, he just leaves the scene as if it's normal for him to leap bodies."

"So what you're proposing," Malone said, suddenly very full of respect for this woman opposite him, "Is that it's not 'Parker' in Parker's body at all to begin with, but someone . . . or maybe *something* else?"

Slave smiled coolly. "Exactly my thoughts. And now that something's moved on from Jenny Yang . . ."

"Into a cat," Malone mused. "I'd already considered that, but dismissed it as improbable. How did you figure it out?"

"Simple enough. You overlooked the time lag between when Jenny reports for work in Parker's body, and when they find *her* body with the cat in it. It's a whole day, right? And the only reason they apparently found her at all was because she was acting crazy. Which means 'she' was behaving normally all the while before. But reason it out—if Parker's 'normal,' why didn't he seek help, call the cops or something, even go home and act 'mad' to his friends or family like Jenny did? So it had to be something else inside him."

She smiled smugly at Soledad. "Of course, the witch here will likely disagree." Her hair parted, revealing her 'SLAVE' scar.

"I was wrong about her being super-intelligent," Soledad retorted in disgust. She stared coldly at Malone. "*Don't* hire her— she's nuts. All those whippings have addled her brains."

"What's so odd about her explanation?" Malone asked.

Their glasses had in the meantime fallen empty. Before answering Malone's question, Soledad snapped her fingers, instantly refilling all three.

Malone regarded the fresh double portion of brandy in his glass. "Is this safe to drink?"

Soledad nodded. "It's from the bar." Then looking aside at Slave, she said, "The problem with your explanation is your stupid body-hopping creature itself. Even if such things exist, and I know enough magic to suppose they do, how'd it ever get free in Boston?" She sipped from her glass, then stared pointedly at Malone. "I'm a witch, right? Maybe I could invoke such a creature if I tried, but, why would I? Something like that would be incredibly dangerous to let loose on the city. And I know *I* didn't raise it, so where'd the creature come from?"

"Maybe some other witch did," Slave said. "There *are* others, you know."

Soledad rounded angrily on her. "Oh yeah? Just tell me why they'd do it?"

"For fun? For a dare?"

"A dare? If you believe that . . ."

"Ladies," Malone said. "You're likely both right."

They stared at him. He nodded back.

"Yes, both of you. What if there *is* a body-shifting creature loose in Boston; only it got in, not through magic, but through an OD?"

The rising anger in both women fizzled out.

"I never considered that," Slave said slowly.

"See? You're not as smart as you think," Soledad said. Her voice, however, lacked cynicism. She now looked sick. Malone wasn't overly surprised at her next words.

"I have to leave," she said coldly. "I've just remembered an appointment."

Slave gaped at her. "Already? I'm enjoying myself."

Soledad looked at Slave like she was transparent. "No, no, you stay—I'm not going home yet." She turned to Malone. "I have to take the car. Can you please bring her back home later?"

"Yeah, sure." He smiled at Slave. "My pleasure."

Soledad Bathory nodded, picked her purse off their table, and in a sudden flash of blue light, vanished from her seat.

Malone was startled by her disappearance; he'd not seen Soledad do that trick before. Around them, there was a sudden hush from those bar patrons who'd also noticed.

Malone looked at Slave, who appeared unbothered at Soledad's abrupt departure.

She met his eyes evenly. "Forget her, she'll be calm by morning. She's just angry at being upstaged; that's why she's showing off by teleporting out of here, like the front door no longer works. Ah, Soly just makes me so angry sometimes. She's been giving me that diva reaction since we were teens."

A flash of blue light in the parking lot outside the bar caught Malone's attention. He looked past Slave's lovely face, out through the glass. Soledad had just reappeared outside. Watching the witch unlock her red Toyota Camry, Malone felt chilled. And it wasn't just from her display of supernatural power—he couldn't shake the feeling that there was something Soledad Bathory still wasn't telling them.

Damn, Steelberg's going to love this, he thought. *We've a bodysnatcher loose in Boston?* He could just imagine the robot cop's reaction on being presented with Slave's analysis. "Look,

Malone," he heard Steelberg saying, "how in the blazes are we supposed to find one cat amidst the thousands of them in Boston? And we don't even know what color the damn pet is."

Soledad drove off. Malone dismissed the case as a worry for tomorrow.

He smiled at Slave, whose brown eyes were pensive and brooding; expectant too. "So I've got you all to myself for the evening. What would like to do?" He faked a scowl. "No spanking."

She grinned, ran a finger round the rim of her glass. "Now let's see, Mr. PI. I figure you owe me at least dinner for helping solve your puzzle, right?"

Malone laughed. "Buying you dinner's the absolute least I can do."

He finished his drink, slid out from the booth, offered her his hand. "Which of the casino's twenty restaurants would you prefer to dine at? There's Mexican, Chinese, Japanese, Indian, Southern USA . . ." his voice faded to a standstill. Raising a hand to forestall Slave's amused question, Malone stared out through the one-way glass wall.

Slave turned and looked out too. "Who're those guys?" she asked on seeing the convoy of departing black cars that had attracted his attention.

Malone ran a finger along the side of his nose. "Sookie Ling's guys. There's too many of them, though."

Malone helped Slave out of the booth. He settled their tab, they crossed to the front door. Before stepping outside, he breathed in deep the bar's cosmopolitan atmosphere—gamblers from everywhere, supplicants gathered here to worship Lady Luck.

"There's going to be big trouble somewhere tonight," he said as they left the Rosebud.

"What makes you say that?"

They proceeded along a walkway that led past the main casino exit. On their left was parked a line of shiny white AG stretch limousines, moonlight glittering off their paint. The long antigravity vehicles formed a solid row, they seemed a hovering barrier against poverty. Malone smiled grimly. Many were the players the gambler's dream brought to Sookie's Golden Dragon; just as many were those the dream destroyed, women and men who left Boston mere shadows of their formers selves, their value depreciated by the roulette wheel, the baccarat tables, the high-stakes poker games, the slot machines, the gourmet food and drink, the sex and drugs . . .

Walking beside him like this, clad in her red leather jacket and pants, Slave seemed to Malone a liquid jewel, like someone had melted down a ruby.

He gestured up ahead at a fresh line of black antigrav cars now approaching the casino exit. "That number of Sookie's goons leaving at once means someone's going to get their ass whipped big time."

Slave affected a delicious shiver. "Oh, God, how I wish that was me."

"No you don't," Malone said sharply, turning to look at her. "Those guys are on their way to kill some other guys."

Slave stared up at him. The motion parted her hair, revealed the letters scarred into her forehead. Her expression was playful. "Lighten up, I was just joking. Being a masochist doesn't mean you're suicidal."

He was impassive. "Being suicidal sometimes means you're a masochist."

A black antigrav Mercedes SUV swept past them. The bearded driver waved to Malone. He waved back.

"Who's that?" Slave asked.

"Stan McCaulkin. Sookie's number one enforcer. Him riding along proves there's going to be major bloodshed somewhere tonight." Malone's brow furrowed, his lips pursed. "But that's strange."

"How so?"

Malone's eyes accompanied the departing convoy. "I keep an ear to the ground. Little happens in this city that I don't hear about, and there's been no hint of unrest in gangland of late." He smiled at Slave. "But please, don't let me bore you with our peculiar brand of Boston badasses. Soledad will expect me to show you a good time; I intend on doing just that. Besides, I owe you big time. So, have you decided what cuisine you prefer?"

Slave punched him playfully on the arm. "There's no need to keep educating me, you know. I'm originally from around here too. I'd heard a little about you from Soly. I only moved to Frisco a few months ago to clear my head."

"The vibes too heavy around here, right?"

"Like you'd not believe. Leaving here then, it was almost like I was running for my life, like something was after my ass to eat it." Her voice had gone flat, like she was back in that dark place.

"I can dig that."

She looked skeptically up at him. "Can you?" Then she nodded. "Yes, I think you can—your eyes have a 'lived in' look, like you've seen more than you care to remember."

They'd now reached the start of the restaurant complex. This was a high rise that flanked Sookie's 'High Tower.' Ten floors, each one home to two different national kitchens, each serviced by the best chefs in the USA. Looking at the building, Malone was impressed by Sookie Ling's version of the American Dream.

"She's the only person I've ever met who runs a system where crime and legality are so mingled they're the same thing."

"Who?"

"Sorry, I was thinking aloud. I mean Sookie Ling." He smiled at Slave. "She's a criminal genius—I wonder if anyone ever bothered testing *her* IQ? Okay, so where'd you like to dine?"

Slave's blues lifted. "Rooftop. Let's do the Seafood Penthouse."

Malone took her arm, steered her up the front steps.

***

High above Malone and Slave, in the penthouse of her High Tower, Sookie Ling stood naked by her bedroom window, a gin and tonic in hand, watching the convoy depart. *Everything good. I soon rid of pesky tranny.*

She watched the cars' rear lights glow away till they faded between distant houses. Sipping her drink, she turned, returned her attention to the two women having sex in her bed.

The older of the lovers—an athletic fiftyish redhead lying on her back and gasping as her vagina was pleasured—was Dallas V. Washington, an ultra-rich Texan millionairess friend of Sookie's. (The 'V' stood for Vegas, because she was addicted to gambling.) The other woman—much younger, compact and dark, and with short black hair—was Tamara Lorraine Carter aka TLC (though

Dallas always claimed the abbreviation meant 'tight little cunt'). TLC was kneeling between Dallas's legs, her tongue fluttering over Dallas's clitoris, her fingers deep in Dallas's spread sex.

Sookie regarded the women's ballet of beautiful bodies in her bed. It was lovely, almost artistic, watching them make sweet sapphic love.

Still keeping fingers sliding in and out of Dallas's sex, TLC slid up her body to suck on her nipples. Dallas moaned and moved her hands from fluttering at random over the silk bedcovers to running them through TLC's shimmering hair.

"Fuck, Tammy, I love you!" she gasped as TLC gripped her right nipple between her teeth and pulled it out, stretching the delicious curves into a tanned cone. She nibbled on the nipple a moment, then let the breast collapse back to its soft roundness. Then she dragged her tongue like a mop down into the valley of Dallas's sweaty cleavage and up over her left mound, up to the nipple, and repeated the process.

While sucking the left breast like a hungry baby, she rolled her thumb slowly over Dallas's clit; clockwise, then anticlockwise, then back again. Dallas gasped and gaped, eyes open at the room. She moaned louder, sweat beading on her brow.

Ah, nice show this, Sookie thought with pleasure. She found voyeurism thrilling, not least because of the amazing diversity of expressions sexual pleasure put on people's faces. Sookie honestly didn't think she'd ever caught the exact same facial expression twice, not even on the same person.

Next, TLC folded Dallas up tight, her buttocks well up off the sheets, knees pressed hard against her shoulders. She stuck her middle finger in Dallas's anus, her index finger in Dallas's vagina. She sawed her hand in and out like that for a while, making the vagina pout wetly as its soft tissue was dragged to and fro.

Meanwhile Dallas seemed to be going out of her mind: her fingers were claws dug deep into the mattress, her face obscured by her red hair; her moans were garbled animal grunts.

"Keep your legs up, baby," TLC instructed, removing her restraining hand from the back of her girlfriend's thighs. Dallas grabbed her legs and held them up in the air, while TLC dropped her mouth down to the yawning wet slit of Dallas's vagina. Her fingers were still in Dallas's front and rear openings, the vagina a frothy white with thick secretion. TLC dug her tongue into the pink hole for a moment, then dragged it up over the red urethral puncture to the swollen clitoris, and clamped down over the sexual bud with her lips. She sucked hard on it, vacuuming it up into her mouth, now slowing the in/out motion of fingers into vagina and anus to a sensual hypnotic rhythm that drove her lover over the orgasmic cliff.

Dallas began a loud climax. Sookie grinned broadly. *He he he! She look like someone killing her. See how eyes bulging with pleasure! Ah, orgasm really little death. At moment for Dallas, nothing else in universe.*

Once Dallas's orgasm subsided, she extended her arms down to TLC. "Hold me, darling," she gasped, eyes shining with love. TLC withdrew her fingers from Dallas's sex and anus and crawled up her body. Their lips clasped in deep passion; tongues entwining, each milked the other's soul. Their breasts pressed hard against one another, the contact, the pricking of hard nipples in soft flesh a sweet erotic dessert.

Hands and legs wrapped tight around TLC, Dallas began gasping like she having another orgasm from their kiss.

"Oh, fuck, fuck, fuck, I love you, girl. That was incredible!"

Sookie smiled. *Good fucking always nice.* Leaving the gasping, kissing lovers, she crossed the bedroom to pour herself another drink. That done, she returned to the window again, observing her reflected nude form, her scaly breasts, as she approached it.

Sipping from her glass, she wondered how her ambush was going. *It fine; stupid fool suspect nothing.* She looked back over at Dallas and TLC who were still kissing passionately. *Oh, yes, Sookie too fuck tonight. But not sweet fuck like friends. I tear up Lucy Tang asshole really terrible!*

CHAPTER 11

Lucy Tang and the Gang

Lucy Tang and her gang stood in the shadows on River Street, a street away from the Beacon Hill Hotel and Bistro. It would have been impossible for Stan to notice them—a building blocked off his view of the four.

The reverse wasn't the case, however.

"Oh, so that's their plan," Lucy Tang said after looking through the intervening building. She turned to her companions. "It's a trap, an ambush."

"I did suggest as much," Bruce said.

(The one thing Sookie Ling and Stan hadn't known [and as such couldn't take into account] while planning their ambush, was the fact that, once high on dragonreich, in addition to being able to dissolve herself, Lucy Tang could also see through solid objects. It was this ability that had saved her life eight years ago when Sookie sent a gang to kill her.)

"You're sure?" Mark Harris asked.

Lucy nodded. "It's a four-story building, right? Well, they've got men on all four floors. She turned back to stare through the brick wall for a moment. "Stan and a black dude are on the ground floor. They're the only ones there—no buyers from Texas anywhere in sight. The gang's AGs are all parked way back, at the next intersection."

"How many others?"

"Too many to count, though I estimate about ten or twelve on each floor; and they've got all kinds of heavy weaponry. Some rocket launchers and . . . shit! . . . flamethrowers too."

"Flamethrowers? Those assholes!!" Jesse thundered. He and Mark both looked horrified. Fire was the one thing the Harrises feared. Transformed (or even just high on reich), their bodies were as flammable as petroleum.

Lucy's was too, but to a lesser degree. On seeing the flamethrowers, she'd turned a little pale.

Bruce, who had no powers at all, was completely unperturbed. He rubbed his hands together gleefully. "Guys, this is just great," he enthused, walking around in a circle by the wall, his mustache quivering like a rat on his upper lip. "We'll ambush Sookie's ambush."

Seeing Jesse about to say something acid, Lucy stopped him with a gesture. A smile was spreading over her beautiful Chinese face. "Guys, this time Bruce is right. Though it's disappointing to not be able to ruin Sookie for good tonight, killing thirty of her goons will weaken her."

"She runs the whole of Chinatown, plus three quarters of Boston," Mark objected, running worried fingers through his curly hair. "Thirty corpses is a drop in her ocean."

Lucy laughed, her teeth glinting in the moonlight. "Not once we start spreading the word about *how* they died. She'll lose massive face. And I know Sookie; she's old-school Chinese. So old school, she'll do anything and everything to regain face. Which means she'll become impulsive in her search for us. Reckless and careless."

"Then," Jesse nodded with understanding, "we'll just walk in and sweep her out."

"What time is it?" Mark asked.

Lucy Tang checked her watch. "Ten-thirty." She nodded to Bruce. "Get the nightmare pods from the car, baby. One box."

Slightly less happily, Bruce trudged off to their antigravity car—a generic silver USAcme sedan chosen to avoid attracting attention to themselves—and offloaded one carton of nightmare pods from the trunk.

There were four pods—white oblong fruits each about the size of a melon—in the cardboard box, tightly packed in with Styrofoam. Bruce carried the carton back carefully. He wasn't taking any chance of a nightmare pod breaking with him near it. The pods grew on trees down in The Groad, the Bizarro-corrupted portion of Hell that lay directly underneath Boston, MA.

Bruce smirked; the Harris Boys were greenhorns at this, they didn't know shit about the pods. Bruce, however, had been Lucy Tang's boyfriend long enough to see several nightmare pods in action. Oh yeah, these fucking things came from Hell alright.

He carefully put the crate down on the floor beside Lucy, "Here you go," then stepped back. He stared at the pods a moment, then smiled nervously. "You know, guys, I think I'll go wait in the car; I'll be there when you're done."

Watching him hurry off, Jesse's ugly face creased into a disgusted scowl. "What the hell do you see in that nancy boy, Lucy? Bruce there is as yellow as they come. The gay guys in the armed forces must be disgusted with him. A hottie like you needs a macho man."

Lucy smirked. "Someone like you? C'mon, Jesse, I don't fuck his courage, do I?" The transsexual woman licked her lips, stroked her breasts. "I'll tell you why I like him: he has a tight ass and an even tighter asshole." She glanced over at Bruce, who was now climbing into their car, then pulled up her skirt. "See?"

Jesse rolled his eyes at Lucy's erection, the swollen organ straining to leap free of her panties. "Doesn't it ever take a rest?"

"I don't like it any more than you like seeing it. It's the bloody reich. The shit makes me so damn horny I could fuck a tigress—"

"And we're all about taking a lot more reich now, so prepare to get even hornier," Mark interrupted from being a taciturn spectator. He held out a jar of dragonreich and a plastic straw. "We'd better hurry up before they suspect we're on to them and leave."

Lucy smoothed her dress down again. Then she took the jar from Mark and toked up, snorting the opalescent powder up in a stream that burst like stars in her head. Feeling like she was the universe, she inhaled yet more dragonreich, till she felt her body trembling with its power.

She handed the jar to Jesse then fell back against the wall. While he and Mark snorted up the rest of the jar's contents, Lucy watched Stan's men through the house, her gaze piercing through eight walls in total.

"They're still there," she said. "I think Stan's getting fidgety. He's pulling his phone from his pocket."

"Let's do this," Jesse said.

Mark nodded assent.

Lucy bent down and pulled the four pods out of their packing. She handed one to Jesse, two to Mark. "Now, boys, we all go at the same time. One floor per pod. I'll do the bottom floor, Jesse the middle one. Mark, you do the two top floors. Make sure you get them through the windows closest to the goons. Okay?"

"Yeah."

"Yeah."

Legs now weak beneath her from the drug, she peeped once more through the wall. "Good. Let's go. Stan's on the phone. I'm sure he's getting instructions from Sookie. Let's hit them before she pulls them out of there."

They three transformed: Lucy Tang altered into a pink creature that was essentially a foot connected to an endlessly lengthening arm with the nightmare pod gripped in its single hand. Two eyes dotted the arm just behind the hand so she could see where she was going. Her erect penis stuck out of the bottom of the arm, a foot above her foot. Her clothes lay strewn on the sidewalk.

The Harris Boys had similarly altered also. Their bodies were still two-legged, but both were now headless, their heads each being replaced by a single long, suckered tentacle, the end of which was wrapped around one of the nightmare pods. Mark's tentacle had a smaller additional tentacle protruding from just before its tip which secured his second pod.

Both Lucy's and the Harris Boys' feet now sprouted thick claws that dug into the sidewalk, rooting them to the ground.

"Go!" Lucy Tang whistled out of the length of her body.

Their three tentacles instantly shot upward.

Leaving their bodies on the ground, the three tentacles extended higher and higher. They skimmed up over the roof of the intervening house, then floated outward over the street beyond. There they paused a moment, as if watching for traffic in the sky.

Then, on another command from Lucy, all three tentacles lashed at speed across the street, towards the house where Sookie Ling's unsuspecting men waited.

A street away, Bruce kept his fingers crossed.

CHAPTER 12

Stan

25 Charles Street

In the lobby of the Beacon Hill Hotel and Bistro, Stan McCaulkin was still on the phone with Sookie Ling.

With him was Abdullah Ibrahim, a negro originally from Chicago, one of Sookie's best gunmen. The black man was stocky with short hair. He and Stan sat by the reception desk, on stools brought in from the bar. The lobby was large, with plenty of space to maneuver, and nooks for concealment in case Lucy Tang made a fight out of things. The glass double doors to the street were both opened so they could see outside.

Stan's pistol lay on the reception desk. Abdullah cradled a bulky machine pistol with an extra-long magazine. His cold black eyes watched the street unerringly.

Sookie was asking Stan, "So, how far waiting game go? She show ass?"

"Nah, Boss, she ain't shown yet."

"She come. Thought of ruin me too strong bait to overlook."

"True." He scratched his beard. "I'm just wondering if word got to the bitch."

"Don't worry, bitch arrive. Try catch alive, though."

Stan grimaced at the phone. *Catch alive? Sookie, are you frigging nuts!? There's no way I'm attempting that nonsense.* "Sure thing, Sookie. With our guys on the upper floors she ain't got half the chance of a snowflake . . . Boss, I'll call you back."

He hung up, stowed the phone away in his pocket, grabbed his gun off the desk.

Something long and thin was falling from the roof of the grocery store across the street and hurtling towards the hotel. "What the fuck is that?"

"Some kinda damn tentacle," Abdullah said.

"Fuck, it's Lucy Tang! She's here!" Both men leapt down from their stools and watched the door with guns ready. Stan made out two other tentacles floating above the one approaching them. He also thought he heard glass breaking on the upper floors.

Then something detached from the approaching tentacle and flew into the hotel lobby. Hit the floor, bounced, stopped. It cracked like a nut, but didn't explode.

Relieved, Stan looked up. The tentacle was retreating. His last sight of it was of a huge pink hand giving him the finger. To the accompaniment of gunfire from the upper floors, the two other tentacles were also retreating.

He looked back down at the object on the floor. A cracked-up off-white pod.

"This is some kinda fruit," Abdullah said. He looked at Stan, his eyes confused. "She's fooling with us?"

"It's a distraction. The bitch is playing mind games. Keep your eyes peeled; You saw those tentacles, right?"

"Yeah. But that weren't too smart; she's given her position away. They're behind the houses, the rocket launchers will reduce them to mincemeat."

"Too easy." Stan scratched his beard. "She's way smarter than that." Stan didn't like this one bit. He still had nightmares about the last time he'd tangled with Lucy and the Harrises. But he'd have looked chicken as hell if he'd backed out of leading this ambush.

He regarded the burst-open fruit again. Now there was a thick yellow gas pouring from it.

"This looks like some kinda teargas thing," Abdullah said. He stepped towards it. "I'd better throw it outa here . . ."

"No, don't touch it!" Stan cautioned. "We need to both get out of here now."

Abdullah looked at him in amazement. "Man, it's just a fruit."

"Don't fucking argue with me. That thing isn't *just* a fruit. Get up the stairs, tell the other guys to evacuate the building right now."

"Man, ain't that what Lucy would want? Everyone panicking out of here?"

The question stumped Stan. Abdullah was right. He was allowing the fear spawned by his last experience to dictate to him. "Okay," he said cautiously, "Throw it out of here." But be careful, very careful. Trust me. I can feel in my bones that this is some real bad shit."

(Had Stan not been in charge here, he'd have lammed it. He wasn't scared of bloodshed; hell, he'd shed lots of blood himself. A gunfight? Bring it, bitch; Stan had the gunshot scars to prove it. Even monsters—that last time he'd been outnumbered, now he wasn't . . . but now, all he was facing was a fruit. A damn busted fruit spewing yellow gas like a leaky propane tank. And he was too fucking scared to touch the damn thing.)

His nervousness had seeped into Abdullah. "It's shaking like it's gonna blow," the negro whispered in horror. "I think you're right, man. Maybe we'd better just—"

Loud noises erupted above them: screaming and yelling. Gunfire. More screaming and yelling. The building began shaking. Outside, gusts of yellow smoke streaked across the street.

Stan looked nervously up at the ceiling, then down again at the fruit on the floor. The pod now throbbed rapidly, parts of its surface bulging then collapsing like fists were pummeling it from within. Visibility in the hotel lobby was becoming obscured by the yellow gas it was still pumping out.

The screams and noises from the upper floors had now grown even louder.

Abdullah gaped at Stan. "What the hell's going on up there?"

"It's these goddamn fruits!" Stan yelled. "Kick it out! Kick it out of here before it blows! Fast!"

Abdullah turned to do so. Before he could punt the swelling fruit out of the lobby, however, it exploded.

Holy fuck! Stan thought as the lobby filled to the brim with the yellow smoke. *The shit wagon just came to town!*

"Man, what the fuck just happened?"

Stan heard Abdullah's voice to his right but couldn't see him. Hell, he could barely see in front of his own nose, the smoke had reduced visibility to mere inches in the lobby.

"I don't fucking believe this shit," Abdullah Ibrahim said. "I can't even see my gun."

"Abdullah, shh!" What most bothered Stan was how he could no longer hear the noises from overhead. And . . . he had the sudden impression of being in a wide open space. *Where the fuck?*

Stan was suddenly aware of an intense musky smell to his left, then of a snuffling sound; like a pig would make, but three times magnified.

The snuffling grew abruptly louder, then louder again. Stan sensed the unseen creature was heading for him. He turned and leapt out of the way, back to where he knew the reception desk was.

He hit the desk, ducked beside it. He gripped his gun in fear, unable to shoot for fear of hitting Abdullah.

Then he heard a loud impact and bodies falling. Then cursing: "What the . . . ? Hey, get off me, you stinky motherfucker!"

Then scratching and the sound of jaws snapping. Then Abdullah began screaming. Then gunfire started. Bullets hit the wood over Stan's head. Cursing the smoke that rendered his eyes useless, he flung himself flat, landed on grass and mud.

In front of him, Abdullah kept on screaming, while something that sounded huge thrashed and flailed. Stan was glad he couldn't see the man being killed. He didn't shoot—he was scared of alerting the monster to his presence.

Abdullah gave a final strangled gasp and fell silent.

And then, like magic, the yellow fog cleared, the gas falling like talcum powder before Stan's eyes.

Stan looked around and shuddered.

His spatial senses had deceived him—they were still in the hotel lobby, only now the lobby had grass and trees growing in it and they weren't alone.

The creature eating Abdullah's remains looked like a huge green snake with legs. It had a long, long tail, and a massive horned head. The dead man lay splayed out in bits across the grass now covering the lobby floor. With razor-clawed hands, the monster was yanking out his guts like they were string. It kept snuffling like a pig as its exploration in the corpse's innards flung blood-flecks high into the air.

Stan ripped his eyes from the horrid sight and looked around. On his left, his gaze locked with that of another monster. This one was a child—a curly-haired boy wearing just dirty white shorts and with an old-man's face in his belly. Both the kid and his belly-face were looking at Stan and licking their lips. Both had needle-like teeth. Behind the monster boy, strange things swung from tree branches.

Stan waved his gun at the boy. "Stay . . . fucking stay away from me! I don't want to shoot a kid, but . . ."

"I'm not a kid," the wizened belly-face replied in a voice even deeper than Stan's. "Andy's the kid. I'm his granddad."

Andy began walking towards Stan.

Stan remembered then that the door was behind him. Turning to run, he found the lobby entrance blocked by yet another huge creature. This one was a metal bird taller than himself.

He winced. The bird had shiny gold feathers and eyes like camera shutters. Behind the giant bird were the front door and the street. Charles Street. Safety from this nightmare.

Conscious of the monster-boy advancing from behind, and the snake-thing slobbering over the corpse on his left, Stan stepped towards his right to work around the bird. It began hopping in place while staring at him curiously. Stan wondered whether to shoot it or not. Whether his gun could harm it . . .

He heard soft footsteps pattering behind him and spun round. *Oh no, no way are that damned kid and his tagalong granddad eating me!*

Andy—the kid with the man in his belly—stopped his rush and grinned innocently, licking his lips like Stan was candy. The granddad-belly-face laughed. "Now, I'd be real darn careful about passing that there bird if I were you, son. You're big and strong, true, but it's gonna eat ya sure as we's gonna do."

"Thanks for the warning, old timer." Stan wished the old guy wasn't in the kid. Then he'd have shot him without compunctions. But still, Granddad had warned him that the metal bird blocking the door was dangerous.

The snake-thing eating Abdullah's remains farted. It raised up from the grass, regarded the lobby with golden eyes. Its mouth was covered with blood. It made several territorial grunts, then, as if satisfied no one was debating its claim to its kill, snatched up one of the black man's legs and crunched noisily into it.

Stan just managed not to puke at the 'krak!' of splintering bone. He quickly changed position so his back was against a short tree. From this vantage point he could watch all three monsters at once. He began racking his brain on how to flee the hotel. *All I gotta do is get past this damn bird filling the doorway*!

He considered, then instantly ruled out, dashing across the hall to exit the back way—there were creatures in there too. Something black brooded in a farther corner. Ephemeral tentacles sprouted from its darkness into the room.

Then, from behind the clump of trees opposite Stan (*How the hell did a woodland sprout up inside here in two minutes?*) two men emerged, one supporting the other. He recognized them as Carlos and Eddie. Both were bleeding, Eddie was missing several left hand fingers. They noticed Stan, waved weakly.

"Hey, Gramps!" the little boy yelped, pointing at the two men. "Here's more food, and they ain't got guns!"

"Yeah, Andy my boy, let's get 'em!"

And while Stan watched like a fool, little Andy leapt right over the snake monster and barreled into Carlos and Eddie. Then, while both were trying to get up again, the boy sprouted a mass of hairy insect legs from his sides and began messily killing the two men, while Granddad laughed and sang like a lunatic.

"Damn, he was scared of my gun," Stan thought aloud as wet bits of Carlos and Eddie began flying through the air. He shut off his ears and conscience to the men's dying screams—things had fallen too far out of hand for such qualms. At this point Stan was simply grateful they'd gotten the monster kid off his back.

Just one more problem to tackle now.

He turned, stared coldly at the golden bird in the doorway.

"Okay, get your ass moving over there too," Stan told the bird, waving his gun at it. Else we're gonna find out if you're bulletproof."

The bird bent its head towards him. It seemed to be listening. He pointed across at Spider-Andy. "Stop gawking at me, chrome-beak. Get your metal butt over there and join the feast. Those two guys are enough meat for all three of you to eat."

He was relieved when the bird took his advice. In a glitter of feathers it launched itself across the room to join in the carnage.

Stan instantly dashed to the door.

He loitered at the top of the steps and looked back. The metal bird was pecking away at Eddie's head, sending brains flying everywhere.

Little Andy, hairy spider legs wagging at his sides, his mouth full of Carlos's intestines, waved to Stan. In his belly, Granddad was chewing on a thigh bone.

Stan staggered down the steps and threw up all over the sidewalk.

When he'd gotten his nausea under control, he backed across the street and watched the Beacon Hill Hotel and Bistro. *Fuck!* There were trees growing in the upper-floor rooms too, blood dripping from the windowsills . . . monsters in the rooms . . . Something like a bat; something else, a hairy spider with a human face.

An eyeless purple head with three mouths, each with too many teeth, roared through a second-floor window at him.

Stan turned and ran. He wasn't waiting to find out if the creatures could get out of the hotel. He was far away from there, zooming through the night in his AG, before he remembered to get out his phone and tell Sookie what had just gone down. And while dialing Sookie, Stan made a silent deal with himself, that, fuck accusations of cowardice, this was the last time ever in his life he was tangling with Lucy Tang. Sookie could go suck dick for all he cared.

***

From the house opposite the hotel, Lucy Tang and the Harris Boys watched Stan flee. All three were back in human form again and very amused.

Mark laughed heartily. "That giant punk'll have quite a tale to tell Sookie about tonight for sure."

"Yes," Lucy agreed. "She's going to be wetting the bed with rage." She laughed. "C'mon, let's get back to Bruce. Just in case Sookie's stupid enough to send reinforcements. We need to leave, anyway. This place will shortly be swarming with Robopol officers. And you know what the robots are like—they're going in there for sure—the hotel will be a fucking war zone."

Jesse grinned. "Robots versus monsters? Wow, I wouldn't mind watching that movie."

"Forget it," Lucy said, "we aren't staying. We can't rumble with the fuzz. You know how those machines are almost indestructible and they've got better hearing than dogs." She pulled his sleeve. "Come on, let's go."

"Alright, sure." Jesse pointed at the Beacon Hill Hotel and Bistro. "What'll happen to that place now? Are the nightmares gonna fade?"

"No, Robopol blowing the building to bits or not, they'll spread—seep through the walls into the other houses—soon this whole street will be a fucked-up zone. It'll take a hell of a lot of cleanup to ever get this area back to normal. I doubt the city council will even bother with the expense—they'll likely just turn it into a tourist attraction, a monster theme park." She grinned, her face exquisite still life in the moonlight. "Good thing for everyone the nightmares can't exit their realm."

She turned from looking at the new nightmare hotel. "Guy's, tonight's definitely been worth it. For me at least." She pointed to her swollen crotch. "Fuck! Now I *really* need to unwind."

CHAPTER 13

Malone / Slave

Malone was surprised by how much he was enjoying Slave's company. They'd dined in Sookie's seafood restaurant on swordfish steaks, oysters, and truffled lobster risotto, and now sat outside on the penthouse eatery's balcony sipping Chardonnay and watching the clouds blow across the Fort Point Channel.

Malone regarded Slave over his glass. He still had difficulty coming to terms with how beautiful she was, and more important, how brainy she was.

Concerns about Lt. Steelberg's strange case hovered around Malone's mind. But if those thoughts were vultures, Malone's psyche was currently a reviving corpse out in the desert, one that the mental scavengers regarded with dismay, realizing they'd wait much longer before dinner was served. As difficult as finding the creature leaping between Boston minds might prove to be, locating its whereabouts was a concern for tomorrow.

Malone liked that, to be able to forget work because of pleasant company.

He still had one worry, though he himself recognized it as unreasonable. Still the intensity of his concern puzzled him: *Is it that I really like this woman, or . . . damn, am I now that insecure?*

Feeling foolish, he voiced his concern:

"You don't have an ex-boyfriend you were about getting married to who's going to turn up suddenly and sweep you away tonight, do you?"

Slave laughed at the unexpected question. "Huh?" Then seeing Malone was serious, she said, "No, I've never been close to marrying anyone. Why do you ask?"

Malone told her. He wondered why he was being so open with a woman he'd just met and who he was still very wary of. (And yes, he was wary of Slave. Even while sharing his feelings now, he was ever conscious of the damning words engraved [branded?] in her flesh, the legend veiled by her bouncy brown curls, teasingly revealed in part whenever the wind blew through her hair, that dark statement of who she was, what she was all about. Still, he kept talking. But *why?* He couldn't answer that.)

"So now you know," he finished with a wry grin. "Guys my age can't take too many blows like that to the heart. I'd wind up needing a pacemaker."

"You're real nice to not blame her for her behavior."

"How could I? Still was shitty, though."

"Yes, I can't imagine how you felt. And no, I've no boyfriend at the moment. I'm not looking for one either. What I want and need is a Master."

"A Master?" Then he got it. "Oh, you mean . . . ?"

She nodded, her face serious. Her expression seemed to insist on a reply from him, so, waving his hands, he said, "Oh, no, I'm not the man for the job. I could never get pleasure from your pain."

Her eyes shone at him. "Have you ever *tried* S and M?"

He shook his head. "I've never found violence attractive."

"But you're in a profession of violence."

"Just for the money. You wouldn't consider a boxer a sadist or masochist, would you?"

She drank, smiled teasingly. "Quite a few are. Maybe not at first, but over time they get used to the pain, come to expect it, cherish it even as validation of their efforts. Remember the classic expression 'no pain, no gain?'"

"Now you're being cynical," he said. Her reasoning, however, discomfited him, sounded too close to truth.

She giggled. "No, I'm being realistic. Deny it all we want, everyone's a sadist to some degree. We all derive pleasure from the misfortune of those we hate. So take it a step further: given the chance to indulge ourselves, we'd get sexual enjoyment from causing them pain. The worse that pain, the greater our pleasure. Like it or not, sooner or later such dark delight always turns erotic."

"That makes sense, but what you're suggesting is my deriving sexual pleasure from the pain of someone I *like*, possibly even love. Sorry, that's beyond me."

Her eyes probed him. "You're missing my point. Imagine for a moment, that it's me you're dominating. Imagine I want you to whip and beat me, to abuse me in countless ways. For *my* pleasure. In that sense, my degradation, the pain I feel, is pleasure not pain."

"You're messing with my head. Pain is pain, pleasure is pleasure, don't mix them up."

"Too logical, but then you're a man anyway—everything's black and white. Try to view this as shades of feeling. In this case, interpretation depends on desire. If one desires pain, it's pleasure to have that desire satisfied, to receive that pain. If I want torment—a flogged bleeding ass—flowers and vanilla sex—no matter how loving or expert—won't cut it."

He pondered that, unconvinced.

Her eyes teased. "Haven't you ever come while beating someone up?"

"What?"

"Don't play innocent. As a PI, you've been in lots of fights. Haven't you ever had an orgasm while throwing punches?"

Malone was stumped. "Once," he finally admitted, again wondering why he was being so honest with her.

Slave stroked wayward windblown curls from her cheeks, an action that made her look oddly vulnerable. She didn't laugh. "How'd it happen?"

"An overload of sexual frustration. Stacy, my girlfriend at the time, had a urinary infection, so we hadn't had sex for two weeks. Meanwhile, the case I was working then had me interviewing prostitutes day and night, and lots of them tried to hustle me into bed." He shrugged. "So when I finally caught the guy—punk was raping some kid at the time—I just laid into him, beat him unconscious. I was aware I was enjoying letting off all the tension I felt, but I didn't even realize I had an erection, I just kept beating the rapist's ass up. It was only when Steelberg dragged me off him that I realized I'd come in my pants." He shrugged. "So there, it happened, but I was completely disgusted afterwards and considered visiting a shrink."

"But you didn't."

"No, I was too embarrassed."

"Embarrassed? And you're telling me?"

"You asked."

Slave giggled, her breasts bobbing. "That's true. Well, despite your rationalizing, Malone, you did have an orgasm during an episode of violence. I think it would have happened even if you *had* been having sex regularly with your girl. And whatever happens once can always recur, given the right stimulus. Oh, there's hope for you yet."

"I don't see the connection."

"Well, if you've experienced automatic sexual release in a completely non-erotic situation, when you weren't trying to, imagine how much easier, and how much sweeter, such release would be in a controlled erotic situation. It's not all whippings, there's some lovely bondage as well."

He frowned. His eyes met hers, tried not to betray his discomfort. "How do I convince you that I'm not interested?"

"I'm not saying you are. I'm just explaining."

"You sound like a sales brochure. Soledad's right, you're too intelligent for your own good."

"Thanks. Brains hardly ever get you laid though. T and A works way better."

Malone checked his watch. "You know what? You're a bit too convincing for my good. I think it's time I take you home."

"So soon? I'm just getting warmed up."

"That's what I'm scared of," Malone grunted. "That you'll shortly convince to bend over a chair with my butt out while you paddle me."

Pouting demurely, Slave finished off her drink.

CHAPTER 14

Lucy Tang and The Gang / Malone

"I wish I could be there to see Sookie's face when Stan reports in," Lucy Tang said, laughing.

The Harris Boys' loud laughter surged forward in a responsive wave from the AG's rear seat. "Yeah, that'd sure be something," Jesse said.

The only person not laughing was Bruce, who currently had his lips wrapped tight around Lucy's erect penis, and was fellating her as she flew the antigrav car along School Street, past the Old City Hall and the One Boston Place (skyscraper home to both USAcme and Robopol). His mouth made slurping sounds as his head bobbed up and down in his girlfriend's lap. She flew the car with one hand; the other alternatively stroked her breasts and ran fingers through Bruce's hair. Her legs were trembling from the sensations in her penis (*Oh, he does it so well!*). As she neared orgasm, it was taking all Lucy's concentration to keep the car on a straight course.

(Neither Harris Boy could handle the antigravity car. Bruce would have preferred to drive, but Lucy was so horny, she'd insisted on driving while he relieved her tension.)

Difficulties at the wheel notwithstanding, there was no way Lucy was going to postpone getting her rocks off. Before she'd commandeered Bruce's mouth, her penis had felt like a stone. Damn that dragonreich.

Jesse, in the rear right seat, had his eyes glued to Lucy and Bruce, the latter leaned over in his seat with one hand pumping Lucy's cock, the other squeezing her balls. Jesse wondered why he was watching them. He wasn't aroused or anything. As it did with most people, the reich had killed his libido. He couldn't understand his fascination with 'all this gay/tranny shit.' Yeah, *shit*—it definitely smelt to Jesse like Bruce had a finger up Lucy's anus.

Bruce pulled his lips almost completely off Lucy's penis, leaving the erection glistening wet purple, like he wanted Jesse to see it. Then he slid his head all the way down again, till Jesse imagined Lucy's 'womanhood' had to be blocking his throat. (*Damn, how's he even able to breathe?*) Lucy shuddered and groaned. "Oh yes, fuck, like that." The AG car shook then swerved left across the road for a moment, till Lucy corrected its course, steered it back to their lane. Jesse was suddenly alarmed. He looked away from the lovers, towards Mark.

"This is fucking dangerous," he whispered.

Mark's ugly face creased up with mirth. "Relax, bro, there's no one else on the road."

Jesse tried to relax. But his eyes kept going to Lucy and Bruce. And now, Lucy had slid further forward in her seat, spread her legs wider. Jesse could clearly see Bruce sliding fingers in and out of Lucy's backside. He began praying Lucy would come quick.

The fingers rubbing Lucy Tang's prostate were really distracting her. Her orgasm hovered like a bird on the horizon, was just about to shoot out of her. Her jet hair flickered in the breeze spilling in through the window. A grimace froze her lovely features; she tightened her grip on the steering wheel. *Damn, this ejaculation will blow Bruce's head off his shoulders*, she thought, then laughed at her violent sexual imagery. But it felt that way, like she'd shortly explode from pleasure. Both her breasts and her testicles felt like bombs about to go off. She giggled from the sex and from the pleasure of screwing Sookie, which was even better than the sex; and this blowjob was fantastic.

Bruce stabbed her ass with his fingers, his tongue stroked her penis. Her legs jerked further apart, her eyes shut from the pleasure. She suddenly remembered she was driving, and jerked her mind back to where she was. She heaved a sigh; she'd not yet flown off the road. (They were up on Washington now, just reaching the Water Street turnoff.) *Okay, that was dangerous,* she conceded, making the right turn. *I'd better talk to the guys to keep some focus.*

"Hey, Jesse," she said, looking up into the rearview. "You enjoying the show?"

"What show?"

"You know."

"Shut up and fucking come, Lucy. I'm terrified that you'll crash us."

"You just wish you were me at the moment, don't you?"

Jesse rolled his eyes and pointedly looked away, out the window at the houses rushing past.

They flew past Benjamin Franklin's statue, toward the Congress Street Junction.

Lucy Tang laughed and rolled her hips deliciously as Bruce kept up his work on her penis. Oh yeah, this was going to be the orgasm of a lifetime. She just knew it.

"Hey," Mark called from the back, "those fruit we hit Sookie's goons with, where'd you get them from?"

"The nightmare pods? They're from Hell—The Groad. Lots of crazy vegetation grows down there."

"We could do with more stuff like that."

She laughed. "Yeah. Easy to say, though. The problem is making it back up alive."

Then Bruce pumped his fist hard on her penis and she forgot Mark.

***

Turning up onto Kilby Street, Malone realized that Slave had fallen asleep beside him. Her excitement at returning to Boston had finally given in to the exhaustion of a day's travel.

He grinned. He felt a bit groggy himself; it was taking a world of concentration to drive. He was glad he didn't own an antigrav car; the alcohol in his system now was a clear recipe for disaster.

The road ahead was empty. Good enough. He sped up, no danger to anyone if he went a bit faster.

He looked across at Slave. Her dozing form shone in the moonlight spilling in through the windshield. She looked incredibly gorgeous, incredibly innocent. But . . .

Malone suddenly decided he never wanted to see Josephine 'Slave' Bailey again. *This is one very twisted lady here, someone I can really do without in my life.*

As if trying to convince himself he could do without her beauty, he looked away from Slave and sighed. *What a damn waste.*

***

Lucy Tang's orgasm hit her like a landmine going off. Her body stiffened; her hips trembled uncontrollably. She felt like she was pumping an almost solid stream of semen out into the center of Bruce's head, like someone was pulling a fat squirming worm out of her penis—the pleasure was almost pain. With one hand she kept Bruce's head firmly in place in her crotch; with the other she kept the car moving steadily ahead, speeding up at little as her tremors increased.

Then Bruce stroked exquisitely deep in her rectum, and while surfing the resultant delicious feelings . . .

Purely by accident, Lucy floored the accelerator.

"Fucking watch out!" Jesse screamed as the AG leapt forward.

"Calm down for heaven's sake!" Mark snapped at him. "Goddam let the woman drive!"

Realizing what she'd done, Lucy Tang panicked. She tried to slow down and correct the car's trajectory. Racked by the throes of her luscious orgasm, it proved an impossible task.

***

Malone looked up from staring at Slave. He was just reaching Liberty Square, the Water Street–Kilby Street intersection.

Seeing the fast approaching lights ahead to his left, he instantly felt a sinking feeling in his gut. Shit! An out of control silver AG was heading directly at him out of Water Street. And the damn thing was coming too fast to avoid.

Damn these damn AG's, Malone thought, bracing himself for the crash.

***

The BMW smashed into the AG's right side, its rear lifting off the blacktop with the force of impact. The black car's airbags inflated, cushioning its occupants. The vehicle juddered to a halt.

The AG, however, took the brunt of the impact. The antigravity car had been turning hard left to avoid the BMW, and the collision, as well as increasing the vehicle's already intense speed, both flipped it over, and flung it high up into the air. Upside-down and now completely out of control, the blue AG streaked across Liberty Square and smashed into a second floor apartment over the shops facing the intersection. It buried itself through the brick frontage. Sparks and smoke flickered from its damaged engines as its four inhabitants slowly made sense of where they were.

***

Malone's first concern after the impact was for Slave. He looked over at her and winced: Slave wasn't moving, she dangled limp in the seatbelt with a cut forehead. Alarmed, he leaned over to her and felt her neck for a pulse, was doubly reassured by the gentle rise and fall of her breasts. He sighed. Already asleep, hitting the airbag had just knocked her out.

Then Malone heard a loud explosion. Looking over the deflated airbags he covered his eyes as an orange flare lit up the previously moon-silver intersection.

Shit! The AG! The antigravity car was on fire now, a furnace. A blacksmith would have been delighted.

He leapt out of the BMW, retrieved the fire extinguisher from its trunk, and raced across the square (past the dragon-melted Hungarian memorial) towards the upside-down car stuck in the building. As he ran, screams spilled at him from the incinerating vehicle. The heat coming from it was intense, it poured over him in waves—the entire floor seemed on fire. Thankfully, this was a mostly un-reclaimed area, the house seemed deserted.

Malone reached the building. (A burning shop sign read Boston Kebab House.) Implanted into its front wall six feet over his head, the antigravity car was an inferno now. He raised the fire extinguisher, began spraying the AG. The extinguisher foam did nothing, it seemed rather to help the fire burn with greater ferocity. Malone kept spraying it regardless. He could clearly make out burning shapes inside the upside-down machine, constantly distorting figures and faces that seemed almost demonic in their fluidity. Those weren't human beings in there roasting. One of the figures—the sole one that maintained a human form—was already frozen in a black rictus.

The screams rose louder by the second—the torments of the damned. Malone was confused by something: It seemed as if the burning people in the AG were unable to free themselves. He didn't understand that. *It's almost like the fire has melted them— they've lost control of their bodies.*

He glanced back across at his BMW—Slave still looked out cold—then returned his attention to the firefight. He stood in a circle of foam that had fallen to earth rather than dousing the burning car.

It was so hot he was drenched in sweat. Water ran in hot streams down his face; his clothes were soaked through by his body's fight to keep him cool.

Still the fire raged.

Malone was struck by a sudden fearsome insight—the understanding that the vehicle burnt so fiercely because its occupants were flammable.

At the moment of Malone's enlightening, a massive flaming tentacle erupted out of the vehicle and dipped towards him.

Thinking it was attacking him, he leapt away from it.

The tentacle detached from the car. It fell to earth, then unraveled into a single wide fiercely-burning sheet. Above it, additional flaming tentacles burst from the vehicle's sides, these however remained in the AG. They flailed weakly, like they were dying.

Malone stared in confusion at the burning sheet on the floor. It had a face in it—a wide smeared face that extended all the way across its six-foot breadth. Eyes larger than footballs, a nose like a car tire, the mouth like a TV screen, with teeth . . .

The burning spread-out face began screaming. Malone directed the fire-extinguisher at it and sprayed.

The foam left in the extinguisher proved just enough to douse the fire on the burning face. Malone stared at it in horror. Whatever help he'd just rendered had come very late—the face was cooked meat now, smoke rose from it along with a sickening smell of roast flesh.

Malone stood staring at the face on the floor. *What the hell is going on here?* The face had stopped screaming, its eyes were shut, and its middle rose and fell as if the sheet of flesh was breathing. And, like they shared a similar mortal control mechanism, the voices from the burning car overhead had also fallen silent.

Also, the heat had reduced. Realizing this, Malone looked up. Thick smoke spilled out into the night air, but the fire had gone out.

The previously burning tentacles now dangled black and limp from the AG's windows. He prodded one of them. It swung lifelessly to and fro. Malone gleaned an idea of what was going on. *Okay, I just rammed a carful of flammable mutants.*

He dropped the extinguisher. It hit the floor with a loud 'klang.'

As though the noise had woken it up, the carpet of flesh by his feet coughed. He looked back down. The massive flat eyes were looking at him.

"Malone?" the spread-out face asked, its voice a weird chitter like the sound of a backyard-full of crickets. "Is it you, Malone?"

A tremor went through him. "Y-y-you know me?"

"Malone, it's Lucy Tang."

He gaped in disbelief at the flat burnt face, that sheet of sickening, glistening wet meat spread out in moonlight. "*Lucy Tang?* Lucy? What the . . . ? How the hell are—?"

"Just listen, Malone. I haven't got much time. I'm fucking dying, and I know it, okay? You gotta do something for me."

He nodded.

"I want you to deliver a message to Sookie Ling for me."

"What's the message?"

Lucy Tang laughed bitterly. "Tell Sookie Ling she can suck my dick."

Next thing, she was dead. The meat-sheet humped up violently once as though lifted by a wind from beneath, then settled and didn't move again.

***

Once he realized Lucy Tang was dead, Malone returned to his car and made two phone calls.

First he called 911. Robopol said they were on their way with a meat wagon.

Next, Malone called Soledad Bathory to make sure she was home. No reply, voicemail. Oops; he realized that put a new spin on things. He looked at Slave, she was more or less awake, but groggy.

She reached a hand across to him. "What the hell happened?"

"Car crash."

Her eyes struggled to focus. "I see airbags. Were we in it?"

He frowned. "Don't talk, just relax. I'm taking you to ER."

"I'm fine, just take me home."

"You need a—"

He stopped. She was out cold again. He sat, staring down the street, his eyes occasionally flickering to the purple sheet of meat that had said it was Lucy Tang and the wrecked inverted husk above it. His mind was troubled, and not just by the four deaths he'd just witnessed.

Malone had the clear sense that his plan to never see Josephine 'Slave' Bailey again after tonight had just been completely derailed.

There was still hope of an escape, however. If he could get Soledad . . . He called Slave's arcane cousin again. Once again he got Soledad's voicemail. He hung up, sat, hands gripping the wheel, staring grimly ahead. Where the hell was Soledad Bathory? Okay, so Slave didn't want a hospital bed tonight; he still couldn't just go and dump her on Soledad's doorstep, could he?

He saw the Robopol AG arrive and went to meet it.

The responding officer, Elroy Bidd (SN. 37R0Y-6166), was just alighting from the police SUV when Malone reached it.

"What happened, Malone?" Officer Bidd asked, adjusting its crumpled hat on its oval head. The robot's navy-blue suit was even more mussed up than its headwear.

Malone explained.

"Lucy Tang, eh?" Bidd said when Malone reached that part. "One of Sookie's girls wasn't she? A drag performer? I thought she left town years ago."

"So did I," Malone said quietly. Lucy's last words were spinning in his head. *Tell Sookie Ling she can suck my dick.* He winced. An old-school Chinese beef had just come to the boil.

"And you're saying this is her spread out over the floor here?"

"That's what she said."

"Wow." Officer Bidd's glowing eyes studied the burnt sheet of flesh. "I wonder how the hell she got so stretched out."

Malone didn't comment, he was suddenly tired out.

The robot next pointed a metal finger over at Malone's car. "And the woman with you? She need the medics?"

"She says she's okay. I'll just take her home."

A ticking sound came from Bidd's head. "I can see some blood on her forehead. The wound's just a scratch, though; nothing a Band-Aid won't fix. Her pulse is normal too. No broken bones either."

They were thirty yards from the BMW. Malone gaped at the white robot. "You can tell that just by looking at her? I can't even see her clearly."

"Night vision; infrared. Body systems monitors. Her blood pressure's normal—she's not leaking fluids anywhere."

"She's asleep, insists she wants her own bed tonight." He shook a finger at the police robot. "Can you tell if she's concussed? That's what I'm worried about."

"Not at a glance, no. But her intracranial pressure's normal—she seems fine, Malone. Take her to an outpatients' tomorrow if she feels or acts odd. Okay, have a good night, Malone. I got some cleanup to do."

Malone nodded and left. Officer Bidd bent and began rolling up the sheet of flesh that had been Lucy Tang.

"One more thing, Malone."

He looked back. "Yeah?"

"You've been drinking yourself. Your Breathalyzer alcohol index is just under the city's permissible driving limit. Now, I can tell from the vehicle angles and trajectories that this crash wasn't your fault, but it could very well have been. So, remember the rules—if you're gonna drive, don't drink." Officer Bidd pointed down at the ground. "You don't take my advice, and next time this could be you I'm rolling up here."

Malone nodded. "Thanks, Bidd. I hear you."

***

Back in his car, Malone again tried getting Soledad Bathory on the phone. Once again he got her voicemail.

"Oh, crap," he mumbled finally at the still slumbering Slave. "Looks like you're coming home with me tonight."

Malone was so upset by this, he didn't even leave a voicemail message for Soledad. He just started up the BMW (to his relief the engine wasn't busted), and drove off.

CHAPTER 15

Rick

I'm in a nightmare, Rick Rogers thought, as antigravity cars made of meat and piloted by demons zipped past him.

It was warm in the Forbidden City. Not overwhelming so; just like being in an air-conditioned room in winter.

The sky was black and sunless, the city lit by radiant white clouds. The clouds glowed like someone had broken up the missing sun and dropped pieces of it in each of them.

Beneath this strange sky, flanked left and right by weird, mind-bending buildings, Rick made his cautious way down the same street he'd been walking for only God knew how long.

"It's called Endless Street," Soledad had educated him before he'd stepped through the OD in her witch's basement. "It leads to just about anywhere you want to go in Bizarro."

"I thought you said I'm going into The Groad."

"The Groad is part of Bizarro. Or if you prefer, Bizarro is what created The Groad."

"Created? How?"

"Bizarro infected Hell; The Groad resulted. What do you care more than that?"

Rick had nodded, pointed at the oval space-time portal, its surface a constant wobbling like agitated jelly. "Okay, so I go in here and keep walking. This Club 66Sex, it's along the way?"

"Most likely, but it might not be. Either way, try not to ask for directions. Making enquiries will mark you as a newcomer in the Forbidden City, and the predators will home in on you."

"Why's it called the Forbidden City?"

"Everything forbidden elsewhere goes on down there. Your most perverted imaginings, whatever they are, are commonplace occurrences. No one bats an eyelid whatever you do. There's little law or order—"

"Sounds just like home."

She scowled. "Here we've at least got Robopol now to keep criminals in line. In the Forbidden City . . ." A visible shudder ran through her elegant frame.

Rick had gotten the point, so now he strode along with fake swagger. His bearing oozed confidence he didn't feel, particularly since he didn't have any weapons. "A gun or knife might be misconstrued," Soledad had said, so Rick had entered the undercity empty-handed. He'd even left his watch ("There's no time down in The Groad."). All he had were the clothes on his back, and a small bag of *Clif* and *Vega* energy bars.

He had no money, because he had no money anyway.

"Don't worry," Soledad had assured him. "Once you meet Anastasia Wormwood and strike a deal, all your financial worries are over."

And where was he? Despite this place lacking a fiery furnace, Rick Rogers didn't doubt he was in Hell. A hell of the mind at least. Even deranged imagination—full-blown insanity—had to have its limits. That clearly wasn't the case down here.

The houses he walked past were all made of meat. Their walls were dripping red surfaces, raw like someone had peeled off their skin. They ran with blood and other fluids. Rough arrangements of bone formed window and door frames. Their roofs were sheets of skin stretched over yet more bones.

Some of the houses had eyes embedded in their substance, staring eyes that watched Rick. Some eyes seemed human, some animal. Some were utterly alien, only recognizable as eyes by their blinking.

From behind the walls of the nightmare houses came both shrieks of pleasure and screams of agony, sometimes from the same place and voice, as if torturer and victim were both the same person. Rick sought to close his mind to this insane mingling of sounds, but even when he plugged his ears with fingers, the noises filtered into his head like thoughts.

He walked faster. Ahead of him was a space without buildings. No buildings meant no sound.

A large brown rat skipped past him, vanished through a bone-framed doorway. Rick shuddered. There were loads of rats down here, huge roaches too.

A meat AG zoomed past him, heading the opposite way. The vehicle's occupants were two laughing women. The AG itself smelt like burnt steak.

Then a demon stepped out from a house ahead. The demon—black, thin, with four horns and an immense potbelly—gaped in alarm at Rick, then vanished into its house again. Rick heaved a sigh of relief. When, a moment later Rick passed that house, he saw through the window that the demon was making a phone call. He quickened his steps even more, just in case the phone call concerned him.

A man was walking towards Rick. Under his hat, the right side of his face was completely melted away, dripped down and congealed like wax over his business suit. As he passed Rick, he grimaced, baring teeth in what remained of his head. Afterwards, Rick realized the melted man had been smiling at him.

He looked down at the sidewalk. It was easier, there were just a few large bugs to see. He replayed Soledad's instructions through his head again:

"The Club you want is called *66Sex*. There's different versions of it though—in some existences it's called the *WTF? Bar*, in others *The Babylon Motel*. There's also a *Hotel Bizarre* version." She'd paused then, scratched her nose while regarding him with intent eyes. "Okay, you need to prepare yourself for this trip. I mean mentally. Don't go there and start freaking out. Club 66Sex is a real weird place. Very weird—you won't believe your eyes what you see there."

"You've been there before?"

"How else would I know where it is?"

"Moot question—you're a witch, you can view places with spells."

"I've been there alright. Trust me, I didn't believe my eyes either. But listen: you get to 66Sex, Anastasia Wormwood will be waiting for you there."

"What does she look like?"

"She's a tall beautiful blonde. Utterly impossible to miss. Totally hot. You'll instantly want to bed her."

"Not me—I just want her money."

Soledad laughed. "Oh, you'll want to do the pig to her alright. And that's the one thing you're not to do, no matter what. *Do not go to bed with her.*"

"Why?"

"She's not just bad news, she's a CNN disaster report. Let me make this real clear: Do not screw, fuck, bone, nail, make love, ball—whatever your favorite expression for penetrating members of my sex is—don't do it with her. You go that route with Anastasia, you won't need Stan McCaulkin cutting off your legs." She frowned. "Dig?"

He'd nodded grimly. "So what do I tell her?"

"She'll start the conversation. Once she notices you in 66Sex, she'll know why you're there and will offer you a deal in exchange for as much cash as you need."

"What if she wants my soul?"

"She won't try to trade for it, too many humans are wise to that now." Soledad raised a cautionary finger. "Just remember . . ."

"No sex with the pretty lady," Rick finished for her. "Don't worry, I won't forget."

At a sudden sense of space around him, Rick's mind jerked out of his thoughts.

He was now through the vale of meat houses, into a wide space fenced by far-off white buildings. He grinned. So long as he could find Club 66Sex, the rest was easy. All he had to do was not bed the lady? Piece of cake; sex was currently the farthest thing from his mind.

He sat on a bench and ate several energy bars, blueberry and chocolate almond. Maybe because there supposedly wasn't time here, he didn't feel tired. Also, so far, he wasn't too worried at being in the Forbidden City. Nobody had bugged him—hell, that potbellied demon had even been scared of him.

Then his eyes caught a motion across the road. After at first imagining the movement was one of the ubiquitous brown rats scurrying through the knee-high grass, Rick squinted to see better.

Then he leapt up to see better still.

Through the grass he saw the ground open up into a mouth, a huge wet mouth surrounded by green tentacles, the tentacles almost indistinguishable from the grass around it. Then the hole in the ground shut up, like there'd never been anything there to begin with.

Rick had just begun thinking he'd imagined seeing it, when the hole suddenly appeared again. Now it was in the middle of the road, just past the double yellow line, on Rick's side. Its many tentacles lay like starfish legs across the road surface.

Rick could now see into the hole—a deep chasm inside which jagged stones ground against each other.

The hole vanished again, leaving the road undamaged and undisturbed.

Rick did a lightning-fast calculation and realized the creature was heading for him, that it was hunting him. He leapt aside just as the hole opened again, this time right under where he'd been standing, its tentacles lashing up to snare him. Rick saw that several of the hole's tentacles had eyes in their tips.

The hole searched for him a while, then vanished again.

Rick had no illusions about where it would appear next. He turned and ran. He kept running till he was again between the rows of meat houses.

There he stopped, and leaning against a parked AG, caught his breath, shivering. *What the hell was that thing? She-it—and it almost had me too!*

After a while, Rick resumed walking down Endless Street. The horror of what he'd just experienced lay heavy on him. He'd learnt his lesson now: he wasn't taking anything for granted down here.

He looked up ahead at the black sky with its lightbulb clouds. *Yeah, the sooner I find Club 66Sex and get this over with, the better.*

Now the horrible screams and mingled moans of pleasure spilling from the house walls were a pleasant reminder to Rick that he was still alive.

CHAPTER 16

Malone / Slave / Soledad

A woman with ginger-colored hair was sucking Malone's penis. Her torso was covered with breasts. All over. She had breasts stacked all up her front and rear; they dotted her arms also. Thirty or forty large and little breasts, each one perfect in its own way, they decorated her.

Her face and legs were clear of the breasts, as were the hands she stroked Malone's erection with.

She dipped her mouth into his groin, slowly drew it up the slick staff to suck hard on the swollen penis head, then dipped down again. And again, and again. Her covering of mammary glands jiggled fiercely with her movement, her many nipples erect with arousal.

He groaned as she fellated him, moving his hands from breast to breast, roving over each succulent white expanse, squeezing and stroking . . . And then suddenly, he had two more hands: then four more, then eight . . . each additional hand joined in his exploration of the fellatrix's flesh.

The woman—he imagined her some kind of goddess—moaned in pleasure and he fondled and teased her nipples.

She rode her lips up over his penis again, looked him square in the eyes. Hers eyes were light blue, like twin skies trapped in skin. Her nose was regal, her lips full. She dipped her head yet again.

"Holy Shit!" Malone groaned as her lips engulfed him completely. He was burning up from the pleasure. Like parched travelers desperately seeking an oasis, his many arms ranged over her landscape of flesh dunes.

The sensation in his penis, the glow in his groin was golden. *Oh yes, any moment now.*

The woman shook herself; her many breasts shook too.

***

Malone woke up.

Pushing against the urge to fall back asleep, he was aware the delicious feeling between his legs remained. A wet dream? But . . . he'd not come yet.

No, someone was definitely sucking his penis. And very expertly too. *Who* . . .

He opened his eyes, saw that Slave was fellating him, her head bobbing up and down between his legs just like his dream goddess's had been. She wore only bra and panties of frilly green lace. Her chocolate hair was spread out over his thighs. It obscured her face as her mouth worked on him.

Last night's events instantly tumbled through his mind again. Dinner . . . the crash . . . not getting Soledad on the phone . . . bringing her cousin back to his apartment . . . . cleaning her cut forehead (she'd had the merest of nicks, there'd been no need for a Band-Aid even) . . . tucking her into bed in the spare room . . .

And now Slave had his pajamas open and was . . .

He made no move to stop her fellating him. She was fantastic at it. Much better than the dream goddess.

Slave realized he'd woken. She slid her lips off his erection, brushed her hair away from her face, then grinned and shrugged. "I came in to say thanks and you had a boner. Would have been a shame to waste it." She giggled. "I like sucking dick. It's fun."

"Hey, I thought you only did the whipping thing."

"That comes later."

Before he could comment further, she dropped her mouth to his penis again and the pleasure resumed. Malone laid back and enjoyed the blowjob, stroking her hair and groaning as the effect of her divine lips on his mere mortal flesh intensified toward the point of no return.

He ejaculated like machine gun fire, pumping weeks of frustrated semen into her mouth. She kept her mouth tight around his penis till he was done.

It was a fantastic orgasm. Malone felt like she'd destroyed him. He lay back, watched her spit his come out into a wad of tissue then crawl backward off the bed.

"Be back in a minute," she grimaced. "Have to brush my teeth. I love sucking you guys, but semen tastes like cod liver oil to me."

He watched her buttocks shake as she dashed off. Slave's rear view was exquisite. Each gluteal globe was painfully tight—no sag whatsoever—like twin full moons filled her panties. Her legs were long and coltish; their pleasant curves seemed to flow down to the beautiful ankles and feet.

Okay, now I'm in this way over my head, he realized. *But, oh yeah, the lady gives great head.*

***

Slave returned and sat beside Malone. In the interim, she'd removed her bra and panties. Her sexual fur was a neat thatch between her legs. They regarded each other's bodies, she stroking his chest and playing with its hair.

"I used your toothbrush," she said. "Hope you don't mind?"

He shrugged back coolly. Despite his wariness of Slave, he had to admit that her body was a wet dream come true. Long, sleek and toned . . . her breasts—neither too small nor too full, just right, with large rosy nipples now engorged by the lust in her eyes. Nipples he wanted to clamp his lips over. Her arms . . . his penis was stiffening again.

"Okay, now it's my turn," Slave said.

Malone tensed; his penis instantly deflated.

"I want you to spank me."

He frowned. "I don't think . . ."

She stared him down, her eyes fires. "I want you to. Do it."

He made to get up. "Slave, I really don't think I'm the man for this job."

She pushed him back down (she was deceptively strong), then rolled her eyes. "You guys are all so funny."

"How?"

"I'd have thought you knew by now that it's us women who decide who's the right man for the job . . ." she grinned, "and . . . what the *fucking* job is in the first place. Get it—fucking?"

Malone had no reply. She saw his tension and said:

"Malone, I know you're a nice guy. That's why I feel I can trust you here. Besides, we clearly like each other—we've chemistry—so why spoil a nice erotic moment, huh?" She smiled coquettishly. "If you smack my butt and don't enjoy it? Okay, then I'll accept that we're wrong for each other and we'll just be friends." Her smile broadened. "How's that for a deal?"

With her putting it like that, Malone felt he couldn't refuse. "Deal," he agreed. "How do we do it?"

She pulled his arm. "Come over to the edge of the bed and I'll kneel across your legs. That way you'll have full access to my buttocks."

"I use my hand?"

"Yes, I don't have any paddles here. Take your pajamas off, I want to feel your erection pressing on my belly."

Malone moved to oblige her, sitting as she directed. She knelt across his legs, her creamy rear globes spread before his eyes.

"Now hit me."

"How hard?"

"Hard as you like."

He gave her a little smack on the right buttock. She sighed then gave him a pained expression. "Stop fooling about. Spank me like you mean it."

He hit her buttock harder, a resounding slap that made them both wince.

"Yes, like *that*," Slave groaned.

He smacked her again, the left ass-cheek this time. "For how long?"

"Just keep going," she gasped. "You'll know when to stop. But keep the strokes firm and heavy—the harder the better. Don't worry, I won't break under the assault."

He smacked her hard again, grimacing as flesh hitting flesh sounded like a gunshot. Slave gasped like she'd been shot. Her buttocks were already smarting a burning red under Malone's hand. And . . . and, he now made out pale scars of previous lust on her cheeks . . .

Malone kept his hand rising and falling against her skin. She was gasping now, flailing like a fish over his legs, clearly in pain, and yet clearly in ecstasy:

"Oh fuck, fuck, give me more."

Slave's sex was drenched, her thighs were drenched. One hand gripped the rug, the other the bed. Her hair, its entire mass slung over her right shoulder swept the floor as she rolled her head in rapture . . .

He hit her buttocks harder; she gasped louder. Malone couldn't understand it: Slave was clearly experiencing deep sexual pleasure from his beating her. The expression on her face told him she'd come soon. And . . .

To his chagrin, Malone had an erection himself. His stiff penis pressed up hard against Slave's belly—there was no way she couldn't know he was aroused. He was confused, wondered if he should stop now and kick her out. One blowjob was just a one-night-stand; it was still possible to cut the cord, to never see this warped woman again.

He decided to see it through: he couldn't deny that what they were doing greatly excited him. His penis was rock hard, feeling like it would punch a hole into Slave's belly.

He kept hitting Slave's buttocks, doing so now with a ferocity he'd not believed he possessed. His erection compelled him to smack her hard, her delighted squeaks and exhortations urged him to hit her even harder. His arm began aching from the effort.

Then Slave began to orgasm, gritting her teeth and snorting like she was possessed, till Malone was scared he'd really hurt her.

"Oh God, oh God, oh God . . . !" she kept moaning.

Malone kept spanking her till she went limp.

Malone's strange lust overpowered him. Suddenly, seemingly unable to restrain himself, he lifted Slave off his legs and flung her face down on the bed. He knelt by her angry, red buttocks, and grimacing, his eyes almost bulging with the intensity of his fervor, masturbated fast and furious over the marks of his fingers in her ravaged skin. He came, spurting all over her behind. This ejaculation was violently unique. He pumped out much more semen than he ever had before for a second orgasm.

Then, as for some reason it seemed fitting to do, Malone rubbed the semen into Slave's reddened ass like it was suntan lotion. She flinched as if the come stung her, then sighed happily as he kneaded each cheek violently. Her flesh felt hot, hot, hot.

Finally, he collapsed by her side. Their eyes met. His were confused; hers were radiant.

"Is that . . . is that what you wanted?" he gasped.

She nodded, stroked his face with soft fingers. "That was the best first-time scene I've ever had with any guy. Did you enjoy it?"

He shook his head, then relented. "I don't know."

"That's odd. You came."

"I had no choice but to come. I felt like a caveman, like my primal desires overran me. I didn't enjoy that."

"That's normal at first. You'll get used to that feeling of power. It's part of the enjoyment of being a Dominant."

"I'm not sure I want to get used to it."

"You're not showing me the door . . ."

"That's the problem: I seem to be unable to—"

Both of them gave a start, as, with a bright flash of blue light, Soledad Bathory suddenly appeared in the bedroom.

* * *

Malone instantly pulled his discarded pajamas up over his penis. Slave made no attempt to cover herself. She rolled over onto her back, purred contentedly at her cousin: "Baby, don't you ever knock?"

Soledad frowned. "I see you've been getting your butt tanned." She looked at Malone. "I'm utterly disappointed in you. Were you that easy to convince?"

Malone's reply was an embarrassed smile. "I hated it."

"Liar." Slave playfully smacked Malone's chest, then beamed up at Soledad. "He loved it—he's just got first-timer's guilt."

Malone looked accusingly at Soledad. "This is all your fault, you know. I couldn't get you on the phone last night."

Before replying, Soledad looked around for a chair. Not finding any, she snapped her fingers. One of Malone's living room armchairs instantly appeared beside her. She sat in it. She crossed her legs and stared glumly at Malone.

"I had some trouble. Big trouble," she began coolly. Then her regal composure collapsed and she appeared close to tears. "Trust me, Malone, I'm not here this early to retrieve the family masochist, and I definitely didn't come to play Peeping Tom. I

104

need your help, Malone. I've got a real monster problem on my hands now."

Malone pulled himself upright, sat back against the headboard. "Go on—what's your trouble?"

Soledad sighed. "Lucy Tang died last night."

"We know that," Slave said. "We were there."

"You were?"

"How do *you* know anyway? It was a deserted street."

"I sensed it. What do you mean: you were there?"

Malone gave her a full description of the past night's events. Soledad listened in silence, then said, "So that's what happened; a completely unforeseeable turn of events." Her worry was now a palpable presence in the bedroom.

Slave yawned. "So what's her death got to do with you? Did you hex her car?"

"No, I didn't hex her car. I hexed *her*."

Malone raised an eyebrow. "Why would you hex Lucy Tang?"

"Sookie Ling asked me to."

Malone sighed. "You mean *paid*, don't you? Well, your hex worked better than you ever imagined."

"You should be ashamed of yourself," Slave said in disgust. "Killing four innocent people. For money?"

"I didn't fucking kill them!" Soledad snapped at her. "And look here—Lucy Tang wasn't any kind of innocent; she'd been murdering loads of Sookie's men."

"Wait a minute, Soledad," Malone said slowly. "If your hex on Lucy didn't kill her—"

The witch frowned. "It didn't. That was purely an accident."

"I get that. So what's the bother? Sookie wanted an enemy dead . . . she's dead."

Soledad Bathory stood up and paced the bedroom. She walked back and forth with long strides, her face clearly distressed. Her long blonde pigtail flopped left and right behind her like it was alive. Slave and Malone were still confused as to what her great worry was. To both of them it seemed 'mission accomplished,' like Soledad should be delighted rather than bothered.

"Or, are you worried you'll have to refund Sookie's money?" Slave asked. "But I don't see how she'll know you didn't kill Lucy if you don't tell her."

Soledad finally stopped pacing. Standing at the foot of the bed, she explained:

"I'm sorry, Malone. I honestly didn't want to, but I lied about not knowing anything about your mind transfers case." She groaned; the sound seemed to vibrate through her. "I'm responsible for that."

A chill went through Malone. "Soledad, what the hell did you do?"

"Sookie—you know how insistent she is once she's got an idea in her head—wanted a permanent fix for her 'Lucy Tang bullshit,' as she called it. Something magic, something foolproof, something also undetectable, but most important, something Lucy wouldn't see coming in a million years. So I suggested *Switch*."

She resumed pacing. "It's a bodiless entity from The Groad. One that can transfer between people's bodies, and then—"

"I knew I was right," Slave interrupted gleefully. "It was something—"

"Let her finish," Malone said.

"Yes, let me finish."

Slave frowned. "No need, both of you. I've figured out where this is going. Now let me see, Soly . . . at Sookie's request, you raised this demon Switch, and instructed it to kill Lucy Tang. You picked it because, leaping from body to body as it does, there's no single person Lucy would be watching her back for—I mean the assassin could be just about anyone, right?"

"Go on," Malone said. "Anyone?"

Slave nodded. "That's the beauty of the plan. The Switch creature could be in anyone. A kid, an old man . . ." she looked pointedly at her cousin, "a cat . . . it does animals too?"

"Yes, you're right," Soledad confirmed. "Switch can inhabit anything with a mind." She raised a hand to stop Slave interrupting. "Please let me finish; it's more complicated than you think."

"Okay," Slave said. "We're listening."

Malone nodded.

Soledad said miserably, "Don't blame me for choosing Switch. The beauty of this plan was that Lucy never even knew there was an assassin after her. It was perfect." Her face fell even further into depression. "Then Lucy Tang died and now . . ."

"What's the problem?" Malone asked gently. "I can't help you if you don't tell me."

"I think I know that too," Slave replied for her, joyful malice twinkling in her eyes. "Now that Lucy Tang's dead, the spell's been reversed, and the demon's coming back after Soly."

Soledad shook her head. "You're right—the spell *has* been reversed. But no, Switch isn't coming after me . . . it's going after Sookie Ling." She collapsed into the armchair and stared plaintively at Malone, looking like she was going to cry. "Malone, I need you to find and stop Switch before it finds and kills Sookie."

"Yeah, now I see what the problem is," Malone said. "And it's a damn big one." He adjusted himself against the headboard, scratched stubble on his chin. "Soledad, how come you don't know where the demon is?"

"I put an obscuring spell on it, the strongest I could work, one even I can't see through . . . or remove." Now she'd explained the problem, she was more relaxed.

"So you're saying that magically, there's simply no way to locate it?"

"None. I've been up all night trying, but no luck."

"There's a whole lot of cats in Boston," Slave said. "Soly, how could you? I mean, what's to happen to all the innocent people who got kicked out of their bodies?"

"I was going to put them back once Lucy was gone. It's not a hard procedure . . ." She shook her head at Slave's enquiring gaze. "No, the rebodying spell won't work until Switch has done its dirty work, in this case on Sookie Ling."

"So we're back to plain old detective work," Malone said. "I'd better call Steelberg, give him the facts—"

"No, don't do that!"

Malone was surprised. The witch's beautiful face was lined with fear. "What is it?"

"Sookie's got ears in all the cop shops. The news'll get back to her, and you know how vindictive she is when she thinks she's been screwed over."

"Not your fault," Slave objected.

"Try telling Sookie that, dear. So, Malone, that's why I'm here and why I'm currently a bundle of nerves: I want you to find and neutralize . . . kill the demon—no it's not a fucking demon—it's an entity, a presence, a crystalized intent, you could imagine it as a mental software program if you like, one from hell. I'll pay you big to stop it before it does a hit on Sookie." She grimaced. "And most important, she mustn't know a thing about it."

Slave grinned. "Ah, the witch is scared of the bitch."

"You don't know her. I don't want to spend my entire future in her bad books."

"I'll do it," Malone said.

"How much will it cost me? I'll pay whatever."

"Don't worry about that. You're a friend of mine."

"You'll do it for free?"

"Yeah, sure." His brow creased in thought. "Besides, I'm sure finding your runaway entity will prove quite a puzzle to unravel. It's been ages since I last had such an interesting case to work on."

Soledad was visibly relieved. "I don't know how to thank you."

Slave grinned, running playful fingers over Malone's crotch then squeezing. "I'll thank him for you. Oh, I'll thank him real good."

Malone felt his penis growing hard again beneath her fingers. That wasn't something he wanted Soledad seeing. He knocked Slave's hand away, then said, "How about, we three all have breakfast and you can tell me what I need to know about Switch."

***

Breakfast was coffee with scrambled eggs on toast. Slave cooked. Malone and Soledad sat out at the dining table, talking. Slave (now, like Malone, dressed in one of his bathrobes) listened through the kitchen door with half her mind.

". . . Switch is only as strong as the body it inhabits, but still, it'll be much harder to kill than that person or animal would normally be."

"That's a contradiction."

"Yes. But remember the body isn't inhabited by a normal mind. Switch transfers some supernatural abilities to the host's flesh. I don't think the creature can feel pain, but *it can* be stopped by bodily damage—when the body simply can't go on anymore. But even reaching that point . . ."

Slave blanked out the conversation. The sweet smell of cooking eggs swirled in her nostrils; she stirred them, taking care they didn't burn.

It was hard to concentrate on food, however. Her mind, her eyes, kept leaping to Malone. How handsome he was too. The memories of his stiffened hand hitting her smarting flesh, pleasure piercing her pain with each loud smack . . . she found herself getting wet again from the memory. Damn! Oh, yes, it had been lovely.

But would it last? He clearly disliked hurting her, which was both a plus and a minus. She wanted a Master who was firm as steel, yet soft as velvet. Malone fit the second category, she needed him to be the first too. There were dark depths of despairing desire in her soul; things she wanted to explore with this man she'd just met, and who, without meaning to, had already surpassed her expectations.

The eggs were done. She killed the fire under the skillet, got the bread out from the fridge. Ah, men; why not just buy *sliced* bread?

Malone's voice floated in through the door: ". . . How hot?"

"Not too much. It'll be noticeable, though: the rise in temperature is a good indicator Switch is in the room. Outside, it's a lot less reliable because of wind currents."

"And the teeth?"

"That's the dead giveaway. The host will start losing their teeth. I don't know why, but it happens very fast."

"Yeah. I remember Jenny Yang—the girl with the cat in her— lots of her teeth were gone."

"So you know what to look for . . ."

Slave sliced up the bread, popped it in the toaster. Checked the percolator. Yes, she really liked this Malone; liked the calm way he spoke, his gentle confidence. She mused: *He has to be at least ten years older than me, but so what? Guys in their fifties date twenty-year-olds, don't they?*

Most of all, Slave knew instinctively that she could trust Malone. He was a good man, the sort most women wanted. (She was surprised he was still single.) Her woman's instincts told her he'd not use her for his own pleasure then discard her.

Herein lay a dark paradox: Being a submissive, Slave's psyche demanded that her lover debase her for his own pleasure. The feelings of being demeaned and disregarded were essential to the joys of her sexual orientation, as pleasant as the pain was; but a good Dominant always understood that he was exerting his will on her at her choice, and that that signed-over choice was a precious thing, something which, in a way, made the submissive much stronger than the Dominant. *I choose to let you whip me, to have your pleasure of my body. I choose this. I am therefore your goddess when you hurt me—I grant you the only honest way to relieve your wicked desires. Your sexual truth is in my pain. My pleasure is your violence, your pleasure is my acquiescence.*

But could Malone take pleasure in her pain? That was Slave's one doubt. She needed him to, needed him to delight in hurting her. She wanted to see him panting like a hound of lust, his cock straining fit to burst as he flogged her like a dog . . .

Her thoughts faded back into the conversation outside. Realizing breakfast was ready, she loaded it on trays and served the others.

***

As Slave exited the kitchen bearing her massive tray of scrambled eggs, Soledad brandished a knife at Malone.

"You kill Switch with this."

He took it from her. "It's made of wood." The weapon was realistically carved, by otherwise spectacularly unimpressive, with no runes or sigils or anything to suggest it had paranormal powers. He ran a finger along its edge. "It's also blunt."

"It'll do the job. Just stab whoever the host is and game over."

Slave laid the tray of eggs between the pair.

"Wow, this smells great," Malone approved.

Slave grinned. "That's two points in my favor." Wiggling for his benefit, she headed back to the kitchen.

Soledad leaned forward and whispered. "You know how this works, don't you? Three points and you're at the altar."

Leaving a bemused Malone examining the wooden knife, she followed Slave to the kitchen to help serve, her leather skirt rustling like bat wings.

They sat, ate.

"So let's recap," Malone said after a sip of delicious coffee. "This creature Switch transfers itself from person to person by contact . . ."

"Any kind of contact—a casual caress, kissing, sex, a fight. The two bodies just have to touch for a short period of time."

"Also, in its bid to kill Sookie Ling, Switch will perfectly fake each host's behavior, and then—"

"How's that even possible?" Slave asked. "I mean, perfectly faking someone who isn't in there anymore?"

"While transferring the owner of the new body out into its previous one, Switch records the person's mind."

"Oh, like I'd do a data backup on my laptop." She nodded. "Then it accesses their memory." She bit into a slice of toast, chewed a while, swallowed, her face thoughtful.

Malone continued: "Then we have the hierarchical thing—it's climbing a 'person ladder' as it were, each time transferring to someone more likely to encounter its target."

Slave refilled Malone's cup with coffee. "The 'six degrees of separation' theory?" She regarded their blank stares with surprise. "Don't tell me you've never heard of that? Okay, it's simply the theory that everyone on the planet is connected by just six other people to everyone else. Take for instance, if I want to meet US president Sara Fischer . . . someone in my circle is bound to know someone who knows someone else who knows someone else who knows her. The point is—the links in the chain won't ever be longer than six people."

"In this case it's just one," Soledad said. "Malone's a personal friend of Mrs. President."

Slave gaped at him, gasped, "You *know* Sara Fischer? She's my heroine." She calmed. "Okay, I'll hero-worship later. All I'm trying to say now is—"

"I get you loud and clear," Malone said quietly. "And you're perfectly right in your analysis. According to Soledad, Switch will keep leaping to people closer to Sookie Ling."

Slave looked at Soledad. She nodded back. "After I performed the ritual, it must have chosen Parker because he was the nearest person to my house with some kind of connection to Sookie, then . . ."

"Jenny Yang works for a company that supplies temps to the casino," Malone said. "She could walk in there any time she likes."

"But she's low-level staff," Slave pointed out, forking eggs on a slice of toast. She'd be very unlikely to actually meet the boss lady." She pursed her lips for a moment. "Which leads us to the cat." Her lovely brown eyes met Malone's. "It likely belongs to someone who knows Sookie very, very well."

Malone nodded. "That's a lead I can set Steelberg working on."

Soledad instantly objected. "You know I can't have Robopol in on this. That's like throwing me to the sharks."

"Relax. Lt. Steelberg sent me to you in the first place—we're already working together on the mind transfers case. I won't spill your beans—I'll just tell it I've a hunch about the cat . . . I'll think something convincing up."

"Amongst other things," Slave said, "have them comb the area where Jenny Yang went psycho. It's likely someone's missing a cat there, and equally likely that person works at the Golden Dragon."

Malone stared at Slave with deep admiration. "I was just about to . . ." He noticed Soledad was sighing. "What's with you?"

"Nothing," she said. "I've a friend's wedding to attend soon. I'm just wondering which dress to wear."

Malone got her point and gulped. He looked back at Slave, who now had a deeply reflective look on her face. Then she looked hard at Soledad.

"Something still doesn't add up," she said.

"What now?" her cousin groaned, stirring her coffee.

"We've a soul missing. Switch is in the cat's body, the cat is in Jenny Yang's body, and Jenny is in Scott Parker's body. Where's Scott?"

Malone frowned at the beautiful witch. "Yes, *where is* Scott Parker? He isn't dead, is he? You didn't just ditch him into the ether?"

Sighing loudly, Soledad Bathory rummaged through her handbag. Finally, she brought out a large transparent bottle and placed it on the table between the tray of toast and the coffee pot.

"Here's Scott," she said simply.

Malone and Slave both gaped in horror at the bottle. It was filled with white gas; only, every now and then the gas congealed into human shape, and the shape had a man's face. The face looked confused, sleepy. Occasionally the 'man' reached out and touched the inside of the bottle before dissolving into smoke again.

"Scott Parker's soul, I presume," Malone said.

Slave stopped staring at the bottled man and instead gaped at her cousin. She began weeping, tears streaming down her face. "Soly, how could you? How in the world could you do something like this to anybody?"

"I was planning to undo everything once it was over," Soledad replied weakly. She looked utterly disgusted with herself.

CHAPTER 17

Rick / Anastasia

Rick Rogers finally found Club 66Sex, squashed between two meat buildings down the walls of which blood streamed into runoff gutters.

He stood regarding the building from across the street. 66Sex was an old two-story brownstone with painted-over ground floor windows. Its faded wooden sign offered no hint of what lay within its walls. Rick realized this was possibly the first completely normal house he'd seen since entering The Groad.

Trembling with anticipation, he crossed the street, then made his way up an aisle of raw-meat stench from the next-door houses to the club's front door.

The cream-colored door had neither buzzer nor intercom nor keyhole. A symbol was painted on it in red: the same warped skull-and-crossbones—the skull having vampire fangs—as Soledad Bathory had on her front door. Clearly an occult symbol of some kind.

Rick knocked—the door swung inward. He pushed it open, entered, found no one waiting. He proceeded through an empty foyer/cloakroom to the room beyond.

He paused in the next doorway, letting his eyes adjust to the dimmer lighting.

On the surface, Club 66Sex seemed like any other recreational establishment: shades of lighting, patrons at tables and booths, scantily clad waitresses, a bar, soft muzak.

The ambience was creepy, however. Rick had felt it immediately he'd stepped through the front door. Now it heightened, stacked on itself in oppressive layers. He suddenly felt weird, like ants were scuttling through his head. It was also much warmer here than out in the street.

Nobody paid Rick attention as he strode inward. He began noticing that both 66Sex's staff and patrons weren't very 'normal.'

The couple on his immediate right were shadows. The man and woman at the table sat there chatting and drinking, but both their bodies were areas of darkness with no filling. They had no faces, no features; just a black suggestion of being, like they were silhouettes of people sitting in other chairs.

Rick imagined they'd turned to look at him; he looked away. He next gave a start. A topless waitress was serving a bottle of wine to a table ahead of him. In a caricature of horns, the young woman had stiff upwardly-curved penises at both corners of her forehead. Also, her large breasts had penises—also stiffly erect—for nipples. She poured her wine, oblivious to his appraisal of her. When she turned away, Rick saw that a fifth penis, this one much longer than the others, depended as a tail between her buttocks. As she departed, the organ wagged between her legs like a dog's tail.

From regarding the waitress's 'tail,' Rick's gaze trailed left beneath the table of the couple she'd been serving—a lady and gent in expensive cocktail clothes. His eyes snagged on a visual hook—the pair had cloven hoofs for feet.

Rick's heart pounded fiercely. *Calm down! Don't forget you're in a part of Hell. This is the sort of thing to expect there.*

"Excuse me, sir?"

He jerked around. It was the penis-nippled waitress.

"Yes?"

She pointed back across the room. "The lady in the corner over there has been trying to get your attention."

Rick looked along her fingers. A smiling blonde in a blue suit was waving from a table. He figured that had to be Anastasia Wormwood.

"Thanks," he told the waitress and strode over to her.

***

Rick discovered Soledad hadn't been lying. Anastasia Wormwood gave him an instant erection. She was utterly gorgeous.

She rose to greet him as he reached the table. Oh, yes, she was stacked alright; Junoesque as a painter's model—jutting breasts, sweeping wide hips, heavy thighs, and long, long legs. She didn't seem so much to be wearing her blue pantsuit as to be wrapped in it, a stick of sexual candy; an illusion perfected by her shoulder-length yellow hair and red lipstick.

They kissed cheeks. Rick kept his pelvis well away from hers. His penis was painfully tight now in his pants.

They sat. "I've been waiting quite a while for you," she said in a smoky, sulky voice, her fingers playing with a brown handbag that sat on the table. "At least I think it's been a long time—it's hard to tell when there's no passage of time as one understands it. A friend of mine called to say you'd just passed his house."

Rick figured that would be the demon he'd encountered, the one who'd seemed startled to see him. Maybe the creature was supposed to have been watching for him and had forgotten. He didn't comment; he was too taken by Anastasia Wormwood's surpassing beauty.

Anastasia pointed at a clock on the wall to their left. "You know it's been nine a.m. here for the past . . . hell knows how many years. You'd expect one would be pleased, right? But having no time is in itself a kind of torment—not being able to tell how long it's taken you to do a thing is as disconcerting as measuring the hours stretching out endlessly while you labor to finish the task." She frowned prettily at Rick. "How long were you walking for?"

"It seemed forever." Then Rick understood what Anastasia meant. His trip from Soledad's place to here had appeared endless, and yet now he had no sense of a past to back up his claim. "You mean it's all an illusion?"

"Not at all. You could have been walking for five hours. If time doesn't pass, it's exactly the same as one second. Just like I might only have been waiting five minutes for you. Impossible to tell."

"Eternity," Rick said softly. He'd never been religious, but now he was scared by the implications of this conversation.

"You mean torment in Hell?" he ventured.

She nodded. "It goes on and on and on because *it seems* to go on and on." She glanced left again. "If the clock doesn't work, you're frozen in that eternal moment, and it had better be a good one, right?"

116

Rick gulped. "I guess." One thing about this conversation was that it had shriveled his penis again. He figured that was a good thing. Soledad's warning rang like a bell in his mind—no sex with this lady, period.

Anastasia snapped her fingers for a waitress. A nude Latina with massive braided hair slid to their side. She too had penises for nipples and horns.

Anastasia smiled at Rick. "What'll you have?"

"Scotch. A double. Neat."

Anastasia nodded to the waitress. "Still nothing for me yet," she said.

The Hispanic waitress nodded and departed.

Rick was now finding Anastasia Wormwood quite odd. Once he peered past her stunning blonde beauty—and *it was* stunning—she struck him as being 'wrong' in some hard-to-put-a-finger-on way. *Well,* he reasoned, seeking to lay his worries to rest, *she is supposed to be a demoness.*

Anastasia silently watched him back.

The penis-nippled waitress was already bringing Rick's scotch over. She reached them, served.

Anastasia smiled at her, her lips a lustrous red curve. "I think I'll have a drink too now, Flor. A Smirnoff Orange if you've got it."

"Yes, Ms. Wormwood." She departed, trailing her massive braids and swinging penis-tail.

Rick felt the world regain just a semblance of normalcy. "Okay," Anastasia said, her blue eyes regarding Rick coolly, "let's deal."

He nodded. He was suddenly unreasonably scared—filled with an immense dread of Anastasia Wormwood. All he wanted was to be done with this as fast as possible and quit this horrible place, quit too this possibly equally horrible woman.

He sipped nervously from his drink, then, to avoid Anastasia's piercing stare, looked around the room. The previous shadow couple had now been joined by two more shadows. Loud laughter carried from their table as the beings jested.

At the table behind the shadows, a tall woman with slit eyes and brown snake-patterned skin was just sitting down. Her red dress was slit at the hip, revealing long scaly legs.

"Hello, Lady Poison," a man thinner than a rake addressed the snake-woman.

Rick gaped. The speaker looked like a string of spaghetti wearing a suit. Even his head . . . *Shit—nothing's normal in here!*

He turned back to Anastasia.

"How much money do you need?" she asked when she had his full attention again.

"Two hundred grand."

She mused on that, grinned. "What are you prepared to trade for it?"

"What are you asking?"

They paused as Flor served Anastasia's drink. The Latina winked coyly at Rick, her penis-nipples wobbling.

He smiled dully back at her. Flor departed. Anastasia sipped her vodka. Rick too, lifted his scotch to his lips again. The booze calmed him. The moment hung in stasis: Rick was too confused to talk, Anastasia seemingly unwilling to.

Then she said: "I'll take your left leg in exchange for the money. Everything up to the hip."

Horror at her suggestion made Rick shudder. He hastily shook his head. "Forget it. What would you do with just one leg anyway?"

"Trade it to someone else who needs one."

Rick grabbed up his glass and took a good gulp of the liquor. He needed the courage the alcohol provided.

Anastasia coughed suddenly. "Damn," she said afterwards, "it's way too stuffy for me in here." Her eyes fixed on Rick's again. "Okay, how about your kidneys, or liver? One eye?"

Rick winced. "Never, I'd look utterly horrible afterward." Now the scotch was working. He recalled Soledad's words: "Just keep refusing till she suggests something you don't mind exchanging."

Rick's being a gambler came in really handy now. Putting on his best poker face, he pulled his chair close up to the table and leaned forward on it. Stared her coolly in the eyes.

"How 'bout something that won't maim me?" he asked.

"Like what?"

"Like my ability to play guitar."

"You as good as Hendrix, Clapton, or Page?"

"Nah, who is? But girls go gaga for my boleros."

"No deal. I'll never be able to offload it. If you had death metal chops, we'd be cool."

She beamed suddenly at him. Rick was instantly confused again; her smile felt like bright sunlight was suddenly pouring over him, burning away his worries.

Beauty incomparable, Anastasia reached over and laid a cool hand on Rick's arm. "You know what? How about we just fuck? I'm quite hard up—I'll pay you for sex. Two hundred grand for the night."

The proposal sounded loud as a thunderclap in Rick's brain. Despite his expecting her to make it at some point, it still caught him unawares. His penis leapt painfully back to attention.

"N-n-n-no . . . No!" he stammered, remembering Soledad's warning.

She scowled at his refusal. "What's the problem now? You're married? I don't see no ring. Or I'm simply not pretty enough for you?"

"No." Rick managed to slur the words out. "You're v-v-very beautiful, b-but no sex." His penis was still stiff, however. He now realized he was quite tipsy—but after just one double? Whatever brand of scotch they served down here packed a punch like he'd never known before.

Anastasia's anger dissolved. "Okay, so what then? Do you want the money or don't you? If you do, you have to trade me something for it."

"Just think of something else."

"Okay." She stood, gathered up her handbag. "But let's leave here. We'll get some bottles of wine and go back to my place. Sit on the roof in fresh air."

"Why leave?"

She patted her chest dramatically, gulped. "Because I'm scared that if I remain in here I'll shortly puke. It's just so damned stuffy."

He got up and followed her.

CHAPTER 18

Malone

Malone drove slowly down Washington Street.

Leaving Soledad and Slave at home after breakfast (he expected the cousins to burn up the morning discussing him), he'd driven over to see Lt. Steelberg at Robopol HQ (up on the tenth floor of the One Boston Place Skyscraper on Washington).

Like he'd promised Soledad, he'd fed the detective the basic gist about the transfers without implicating her in them. Steelberg had been delighted. For a robot, any kind of logical lead was better than shooting in the dark.

Slave's suggestion had proved right: Mia Wong (a thirty-year-old Golden Dragon croupier who owned a cat) lived on Grove Street, three streets away from where 'Jenny Yang' had been picked up by the medics. Malone figured that made sense—Mia's cat remaining in its own neighborhood. The animal, not self-aware, had had no way of calculating the difference in itself, and as such had attempted to continue its normal pattern of behavior.

Miss Wong, however, hadn't seen her cat, Bubbles, for two days now. That was by no mean conclusive evidence/proof—Bubbles had a tendency to roam, had once stayed away from home for a week.

She also didn't see what Robopol (and Malone of all people) wanted with her pet. "Did he murder someone? Cats can't commit crime, can they?"

They'd chosen not to enlighten her. "We're researching low-level genetic mutations across a pinpoint sample population of Boston felines," Steelberg had said vaguely. "Your cat's in the database."

"There's a high chance of cross-species viral infection here," Malone had added when she'd looked unconvinced. "Don't, don't, don't *for any reason* touch the cat when it returns. Just lock it in a room and call the cops."

The viral scare had spooked Mia Wong. She'd agreed to call Steelberg once Bubbles got in.

So now we wait, Malone thought. *We wait.*

Mia Wong had given them a picture of Bubbles—a chocolate Manx. Steelberg had forwarded it to all the city's Robopol officers. So the cat would be found. (It being a Manx—meaning it was tailless—narrowed down the search a whole lot.) It might just take a little time. Hopefully before its inhabitant body-hopped again.

He swung the BMW onto Milk Street, turned his mind onto his own concerns.

There was really just one; it cruised slowly through his head: *Slave.* What to do about her?

His mind filled with the memory of the morning's sex, of his own reaction to spanking her. He couldn't recall being that turned on in a long time. Okay, he'd not had sex in a long time, but it was way beyond that—Slave had aroused something in him—a dark lust he was very uncomfortable with.

I beat her, then jerked off over her smarting buttocks and rubbed my come into them? Shit! And I don't even watch porn!

He replayed the scene in his mind. He'd felt dirtied by Slave, but at the same time—paradoxically—freed to be himself. A different version of himself. She seemed like a door to a room in which there were no restrictions on sexual behavior. No limits.

The question was: did he want to—did he dare to—enter that room?

He pulled out of his thoughts. Across the road up ahead, a couple were stepping out of an old brownstone building. *66Sex*—some club Malone had never heard of before.

He instinctively slowed a little—the man looked familiar. Yeah, it was Rick Rogers, a sometime friend of Sookie's.

He mused; it had been ages since he'd last seen Rick. He'd heard the man had fled Boston over gambling debts; Sookie could be a cold bitch at times.

And the blonde with him? Malone whistled. Damn, she was a looker—almost like she'd taken sex appeal injections.

Passing the couple, he grinned. Rick was drunk; the blonde bombshell was holding him up with one hand, flagging for a taxi with the other. Looked like the pair were still planning on some heavy drinking—the necks of two wine bottles peeked from the plastic bag Rick seemed in constant danger of dropping.

The blonde flicked something—it looked like a black snake—off her shoulder.

Watching in the rearview, Malone saw an AG cab slide to the curb and the couple get in. The odd thing was, looking back at his passengers, the cabbie appeared to have no face—just a featureless expanse under his mop of dark hair.

No, that was definitely a trick of the light. The cab floated off out of sight.

Malone rolled past the Arch Street intersection. He recalled his morning's conversation with Steelberg, who'd just been returning to the cop shop from a homicide scene over in Beacon Hill. It had been there most of the night. (As USAcme were always fast to point out, that was another benefit of a robot police force—the machines worked 23-hour shifts.)

"Last night, someone dropped several nightmare pods into the Beacon Hill Hotel and Bistro," the robot cop had said. "The building was full of Sookie Ling's guys at the time." It shook its egg-like head. "Thirty-four corpses—well not really corpses, Malone; only skeletons left . . . most of them incomplete at that."

"Any survivors?"

"Stan McCaulkin. You know the guy—the big old biker chap? He got lucky, was apparently downstairs in the lobby when hell broke loose. He bolted." The machine gave a metal laugh, waved a metal hand. "You should have seen some of the monsters we found in the building: massive legged snakes, crazy dinosaurs; some redneck kid with a head in his belly . . . There was also a two-headed old woman wearing foot-high platform boots, with razor-like fingernails long enough to break all the Guinness records . . . three metal birds . . . a hungry grandfather clock—"

"Can you control them? There're dangerous. And from what I recall, except using dream weapons, nightmares are almost impossible to kill."

Lt. Steelberg's digital brain had audibly ticked a moment before it replied. "That's the odd thing, Malone. The monsters can't leave the hotel. They try, but something forces them back in. So, for the moment it's fine. But . . . the building itself is quite damaged. The monsters kept attacking the officers who went in to retrieve the bodies, so it was a shooting gallery over there last night . . ."

Malone hadn't commented further. He'd grimaced, imagining the hotel strewn with human gore, prowled by ravenous dream beasts. Then a memory: *Oh, so that's where Sookie's guys were all headed yesterday? But for what?* But he already knew the answer: *To kill Lucy Tang, but she apparently struck first . . .*

Nearing his house, Malone's concerns again shifted to Josephine 'Slave' Bailey. What bothered him now, much more than his own confusion over her, was how pleased she'd been with his 'performance,' if that was the right expression. She'd seemed utterly delighted. Which meant she had no plans of leaving.

But even more worrisome was the fact—he finally admitted this to himself as he pulled into his driveway—the fact that he didn't want Slave to leave.

Something about her utterly magnetized him.

Parking the BMW now, Malone was suddenly filled with panic that he'd not meet her in his apartment.

CHAPTER 19

Slave / Soledad / Malone

Slave shut the drapes, then nodded across the living room at Soledad, who sat cross-legged on a green sofa fiddling with the end of her pigtail.

"Okay, he's home." Her voice was nervous.

Soledad let her braided hair fall. She uncrossed her legs, dropped her feet to the floor, and leaned forward, elbows on knees. "You're sure about this? I mean, you just met the man yesterday and—"

"It's not love at first sight. But I'm definitely not letting him get away from me." She slid her robe aside, bared her reddened buttocks at Soledad. "He's got definite potential."

"I'm sure he hated it as much as you loved it."

"His penis said differently—you need to have felt how hard it was." She scratched her 'SLAVE' scar with worried fingers. "Okay, I just heard the elevator stop. Now, Soly, do not dare fuck this up for me."

"O.K."

***

Malone pushed open his front door to the scene of Slave and Soledad Bathory in a catfight. Both women were rolling around on the floor, beating and kicking at each other while shrieking at the top of their voices.

"You stupid magical terrorist!"

"Masochist slut!"

"Paranormal idiot!"

"Fatass loser!"

Malone ran into the confusion. "Stop it, stop it! What the hell are you two doing!?"

He grabbed Slave off Soledad, managed to prize her opponent's pigtail from her grasp, and then to dump her on the sofa. Then he returned to help a confused-looking Soledad off the floor. Once his back was turned, however, Slave leapt off the sofa, charged past him, and leapt atop her cousin again. The hair pulling and shrieking resumed:

"Smartass,"

"Retard!"

"For God's sake—stop fighting . . . ouch!"

"Miss know-it-all!"

"Cobweb-pussy!"

"Fucking pervert!"

After several times of grabbing hold of one cousin in the rough-and-tumble only to find out he was actually holding onto the other, and catching several vicious blows to the face for his troubles, Malone finally managed to separate the battling women. They sat in opposite chairs either side of him, breathing like boxers in the interval between rounds, while he stood between them, refereeing their emotions.

"Now calm down. What's going on here?"

"It's her fault!" both yelled at once.

He lifted his hands in a placating gesture. "Yes . . . but what is the matter? What's the argument?"

Neither woman replied him. They sat staring knives at each other.

Malone looked from one to the other. Soledad was dabbing blood off her cheek with a blue tissue. Malone winced—the witch looked a total mess: her top was in shreds, her braided hair wrapped twice around her neck (Slave had been throttling her with it), her left breast almost free of her bra.

He looked the other way. Slave looked just as bad: Her bathrobe was all ripped up and she had a slight nosebleed and some fingernail scratches across her shoulders. Her bared breasts were heaving with her violent breathing. Her brown hair, already curly, now looked like a bird's nest (to enhance that illusion, a short length of parcel string had gotten tangled in it).

But what the hell were they fighting over? He chalked it down to estrogen rage.

Soledad stood up. "I'm leaving," she told Malone. "I don't want to see that bitch again." She pointed a finger at Slave. "I'm warning you—don't bring your perverted ass anywhere near my house. If you do you'll regret it!"

Slave immediately leapt up and rushed at her. Malone got between the pair just before they smacked angry breasts together. "Oh yeah, and what the fuck will I regret, huh?"

Soledad smiled evilly. "Consider this a hypernatural restraining order: if you show your ugly mug anywhere near me, I'll hex you into a piglet."

"Your magic's not that good! Damn cut-price Walmart witch!"

Soledad's smile widened. "Isn't it? How 'bout we find out now, huh?" She raised clawed fingers as if to fling something at Slave.

"Please, please, please, ladies!" Malone pleaded, totally at a loss. (He currently felt way, way, way out of his depth. Fighting crime was one thing, settling female disputes completely another. The former played by fixed rules, the latter seemingly had none, other than to avoid getting hurt oneself.) "Soledad you *can't* magic her into a pig—she's your cousin."

He flung a warning glance at Slave, who, still panting angrily, snorted the threat off.

"Damn bargain basement sorceress."

"What?"

"You're a garage-sale witch!"

"Okay, that's it! You're getting it." Ducking Malone's attempts to stop her, Soledad's hooked fingers ripped against the air. The action released five black energy traces that combined into a single beam of darkness which streaked at Slave and hit her in the forehead.

Blue light flashed and burst around Slave's head. She staggered back at the impact, then growled at Soledad.

"That the fucking best you've got? See, I told you you couldn't do shit!"

In response, Soledad smiled smugly at her. "I can't, eh? You actually sure of that?"

Then Slave gave a start. Malone watched her part her hair and run fingers across her forehead, then her eyes widen in shocked rage. "You bitch, give me back my scars!"

Malone was himself shocked: her forehead no longer bore the damning 'SLAVE' marking. It was smooth, clean skin.

"Give them back! Now!"

Soledad laughed spitefully. "No way, girl. It's an improvement; now you look like a *normal* woman. I'm sure Malone thinks you look better too. Don't you, Malone?"

He refused to comment. She did look better—much less threatening anyhow.

Slave was meanwhile steaming. "Give me back my scars . . ." her eyes flickered around the room, "or else . . ."

Soledad raised her hand threateningly again. "Can it, okay? Know when you're beat. Any more nonsense from you and you'll be a pig for the next month."

Slave said nothing. She ran distracted fingers over her bare forehead and looked traumatized.

"Don't . . . please," Malone begged Soledad.

"Why not? I'd likely prefer the pig as a relative. It'll be less screwy in the head." But she lowered her quavering hand. "Okay, Malone, I won't—just 'cos of you. But back to what started this: I don't want her ass anywhere near me."

"But we're all working on resolving your case."

Soledad smiled coldly. "So? Keep her then. She can fucking stay here with you. Make the bitch pay rent if you like—she's loaded, our Uncle Ernie left her a chunk of money. She just doesn't come to my place for anything. For no reason."

"Hey, what about my things? I need my damn clothes and all! Everything is still over at that dumpster you call a—"

"Watch your mouth before I seal it permanently shut." Soledad mused a moment. "Okay, fair enough—I'll deliver your trash here myself." She looked coldly at Malone. "She stays here, right? You'll keep her away from me? It's either that or she's in the pigsty."

Malone nodded, amazed at the suddenness and totality of their familial meltdown. He was suddenly very wary of Soledad. The way she'd just stripped the scars off Slave's face . . . damn. "Yeah, yeah, sure, till I find her a place. Just don't hex her."

"Whatever, man." And with that, in a flash of blue light, Soledad Bathory vanished.

"I can't believe that Soly's such a cold, heartless bitch," Slave spat after her, still feeling her forehead.

"She's just angry. Here, you sit down."

She sat on the green sofa; he sat beside her. "It'll be okay," he said. "She'll calm down."

"I just can't believe . . . she stole my scars!" She buried her face in his chest and began sobbing.

And I'm delighted she did, Malone thought. He wrapped an arm around her shoulders and pulled her close. "It's okay, you can always get some new scars. And you're welcome to live here for now." He found it hard to hide his delight. Oh no, she wouldn't be leaving his apartment anytime soon. Malone figured he could easily find reasons—both real and imaginary—to put off getting Slave a place of her own.

Of course, there was the jagged route of her perversion to navigate, but that could be . . . or maybe it couldn't. *You can take the scars off the woman,* he mused, *but not her desire to be scarred.*

His thoughts fractured as a suitcase appeared in midair in the living room and crashed down on the rug. Then it began raining shoes.

"Hey!" he shouted. "Put them in the bedroom!"

Like Soledad Bathory could hear him from afar off, the footwear rain ceased, to be replaced with loud telltale sounds from further inside the apartment.

***

At the noise, Slave instantly jerked out of the manly warmth of Malone's chest. Regretfully, she exited that safe haven of Eau de cologne and sweat.

It worked! He offered me his place to stay! She hid her delight, however, with a scowl of almost palpable misery, moaning, "Shit! How could Soly do this to me!" Inside, though, she was thinking: *Oh, Soly, I totally owe you big time for this! Yes!*

"You okay?" Malone asked solicitously. He looked around at the strewn shoes. "I'm myself shocked at Soledad's behavior; it's as if she just snapped."

"Forget her—some women use PMS as a mask for sadism, she's sure to later claim it was just that bad time of month." Slave grabbed Malone's hand and pulled him towards the bedroom. "Come. I have to see . . . I'll kill the bitch if she's broken any of my stuff."

Malone followed her.

***

They stood together in the bedroom entrance. It was raining clothes over the bed—panties and pantyhose and bras, thongs, tops and trousers, an assortment of latex gear, other more arcane female paraphernalia.

Slave made a disgusted face. "The damned showoff is scattering my stuff everywhere."

The clothes-rain ceased. To a blue thunderclap, a suitcase dropped out of the air in a corner; another followed, then a shoe rack. Then appeared several metal apparatuses that Malone didn't recognize, like exercise equipment without the gears; then came something he did recognize: a set of stocks—head and hand holes in a wooden frame with chains to restrain the ankles too.

Malone stared bemused at Slave. "How'd you get all this back to Boston? A U-Haul?"

"I left it at Soly's. She has loads of space. Shit, I'm real sorry she's flooding you with junk like this. If I'd known . . ."

A final in-house thunderclap released a mass of leather bondage clothes onto the bed, along with a pile of whips, floggers, handcuffs, bracelets, necklets, and paddles—

"*You* pissed her off—*you're* cleaning this mess up," Malone said grimly.

—and one more thing: A large frame like a playground swing without the chair appeared by the bedroom window. The frame was taller than Malone and had sets of handcuffs attached by chains to its upper crossbeam and uprights.

Malone nodded at it, his mouth suddenly dry. "What's that?"

"My bondage frame." She giggled. "Let's try it out."

"Oh no." He felt weak; the sheer profusion of instruments of torture on display now the apparel rain had ended flabbergasted him. Nipple clamps, candles, spiky dildos, gagballs, masks, latex gloves—all lay piled everywhere like his bedroom was a sex shop.

"C'mon, let's do it," Slave said, discarding her robe. "You know you want to." She placed a foot on the bed and put on a show of stretching.

"No." It was however a weak, half-hearted protest. He was violently aroused by the suggestion of tormenting her again. *But so soon!?* his mind screamed. *It was just this morning! What the hell is wrong with me? This isn't me!*

"No," he responded to her 'come hither' gaze. "Your bottom has to still be hurting—you couldn't bear it."

Slave laughed at that; he got the clear impression she was mocking him. She leapt on Malone's bed and rooted through the assorted piles of her belongings. She pulled out a riding crop and shook it at Malone.

She smacked the flail hard against her hip. He started like she'd hit him. He stared at the crop in a haze like disbelief. His mind cut off thinking—he had no idea what to think anymore. Thought seemed irrelevant, mainly because it wasn't explaining anything: each attempt to reason out his strange attraction to Slave left him more confused than before. Blood filled his penis, thickening it so it jerked in its confinement.

Slave strode into his fugue. He felt her soft hands undoing his belt and pulling his pants down, then freeing his penis, which leapt out at her. He heard her giggle, felt her take him into her mouth; only the swollen head at first, then more and more of him, deeper, till he hit the back of her throat. She remained there like that—head impaled on his cock—while he, like one sleepwalking, removed his jacket and shirt.

Gagging, she slid her mouth off his penis. "Nice prick you've got here. I could do with more of it in my life."

He garbled out a reply that made no sense to him either; then sat down on the edge of the bed and removed his pants and shoes.

It seemed to Malone now that he existed in a dream; he'd somehow staggered down into a cavern of wonders, in which Slave was the genie of the lamp.

"Don't be afraid of what you feel," she said. "Be true to the real you."

He found words. "I've no idea what I feel."

She laughed, tugged on his erection. "In that case, don't knock it till you've tried it."

Pulling him by the penis, she led him like an erotic angel towards the frame where their sexual violence would take place. He followed in a sort of daze, his eyes riveted to her still-red buttocks, impressions of his fingers still clear in the soft flesh. He could still refuse to do this, but suddenly, he didn't want to. No, it was more like he felt a sense of inevitability about all this, like fate had led he and Slave together, and this thing (Hell, it wasn't even a relationship yet!) wouldn't be complete except he fulfilled her . . . fulfilled himself . . . fulfilled whatever their joint karma was; he didn't know what.

He knew, however—was intensely certain—that he wasn't about to whip a woman just because he was bored.

Slave cleared a way through her spilled paraphernalia to the frame that now in its turn framed the bedroom window.

She pushed the riding crop against Malone's chest, then, her beautiful face now serious, turned to the frame and stepped under its crosspiece. She stood looking out over the Boston afternoon, arms spread overhead, her svelte body forming a 'Y.'

"Strap me in. Make the cuffs good and tight. It has to be realistic, with no way I can break free."

He did so quickly, with much more enthusiasm than he liked. His penis remained hard all the while, and when their bodies touched as he spread her long legs and fettered her ankles, it felt like electricity tingled back and forth along his manhood. He found the sensation astounding.

Finally, he had her bound up.

Lust or not, however, Malone was conscious of Slave's safety. Reason cut like a knife through the black veil of his arousal. True, he knew little about S and M, but he knew one important thing about conducting a session:

"What's the safe word?" he asked, keeping his voice level with difficulty.

She looked back at him, face flushed with anticipation, pupils dilated. "Fuck my ass!" she gasped.

"What?" A shocking disappointment flickered in him on realizing she was suddenly calling it off.

"'Fuck my ass' *is* my safe word."

He scowled. "What kind of crappy safe word is 'fuck my ass?'"

"The best ever. All you men want anal. It takes precedence over vaginal sex any day. I wonder why. You don't all think women are shit, do you? Anyhow, you can't really be sodomizing someone and whipping them at the same time."

"So I lash you till you yell *that*; then what?"

She winked, her lips curling wickedly. "Then you simply do what comes naturally."

***

"Oh please do it, baby!" she gasped. "Don't torture me by keeping me waiting like this."

He balanced the riding crop on his hand for a final moment in an agony of indecision, then swept it back high and brought it down hard across her waist.

She jerked stiff with the impact as though it was unexpected, then went limp again, gasping for breath as the feeling flooded her. She looked back at him, then away again: it was always better to anticipate the strokes, the wait made the pain sweeter, sharper.

Moisture flooded her vagina.

He flailed her again with the crop, firm and hard across her lower back, with more assurance this time. Then again, and again. At first he flinched when she did, but soon he became entranced in the act, as if he—the accidental sadist—was in reality a sexual wizard, and making those red lines appear on her pale flesh by magic, not violence. And now, he smiled as he whipped her; a cold smile, not one of pleasure, but of primal satisfaction. His cock throbbed hard in his crotch. He stroked it once, then held it in his fist—the penis felt hot, as if boiling water, not blood, inflated it.

"Give it to me! Whip me!" Slave gasped, sensing a lull in their communion. "Oh, oh, oh, oh!" she moaned as the lashing resumed, as the evilly delicious pain once again destroyed her flesh. She peeked back over her shoulder. As his arm rose and fell, Malone's eyes were bright with intense concentration; she imagined he was looking at her buttocks (which he'd so far avoided touching). A moment later she had confirmation—her ass stung! She leapt off the floor from the pain, then landed, tried to slump but the leather bracelets held her up. More lashes stung her buttocks, more hot pain made her start as it converted into liquid pleasure that flowed like milk up into her breasts. *Oh, yes—this man is just fantastic!* Her vagina clenched hard and fast like it sheathed a stiff penis. The stop-start pain moved down to her legs. She climaxed when the riding crop bit into her thighs, her body shuddering with her orgasm, her sexual fluids gushing from her vagina, dripping down her legs. She felt glorious.

"More," she moaned. "More!"

His breath loud like a car backfiring, his eyes staring with almost manic concentration, Malone beat Slave with the riding crop. He fought to control himself, to not degenerate into the caveman he feared lurked within—it was almost impossible to not let go and simply flail her wildly. He couldn't understand this—the sight of Slave's luscious body, her back covered now with red crisscrosses, had him more horny than he ever remembered being before. Placing each fresh strike across her large buttocks felt almost like stabbing his penis between them. His arm fell, an evil welt appeared between her shoulder blades. His cock leapt high at the sight and throbbed, his balls twitched. He felt close to orgasm without even fucking her or masturbating. *I'm an animal,* he thought in dismay. *She's turned me into an animal.*

He watched the glistening trails of moisture on her crop-marked thighs; he'd seen her shudder and moan and shake, knew she'd already come. Maybe more than once, even.

"Haven't you had enough?" he pleaded desperately.

"No, baby! More!" Then, when he dallied, she gasped, "Do it, you son-of-a-bitch!"

Chastened by her displeasure, he whipped on. Now, however, he'd regained control over himself. Now, he took his time, teasing her with each lash, making her feel like he'd not hit her, then when he finally did, cutting her sharply.

"Is this what you want, Slave!?" he grunted.

In response her body juddered through another orgasm. Malone beat her through this one also. And now, though his arousal hadn't lessened—his penis was still as hard—it was less frantic. He realized with dismay that now he was enjoying Slave's pain, enjoying her tremors. There was dark delight in making her twitch and shudder, not for her pleasure, but his.

He measured her body for an unbruised area of skin, then stepping to the side of her, laid the riding crop right across the top of Slave's breasts. Another purple welt rose.

"Take that, you slave!"

She slumped against her restraints so she was swinging limp from her arms. This was just fantastic. She'd already had three orgasms—her entire body felt like a sponge soaked in honey—and was now dizzy from the pleasure. Her mind seemed to float above her head so she could view the entire world. Yes she'd love to climax some more, but there would be other times. This was dangerous pleasure, one drank it in small draughts.

"Fuck my ass!" she gasped. "Fuck my ass, Malone!"

He stared at the bruised expanse of her skin and felt a horrible potency, an immense power rise in him. He laughed loud, whipped her again, then bent tantalizing close to her ear and whispered: "What did you say, Slave? Louder, Slave? I didn't hear you, Slave. That's what you are, isn't it—my slave?"

"Oh, yes, I'm your slave, baby."

"Not 'baby.' Master." He lashed her legs again. "Now what did you ask me to do?"

"Fuck my ass, Master!"

"Beg! Plead like the little bitch dog you are!"

"Please fuck my ass, Master! Please fuck my ass!"

Feeling like she'd just damned him to Hell, Malone flung the riding crop aside. Spitting on his penis, he stepped forward. He gripped Slave by her hips, jerked her up from her slump and forced his cock up hard into her anus. Slave's hole was tight as shit; she shrieked with the violence of his penetration. Malone didn't care if he hurt her or not, he stabbed the organ as deep into her body as he could, thrusting hard and fast as he liked.

She instantly began moaning, "Yes, yes, yes, Master. Harder! Hurt me good!" then began coming again. Beyond her, outside the bedroom, the afternoon continued.

Malone reached around her and squeezed her breasts roughly as her juices flooded her thighs. Her buttocks squashed his hips. "Is this what you want, slave!?" He now found it hard to separate her name from the concept of her. Slave *was* a slave. And he? Buried deep in the all-compassing warmth of her rectum, a sort of understanding came to him then—of what she wanted, of what she was all about.

Digging his fingers so deep into her breasts that she squealed with pain, he came. It was a hot, painful orgasm, the semen forcing itself past the crimp in his penis caused by her contracting sphincter, and blowing out into her ass. He had the impression of his come as bubbling lava, its molten flow scalding her interior tissue, burning its way to the core of her.

Slave moaned as Malone emptied his seed into her. Her moan was animal reflex—she was barely conscious of her surroundings. She felt his body inside hers—her rectum warm around him, cocooning him—as the elements of delirium, solidified images of a delicious dream. Her anus felt wondrous gripping him. His sweat burnt in her wounds; his body hair scoured them, made them bleed anew. She felt him bite her neck, deep; the pain blew through her in gusts like wind over a body desert. She burnt, she bled; the pain penetrated her afresh as little pinprick penises. The pain fucked her, tickling her already overstimulated nerve endings.

Oh yes! she thought as he collapsed on her, his penis spent of its spasming effusion. *I want this man. I really do want him . . . possibly forever.*

They remained like that for a good while; him leaning on her, his manhood stuck inside her, two people become a violent, but undeniable, one.

Regretting that he had to, Malone finally pulled out of Slave's anus, letting his semen fall free from her spread hole and splatter the rug. He still couldn't explain what had happened, but something had. Some communion of spirits had occurred—this sadist/masochist experience had completed something in him, just like it had in her.

After clearing the bed, Malone freed Slave from the bondage frame and tenderly, lovingly, carried her across to the satin sheets.

They lay there, his arm wrapped around her as if to protect her from himself. Waiting in the moment.

She finally said, "Please don't be ashamed or disgusted with me. You only gave me what I wanted. What I needed. Remember that—you satisfied me. Being a slave is to willingly refuse to have a will of one's own—to give oneself away to another's whims and

135

caprices." Her voice was soft as silk, happy and sated yet vulnerable as a butterfly's wings.

He recognized her fear of his reaction now she'd shown him— no, confirmed to him (she'd already teased him with his inner darkness during their morning 'spank session')—another side to himself. He bent her face up to his, kissed her tenderly. "Don't be afraid," he said. "I don't hate you or anything."

Emboldened now, she asked, "So, will you be my new Master?"

"Only on probation. I'm still not sure I can handle you. You scare me more than any woman I've ever been with in my life."

With a squeal of delight, Slave grabbed Malone's head in both hands and kissed him deeply. She flinched with pain when he grabbed her sides and kissed her back equally hard, but it was a delicious pain, the sweet agony of a blooming sadomasochistic relationship.

***

Afterwards, they drank coffee in the living room, looking out over the city as the shadows slowly lengthened.

"Don't you hurt badly from the whipping?" Malone asked Slave as she lounged carelessly on the green sofa.

She smiled coyly. "Yes, it stings, but it's my kind of pain. Besides, it reminds me of your cock in my ass." She giggled. "You know, Malone, one thing they never show in porn is how you guys always get a woman's shit on you during anal. Up inside your penis, even. And considering symbolism, I guess its empowering for us ladies—we get to poop on the patriarchy." Amused by the blank look that came over his face in reply, she picked up a chocolate cookie off a tray, bit into it and chewed a bit, her expression pensive.

Malone just watched her, impressed by her brunette beauty. Impressed by her delectable mind. Watching Slave sip at her coffee (full of milk and sugar—she had a surprising sweet tooth), he felt a sudden welling of warm emotion burst up inside his chest. No, he was certain this wasn't love (*We only just met yesterday!*), but it was a nice substitute.

It's odd, he felt. *Now it's over, we seem like your average couple, almost like a postcard picture even—that classic picturesque scene of a gorgeous woman by a window while her man looks on . . .*

The day's mundanity perplexed him: *Is this how this works out? Sadomasochism as a new kind of normal? I've just whipped her to orgasm and now . . . now it's really no big deal—it's just what we do? Part of our everyday life? And 'we?' What's this 'we' anyway? Am I really, for the life of me, seriously considering remaining with her? Yes, I want to, but I also don't want to.*

Slave noticed him staring at her. "What's bothering you, baby?"

"Your cousin's mind transfer case," he replied smoothly. "I was coming home to update you and Soly on developments when I met you fighting."

She sipped coffee, her eyes urging him to explain.

He was glad of the distraction. Staring at Slave sitting there, demure and lovely, long legs bared through the parting in the bathrobe with the occasional flash of brunette pubic curls, was turning him on again. "Okay," he said, "we've narrowed it down, we're looking for a chocolate-brown male Manx cat . . ."

"Those are the tailless ones, right? Can't be that many of them in Boston."

"Uh huh. But—"

She winced. "But yeah, you have to find it before it body-hops again . . ."

CHAPTER 20

Steelberg

In its office on the One Boston Place's tenth floor, Robopol Lt. Steelberg was currently pondering the same puzzle as Malone. Where in the whole of Beacon Hill—no, the search area was more correctly the entirety of central Boston—did one find a single Manx? According to its owner Mia Wong, Bubbles still hadn't yet returned home. So where had America's most wanted feline got to?

The white robot thought on, its thought processes blindingly fast. The robot mind is miles quicker than the eye. Steelberg analyzed and collated strips and flecks of info that to a human would be meaningless: doing such things as rewatching (in its mind) the eye-cam videos of it and Malone's interview with Mia Wong, and reanalyzing her speech patterns, facial expressions, retinal blood flow and pupillary contractions, all in an effort to determine if she was lying.

The results were a conclusive negative—she didn't know her cat's whereabouts.

Steelberg's mind next switched to analyzing its mental photocopy of the picture of Bubbles that Miss Wong had provided the police. It quickly determined the cat's paw sizes (for all four paws).

Then there was that odd detail Malone had mentioned: the teeth. The cat would have gaps in its smile.

"Excuse me, sir."

Steelberg looked up. Sgt. Olive Banks (SN. 07173-64nk5), a passable white plastic model of a human woman (complete with long bronze hair and emphasized feminine curves her uniform barely concealed), stood there.

More important, Sgt. Banks was carrying a cat. A chocolate-brown Manx. Lt. Steelberg instantly recognized it as the missing Bubbles.

The robot stared at the cat; it stared back.

"Where did you find it?" Steelberg asked, reaching out metal fingers and stroking the Manx.

Sgt. Banks put Bubbles down on Steelberg's desk. "We didn't, sir. It came to us. It said it wants to see you."

"It wants to see . . . ?"

The robot policeman worked out the implications of the statement a nanosecond before the cat said, in a high-pitch purr that conveyed its deep confusion:

"I'm Mia Wong. Bubbles came home two hours ago. I touched him and . . . I found myself *inside him*." The voice was cartoonish, the animal's larynx wrong for making human sounds.

Steelberg instantly noted that the cat was missing several teeth. A telling and conclusive sign.

The robot was lost for words, finally saying sternly, "But . . . but . . . but, Miss Wong, we *warned you* not to touch it. We were very specific on that instruction."

"I just want my body back!" the cat screamed pathetically. "I want my body back!"

"Please calm down, Miss Wong." Sgt. Banks stroked 'Bubbles' in an attempt to soothe it, then looked at Steelberg. "What do we do now, sir?"

Detective Lt. Steelberg made the robot equivalent of a perplexed groan. Then, swiveling its gaze between the cat and Sgt. Banks, it picked up the desk phone. "Only one thing to do—we call Malone."

CHAPTER 21

Sookie

Uncharacteristically for Sookie Ling, the party had begun early today.

With the blinds half-open, mid-afternoon sunbeams filtered in through the silken drapes of Dallas Washington's fourth floor hotel suite. A light breeze shifted the drapes, casting dappled shadows on expensive Persian rugs.

Sookie, Dallas Washington, and TLC were in Dallas's bedroom.

The couple were playing poker; Sookie was dealing the cards. All three women were naked.

The atmosphere in the suite was celebratory. The tray by the card table held beer for Dallas, wine and a vial of cocaine for TLC, and another glass of wine and a vial of dragonreich for Sookie. A mirror with several prepared lines of coke, a credit card, and a half-unrolled hundred dollar bill lay by TLC's elbow.

There was no money on the table. No chips either. The lovers were playing fisting poker, an invention of TLC's. There was a thick delicious smell of wet vagina in the air and TLC's hands showed smears of lube, the uncapped bottle of which lay on its side on the queenly bed.

In contrast to her raven-haired, cool-seeming girlfriend, the redheaded Dallas looked totally disheveled and well-fucked— she'd lost four games so far. Every now and again, she groaned, the sound a combination of pleasure and hurt.

Sookie dealt the last round of cards. "Okay, everyone show hand now," she said. "Who win this?"

Wincing, Dallas spread her cards. Two jacks, a seven, a five and a nine.

"Horrible bad hand," Sookie announced. "Only jack and seven in same red suit. Look like you spread legs again."

Rolling her green eyes, Dallas Washington pointed a ring-covered finger at her grinning girlfriend. "Okay, let's see your hand," she said in a tipsy voice.

"Royal flush, baby," TLC leered. She spread her cards. "Read 'em and weep."

On seeing the perfect set of ace, king, queen, jack, and ten of spades, Dallas Washington did begin weeping, moaning: "Oh no, not fucking again. I can't take it! When am I ever going to—" She glared at Sookie, boozy eyes suspicious, small breasts indignantly raised. "Hey! You're not stacking the deck against me, are you?"

Sookie laughed boisterously. "How I stack deck? All of us naked here. Ah, you think cards in Chinese hole." She leapt up, placed a foot on the table and spread her vaginal lips. "See, empty pussy!"

Dallas winced at the sight of Sookie's vagina, all warped red and scaly from her dragonreich abuse. "Damn, girl, put that thing away."

Sookie laughed, she fingered her large clitoris. "What? You scared it eat you? Honest, I wish drug not kill sex desire—ten years not fuck bad for vagina—I sure it already forget what God design it for." She reached fingers for the reich vial. "Still, drug have benefits."

"What benefits?" After this question, TLC bent to sniff up two lines of coke. Then she jerked back, looked completely stupefied for a moment as the high kicked in.

Sookie explained: "No romance drama. Maybe I like man, he not like me, maybe I kill him from disappointment. Or he like me, I hate him? He angry, try kill me. Or both like, but I not in mood . . . I have headache—have to know different kinds of headaches. Or he forget birthday? See many complications?" She snorted some reich. "Drug not make demands on woman." She squeezed her clitoris, her other hand stroking her scaly yellow breasts. "It sad though, no feeling at all in love bud—like dead fish . . ." Then the drug high hit her. "But I always feel dragonreich love me deeply . . ."

"You can't substitute a chemical for a relationship," Dallas said.

The drug having fully infiltrated her now, Sookie raised a hand in correction. "Not substitute for penis. Man always man, always best—but chemical relationship best of all." She finally dropped her foot from the table and grinned broadly, her hawkish face and lime-green eyes expectant. "But forget Sookie's tight ass, we playing fisting game!"

Dallas, who'd been hoping the discussion with Sookie would prove sufficient distraction to get her off the hook, groaned as TLC began womanhandling her out of her seat. "What're are you so happy about today, anyway, Sookie?"

"Ah, things turn out great for me." Sookie watched Tamara Lorraine Carter drag the protesting Dallas to the massive bed and push her down on it.

Dallas pleaded, "Later, darling, later."

"Don't be a sore loser, baby."

"*I am* fucking sore! If you fist me again, I won't be able to walk for a week."

"No, spread your wings."

"How 'bout we go shopping instead?" She blew TLC a kiss. "I'll buy you a big fat diamond ring? No? Okay, I'll buy you a new pink Mercedes, one of the new AG models . . . ?

TLC shook her head and grinned sweetly, her eyes twinkling. "No. Aw, poor little's pussy's tired out, is she? How 'bout I do your ass this time?"

Scowling, Dallas promptly spread her legs wide, exposing her vagina like a flower. "Hell no! I'm no damn prolapse princess. Do the pussy, now! I said: fist this damn pussy right now!!"

Sookie drew up a chair to the bed and watched while TLC lubed up both her hands past the wrist and slowly, with a touch of loving malice, slid her right hand into Dallas's sex.

Sookie watched the insertion with fascination, licking her lips as TLC's hand spread the wet vagina wide to what seemed ripping point, the labia taut around her knuckles and palm . . . (During the penetration, Dallas's breath exited her in a series of gasps. "Slowly . . . slowly . . . okay . . . just hold it there. Damn, it feels so big . . .") And then, almost like magic, with a slurping sound and the loud queef of expelled air, TLC's hand was fully inside Dallas.

TLC twisted her hand inside the stretched vagina. Leaning forward, she kissed Dallas on the lips with exquisite tenderness.

She pulled back, looked down into Dallas's eyes. "I thought you didn't want it," she said softly. "Should I stop?"

"I . . . I-I-I . . ." Dallas groaned as her girlfriend's mouth dropped to her breasts and sucked her nipples. "Just fuck me, darling, oh please."

TLC giggled. "Okay, remember you asked for it . . ."

She began sliding her fist back and forth inside Dallas's vagina. Dallas twitched, twisted, and turned on the bed, gasping, "Fuck, fuck, fuck!"

Sookie watched the deep penetration between the women for a while, then got up and proceeded to the card table for another hit of dragonreich.

Behind her, Dallas, her tanned limbs taut and sweaty, her fiery red hair mussed up even further, gasped, "I love you! I love you! I love you, TLC! I'm coming, dammit!"

Always problem with relationship, Sookie opined with a cold smile as she toked up, *woman always pretending to not love being fucked by lover until actually fucking. Reich much better—never play games with me.* Her smile broadened considerably. *Oh yes, Dallas baby, I very, very happy today. I not tell you idiot Lucy Tang dead!? Ha ha ha! Dumb bitch fry like Chinese dumpling!*

For a moment, Sookie mused: *Ah, so no need hire Soledad after all—Lucy destiny outsmart magic. Money wasted. But still, paranormal backup plan good to have. What if Malone not available, eh?*

Her eyes dropped to her cellphone. *Ah so, I make phone call.*

CHAPTER 22

Malone

Malone (driving back up to Robopol HQ after Steelberg's call about Mia Wong being trapped in her cat) had just turned onto Washington Street when his phone rang.

He picked it up off the seat, checked the display picture: Sookie Ling.

He accepted the call. "Hello, Sookie."

Houses and walkers scrolled past him as the dragon lady's voice came through the speaker. "Hello, Malone, long time no see; what cooking? You forget Sookie?"

Malone instantly realized she was inebriated. Maybe stoned as well—her voice was suitably slurred. "Everything's fine, Sookie. I was over at the casino just last night—"

"Ah, Malone, you very good friend of mine, maybe best ever. I call say thank you for killing Lucy Tang for me."

"W-W-What . . . ?" In his shock, Malone almost swerved his car off the road. A startled Mexican man in a dark coat gave him a one-finger-salute. He waved his apologies. "Sookie, I didn't kill . . . it was an accide—"

"Ah, Malone, you always modest—what girls love best about you. Not just big manhood make a big man—little manhood, big mind, big plans, always better. Kill is kill, bottom line, Lucy Tang tranny ass dead as delicious dog meat. So, thank you for murder her. You do me favor, I repay sometime. What do later today? Meet me and beautiful friends?"

Still shocked, Malone decided to humor her. "You're welcome, Sookie. Later? I've a date with—"

"Yes, I understand: After kill enemy, hero fuck woman hard, replace lost energy. Good pussy better than blood tonic—"

Scared he'd shortly drive off the road again, Malone parked the BMW behind an AG minibus.

"Hey, Malone . . . you still there?" the slurred voice enquired.

"Yeah, Sookie. I was just . . ." He became suddenly aware of wet slurping noises coming from the phone, followed by a loud 'Oh my gosh!' "Sookie, what's going on there?"

"Oh, that? You hearing noise? Oh, beautiful girl friends I want you meet. Dallas and TLC—tight little cunt. They playing fisting poker. Ha ha ha!"

Malone's mind boggled. "Fisting poker?"

"Normal card game. No money stakes. Winner fist loser hard as like . . . make loser much looser. Ha ha ha! Ah, Dallas very bad card player; poker face always telling truth. Lose five times already. Good thing she only like girls—cunt like train tunnel now, no more grip for penis again, except maybe horse cock."

Malone gulped. "Yeah, I get it." More moans of ecstasy spilled from the phone. Looking at passing pedestrians without seeing them, he suddenly felt impossibly surreal. His thoughts fluttered like confused birds in his head: *This morning I whipped a beautiful woman I might be falling in love with till she came. Now, I'm listening to a pair of fisting women while being thanked by a fourth for offing a fifth who I didn't—*

". . . No lie, Malone," Sookie was saying, "You truly best PI in Boston, possibly in America . . ."

Malone grimaced. *Hurry it up, Sookie. I've got to see the cops . . . and it's to prevent your drunken ass from getting killed by your own damn spell!*

First, however, he winced to the sound of Sookie snorting up a palmful of dragonreich. ". . . So what I want say before? Ah yes, maybe I hire you find runaway debtor. Good friend Ricky Rogers hiding from Sookie, but Sookie find him, remove both of two legs. Cocksucker run, but far away not far enough. Stan eyeballing for him now. Say, Malone, you see Ricky anywhere?"

"Rick . . . Rogers?" Malone remembered seeing the man earlier in the day, draped over that knockout blonde bombshell outside that bar. *What was the place's name again? Yeah—Club 66Sex. Damn! Sookie wants to cut his legs off?*

"No," he replied, "I haven't seen Rick in months."

A loud moan sailed out from the phone, followed by louder breathless panting. Sookie laughed over the noise. "I think Dallas play enough poker today," she told Malone. "So you not see Rick, no problem; but if see, grab runaway prick hard for me. I pay big bonus. Okay, now I go—Dallas not tired yet; still want win cards against TLC. I think girl just like fist. Ah, Malone, thank again for killing stupid bitch Lucy Tang. Come casino anytime, meet Dallas and TLC."

She hung up. Malone stared at the phone, bemused.

She's fucking serious, he realized. *She really is grateful to me for killing Lucy Tang. And she also has utterly no idea of the danger she's in herself. Damn!*

He restarted the BMW, eased out of parking into traffic, resumed his journey to Robopol HQ.

CHAPTER 23

Stan

Stan shone a flashlight down the darkened corridor. He made certain it was empty before stepping into it. Empty of life anyway. Dust, plaster, and wall debris lay everywhere, battle residue from the monsters' fight with Robopol. Here and there, Stan saw severed hands and legs, occasionally an gouged-out eye, or ripped-of ear. Bloody odd-shaped bones. Lots of innards and slime, beastie gore. Red scraps of human clothes. A single brown brogue with a foot in it.

No mechanical parts though—robot cops were hard (well nigh impossible) to dismantle. He doubted any of them even shook a bolt loose while pacifying this place.

Pacifying. To Stan, that was the key word here: *Pacified.* (Wasn't that what the robots' COP acronym stood for—Criminal Offensive Pacification?) Yeah, the damn Beacon Hill Hotel and Bistro seemed pacified alright. No noise, no monsters. Which was good.

Stan wondered what the fuck was wrong with him, coming here again. Big guy or no big guy, loaded machine pistol in hand or not, this wasn't somewhere he needed to be again, not just right now, but ever.

So what if Sookie wants Rick? She can damn well catch him herself! But it was a halfhearted resistance. Money always talked, and here it was yelling loud and clear in Stan's ear. With the sort of bread Sookie laid on him yearly—a million even, plus bonuses—he'd be a fool not to risk his life to keep her happy.

But, he thought nervously, tugging on his beard while making cautious strides in the darkness, *I'm being equally foolish coming back here after what Lucy Tang did. And why the hell did come I alone? This is just plain suicidal.*

Why was he here? Because some dealer named Juan Tevez had called and said Rick was hiding out here in the hotel, that was why. And it made sense, Rick hiding—

Stan slipped on some gore. Losing his gun as he tried to right himself, he fell sideways onto something that was hard yet pillowy.

He leapt up; was it another monster?

His flashlight revealed the object that had broken his fall to be a huge severed scaly leg—a tyrannosaur's leg—by the wall. Cussing, Stan retrieved his gun, then sat on the monster leg. *How the fuck did I get so caught up in thought I didn't notice that?*

Falling had really startled Stan. Dimming the flashlight beam, he leaned back against the wall to calm himself. The world contracted into the circle of light cast by his flashlight in the corridor. The light outlined his feet in spilled dinosaur blood. All around him was darkness—he felt abandoned in it. His heart beat extra hard; his mind replayed unwanted images of last night . . . Abdullah Ibrahim getting eaten . . . the nightmare boy Andy with the 'granddad' head in his belly . . .

With a sudden start, he switched the flashlight fully off. He'd heard a sound—footsteps. Soft furtive ones, like some extra large rat was walking . . . Shit! Why the fuck had he thought that? A *rat?* No, it had to be that bastard Rick Rogers.

The footsteps grew louder, but they weren't coming along the corridor. They sounded confined. Stan listened hard, trying to work out their source.

He made out that the footsteps were coming from the other side of a door about ten meters away. And now that Stan had flicked off his own light, he could see a beam of light projecting from that same door and forming a diffuse mushroom shape on the opposite corridor wall. A keyhole.

Silently pulling his large frame to its feet, Stan McCaulkin padded forward to the door and peeked in through the keyhole.

Then—before he even realized what was happening—in a sudden inexplicable painful transition, Stan found himself sucked in through the door.

Next thing he knew, he was inside the room. But that was the least of his problems—he was also tied down on a bed, bound hand and foot. He was staring up at a glowing lightbulb.

Confused, trying to work out what the hell had just happened, he looked desperately around. This room was a bedroom, lit by the single dangling bulb overhead. The bed to which Stan was tied was positioned in the room's center. The door was out of view, likely behind his head. His gun and flashlight lay on a chair on his right. On his left, a woman with glossy black hair and dressed in a business suit stood looking out of a window that framed a black sky with glowing white clouds.

Stan's mind made the instant connection: *That's The Groad— Hell—outside!*

The woman by the window turned to face Stan.

He felt his blood run cold in his veins—felt like his ageing heart would stop.

She had no face. Her flawless raven hair framed a featureless expanse with just a mouth—a lipless smiley-face semicircle—in its bottom half. But no eyes, eyebrows, or nose, and no contours, just smooth skin marbled with the faintest tracing of blue veins.

The faceless woman grinned at him. Her teeth were long and very pointy. "Hello, Stan."

Stan knew he was close to peeing himself from fear. He was trembling so much—it was her teeth. He could practically feel them biting into his flesh.

"I-I-I ain't looking for trouble," he managed to get out.

She walked over and picked up his machine pistol. "I'd say you were." She grinned that sharp display of teeth at him again, her tongue massive and pink between them. "And I dare say you've found it."

"Who are you?"

"Aunt Corpse."

The answer, spoken matter-of-factly made no sense to Stan, though he now became aware of a smell of decay coming from the faceless woman. Thoughts and fears ran riot in his head; his dread of this grotesque woman enhanced by the view through the window—the understanding that he'd somehow stepped down into Hell. He flexed his huge muscles against his restraints to no avail. *Shit! I'm utterly helpless, strapped to a table, and this lady with the bear-teeth plans on eating me for sure! What the hell is going on here!? I entered the hotel to find that bastard Rick and now—*

He deduced that Aunt Corpse was watching him with interest. He got that impression from the angling of her head. Rick wondered how the fuck she could see without eyes. Or did she use her ears like bats did?

"What do you want with me?" he asked.

"Rick Rogers asked me to kill you," she replied.

"Rick? That spineless little punk?"

She nodded, then laughed uproariously. "You should have left Rick alone, man. Now you'll never collect that debt."

Stan gulped. "Okay, let me go. I'll leave Rick alone." It hurt his masculine pride to say the next words, to beg: "Please, please, please, let me go!"

She laughed again, her mouth a pink hole filled with teeth in the lower half of her face. The stench of rot seemed to flood out of her mouth and fill the room. "Too late, Stan. Some friends of mine want to eat you."

Stan heard the door open behind him then close again. "Hello, Aunty Corpse," a familiar young voice said.

"Why hello, Andy, my little darling."

Stan didn't bother to restrain his bladder from emptying this time as the little boy walked around the bed. Andy's black spider legs were already sticking out from his naked sides and scratching impatiently on the floor. 'Granddad' was asleep in his belly, drool dribbling from the old man's cracked saggy lips as he snored loudly, and trickling in a mess through his stubble of beard. Andy himself was covered with blood and held a well-gnawed forearm bone with fleshed fingers attached.

Andy's eyes widened on recognizing Stan. He began slapping Granddad's big nose hard.

"Hey, Gramps, wake up! It's him from last night. The big meal that ran away! Wake up! Food! Food!"

Granddad sputtered awake. "Fo-fo-food? D-did you s-s-say fo-fo-food? Where, boy, where?!" Seeing Stan, his rheumy eyes lit up with pleasure.

"I caught him for you, old timer," Aunt Corpse said.

The rotted meat stink from the faceless woman had now literally paralyzed Stan like curare. His mind kept seeking a way of escape. All he could do was mumble, "Please, please, please."

"Thanks," Granddad said, slurping his lips loudly. Andy flung the bare forearm away, began dancing in glee as he regarded the captive Stan, his spider legs tapping noisily on the floor. "Let's kill him now, Aunty Corpse! Can I have his liver?" He smiled disarmingly at the faceless woman. "Please . . . please?"

"Liver's mine!" Granddad yelled from the boy's belly. "The greedy brat just ate three in a row."

Aunt Corpse frowned. "Neither of you get it—Mr. Chews already asked me for Stan's liver and I agreed."

Mr. Chews? Stan's vapor-addled mind fuddled. *Who the . . . ?*

"Aw, not Chews again!"

"Yes, Aunty—he's always eating our grub!"

Aunt Corpse turned toward the window. "Ah, speak of the devil. Here comes Mr. Chews now."

Stan turned his face toward the window too. A monstrous black snake with burning red eyes had just slithered up onto the windowsill. Stan watched in disbelief as the black serpent transformed into a short muscular negro clad only in boxer shorts. Stan gaped. Mr. Chews stalked into the room like a panther.

Aunt Corpse and Andy bowed deferentially to him.

Mr. Chews peered down at Stan and grinned. The negro's eyes were red pits, his mouth another pin-filled slit. His expression was one of intense hunger. He felt Stan's muscles, nodded his approval. "Yeah, Ms. Corpse, Rick really put us onto some prime meat this time." He looked at her slyly. "Did Ricky pay the full amount for offing this motherfucker?"

"Oh, he sure did," Aunt Corpse replied.

"Hey, don'tcha swear around the kid!" Granddad added.

Pay! That's it!! Stan's mind latched onto this sudden hope. *I'll fucking buy myself out of this!!!*

He put all his energy into his words, to ensure they heard him over themselves. "Whatever it is Rick's paying you to kill me, I'll pay you triple! Five times as much, even! Just don't eat me!"

Mr. Chews looked down at Stan. "Five times as much? Hmmm." His dusky face turned pensive. Stroking his square jaw reflectively, he considered the proposal for a full minute. Then he shook his head. "Nah, motherfucker."

"Please, please!"

"Five times as much is good money, Chews" Granddad piped up from Andy's belly. "Maybe we should reconsider."

"Yes, yes!" Stan hoped aloud, desperately.

"No." Mr. Chews said. "I still say we're gonna eat this motherfucker."

"Eat, eat, eat, eat, eat!" Andy began singsonging. He ran up the wall onto the ceiling and dangled over Stan upside down, like he'd fall on him.

"Don't eat me," Stan screamed feebly. "Okay, I'll give you all the cash I've got! Everything! Nine million bucks!"

"Damn," Mr. Chews said. "It's just like Rick told us—you really are one sick, greedy motherfucker."

"I don't understand."

The negro rolled his crimson eyes, then struck a pose that pumped out his muscles. "It's like this, you damn douchebag: If you knew you were willing to give us all your money to set you free, why not offer it up the first time? The damn cash is useless to you if you're dead, right? Where's a corpse gonna spend money, eh? Hellmart? See, you're so fucking greedy you're still trying to screw us with your life at stake"

"I'm sorry. I wasn't thinking." Stan sighed with relief. "We've got a deal then? Everything for my life?"

"Hell, no! We're still gonna eat ya. And I'll share your liver with the kid."

"Yaay!" Andy yelped from the ceiling. "Thanks, Uncle Chews."

"Don't mention it, little brother."

Stan slumped back down.

"I'm hungry!" Andy yelled, now swinging back and forth on his many legs like a wind was blowing him.

Granddad growled. "Yeah! Are we'es gonna eat this here bastard or grow old discussin' it?"

Mr. Chews grinned broadly, his pointy teeth shining white. "Hell yeah! We gonna eat the motherfucker. Do him in, Ms. Corpse."

Watching Aunty Corpse step towards him, his gun clutched in her bone-white hands, Stan lost all hope. He peered once out of the window at the black sky, then looked back in again, his gaze locking with that of Granddad, who now leered down at him from overhead, spittle dropping like thick rain from his mouth to splatter Stan's pants.

Aunt Corpse reached the bed. Staring at her eyeless, noseless face, Stan had only one question for her:

"I don't get it—I just offered you bastards everything I own in this damn world—nine million fucking dollars—and you're still gonna kill me? The fuck why? No way did that debt-ridden punk Rogers offer you even one percent of that—he's broke!"

Mr. Chews replied as Aunt Corpse bent over Stan, her 'face' an evil smiley of just teeth. "You don't get it, do you, Stanley? You're a complete asshole—a nasty person."

"Yes," Aunt Corpse agreed, her stink of decay pouring on him like spilled sewage. "That's it exactly: We *like* Rick Rogers; we don't like you."

She pulled the machine pistol's trigger and kept it held down.

The spray of hot metal bullets ripped Stan's head clean off his shoulders.

***

Stan jerked awake. He was covered in sweat, like he'd been working out in Gold's Gym. His breath was running hard and fast, his heart seemed to be going even faster.

A dream? A fucking dream? Me . . . Rich hiring some . . . Thank God it was just a dream. Hey, I didn't actually piss myself, did I? No I didn't.

He swung his feet out of bed, sat up rubbing his eyes, looked out the window at the day. A glance back in at the wall clock confirmed his deductions: it was late afternoon—half past three.

(He had the ghost of a headache, like a hangover had tried to get its hooks into him during his sleep but had been scared off by his nightmare.)

He'd not slept last night. Once through explaining to Sookie what had happened, Stan had returned to his quarters and sat awake drinking. The brandy didn't work, however; each time he'd shut his eyes he'd see his men being ripped apart like vultures savaging roadkill . . .

So he'd drank till seven in the morning . . . then Sookie had called him about Lucy Tang's death and he'd gone to see her . . . then he'd returned here and lain in bed staring blind at the ceiling . . . then fallen asleep . . .

And now it was almost evening.

He scowled at a memory. He'd been white-faced with fright when he'd got back to Sookie last night. And for the second time running, Sookie's poker-faced advice to him for getting over the willies had been the same:

"Ah, Stan. Find pretty woman, fuck hard—worries and fears become semen, explode out into vagina. When I hooker, I cure much hypertension—Dr. Sookie men always call me."

Stan wasn't amused in the least. The one thing he could do without was Sookie thinking of him as a scaredy-cat. Once that happened, he could kiss his right-hand-man position goodbye.

He looked out the window again, at the overcast sky with white clouds like . . . like those shiny clouds in the black sky in . . . His mind leapt back into his dream, to the weird people in the room: that horrid, horrid creepy little Andy (*no wonder I never wanted kids*) . . . and Granddad.

And Aunt Corpse? The negro Mr. Chews? Damn, how the hell did I think those two up? He tapped his temple reflectively. *Wow, the unconscious mind is one seriously fucked up place. No wonder shrinks get paid so much.*

Stan's unease slowly became irritation. Irritation directed at one particular person: Rick Rogers. *Yeah, I gotta find that li'l punk and collect for Sookie—I've gotta stop looking incompetent.* His anger was buffed by fear carried over from his nightmare, as if Rick had sicced the bad dream on him.

Then he beamed at a pleasant thought. *So, Lucy Tang is dead? Malone killed her? Malone 'goody two shoes?' Ha ha ha!*

Stan was immensely relieved that he'd never have to tangle with Lucy Tang again.

He began planning the evening. Time to go looking for Rick. He and Sookie had earlier gotten word (ironically from the same Juan Tevez who'd given Stan pointers as to Rick's whereabouts in his dream) that the son-of-a-bitch had fled home, hadn't slept there last night.

154

Stan grinned—assholes will be assholes, no telling where the punk would have run to now.

Stan didn't mind chasing Rick Rogers around Boston. In fact, he'd be disappointed if Tevez was wrong and he found Rick at home waiting meekly for him. Stan planned on beating the bullshit out of Rick when he caught him anyway, and wanted a good excuse so the little wussy couldn't weasel out of the grievous bodily harm coming to him. Blame fucking Lucy Tang, Rick—your ass is collateral damage.

Stan flexed his arm and flung a shadow punch, imagining the air was Rick's nose breaking. Yeah, a little display of his superior masculinity over an inferior physical specimen was certain to prop up his flagging ego.

Stan considered a bit more: Yeah, along the way, he'd take the boss lady's advice: pick up some woman and fuck her hard. Extra, super hard. He squeezed his crotch, suddenly feeling a little like his usual violent self again. *Yeah, I've got a whole lot of fear and worry to empty into that tight vagina of yours, honey. So much fear and worry, you'll be slack for life when I'm done with ya.*

He laughed, then went to the bathroom to have a piss and brush his teeth. Time to go hunting.

CHAPTER 24

Rick / Anastasia Wormwood

The antigrav taxi pulled out of an aisle of skin-covered buildings onto a broad plain.

"Where are we going?" Rick groggily questioned Anastasia. He'd regained control of himself during their trip through the Forbidden City. (He had no idea how long they'd been journeying in the cab—seemed like forever. It also seemed like five minutes.) The two bottles of wine lay between him and her.

The gorgeous blonde, her smile cherry red, pointed to the single building approaching on their left. "My place; we'll be worlds more comfortable out there—the house has a lovely rooftop view."

Rick looked out. Flanking them in the distance were lots of immensely high white trees. Below the trees were a few red buildings. The trees appeared to be moving. He looked back inside the car. His attention was for a moment held by the faceless taxi driver. He shuddered. It was impossible—the cabbie seeing without eyes. In addition the man hadn't said a single word since they'd gotten in. *Or did he, and I was too out of it to notice? And that's another thing I don't get: how the hell does one get this wasted on just one drink?*

Anastasia patted his arm. "Don't worry, baby."

He grimaced. "Oh, I'm worried alright. We've still not yet reached a deal and my time's running out. Time waits for no one."

"Nonsense. Time waits for everyone here in The Groad. I already explained as much to you."

Rick shook his head to clear the last of the booze from it.

The cab slowed and stopped. They got out. Anastasia paid the cabbie.

Rick now had his first real look around.

"Are we still in the Forbidden City?" he asked.

"Never left it." She pointed out across the plain. "The city is all around us."

Rick looked to the limits of his vision. The plain was wide, wide, wide, with the impressions of crystal high-rises on its outskirts. Far back the way they'd come, he could still see the moving white trees. "What are *those* things?"

Anastasia took his hand. "Come upstairs. The view's way better from the roof."

They walked up the drive to the solitary house, a three-story building that—to Rick's immense relief—looked normal enough: White stucco walls, black-tinted glass windows, an extensive porch, upper verandas. Just an everyday rich woman's villa.

The ornate wooden front door opened just as they reached it. Rick almost leapt back in fear. The woman who'd opened the door had no face—no eyes or nose, just a 'smiley' grin of pointy teeth at the bottom of the smooth white expanse of skin fronting her head. Thick, well-dressed black hair fell to below her shoulders.

"Welcome back, madam," she said.

"Thank you, Aunt Corpse," Anastasia replied with a smile.

Rick was aware of a horrible stink of rotting meat issuing from Aunt Corpse as she stood aside to let them in. He hurried past her, taking care that their bodies didn't touch. He imagined he heard her laughing softly after him.

They walked into a compact living room. Bright lights, dark furniture, pale walls.

Anastasia flung her handbag down on an armchair. She took the bottles of wine from Rick and handed them to Aunt Corpse. "Chill one of them; serve us the other with ice. We'll be up on the roof."

Aunt Corpse smiled knowingly, her teeth long and white and sharp. "Business, madam?"

"Of course. You know what they're like downstairs—profit must be made." Her voice now assumed a histrionic, melodramatic, mocking note: 'Profit must be made, Ana, or our financial Titanic will sink, it's hull shattered on the iceberg of human bad debts." She fell silent.

Aunt Corpse nodded. "It's a horrendous lot of work keeping any company afloat, madam."

Rick was relieved that that was the end of their conversation. The mouth-faced woman escorted them to a recessed elevator, then departed to fetch glasses and ice.

As the elevator doors closed, Rick studied the departing maid. The odd woman walked with very prim and proper steps.

"Aunt Corpse? That's the weirdest name ever."

"She's an aiis," Anastasia explained as the cage rose. "They're a tribe from the lower Groad."

"And they're all like that? No faces, just mouths?"

"The aiis sport all kinds of different mutations. Some have just eyes, some only noses, then others . . . well you saw the cab driver just now—no facial features at all." She ran fingers down Rick's back. "Lots of strange folk inhabit The Groad."

"You can frigging say that again," Rick said, remembering that Anastasia Wormwood herself just looked human, he had no idea what kind of being she really was.

Almost like she'd sensed his thoughts and was angered by them, she didn't reply. They rode the rest of the way in silence.

***

They sat together on the roof, on soft cushions at either end of a white-painted metal bench. Anastasia kicked her shoes off, flexed her toes on the concrete.

Aunt Corpse appeared almost immediately with their wine. She set the tray down on a small foldup table, opened the ice bucket and began serving.

While she filled their glasses, and while Rick tried not to puke from the horrible smell of her (He didn't get it—she didn't seem to be rotting anywhere, yet this sickly odor just oozed from her.), Anastasia stripped off her business suit to reveal the skimpiest of white silk bikinis. She handed her clothes to Aunt Corpse, who after retrieving her mistress's shoes as well, instantly left the roof. Anastasia sat facing Rick again, posed to maximum effect with an arm draped over the rear of the bench and a foot up on a cushion.

"Damn it's hot up here," she said, picking up her drink. "You should bare some skin too."

"I-I-I . . ." The words failed him. His eyes rode along her sleek thighs to the strip of white material barely concealing her pubic

158

plot, her sexual lips pouting against the sheer fabric. Gulping, his gaze rose further up her stacked form. His erotic distraction only increased: In addition to her movie-star good looks, Anastasia Wormwood had a sex goddess's body, all curves and more curves. Rick's head spun at the perfection of her; he imagined he'd have an epileptic seizure just from staring at her breasts, the nipples of which seemed about to puncture her bikini top.

His penis stood to attention again.

"I-I'm fine," he sputtered, picking up his glass and draining most of it in one gulp.

He sat back, not looking at her, but instead out over the landscape, his eyes traveling the strange countryside. "Okay, so we're up here like you wanted. Let's deal." His eyes now focused on a moving distant object. He was shocked. The white trees he'd noticed on his way here were animal legs. Long, long, legs (furry white like a polar bear's, but impossibly stretched) that ended up inside the fluorescent clouds overhead, making it seem like the clouds were walking. *What the . . . ? Some of those legs must be miles—*

Anastasia's voice cut into his thoughts. "We're in stalemate, Ricky; you're yet to offer me anything I can use."

She poured them both fresh glasses of wine, smiled disarmingly. "So, that's the fifth-of-a-million-dollar question: what can *you* offer *me?*"

Rick grinned back shrewdly. "You know, so far this has all been one-sided. All I'm hearing from you is 'I want this and I want that.' How do I even know you can get me two hundred grand?" He raised his glass to her. "You know, this wine's got a real kick to it. You're trying to get me drunk, right?"

"You're very cocky for a man about to lose his legs." Then she shrugged. "I can—Aunt Corpse is already on her way up with the money."

They waited. To Rick the pause felt like a break in transmission, like he was an interrupted radio broadcast.

The rotting-meat smell announced Aunt Corpse's arrival. She handed a briefcase to Anastasia.

Anastasia flipped open the brown leather case, then spun it toward Rick. "Count it."

He gulped at the sight of the neatly bundled hundred dollar bills. "No need."

Anastasia shut the case again, dropped it down behind the bench. She smiled sweetly at Rick. "You're convinced now that this is the real deal?"

He nodded. "I just can't think of anything to trade."

Aunt Corpse smiled at him then. Her smooth-skin face gave Rick the creeps.

Anastasia giggled. "Aunt Corpse likes you, Rick. Don't you, Auntie?"

The eyeless, noseless woman nodded back. "I really do, madam. He's cute—the kind of man I wish my niece Tammy would hook up with, not that—"

"TLC? Is she still dating Dallas Washington?"

Aunt Corpse nodded sadly, the emotion conveyed by a frown and despondent sag of her shoulders. "She still is, madam. Dallas has cast a spell over Tammy with her money. From what I gather they're whooping it up right now with Sookie Ling."

Rick practically froze solid on hearing that.

Anastasia nodded back sagely. "Don't worry, Auntie. Girls will be girls—sometimes they want sugar mommies, the richer the better—pussy and cash is always a winning combination. Sooner or later young TLC will realize stability is more important than money and endless fun."

Aunt Corpse sighed. "I've nothing against women being together, madam, you know that—I've had girlfriends myself . . . but that Dallas Washington, she's a bad seed, mark my words, she'll get my Tammy into a world of bother." She smiled at Rick again. "Likely break her heart then leave her broke. Not like this gentleman here—I can tell." She stroked Rick's arm with her fingernails; he fought not to flinch at the bug-like contact, like furry spiders were walking on his bare skin. "You're reliable, sir, aren't you? Not one to break a trusting woman's heart?"

Rick gulped a confirmatory nod.

"So sad," Anastasia Wormwood said. "I really wish I could help you, Aunt Corpse; but Dallas Washington's so stinkingly rich. I think she's got half a billion dollars, more even by some accounts. Now if she somehow went broke overnight, and came here to deal..."

Aunt Corpse seemed satisfied with that; she smiled again.

"So back to us," Anastasia told Rick. "Unless you can somehow get into Dallas Washington's pants in TLC's place, you're stuck with me for your financial redemption. What'll it be?"

Aunt Corpse left them then. Rick felt weird. His impression of how much time had passed since they'd been up here on Anastasia's rooftop—none at all—was doing his head in. *And we're still no closer to a deal?*

Then Anastasia undid her bikini bottom and slipped it off. Spreading her legs wide, she bared her vagina with forked fingers for Rick's inspection. "Stop being a pussy; how 'bout you just eat mine?" She licked her lips. "Two hundred G's for some head has to be a bargain, right?"

Rick sputtered the wine he'd been about swallowing. Her vagina looked so tasty, the pink slit so inviting, its dark cavern brimming with white secretion. He could smell its musk like a sweet perfume. He imagined his tongue lapping up her sweet white cream, swirling inside her hole like it was mining for more, riding up to her clitoris, then . . .

Then Soledad's warning flashed through his mind: *'Whatever you do, don't fuck her.'*

But it was a weak caution—the wine was too heady, too entrenched in his psyche now. He shrugged the dire admonition off. Besides, Anastasia Wormwood's blonde pussy looked so delicious. Like it would a total gourmet joy to eat—appetizer, entrée, dessert all in one. And . . . Rick felt a strange force coming from the spread vagina—like a sci-fi tractor beam was pulling him down to it.

He bent forward under the hole's magnetism. Then his bladder twinged painfully.

He got up. "I need to pee."

Anastasia paused in pouring the last of the wine into her glass. She sighed, pointed across the roof to a hut he'd previously not noticed. "There. Don't talk to strangers."

Pondering her weird caution, Rick dashed across to the hut.

***

Inside the hut looked like a public toilet—a wall of urinals, several washbasins opposite those, and three cubicles at one end. The room seemed larger than the hut did from outside.

Rick unzipped and got down to business.

He was sighing with relief as the amber stream arched against the tiles when the front door opened.

He glanced back at it, then froze in shock.

A huge black snake was slithering in through the door. The creature was almost anaconda-sized and had glowing red eyes.

The snake fully entered the toilet and slid towards Rick.

He unfroze, leaping away towards the cubicles, pissing into the air as he did so. Some of his urine splattered the snake. He hastily packed away his member, began looking desperately for an escape route. The snake was blocking the door; his best bet seemed to lock himself in a cubicle and yell.

He backed into the closest cubicle, then froze again in the doorway . . .

The black snake was altering. Rick watched it become a man. A stocky black man with the same glowing red eyes the reptile had had. The negro was naked except for boxer shorts.

He looked angrily at Rick. "Hey, motherfucker—how you gone piss on a brother like that? You a racist or something?"

He had pointy white teeth.

"S-S-Sorry," Rick gasped.

"Don't worry 'bout it." The black man turned to a urinal, freed his penis, and began urinating. "Name's Mr. Chews," he said while doing so. "I came by to offer you some advice, man."

Rick gaped. "Advice?" He remained in the cubicle entrance, ready to slam the door shut if the negro became a snake again.

"Yeah, man, advice." Mr. Chews finished his peeing, then crossed to wash his hands. As the water flowed he frowned over at Rick. "Motherfucker, didn't your mama train you better? Get your punk ass over here right now and wash your damn hands. Shit, no wonder the world's full of diseases nowadays."

"Yeah, sure." Rick padded over to the washstands, began soaping up. His reflection in the mirror over the sinks looked haggard and hungover. Beside him, the negro's eyes blazed like fire.

"Now, listen here," Mr. Chews said, holding his hands under the dryer. "I know you're here to deal with Cousin Wormwood."

"How'd you . . . ? Sorry, just go on. I'm listening."

"She's just talked you into giving her head for money, right? That's cool—just don't lick her ass."

"What?"

"You heard me right. Eat all of Blondie's pussy you want, just don't do no rimming."

"No?"

The negro nodded. "No, man—no sticking your tongue in her brownhole like you're wiping her ass for her." He shook raised palms at Rick. "Don't do that, and not just 'cos it's dirty."

"Why then?"

"That's the trap, see? Girls *all* love it when you lick their crack; sure they'll tell you they don't, maybe even push your head away, but insist on licking that asshole and next day, they be boasting to all their friends; she'll be prancing about, shaking that fat ass like she a queen or something. Cousin Wormwood—Anastasia—on the other hand, she gone practically force your mouth down to her anus. Like I said—don't. No anal. You wanna live to spend that good money—blessed be Benjamin Franklin forever—you remained focused on the damn clit. That's what the lady needs-damn satisfucktion. Suck up some pussy juice if you want—that stuff's more nutritious than breast milk—but lick that clitoris like your life depends on it." He glared at Rick. "'Cos it does, mofo—I saw Stan McCaulkin a while back and he's gunning for your legs."

Rick felt cold. "You saw Stan? What did he say?"

"Motherfucker didn't say shit—he was asleep and dreaming. But trust me, that son-of-a-bitch ain't fooling about. He gone kick your ass halfway to Springfield before amputatin' your walkers."

Rick sagged against the ceramic sink. He feebly extended his hand to the negro. "Thanks for the warning, man. I appreciate it."

Mr. Chews regarded Rick's hand with suspicion. "You use enough soap just now?"

"Yeah, fucking loads."

"Well, alright then." Mr. Chews grinned and shook Rick's hand firmly. "Now stand back and don't freak out—I'm gonna become a snake again."

Rick nodded and did so. Two moments later, Mr. Chews had become a huge black snake again and was sliding back out the toilet door.

Rick watched the serpent's tail disappear, then he unzipped his pants and finished off his pee.

Then he washed his hands again. Real clean, just like the negro had insisted.

**

"Enjoy yourself in there?" Anastasia asked when Rick rejoined her. "You didn't talk to any strangers, I hope?"

He shook his head. "No one."

She smiled like strawberry ice cream, pointed down at her crotch. "So what'll it be: trick or treat?"

Rick gazed at her naked sex, a gorgeous pink flower, its petals creamed white, then looked back at her face. A beautiful, possibly devious face.

"Are you trying to treat me or trick me?" he asked. In the interim their empty wine bottle had been replaced. He poured himself a glass, sat, sipped while gazing between her splayed legs like a special truth resided in her vagina.

"Maybe one, maybe none, maybe both; that's for you to find out, but for me to know." She shook her head; her blonde locks flared, catching the light like sequined silk. She pouted prettily, her lips a fellatio invitation. "You worry too much."

"I should; I've only one life."

"Only two legs too."

"Horrid pun. But okay, deal—I'll perform cunnilingus on you." He bent forward to grab her thighs and position her crotch on the edge of the bench.

Giggling, she pushed his questing fingers away, leapt to her feet. He sat watching her, a sex goddess outlined against the black heavens, her perfect figure illuminated by its flashing white clouds.

She slipped out of her bra, flung it away. Posed for him against the dusky sky. Freed from confinement, her breasts floated against the dark backdrop—two pink balloons. He drank in the delightful vision of her bared chest like soil drinks in rain. His penis again stiffened, this time for real.

She reached out a hand, drew him to his feet. "Come. We're going downstairs to the mistress bedroom." She winked. "We're taking our time with this. Baby, you've never sex where there's no time factor involved. My orgasm literally seems to last forever." She winced. "And paradoxically never long enough."

He pointed to the briefcase with the money.

"Leave it," she said. "It's not about running off to bank itself."

After downing the rest of his wine, Rick followed Anastasia Wormwood across the rooftop to the elevator door. It was a normal enough scene: two tipsy lovers, she leaning against him while fondling his cock through his pants.

Still, Rick couldn't shake an image from his head: that of a stupid lamb being led to the slaughter.

He smothered his fear. *No, I've got this covered. Mr. Chews made it clear—no anilingus. Pretty lady's in for a shock if she expects me to rim her.*

Once inside the elevator, a sudden passion seemed to seize Anastasia. She quickly pushed Rick down to his knees. Then, leaning back against the metal wall, she spread her legs and pulled his face into her dripping crotch. "Dammit, I can't wait till we're downstairs. Start eating me now."

Rick was already eating her, his mouth pressed tight as a leech's against her vagina. Her musk filled his nostrils, corrupted his senses. Soon, his mind was a ship adrift at sea, propelled to and fro by musky winds, blown too far from recalling any of the warnings he'd received.

His only odd impression was that she seemed much taller. Then he looked down, saw that her shoes had gotten higher. Almost a foot higher.

Hey, he vaguely pondered as he tongued her clitoris, *didn't she take her shoes off earlier? When did she put them back on?*

CHAPTER 25

Malone / Soledad

The Freak Dungeon Bookshop was two buildings down from Robopol HQ. On leaving Lt. Steelberg, Malone made his way over there.

Despite its name, the bookshop was on the building's seventh floor. Pushing open its black front door, Malone felt wonderfully embarrassed, like a fugitive from moral justice, an impression twice reinforced once he was fully inside amidst the shop's decadent ambience, surrounded by its shelves of sex toys and displays.

Yeah, now I'm a pervert, he though glumly. *What the hell am I doing inside here? All I wanted today was to check out the girl in the cat.*

Well he'd checked out the girl in the cat, alright. Time enough to review *that* madness once he'd gotten *this* madness over with.

The Freak Dungeon Bookshop was well named. Malone felt like he really was underground. Maybe it was all the kinky equipment on display: the stocks, the racks hung with floggers and latex and leather clothes, the miscellaneous paraphernalia . . . The singularity of function of all its displayed apparatus gave the large room the claustrophobic feel of a medieval torture chamber.

We're only missing the inquisitors, Malone thought, his gaze drawn to the room's several floor-to-ceiling aisles of books and DVDs. *And if I pull Soledad's monster-hunting knife from my jacket now I'll instantly fill that old-time role.*

Thankfully, he wasn't the only customer. Ironically though, the other bookshop patrons made him feel even more out of place, they all seemed so at ease in this fetish universe. On his right, a man and woman giggled while examining a huge green dildo. (Malone

166

couldn't help wondering which of them was going to use it on the other.) Behind them, a nerdish brunette in a severe gray pantsuit (who'd apparently already selected several whips—they were draped over her arm) perused a thick leather-bound volume. Directly in front of Malone, two buff men examined a black leather suit fitted with a scary mask—it looked like something from WWII. The younger man smiled at Malone as he passed towards the sales counter.

He nodded back, next passing a man examining a *Bath Time: Golden Shower Tales* DVD. He winced. *What the fuck have I gotten myself into by meeting Slave?*

The attendant at the counter—slim and dark with a handlebar moustache and dressed in a ripped 'Tainted Love' tee shirt and red leather pants—nodded sagely as Malone explained what he wanted.

"What kind of book, sir? I mean, what BDSM level? How experienced are you and the lady in question?"

"She's very . . . I-I-I'm not even a novice," Malone admitted. "She's asked me to be her Master. I want something that gives pointers about how to handle her safely. . . sort of like *S and M for Dummies*, if you've anything like that."

The man gave Malone a knowing smile. "Nothing to be embarrassed about, sir. It's a common situation—wanting to experiment in a relationship. Please excuse me for a moment."

Malone nodded. The man vanished left into an aisle of books.

Feeling less out-of-place now he'd made his order, Malone sat on a leather-covered stool by the counter to wait. He heard the seller pulling books from shelves and putting them back again. His eyes met those of a pretty Goth girl fondly stroking a spanking horse. He winked; she looked shyly away. A moment later a handsome young denim-clad man joined her. The pair began arguing heatedly, with her shaking her head and pointing insistently at the horse.

Malone laughed. *Ah, so you have a Slave of your own, do you? Or are you the slave?*

While waiting, Malone's mind slipped sideways, back to Steelberg's office at Robopol HQ. The talking cat. Or more accurately, Mia Wong stuck in her cat. It had been a harrowing, hellish interview. Mia Wong kept breaking into extensive weeping bouts, in between explaining how she'd gotten home . . .

Malone suddenly felt his guts clench. The pain was so intense he first thought he'd been shot. Then the pain repeated, along with a telltale belly rumbling. He grimaced. *Damn, I need to use the toilet! But what the hell? Now?* The pain abated; the discomfort continued, an ominous sensation that caressed his rectum with creepy fingers.

He looked around for a toilet, but too many displays, bookshelves and people were in the way everywhere. (The couple who'd been arguing by the spanking horse were now kissing by it; the bookish brunette previously perusing a leather-bound volume was now weighing a vibrator in her palm.) Malone scowled. *I really need to use the john; no way is this shit keeping up my butt till I'm home.*

The shop attendant returned then. With a satisfied smile, the man dropped four books on the counter in front of Malone.

"Ah yes, sir. I've found just what you need." He spread the books out. "*Knowing Your Whips* by Lisa Lash . . . *How to Dominate Your Slave: A Master Training Manual . . . Well Flogged: A Buttock's Tale*—" He saw Malone wince. "Are you alright, sir?"

Malone winced again. "Where's the gents'? I'm on laxative call."

The attendant's eyes widened. Stroking his mustache, he pointed behind Malone. "By the *Boston Decadence* poster, sir. Steps lead right down to it."

"Thanks." Malone turned and dashed off for the indicated door, pausing to say, "I'll take all four books, pack 'em up for me."

***

The stairs ended in a rosewater-scented room with two cubicles, one each for female and male customers. Malone rushed through the left, male, door, hung his jacket on the hook behind it, pulled down his pants and underpants and sat.

He concentrated on defecating, while his bowels churned like they were angry with him. He gripped his knees, focused on the border of blue rug visible under the cubicle door,

He felt embarrassed to be caught like this in public. The way he'd fled the bookstore, everyone would know he had the runs. Yes, but what had triggered it? Slave's cooking? That was unlikely—she'd only made bread and scrambled eggs. Ah, it had to be last night's seafood dinner at the casino—the fish must have been off! But it hadn't tasted bad, and Slave hadn't shown signs . .
.

Malone smiled on remembering Slave. She made him happy—happier than he'd been for ages—which was odd, because she had him really confused too. He'd not be here right now but for her . . .

His bowels finished ejecting their contents. Relieved, Malone reached for the toilet roll.

Then he froze on the seat.

There was a little plastic doll—a blonde Barbie doll in a frilly pink dress—sitting on the toilet roll.

The doll waved its plastic arm in a stiff motion. "Hi, Malone, it's Soly."

His alarm lessened. "Soledad Bathory?"

The doll nodded. "Yeah." Its voice seemed to come from a tiny speaker on its back. Its body movement was creepy, like human hands bent its plastic form. It was a doll alright, no doubt about that. A demon doll now, one possessed by a witch.

"Soledad, what the hell are you doing here?"

"I just thought to check on developments."

"In here? I'm on the toilet." He remembered his pants were down, checked to ensure the front of his shirt hid his manhood from her view. "Okay, get going. Leave. Go wait in my car."

"We need to talk."

"I need to wipe my butt, Soledad. Get off the toilet paper."

In response, the Barbie doll sat back comfortably against the wall, and crossed her legs on the tissue paper. It wasn't a convincing pose for a toy, but Malone got the point.

"Okay, okay," he groaned. "Just hurry it up, they're waiting for me upstairs. I just bought some books."

"Yeah, books on how to whip freaky's ass. Damn, Malone, I never thought you had it in you."

"Soly, why can't you just be normal-sized?"

"Answer that yourself—both of us can't fit comfortably in here."

"Okay, what do you want to know?"

The doll tilted its head. "They found the cat yet?"

"You don't know? You're following me about, aren't you?"

"No, I don't know, and no, I'm not stalking you. I was driving past and saw your car."

"Okay, so . . ."

"Hey, aren't you in a hurry to get back up to pervy paradise? Just tell me what happened. Have they found the cat, or what?"

"They found it too late. Your pet demon's in someone else now."

The doll scrunched up its plastic face, a painful-looking maneuver even for a toy. "Shit! Do they know *whose* body?"

"Its owner's—Mia Wong, one of Sookie's croupiers. She opened her front door, knelt to pet her cat, and the blasted feline attacked her. Dug its claws into her and . . ."

The doll almost fell off her commandeered roll of toilet paper. "Shit! It's getting closer to Sookie."

"I don't think so. Mia's a low-level casino employee, not someone guaranteed to have contact with her boss. All her interaction will likely be through her superiors. By your cousin's 'degrees-of-separation' explanation, Switch will likely try to infect one of those. Mia hasn't been into work today anyhow."

"The damned thing is just biding its time." The doll steepled hands in front of its face, then asked in a tiny worried voice. "Does Steelberg know this?"

"No, he's just tired of having to explain to folk why they're in different bodies." Malone was suddenly aware of the stifling smell of poop in the cubicle. *Shit, how I wish this was France—this could never happen if we all used bidets!*

The doll faked a bow. "Okay, thanks, Malone. I owe you big time."

He waited for the doll to leave. To his horror, it didn't.

"C'mon, Soledad, give me a break, the shit's drying on my ass."

Instead of leaving, the Barbie doll covered its eyes with its hands. It giggled. "You can wipe your ass with me here. I'm not looking, see?"

Malone saw his chance. Moving like a flash of light, he grabbed the Barbie doll off of the reel of toilet paper and flung it outside, over the top of the cubicle door.

Hastily unreeling toilet tissue, he heard a loud, heavy thud on the floor outside. He paused, a long strip of tissue paper in hand. Shit. That didn't sound a doll falling.

"Ouch, that fucking hurt!!"

The next second, a life-sized, flesh and blood Soledad Bathory was inside the cubicle with him. Malone realized she was right: there really wasn't enough space in here for both of them. Her crotch was practically in his face.

He also saw that Soledad was furious. She was glaring down at him in a total rage. She also had a bloody nose, the red liquid still streaming down to her chin and onto her top.

And Hell hath no fury like an angry witch.

"Sorry, Soly, I didn't mean to—"

"Man, can't you take a damn joke!? I was about leaving, and then you go and bust me up. Shit! I think you've broken my damn nose!"

"Soledad, calm down! I'll—"

"I'm going to fucking get you for this, Malone."

She snapped her fingers twice and was gone.

A moment later Malone realized all his clothes were gone too. Jacket, shirt, pants, underwear, socks, shoes; he was completely naked and barefoot in a toilet. And not just any toilet; a BDSM shop's toilet.

He frowned. *Well at least she left the toilet paper.* He tore off a good length and took his time with wiping his ass.

That done, Malone said, as calmly as he could manage, "Hey, Soledad, I know you're still here. Please give me my clothes back."

There was no reply. Malone was playing a hunch that she'd not yet left, that she was lurking around invisible to make him suffer.

"C'mon, Soly, don't be a bitch."

Her voice floated from the other side of the door. It sounded completely disembodied. "No, unless you come out naked from the toilet."

"Naked? Aw c'mon, Soly, I can't do that. C'mon, you know I'd never try to hurt you. I didn't know—"

"You come out naked or no clothes. Hands on your head."

"Is this just a ploy to see the size of my dick?"

"I already saw it this morning." He could practically hear her smirk. "Do you want your goddam clothes back or not? Or maybe you don't mind wearing some of the bondage gear upstairs. I'm sure the family freak will be delighted."

Cursing all witches, and vowing in his mind to help permanently stamp out their infernal breed if he could, Malone stepped out, hands-on-head.

To his relief, Soledad Bathory was nowhere in sight. At that exact moment, however, a woman came down the stairs to the toilets. It was the bookish woman in the gray suit who'd been examining the dildos upstairs.

Malone was caught. He stood staring, a flasher, expecting her to bolt screaming.

Instead, the brunette's eyes flashed with calm, cool interest. She spent a long time regarding his body, then, licking her lips, took a card from her purse and handed it to him.

"My name's Lisa Lash," she said softly, running manicured fingers through the hair on his chest. "I just *love* your cock. Come see me sometime; we'll have fun." She stepped up close and kissed him on the lips, then entered the female cubicle. Her perfume lingered after her.

Malone was pulled from his bemusement by Soledad's amused giggling. He still couldn't see her, though.

Pursued by her mirth, he retreated back into the male cubicle. "Listen, Soly," he whispered angrily. "Okay, you've had your damn fun. You knew that woman was coming down here, didn't you? Now look, if I'm not fully dressed in the next five seconds, I *will* walk upstairs naked and buy some bondage gear to wear; but I swear to you, I'm heading directly from here to the casino to tell Sookie about your screw up."

Sounds of Lisa Lash flushing came from the next cubicle. Then came the creak of the door opening and the soft footsteps of her departure.

Malone began opening the toilet door to follow the brunette. "Okay, witch, call my bluff if you like."

A loud gasp like a soft thunderclap followed. "No, don't . . . please."

"Give me my fucking clothes back then. Right fucking now."

The next moment, Malone found himself fully dressed again. He examined himself, nodded. Damn, Soledad was *really* scared of Sookie Ling—she'd even pulled up his pants for him, tucked his shirt in, and done up his zipper.

Hiding his relief that she'd quit her game, he strode out of the toilet, examined himself in a wall mirror.

Soledad's disembodied voice said, "I'm real sorry; real, real sorry. I was only joking."

"For real? Invisible Lady, I'm not even angry with you." He frowned. "But I know someone who is. You know who, right?"

A bulgingly pregnant pause after, Soledad Bathory appeared beside him. "Forget it."

Her nose was still bleeding. Malone handed her his handkerchief. "Soly, go and apologize to Slave."

"Thanks. Hell no, I won't."

"Soly, go and tell her you're sorry you kicked her out. That was an utterly nasty thing to do." Suddenly worried that he was opening up a door for Slave to leave him, he hastily added: "She can still stay with me, but just make up with her, please. Do it for me."

Soledad smiled sarcastically. "Should I give her back her 'SLAVE' scars too?"

He gave a violent start. "Hell no!"

"I knew you'd say that. Okay, I'll go see her."

She vanished to her trademark blue flash.

Malone made his weary way back up the stairs to pay for his purchases. From the interested/amused looks he got on arriving upstairs, he was certain they all thought he'd been masturbating in the toilet.

CHAPTER 26

Switch

The entity called Switch moved amidst a fog of impressions. Here in Mia Wong's body, it reasoned largely as she would, the echoes of her thoughts providing its latest mental framework.

For all intents and purposes, the soul currently inhibiting Mia Wong's body *was* her—indistinguishable to the nth degree.

Except one: Like Bubbles the cat and Scott Parker and Jenny Yang before it, the creature kept losing teeth. 'Mia' had so far lost four including both upper left incisors. Now another—a bottom right premolar—popped out by its roots, leaving a red pulpy crater. Switch spat the tooth out, then regarded it with distaste—human bodies were so puny.

Switch currently sat in a darkened upper room of the building right opposite the Beacon Hill Hotel and Bistro. It was here because it felt kinship with the nightmare creatures it saw frolicking inside the hotel. It didn't attempt to cross the street to them, however. It knew they would attack it, kill and eat its current mortal body, and that would defeat the purpose of its summoning.

And its purpose was clear—to kill Sookie Ling. And it *would* kill her. Switch didn't consider the possibility of failure. Such understandings were outside its nature. Sooner or later, moving ever closer like one climbing a series of ladders to successively higher floors, it would accomplish its objective.

At the moment (as Soledad Bathory had surmised), Switch was biding its time.

And so 'Mia Wong' sat in her darkened room, watching monsters.

After a while, she spat out another detached tooth—a bloody molar this time.

Then she spat out one more.

CHAPTER 27

Malone

Walking the corridor from the Freak Dungeon Bookshop to the elevator, Malone pondered where Switch could possibly be. Steelberg already had a citywide Robopol APB out with Mia Wong's picture. So far, however, the robot police force hadn't reported any sightings of the missing woman.

Switch was cunning, that was certain.

Malone knew time was running out to catch the creature. Any second now, it could jump from Mia Wong's body into someone else's. Then they'd be back to square one.

He reached the elevator and pressed the call button. The indicator showed the cage descending from the eleventh floor.

Waiting for it, feeling the bag of books he carried under his arm press Soledad's wooden knife against his belly, Malone really wished he could simply tell Steelberg the whole story. Everything would be way easier then. However, he acknowledged the impossibility of doing so. *I have to protect Soledad. Not least because I'm sleeping with her cousin.* He grimaced. *On the first hint of Soledad's involvement in this mess, Steelberg is sure to lock her up for disturbing the peace. Though she'll equally likely magic herself out of her cell . . .*

He regarded his haul of books. Some good had come out of his visit to the bookshop. More than just a little, even. Meeting Lisa Lash (on getting back upstairs he'd realized he was buying one of her books and asked her to autograph it for him, which she'd done gladly) was fortuitous. The card she'd given him in the toilet was safe in his breast pocket. Malone aimed on using it; not to sex Ms. Lash up (like she clearly intended) but for advisory help if things threatened to get out of hand with Slave.

The elevator arrived and opened. It was occupied by two people: a naked, stacked blonde in ridiculously high heels and a dark-haired man on his knees between her legs, his mouth pressed into her crotch. The woman's eyes were closed, she moaned deliciously at the cunnilingus, her hands making waves in her partner's hair.

Malone shrugged. *Elevator sex? I guess this is the right building for it.* He entered the cage opposite the couple, punched for the ground floor.

The elevator door shut. Malone now realized he'd seen this groaning beautiful woman before. Where? Yes, she'd been the one outside that Club 66Sex place, escorting a drunken Rick Rogers.

He regarded the kneeling man with fresh interest. Was this . . . ?

He quickly tapped the kneeling man on the shoulder. "Rick? Rick?"

Rick Rogers kept licking the blonde's vagina like he both couldn't hear Malone or feel his touch.

Malone shook him harder. "Hey, Rick, man, fucking pay attention!"

The blonde opened her eyes. They were a lovely cool blue; she lifted her hands to her breasts and squeezed them. "Don't disturb us," she gasped at Malone. "He's soooo good at this!"

"Can't you two wait till you find a bed? We're almost at the ground floor."

She groaned. "We're going a lot farther down than you think, man."

Malone gestured at Rick, who still gave no indication of hearing their conversation. Rick was lustily lapping the blonde's sex, his tongue flicking up, down, and sideways amidst its pink folds. His mouth, chin, and nose were wet with a mix of saliva and her sexual secretions.

"Why can't he hear me?" Malone asked.

"What do you want to tell him?" she parried. "Personally, I'm glad he can't hear you—you guys get sidetracked too easily. I really appreciate his deep commitment to my orgasm."

Malone was about retorting when he realized the naked woman was having a weird sexual effect on him. He'd begun feeling horny himself, suddenly had an erection. He felt like yanking Rick away from the blonde's sex and taking over servicing her. *Okay, now it makes sense: The height of her shoes—they're well over a foot high—gives perfect access to her vagina. It's a wonder she doesn't topple over though . . .*

Then he caught a glint of . . . something . . . in her smoky blue eyes—a flicker of carnivorous lust like that in the eyes of a lioness just before the kill.

Her predatory look chilled Malone. His erection deflated. He suddenly wanted out of the elevator, and fast at that.

The bell chimed for the ground floor. He shrugged. "Okay. Tell Rick that Sookie Ling's after him. She's sent Stan McCaulkin out after his legs. Tell him Malone said so."

The elevator opened into the lobby. The blonde laughed through her sexual enjoyment. Dropping fingers from her breasts back to glide through Rick's hair as he licked her, she replied, "Oh, that little matter? Don't worry, it's all taken care of. He's gotten the Queenpin's money for her."

"How would you know about that?"

She grimaced. "How else, Malone? I'm Rick's fucking banker. Now please get out of the damn elevator, will you? You're messing up my sex life."

He stepped out, glad there was no one presently in the lobby to view this weird scene unfold, then turned back to face the copulating pair.

Groaning and grinding her hips, the blonde bombshell pinched her stiff left nipple. Her other hand forced Rick's head harder against her crotch—his mouth was now invisible amidst her sexual folds. "Don't worry, I'll give Rickie darling your message!"

"Aren't you two getting out here? There's no basement."

She winked. "Says who?" She pressed the elevator controls, then waved. "Bye bye, Malone. Like I told you before: Rick and I are going farther down."

The elevator door shut.

Malone curiously watched the floor indicator. It now began registering floors in the opposite of normal: −1, −2, −3, −4 . . ."

He left when it showed −35.

"The elevator's out of commission," he told a bearded man who was walking towards it. "Take the stairs. Less chance of being spooked."

***

Out in the street, key in the lock of his BMW, Malone tried to get his head around what he'd just witnessed. *Why the hell would Rick keep on . . . ?"*

"Hey, Malone," a gruff voice said.

He looked up. It was Stan McCaulkin. Malone regarded Stan with unease. The fading day made the big old guy look eerily sadistic in his black leather getup.

Stan stroked his silvery beard and grinned at Malone, his eyes obscured by his shades. He pointed across the street at his shiny black AG Mercedes. "I was floating past, saw your car."

"How's it going, man?" Malone saw this wasn't a conversation he could avoid; Stan seemed to want to talk.

"Sookie says thanks about Lucy Tang, Malone."

"C'mon, Stan. It was an accident."

Stan laughed. "You think the boss lady gives a crap if it was?"

No, she doesn't, Malone conceded to himself, remembering her phone call earlier in the day.

"I spoke to Sookie about an hour ago," Stan continued. "The woman's pleased as pie, whooping it up a storm with some friends of hers—"

"What are you doing around here anyway?" Malone interrupted. He pointed up at the building's higher floors. "Or are you a member of the Freak Dungeon Club?" He was relieved he'd gotten the question in first, else he'd be the one having to answer it.

Stan made a face. "Man, screw that freaky shit. In my book, any guy who can't get it up except he's whipping a chick, or she's whipping him, ain't a real man." He shook palms at Malone. "Me? I'm straighter than an arrow—ain't got no sex issues."

Malone winced at the reply; the big man didn't notice. He removed his shades, peered up and down the street, then put them back on. "I'm looking for Rick Rogers. Sookie's got it in for the little worm. I've already been to his house, can't find the shithead there. Nor anywhere else."

Malone nodded. "More gambling debts?"

"Yeah, like he thinks money grows on trees." Stan scratched the side of his nose. "You seen him anywhere?"

Malone shook his head. "Nah, not for like six months."

A woman walked out of the Freak Dungeon building's front door and down the front steps. It was Lisa Lash. The brunette blew Malone a kiss, then sashayed over to her AG, a yellow corvette convertible.

Stan watched her shake her hips. "Now there's a hot number," he muttered to himself. "Lose those nerdy glasses of hers and I wouldn't mind . . ." He seemed to run out of libido. "Okay, Malone, I've gotta run after Rick's legs. Hope to see you around the casino sometime."

Malone laughed. "No gambling for me, Stan. I don't want to wind up with you after my legs too."

Stan laughed uproariously at that. He crossed the road back to his Mercedes.

Malone remained on the sidewalk awhile, watching Stan and Lisa's antigrav cars depart in opposite directions. Remembering the odd scene with Rick and the blonde in the elevator, he looked back up the building steps. Then he got into his BMW and headed home.

Time to go see Slave. Finding Soledad's monster could wait till tomorrow.

The sun set.

CHAPTER 28

Slave / Soledad

Soledad sat smearing salve across Slave's slashed skin.

"Damn, girl, Malone whipped you like a dog!"

"Yes," came the dreamy reply, "It was fantastic."

"You're a complete hot mess. You know that, don't you? Does he suspect we planned our bust-up?"

"Nah, not a thing. I didn't know I was that good an actress."

"I was better than you. Okay, turn around, look at me. We need to talk seriously."

"What's on your mind, Soly?"

"Malone is."

"What? You like him too? I'm not sharing."

"Slave, Malone is a good guy. A boy scout, maybe, but he's a good person. I don't want you hurting him, messing him about like you did—"

"That's past, honest. I was younger then, not sure what I wanted."

"And now?"

"I want Malone."

"But for how long, girl? That's what worries me. I really don't want you hurting this man. I like him."

"Are you in love with him yourself?"

"Would I help you get him if I was?"

"I thought you just wanted me out of the mansion 'cos I mess up your spells."

"That too, but . . . let's be serious. All I want is your assurance that you'll be straight with Malone. I think he's falling in love with you."

"He is?"

"Slave, he was at Freak Dungeon a while ago buying S and M books. If that's not commitment to your fat ass, what is? And . . . Lisa Lash gave him her card."

"Lisa? I'm her greatest fan!"

"This morning you were Mrs. President's greatest fan."

"My heroine worship changes with the hour of day."

"You still haven't answered me: Are you going to be good to Malone, or do I tell him we scammed him and leave him to find someone who honestly cares?"

"C'mon, Soly, don't do *that!*"

"So promise you'll keep your ass in line and treat him right then."

"I promise, I promise. I can't really help myself; I think I'm falling in love with him."

"That fast?

"I mean it, Soly. Okay, I know love at first sight is overrated and all that—"

"Love at first sight is just horny wet pussy."

"—But I really, really want Malone. Really, really, really, REALLY want him."

"Tell me something: has he been in your vagina yet?"

"No, we've only done anal. Why?"

"Yeah, you really do love him—you're saving the best for last."

"So?"

"Okay, I won't rat on you. Shit!"

"What's the matter?"

"It's Malone—he's outside the front door! Remember the story: I came over here and begged you; then you said . . . improvise the rest however you like. See ya."

With a spark of blue light, Soledad Bathory vanished just as Malone pushed the front door open.

"Darling," Slave beamed at him, leaping up naked from the sofa and rushing into his arms. "You won't believe what happened after you left. That horrible bitch Soly came over, and started begging me to forgive her."

He kissed her tenderly. "And did you, slave?"

She pouted, slipping smoothly into her role in their D/s play. "I said I'd think about it, Master. I'm not really sure I want to, though. She was just so nasty—"

"You must. She deserves another chance. But for her, we'd never have met."

"Mmm, that's true. Here, let me take your package. What is it anyway?"

"Just some manuals. I'll show you after dinner. How's your back?"

"Still hurts wonderfully, Master. Please come, help me rub the damn salve in . . . Ouch! Yes, painfully like that, Master . . . ouch!"

"On your knees, Slave. Suck my cock till I come, bleed out the stress of the day from me—you have no idea what kind of day it's been."

"Oh, yes, Master . . ."

CHAPTER 29

Stan

The night was cooler than usual. Sipping from a can of Bud while cruising in his Mercedes, Stan wondered where in the world Rick had gotten to. He'd already thrice checked out Rick's Joy Street residence without success.

The punk's not left Boston, for sure. He wouldn't dare. Or would he?

He swung the AG round a corner onto Charles Street. The car hugged down tight to the blacktop like it still had wheels. He straightened the car into the street.

Prompted by the nightmare that had woken him, Stan had come to look over the Beacon Hill Hotel and Bistro on the odd chance Rick might actually be hiding in it.

No way was he entering the building, though—last night's horrors were still with him, a dark specter riding shotgun on his soul.

He slowed as he reached the hotel. It was hard not to gape. The building's walls were now frames full of holes. Bricks lay out across the street. On the third floor, a four-poster bed hung half out of the front wall, its sheets waving like flags. Chunks of busted-up furniture lay everywhere—a chair was even stuck like fruit in a treetop. Stan gulped beer then grimaced. *Damn, the cops really did a number on this joint.*

In moonlit windows he made out vague moving shapes. A tentacle flailed, a huge eye glinted. *The monsters,* he realized and shivered, his willies returning.

He kept the Mercedes floating slow till he was past the hotel— *No, the son-of-a-bitch ain't in there, and if he is, the monsters can keep him!*—then sped up, relieved to be away from it. He definitely wasn't coming back this way for a long, long time.

More relaxed now, he flung his empty can down into the passenger foot well, picked another Bud off the seat and opened it. *Fuck Rick,* he thought, drinking deep, *it's high time I took Sookie's advice and got laid.*

***

Zipping past a dilapidated Starbucks, Stan was nearing the Revere Street corner when he saw the woman. Dressed in a denim top, shorts, and sneakers, she was walking toward him in the shadows, her face hidden. He slowed, admired her figure a while, then whistled. *Ooh yeah, man, this is just what I need tonight!* She was slim, but with high breasts, wide hips, and long legs.

Her face was finally revealed. Stan recognized her—one of Sookie's croupier girls, Mia something . . . yeah, Mia Wong.

He instantly shrugged off his disappointment that she wasn't a hooker. *So fucking what? She's a woman, ain't she? They're all hookers in disguise—all just in it for the money. I need to get laid here and now. This bitch is sucking my dick tonight for sure! If she don't like being my stress relief, she can complain to Sookie afterwards. Yeah, like the boss lady gives a shit . . .*

It wasn't the first time. Stan didn't really consider it rape: In his view, some women didn't know their own minds; you had to force them to realize they wanted to fuck you.

He was now alongside Mia Wong. He parked the Mercedes, leapt out and grabbed her roughly.

"Come over here, girl! I need some lovin'."

"Let me go!"

He laughed at the fear in her eyes; his penis leapt in his pants. "Let you go? Girl, get down on your knees and suck my dick!"

"Please, Mr. McCaulkin. I don't want to."

"Call me Stan; we're lovers now." He saw her opening her mouth to yell. "If you dare make any noise—" Stan gaped in horror at Mia's open mouth. About half her teeth were missing, just bleeding red pits everywhere. Looked like some sort of disease. *Oh, no way I'm sticking my dick in that mess!*

"Please, Mr. McCaulkin, let me go!!" (Oh yes, her mouth was a total disaster zone. What the hell?)

He scowled at her. "Shut the fuck up, Mia. I'm not letting you go. I'm fucking you here and now. You can either like it or hate it, but it's happening. And stop fucking crying." He shoved the weeping woman forward, bent her over the car hood. Held her in place with a palm while he polished off his beer. He crumpled the can in a meaty fist and flung it away, back over his shoulder, across the road. "Looks like we ain't doing no foreplay either, girl. That mouth of yours . . . shit, don't you ever brush your teeth?"

"No, no!" Mia yelped as he pulled her shorts and panties off. She looked back at him over her shoulders, tears streaming down her face. "Don't, I don't want to, Mr. McCaulkin! I'll report you to Madam Sookie!"

Stan clouted her hard on the ear. "I've told you to shut up. You're going to experience my penis here and now. It's the real reason I'm sometimes called 'Big' Stan."

He kicked her legs apart, spread her buttocks and inserted himself. "Oh yeah, Mia," he gasped as he slid in, "you've got the sweetest pussy a guy ever did fuck."

She screamed weakly as he forced himself fully into her vagina. Blood instantly squirted from a tear.

Stan, drunk and feeling completely in control of the situation, laughed and laughed. Yeah this was fantastic—just what he need to bolster his flagging sense of masculinity after all that Lucy Tang nonsense.

Then . . .

Suddenly Stan was aware of the most horrible pain between his legs, like someone was sawing his penis off. And he wasn't looking down at Mia Wong's buttocks anymore, but sideways at the windshield, and the hood, hot from the car engine, was burning his cheek.

What the hell? The pain between his legs felt like something huge was being forced in and out of him.

He looked back up over his shoulder, saw his own face—red-eyed from booze, spittle flecking his lips and running into his beard—staring back down at him. He was grabbing his own hips and pumping hard back and forth.

In horror he realized what had happened: he was now inside Mia Wong's body and being raped.

"Stop, stop!!" he screamed in panic as the penis continued to tear into 'his' vagina (there was no other way to think about it—he felt Mia's body completely as his own). The pain was indescribable, accompanied by an even more indescribable feeling of being destroyed—of being rendered utterly worthless—by someone else.

Oh, I'm sorry, I'm so, so sorry, he moaned in his mind to every woman he'd ever had sex with against her will. *I had no idea it felt like this!*

"Please let me go!" he screamed up at himself, as the penis ripped his vagina apart. "Please!!"

(Fighting against the hands holding him down over the car hood was useless. 'He' was twice as big as 'Mia.')

"Shut the fuck up, bitch!" his own voice replied him, its familiar sound doubling his horror. Next came a slap to the side of his head that stunned him. Then he felt the huge penis being withdrawn from his—Mia's—vagina and—

"No, please no!" he moaned feebly. "No!!"

—Being forced into his anus.

"NOOOO!!!" he screamed as the penis entered his new body afresh and he felt the virgin anal and rectal tissue rip and blood spill out of him. "Stop!"

Another blow to the side of his head made him see stars, then: "Oh yeah, bitch," his voice replied. "You've got the sweetest asshole a man ever fucked in his life."

Stan's rectum now felt like someone had stuffed a watermelon inside it—just a world of pain. He was bleeding profusely, he could feel the blood running down his legs, mingling with that from his vagina. His mouth too hurt like from botched dental work.

The massive cock began sliding in and out of his anus, it felt like the opening was being sandpapered . . . Stan screamed, and screamed and screamed . . .

He was clouted again and again.

Stunned, in indescribable agony of body and soul, Stan lay there draped over the AG's hood being raped by 'himself.' His life became the violent rhythm of the hips slamming against his buttocks, of the penis tunneling in and out; the recurring feeling of being ripped apart afresh, of his anus gaping ever wider open.

(He was almost oblivious to the fact that he was crying. The tears pumped from his eyes, running down his cheeks, his mascara had long since become a stream of black droplets on the car hood.)

He now regretted ever bumping into Mia Wong tonight. *Oh, God, if I ever get out of this, I'll never ever force another woman to . . .*

Finally, almost out of his mind from shock, Stan had respite. With a stiffening of his hips, his body ejaculated into Mia's ass. The massive penis pulled out of his rectum. The bloody semen spurted from the destroyed anus, ran down his legs, splattered the road.

Oh, thank God, that's over . . . He wanted to find the deepest darkest hole in Hell and die in it.

But his ordeal *wasn't* over. Next thing, he felt two thick hands—his own hands!—grabbing him tightly around the neck and squeezing. Choking him out.

Horrified, he looked back at himself. The sadistic smile on his face told him everything he didn't want to know. He was being murdered by himself.

"No!" he gasped, kicking weakly as the hands tightened their stranglehold, and his/Mia's face turned a violent purple. "You already raped me; why do you want to . . . ?"

He ran out of air, ran out of strength . . . could only lie on the hood dying.

Then, as the darkness overwhelmed him, he was glad he was dying—glad he'd never have to deal with the emotional consequences of being sexually violated. God, he'd never have imagined in a million years that being raped felt as horrible as this to a woman.

To Stan, it had always just been fun.

***

Once Stan/Mia Wong was dead, Switch pulled the body off the hood, got into Stan's antigrav Mercedes and drove off.

After a while he spit out a tooth, then another.

The bruised broken bloodied body lay there in the road; just another poor unfortunate woman who'd run into the wrong man at the wrong time.

Above Charles Street, the moon continued its slow cold journey through the night.

CHAPTER 30

Malone / Steelberg

As the morning sun rose higher over the housetops, Malone sat in bed reading Lisa Lash's book *Knowing Your Whips*.

Slave lay by him, asleep on her belly, her marked back exposed. Occasionally he reached across, and gently, wondrously, ran a finger over one of the welts on her skin. The sight of them still bemused him. *I did this to her? Bruised her up so?* But (and this baffled him even more) concurrent with his strange state of detachment from his actions, came arousal. His penis stirred fiercely. Once again, he felt the compulsion to hurt her for both their pleasures. And it was for *both* their pleasures. It was scary, seeing . . . feeling . . . how pain turned her on. He could have sworn she'd even orgasmed while he'd been rubbing salve into her welts.

She turned then, rolling backwards onto her side so she faced him. She seemed angelic, her face innocence framed in chocolate curls. He gasped again at her organic, natural beauty, as heady as wine to his senses. His heart leapt in his chest as it did each time he looked at her.

His gaze rode down her slumbering form, over the large natural breasts with their brown nipples, over the smooth barely-muscled belly, the tight waist, the flaring of the hips. It lingered for ages between her legs, staring at the source of her power . . .

He was becoming distracted, his erection insistent. If he didn't control himself, he'd shortly roll her onto her back, lift her legs to her shoulders and insert himself. Without waking her. She'd already explained to him that her being his slave meant he could use her as he liked. Hard and roughly as he chose, when he chose.

She didn't have to like it; indeed her pleasure was that she didn't like it.

"You own me now," she'd said. "I'm your property. Do with me as you will."

Malone disliked his excitement at the concept. It was heady, intoxicating, knowing that this beautiful woman lying beside him 'belonged' to him. Was his plaything, a toy to satisfy his whims. The ownership of another seemed sexist, particularly across genders, but she clearly wouldn't have it any other way.

Nor would I, he thought, his tortured emotions bordering on outright desperation.

Ignoring for the moment his desire to use Slave for his sexual relief, Malone resumed reading Lisa Lash's book. It was a good one. In a way it buttressed Slave's arguments of her achieving ultimate sexual and emotional power through powerlessness, but it also dispassionately analyzed the BDSM scene and lifestyle. Like in this paragraph:

'The true power of the S and M relationship lies in consent. It also lies in trust, in you knowing that the other person cares enough about you to degrade you for your pleasure. A D/s relationship isn't rape or abuse or torture, though to the uninitiated and unenlightened it often looks that way. A man or woman moaning in pain and enjoying it, cringing with each blow yet begging for more? Being peed or shat on and thanking the person doing so to them? Oh yes, we in the BDSM lifestyle do harvest fruit from the dark fields of the psyche, and equally yes, our erotic joys, our sensual pleasures and satisfactions are on par with those of the vanilla sex community, may in many cases even supersede those, if only because we have accepted who we are . . .'

Yes, Lisa Lash was someone Malone would like to talk to. The phrase 'harvest fruit from the dark fields of the psyche' practically sang to him.

His phone buzzed. He picked it up: Lt. Steelberg. He was instantly alert and tense. For the robot cop to call him at this early hour meant something big was up.

Carefully, so as not to wake Slave, Malone got out of bed and padded to the living room to accept the call. Then, alarmed, he rushed back into the bedroom and began throwing his clothes on. Thankfully, Slave slept on.

Once dressed, Malone strapped on his gun and slid the wooden knife Soledad had given him into a jacket pocket.

Then he rushed out of the house.

***

Lt. Steelberg pointed to Mia Wong's corpse. "That cat in my office is going to be very upset by this."

Malone didn't immediately reply. The dead woman was a harrowing sight. More obscene than her horrified face, her eyes bulging like they'd been about to pop from their sockets, her tongue a fat slug that filled her mouth, the dark finger marks of strangulation on her throat, was the terrible sexual abuse she'd suffered before dying. There was a thick pool of dried blood around her hips and legs, and peeking out between her buttocks, strips of shredded pink flesh, like someone had pulled her rectum out through her anus.

Malone felt sick. "I'd like to meet the bastard who did this to her," he finally growled through grit teeth. "I'll teach him to treat women better." This sight of dead Mia Wong (okay, she wasn't actually dead, but someone was . . .) was a complete blight on his soul.

"It wasn't a man; it was the monster," Steelberg said. The white robot, its suit and hat as rumpled as usual, knelt by the stiff, violated corpse. It ran a finger over her staring face, turned to Malone. "Half her teeth have fallen out." It picked one of Mia's teeth out of her hair, studied it for a moment, then pulped the tooth to dust between thumb and forefinger.

"You're destroying evidence," Malone pointed out.

"I've recorded everything of importance. It was her second upper right premolar, detached by . . ." The robot stopped speaking and stood up. "What I don't get, Malone, is why the creature killed the girl? It's a change from its normal MO."

"It killed her because she recognized it. Or would have recognized it, I mean. The person who left Mia's body knew her abuser."

192

"That is almost logical." Steelberg stuck hands in its pockets. "And it does provide a motive."

"The creature seems to favor this area," Malone noted. "It jumped into the cat not too far from here too."

"Likely coincidental—home turf of most involved parties. Good though if it helps us narrow the search."

"Nah, I don't think so. Now it's killed someone, it won't be hanging around to get caught."

Steelberg raised a hand. It looked around, its head making the whirring noise that indicated increased mental activity "Hold on a minute, Malone."

"What's up, Metal Guy?"

The robot was already in motion, crossing the street with fast purposeful strides. Malone watched Steelberg head for the house opposite them. Once there, it kicked in the front door and entered.

A short while later Steelberg reemerged. Now it wasn't alone; it was carrying a protesting, kicking man, lifting him off the ground by the collar of his shirt. Behind the approaching pair, a half-clad woman appeared in the demolished doorway. She stood watching, but made no attempt to follow.

The pair reached Malone. Lt. Steelberg kept the man held off the ground, shifting his grip so his burden wasn't choking. (Malone was once again surprised by how strong Robopol machines were. Steelberg's right sleeve had also slipped down to its elbow, revealing the arm's built-in machine gun tube.)

The man, short and stocky with harried eyes, protested, "Hey, robofuzz, let me the hell go now! I got my rights, and I haven't done nothing!"

"What's he done?" Malone asked Steelberg.

"I haven't done nothing!" The man goggled at Mia Wong's corpse like he'd piss himself from the horrible sight.

Steelberg said, "He saw the perp. I heard him telling the woman back there how he saw what happened to Miss Wong."

The fight leaked out of the dangling man. He gaped at the robot in shock. "You *heard* us?"

Steelberg nodded. "I've got the best ears USAcme's money can buy. Would you like me to replay your conversation?"

The man shook his head. "C-Can you please put me down?"

"No," Malone said coldly. "You stay up there till you tell us what we want to know. First, what's your name?"

"Tony. Tony Ramone." He pointed back across the road. "That's my wife Lisa."

"Okay, Tony," Steelberg said. It pointed down at the raped and murdered woman. "What did you see last night?"

Tony cringed. "I-I-I . . ."

"C'mon, Tony, don't be a jerk," Malone said unsympathetically. "This is a murder investigation. You're not a suspect yet, but you'll be an accessory if you don't talk."

"Yeah, Tony," Steelberg assented in metal tones. "You're still in the clear, best you remain there."

"Talk, Tony," Malone insisted. "It clearly wasn't you who did it. No way you're gonna pull this shit and hang around the neighborhood. I'm surprised you're even still here now after seeing what happened."

"What are you doing living on this deserted street anyway? Peddling dope?"

"My wife likes the house. She insisted."

"Okay, so you two keep playing happy family." Steelberg pointed a white finger at the corpse. "We're police—here to protect innocent citizens like you. Besides, nonsense like this drives down property values. You don't want potential neighbors thinking it's an unsafe neighborhood now, do you?"

Tony Ramone gulped. He talked.

"About two in the morning, I heard a car stop across the road, then two voices. Lisa was sleeping. I didn't wake her, I came downstairs to see . . . a black AG Mercedes . . . there was this man, he was real big. The moon meant I saw him clearly."

"What did he look like?" Malone asked.

"Huge, giant guy. Looked like a retired biker—long beard, ponytail, black leather and boots . . ."

Malone winced at the description. Tony Ramone was clearly describing Stan McCaulkin. The black Mercedes clinched it. *Fuck! Switch has struck the mother lode.* Slave's 'degrees of separation' explanation made Stan McCaulkin the perfect host for Switch to transfer itself into. Stan had guaranteed access to Sookie at any time of day and night. Also . . . Stan would be able to finger Switch in his body afterward—he and Mia both worked for

Sookie—which provided the perfect motive for the murder. Malone patted the wooden knife in his jacket. But . . . to die like this, mercilessly ripped apart . . . or (the thought leapt into his mind like a wallaby) . . . had Stan tried to rape Mia and gotten more than he'd bargained for?

Tony was saying. ". . . That's why I didn't say nothing: He was so big, so violent, I was afraid if I called attention to myself, he'd come over and rape Lisa too."

"You didn't have to let her die," Steelberg said sternly. "You could have called 911. Even this morning you didn't. And she's right opposite you. We only found the body because a motorist called in."

"I'm sorry," Tony blubbered. "I wasn't thinking right. I was too scared. All that was in my mind was protecting my Lisa."

"Put him down," Malone told Steelberg. He was sickened that Tony hadn't done a thing. But self-preservation was an instinct too, as in this case. He grimaced. *Damn!* Now there'd been a murder, he really had to protect Soledad. If Steelberg got even the slightest inkling of what this was really all about . . .

"One more question," Steelberg told Tony. "Did you get the perp's car's number?"

"No. I was too distracted."

"Too bad. It would helped immensely." Steelberg lowered Tony Ramone to the concrete. "Okay, we have a description of the criminal and your recorded statement. Go back home to your wife and continue being a good citizen. If it's necessary, we'll invite you to the station for further questioning." It paused a moment. "And try to be more contentious in future. It's a pity I can't book you for criminal negligence."

Tony stared glumly at Malone. Malone nodded. "Go, and for heaven's sake, next time use the damned phone, man."

Head slumped in shame, Tony Ramone trudged back across the street to his waiting wife.

Steelberg looked at Malone. "He was telling the truth; there were no fluctuations of his vital signs."

"The description he gave could be anyone."

Steelberg gestured at the corpse. "Good thing the murderer left his DNA in the victim them. I'll have forensics do a semen analysis. It'll take a couple of days, but we'll know who we're looking for." He looked across at the Ramones' residence, where, with occasional worried glances over at Steelberg and Malone, the couple were trying to straighten their damaged front door. "I can also have him come in for an Identikit session."

"Not yet," Malone said quickly.

The police robot assumed a musing pose in its crumpled clothes. "Why not? You sound worried."

"Because . . ." Malone searched for a suitable explanation. "Well, firstly, because it was late at night, there's no guarantee Tony won't describe the wrong person. And what if you put out an APB and the creature realizes you're onto it? Then we'll again be back to stage one. Also, from Tony's description, this creature's current body is the best it's had so far. Big and fast. It's unlikely to jump ship again—figuratively speaking—so long as it thinks it's anonymous. And with the body's original owner dead—remember it had no idea Tony saw it—it must think it's safe. So take your time with the DNA analysis. Once we know exactly who we're looking for . . .

Malone hoped he'd successfully diverted Steelberg from doing an Identikit and fingering Stan McCaulkin. (As it was, he knew the only reason Steelberg wasn't currently considering Stan as a suspect was because it didn't know the fugitive creature was after Sookie.)

He stared down again at Mia Wong's mauled, bloodied corpse, quickly looking away from the exploded shreds of anal and rectal flesh poking from her buttock cleft, a bloody mess that looked like strips of uncooked bacon in spilled ketchup. *Oh, yes,* he thought grimly, his mouth flooding with bitterness, *taking down this monster Switch is a job I want to handle myself.*

And now, he had to get over to the Golden Dragon Casino as fast as was humanly possible. And just hope he got there before 'Stan' did.

"Gotta leave," he told the robot. "I'll go check out a hunch over at the casino."

Steelberg attempted straightening out its hat. "Yeah, sure, Malone. Thanks for your help."

Malone rushed to his BMW and drove off.

CHAPTER 31

Sookie

The new morning streamed in through the parted drapes, pooled in shadow on the floor, then realized it was being ignored.

The bed was full of naked women. Their curves stretched out over the queen-sized expanse like dunes. Several of the women were grappling together, their bodies rolling and twisting as they touched each other and moaned.

A woman gave a sudden sharp yelp and went limp; her partner's head rose from between her legs. Licking her lips clean of its wet smearing, she slithered up along the other's body to kiss her deeply. They snuggled, slept. The sapphic ballet was repeated in tandem elsewhere on the bed.

It was Dallas Washington's and TLC's bed. Both women were somewhere in the midst of the luscious female tangle, but currently obscured from view by everyone else, as invisible as the trails of sweat and sweet fragrance that marked all those in the bed as women.

Sookie Ling extricated herself from an arm draped over her shoulder and a leg thrown over her buttocks and got out of the bed. She looked back to see who'd been holding her. It was Baroness Olga Wollscheid. Olga's wife Michelle was visible across the bed as a mop of blonde hair bobbing between a pair of olive-toned thighs. On Michelle's right, another married couple, Mrs. and Mrs. Robinson—two Californian platinum blondes—slept arm-in-arm.

There were two tables in the room, both crammed with empty wine bottles and crunched beer cans, salad and sandwich leftovers, cigarette and joint butts, TLC's mirror with its lines of coke . . .

197

Sookie's plump lips spread into a jaded grin, her lime-green eyes flashed with amusement, she stroked her nippleless breasts. In Dallas's suite the party just went on, and on. And on.

And, oh yeah, the sex had been great fun to watch too.

***

Sookie, Dallas, and TLC's frolicking of the previous day had paused late evening so Sookie could attend to casino business. A party of businessmen were flying in from Florida, and she had to meet them in person. (This was a big money deal; drugs she could have delegated to Stan.)

By then, TLC had roundly defeated Dallas Washington fifteen times at fisting poker. Dallas hadn't won a single hand of cards, and TLC, with a sequence of increasingly evil smiles, had insisted on collecting each 'pussy payment.' It hadn't mattered at all that Dallas kept moaning her way through orgasm after orgasm, finally, she'd broken down in tears and begged off the fifteenth fisting. TLC had been cokehead insistent. Dallas, however, had been too sore by then to go on. "I think she learn lesson now," Sookie told TLC. "She not Mrs. Horse." Dallas had paid for her escape from fisting number fifteen by buying her girlfriend a diamond-studded tiara and matching earrings.

Sookie had left for her business dealing. On returning six hours later, she'd met the bedroom full of women. All shapes and shades of them, with only one thing in common—they were all drop-dead-gorgeous.

Sookie had gaped at Dallas, who was still as unclothed as she'd left her. Across the room, an equally nude TLC was bent over some lines of coke, a straw up her left nostril.

"Who people?"

"The beautiful people. Some close friends of mine," Dallas had explained, then cocking her head, added with a wink, "And a few working girls."

Sookie gasped, "You turn room to brothel?"

"Do you mind?" Dallas asked throatily, before accepting a glass of wine from a busty brunette, then turning to kiss the woman and fondle her between the legs. "It's just a little private pussy pajama party." She dragged her brunette towards a chair. "Come on and eat me; my vagina's had a really hard day."

Sookie watched them go. "No, not really mind much." She pulled up a chair and settled down to watch.

After a while, the tentacles ringing her anus began wiggling in response to her excitement.

***

Now, Sookie finally made out Dallas Washington amidst the tangle. Dallas was on her belly, moaning while a woman with a black buzz cut licked her anus.

Ah, Dallas always fuck like entire team of football cowboys. Insatiable fuck up 24/7 if possible—maybe woman miss love as baby. Or think cunt source of longevity.

While scratching her cheek with a six-inch green fingernail, Sookie made an attempt to count the women in Dallas's bed. She gave up at sixteen; she kept mixing up those sleeping with those having sex. She couldn't help but admit it was a lovely sight, though—so much gorgeous female flesh all in one place at one time, lovely hair, beautiful faces, tanned and pale skin, toned bodies, breasts and buttocks of all kinds, vaginas of all designs . . .

The moanings from the bed went on and on. She watched a vagina spread wide open and fingers slipped in, then an entire hand. The brunette being fisted gasped loud. She arched her back; her eyes rolled up into her head till only their whites were visible like someone had replaced them with hardboiled eggs; her legs visibly trembled. Another woman bent and sucked on her erected nipples. The sucking woman's red hair dangled like a silk curtain, obscuring her face.

Sookie watched the fisting for a moment. The act always both amused and appalled her—such a large thing entering such a little hole. To Sookie, fisting wasn't just invasive, but abusive. And yet, she recognized the contradiction in herself: way back when she'd worked as a prostitute, she'd been fisted many times, usually by male clients (who had even bigger hands), and had often enjoyed it immensely. But still . . .

Pussy best for cock entrance and baby exit. What hand look for inside it?

As if to contradict her, the woman on the bed began coming. As the fister twisted and slid her hand inside her, it was impossible to deny the climaxing lady's delicious sensations. Sookie shrugged. *Ah, too much dragonreich destroy memory of sex anyhow. Ah, where put my lovely reich?*

She turned away as the woman who'd just been fisting was pushed flat on the bed by another woman who slowly slid a greased hand up her anus. Then two hands.

***

Sookie located her handbag amidst the pussy party's pile of discarded clothes. As she rummaged through its contents for her spare bottle of dragonreich, her cellphone beeped. Stan McCaulkin.

Forgetting the reich for the moment, she walked across to the window to accept the call. The tentacles between her buttocks swayed with her motion as if they were underwater. Once at the window, she wrapped herself in the drapes while her eyes watched the world outside.

"Hello, Stan, Boss Sookie here. What calling so early for? You collect Richie Boy's legs yet? . . . Not find asshole? Stan, how asshole so hard to find—just squat naked over mirror! Ha ha ha! . . . Of course, yes, I joking. . . . What that? . . . I see. . . . WHAT!? (Then she remembered there were other people in the room and controlled her agitation.) Lucy Tang? Tranny bitch dead, not so? . . . It complicated, you not talk on phone? . . . Yes, yes, yes . . . no, I not in Boss Lady suite, I with Dallas. . . . Yes, fourth floor. . . . Yes, I wait you here. . . . Okay, hurry."

Sookie hung up and stood looking perplexed. *Okay, not understand this. Stan say bitch Lucy dead, but still plan kill me? How possible? Zombie? Or contract killer? Maybe I need Soledad Bathory again? Very strange this.*

Behind her, the impassioned female moanings from the bed had intensified. Sookie turned and sort-of-watched it, the erotic images making little impact beyond her retinas.

Baroness Olga Wollscheid had now woken up, had donned a black strap-on, and was fucking her wife Michelle hard from behind.

"Take that, you! Your pussy is mine, all mine . . . !"

"Yes, honey, this tight little cunt's all yours."

"Hey, stop that plagiarism nonsense!" a sleepy voice piped up. "TLC is *my* nickname!"

"Go back to sleep, Tammy darling," Dallas chided gently. "You're dreaming."

"I am? Oh, that's alright then."

Sookie mentally faded the voices out, turned again to the window, returned her attention outside. *Hmmm, plan to kill me, eh? First, hear what Stan say, then—*

Her phone buzzed again. She felt great relief on looking at the display. *Ah, fantastic—it Bud Malone! Just macho man needed at moment.*

"Hello, Malone, Sookie on line. . . . What!?"

CHAPTER 32

Malone

Malone told Sookie Ling the one story he was certain would get her attention:

"Sookie, Stan's coming to kill you. He and Lucy Tang were lovers."

There was a shocked gasp on the line as he turned from Arlington Street onto Stuart, then Sookie whispered: "Not believe, Malone. Stan most loyal employee."

Malone had expected that. "*Was*, Sookie. He *was* your most loyal employee. Remember how beautiful Lucy was . . ."

"Looks mean nothing, casino full of cutie girls. Stan have pick anyone like. How find out traitor anyhow?"

"I'll explain later. Where is Stan now?"

"He just call me. He coming over now."

"Shit. Don't let him in."

"Malone, you not just raising false alarm?"

He racked his brain for something to make her suspicious. "Sookie, don't you find it funny that Stan was the only survivor of Lucy's killing your men? I mean, *only* Stan got away?"

There was a pause, during which Malone thought he heard female giggles and someone moaning "Yeah, fuck my ass, darling!" in the background, then Sookie's voice came over the speaker loud and clear:

"Malone, I kill that Stanley son-of-prick!"

"What, Sookie?"

"You right, you right. I not repair puzzle before. Stan survive Lucy Tang attack, not once, but twice. Why only him get away, eh? Stinky."

"There was a *previous* attack?"

"Explain later when you also explaining."

Malone made another turn. "Fine, you believe me now?"

"Very believe you. I just blind to not see early." He heard her smack her head. "Okay, Malone, what you want I do? You coming here?"

"I'm on my way over to the casino now. Are you up in your suite?"

"No. I downstairs, fourth floor. Dallas and TLC's room— friends I mention yesterday, remember? Ask reception—you find easy."

"Yeah, yeah. Okay, stay in there. But fill the place with guards." He paused. "From what I can tell, Stan's jacked up on some drug that gives him superhuman strength. And remember, he's already a big guy."

"He not bulletproof, Malone. I gonna shoot son-of-prick!"

"He *might* be bulletproof, Sookie—I don't know. Let's play this my way, okay? Keep you safe."

"Okay, but I not happy hiding. I want shoot bastard personally." A loud burst of moaning came through the phone, followed by Sookie yelling, "Hey, Michelle, lower volume of orgasm; Boss Lady do life-or-death conversation!" This was followed by even louder moaning. Sookie's voice resumed, "Ah, response to deep penetration hard to control. Oh, Malone, this so bad—Stan betrayal. Second-in-command fucking enemy. Ah . . ."

"Sookie, calm down. You're in *huge* danger. Stan might already be in the casino. You're in your friend's bedroom? Fill her living room with security guys—the best you've got. Hurry it up."

"Okay, I do once you hang up."

"Damn, that's right, I'm delaying you here." A thought occurred to him. "One last thing: It's very important you trap Stan in your room so I meet him there. Don't have anyone attempt to stop him from getting upstairs. Don't alert him in any way that you're onto him."

"I thinking of doing that."

"Don't, Sookie. Trust me, you won't like the results if he escapes."

"Okay, Malone. You big hero friend. I trust you. Only guards. Just hurry up come save me please."

She cut the call.

Oh, I'm coming alright, Boss Lady. Malone sat back in the BMW's seat and floored the gas pedal. He raced through the waking morning, driving like hell was after him till he saw the Golden Dragon Casino's gleaming gates up ahead.

CHAPTER 33

Rick / Anastasia

The elevator kept descending. Trapped in a haze that eliminated time and space, Rick worked hard at the cunnilingus. Oh yes, he worked hard—his legs depended on it. At some point, he'd imagined Anastasia was talking to someone—a man—but then the haze had smothered him in its coils again, and Anastasia Wormwood's vagina once again became his god.

He remembered well what Mr. Chews had said—he kept well away from 'Cousin Wormwood's' anus. To his relief, she didn't suggest he lick it.

After a while Anastasia slid to the floor and pulled Rick atop her in a sixty-nine position. He found he was naked and that her ridiculously tall shoes had vanished again.

He forgot his missing clothes, dissolved into her universe of passion. They sucked and slurped each other, moaned and groaned together. He pumped his hips up and down, smearing her red lipstick all along his penis as he enjoyed her mouth, plunging his cock ever deeper into the wet velvet grip of her throat.

And all the while, the elevator grew warmer. Then Rick noticed its walls were now shimmering, glowing like silver lamps.

It's an effect of the heat, he thought. *Hot-air haze. She's a demoness . . . I think. Her body naturally gives off heat.*

Rick's pleasure became much more than he could handle, his body tensed like it would break. He gasped and came.

On feeling Rick's orgasm starting, Anastasia clamped her lips tight around his penis. She sucked his glans so hard while he ejaculated that Rick felt he was dying from the exquisite agony of the sensations. The semen seemed to flood out of him. He momentarily forgot Anastasia's vagina and focused on emptying his testicles into her mouth.

When he was spent, Anastasia—thick lines of Rick's semen now trickling down both her cheeks—raised her head and moaned. "Keep licking me, baby. We're almost there. Oooohhh."

We're almost there? Rick wondered, swiping his tongue over her clitoris. *Hey! That sounds like we're travelling. I thought we were just headed downstairs, and it's taking forever 'cos there's no time here . . . Oh, it's a slip of tongue. She means: 'I'm almost here . . .'*

Drained by his orgasm, he lifted his head from between Anastasia's milky thighs and looked around.

He stared in disbelief.

***

Rick watched the elevator vanish, its walls giving way to an unimaginably vast vista, a massive cavern circled by immense black cliffs. He twisted his neck, peered up. The cavern rose into limitless blackness; its bright orange lighting all came from below.

It was fucking HOT.

The metal floor had also disappeared. Rick and Anastasia now lay on black obsidian stone.

He looked closer at the stone and felt chilled despite the oven-like heat. Frozen human faces stared back at him. Worse still was the expression on the faces. Their eyes gaped, their mouths shrieked out unutterable torments.

Rick gulped, utterly horrified. *What the hell?* His fresh erection instantly wilted.

"What's the matter, baby? You've gone all soft on me."

Rick didn't reply. He couldn't—words had fled his tongue. He just kept looking down and around, mouth gaping wider as his disbelief increased.

He and Anastasia were perched atop an immense black stone crag in the middle of a lake of fire. The lake's glow was the sole source of the cavern's lighting. The lake's yellow surface bubbled like boiling soup. The bubbles popped, releasing green gas.

But that wasn't the worst. There were *people* in the lake, *human beings* burning in the fiery red flames that raged over the yellow liquid—women and men being tortured by mobs of winged demons with blazing pitchforks and by other creatures hard to describe.

The tormented people screamed with the same horror as those frozen in the rock under Rick, while they were punctured, decapitated, mutilated, raped and exploded, only for their wounds to instantly heal up so they could be abused again. And again. And again.

The winged, pitchfork-bearing demons appeared more reptile than human, almost like pterodactyls. Still, Rick's mind could disregard them—compared to the other monsters in the flaming lake, they seemed mundane.

(Rick had watched any number of horror movies, but he'd never seen *anything* like the abominations tormenting those hapless multitudes below. Some of the tormentors/torturers/abusers seemed combinations of different animals, insects, birds, and even plants. Others looked like buildings made from parts of human bodies. Yet others resembled glass octopi, with rainbow liquid limbs and full-sized metal elephants for heads. And these were those that Rick's mind could wrap itself around. There were yet others—many others—so alien in appearance and concept of being, no words existed to explain their physical composition.)

"Welcome to Hell, baby," Anastasia said.

With a start, Rick remembered he'd not come here alone, that he was perched over Anastasia, his head positioned so he could lick her clitoris.

But something was wrong now: her pubic hair had suddenly vanished and her vagina . . .

Suddenly even more frightened than before, Rick turned himself to stare at Anastasia. Then, his body lying across hers, he froze again, nerveless, trying to contain his shock.

Beneath him, Anastasia Wormwood was changing. Her skin had turned a bright crimson, redder than freshly spilled blood. Her lush blonde hair had all vanished, leaving her completely bald. While Rick trembled, two curved black horns erupted out of her forehead.

She was growing too, was already much larger than Rick, a red giant beneath a pale pigmy, her breasts larger than pillows beside his head. A sudden growth spurt trapped him atop her body before he could leap off. He floundered a moment between her belly and breasts, then helplessly rolled sideways off her.

She grabbed him before he slid away off their stone perch down into the fiery lake. Pulled him back onto her belly.

"Hell?" Rick croaked weakly, terrified by the horrible change in her. "Did you say *Hell?*"

"Where else could this be?" came the amused reply.

Her naked red body—still voluptuous—kept growing and growing. Watching her change, Rick fought to remain sane. *She's getting bigger and bigger and . . . !*

Anastasia smiled and licked her lips. "Soledad Bathory warned you not to fuck me, didn't she?"

Rick gaped mutely at her.

"Oh yeah, and this really handsome guy called Malone? He said to tell you Sookie's sent Stan McCaulkin after you."

And now, suddenly, the veil of silence cloaking the damned below was lifted.

Their piteous screams assailed and chilled Rick. They were a wall of sound unlike anything ever conceived in human imagination—a barricade of hatred and horror; a wailing wall of regret and repentance, a fortification of agony, anger, and angst.

Overhead, the impossible blackness that roofed the cavern fell toward the burning human furnace that fried the damned. Between darkness and light, the dinosaur-like demons, several biting flesh from women and men impaled on their pitchforks, frolicked, soaring aloft with loud beats of scaly wings.

The tormentors shrieked with delight. The damned screamed in agony. Rick quailed before the sound of their terrors. He was himself terrified. The relentless audio assault threatened to drive him out of his mind.

 And Anastasia . . .

Anastasia Wormwood was now simply immense. Her red form glowed a shapely crimson in the light from the burning lake.

She still reclined on her back. Rick was standing on her belly, a belly wider than a sailboat's deck. Her arms and legs were like pillars, her fingers thicker than his legs.

Her breasts were simply HUGE.

Rick held firmly onto one of her immense nipples to keep from slipping off her body into the burning lake below. The nipple was much bigger than his head. Each of its pores was a mouth, with teeth that nipped at his fingers as he gripped it desperately.

Rick was quaking with fear now, all alcoholic haze left in his system drained away like piss. Anastasia's body extended down the rock they rested on, her black toenails dipping in the pool of fire.

"Please let me go," he whimpered.

She sat up a little and craned her neck to see him better. She smiled, then licked his head.

"You can leave after you satisfy me," she said. "That was our deal, wasn't it? Don't be selfish—I haven't come yet."

Despite his terror, Rick was flabbergasted. "How?" he gasped. "You're a hundred times larger than me."

"I have ways and means," Anastasia replied. "You *will* satisfy me, and afterwards, I'll pay you for doing so. Remember the money's on the roof upstairs."

She grabbed hold of Rick. He fought to hold on the nipple, but its teeth bit him deeply and began eating his palm.

He yowled in pain and let go.

He was raised aloft. Blood poured from his wounded palm onto Anastasia's massive fingers.

She lowered him to her crotch.

"What do you want with me!?" Rick screamed as he approached the V of her legs, those legs like shapely red towers. Like the lake below reflected in a mirror, fire burnt around her sexual lips.

"Sex, you idiot!" the demoness yelled back, her head seemingly miles above him. "What else does an aroused woman want from a man!?"

She slid Rick into the crevice between her legs and pushed him head-first into her enormous flaming vagina. She shifted her grip so she was holding his ankles, then pushed him DEEP inside her.

Sighing, Anastasia relaxed back on the rocky crag and began masturbating, using Rick as a dildo.

CHAPTER 34

Soledad

Soledad Bathory was crossing her bedroom to get a hairbrush when darkness wrapped itself around her.

The witch instantly felt like she'd been painted black. She was suddenly petrified in a *no-space* that resounded with malevolent evil, floating in a black void—a *nowhere*.

A window ripped open in the unreality surrounding her. Through it she watched Rick kneeling between the legs of the moaning Anastasia Wormwood. She watched him dip his mouth into the demoness' sex and lick her. She watched what came after.

Evil's black sheath unwrapped itself from around Soledad, leaving her drained of vitality. She staggered to her bed and collapsed face down on it, her buttocks jutting up like twin mountains of flesh.

Fingers weakly playing over her blonde pigtail like it was a string of worry beads, she moaned softly, her mind filled with horror at Rick's mistake.

Dammit, dammit, man! I warned you 'bout this shit!

CHAPTER 35

Rick / Anastasia

Inside Anastasia's sex, Rick was now *really* terrified.

The cunt was tight. It pressed in on him like anaconda coils, gripping him like a fist, not permitting him any motion other than of his head.

Rick looked forward.

The walls of Anastasia's vagina pulsed with a soft red glow. A dim glow around what appeared an endless black tunnel ahead.

A tunnel that approached and receded as Anastasia fucked herself with Rick.

Her inner tissue was rough, like sandpaper made from glass shards. Rick's skin rubbed off as she slid him in and out, till soon his entire body excepting his head was raw and bleeding.

Anastasia's vagina lubricated with Rick's blood.

The pain was unbelievable. Rick screamed as first his skin, then his flesh, peeled off his bones.

Anastasia, however, was getting off big time. The demoness' tremors of pleasure transmitted to Rick through the walls of her sex. Her grip around his calves and feet was so tight he no longer had any sensation in his lower legs.

Then Anastasia thrust Rick savagely into her cunt, fracturing both his ankles with the intensity of her infernal passion.

Rick's mind was now a fester of horror, fear, and confusion. Mixed in with these tortured emotions was self-reproach and intense dismay: *Soledad warned me not to fuck her, not to fuck her, not to fuck her . . . But that snake man, Mr. Chews, he said . . . and I didn't lick her anus! I didn't! Shit! The bastard lied to me! He lied to me!* The accusation shrilled in his mind, wedded companion to the agony ravaging his body.

In out, in out, in out, Rick slid. He kept screaming and screaming into the blackness ahead, "Oh, God! Help me! Help me!"

It was the logical cry: In Hell, what else *could* one pray for, but the Almighty's intervention?

God didn't help Rick.

Instead, the blood-smeared walls of Anastasia's cunt opened little red vaginas that disgorged insects into the tunnel.

Rick almost lost his mind for real when he saw what the insects were—metal crabs with little human-baby-faces and mouths full of metal teeth.

"No!" Rick yelled as the crabkids swarmed all over his head, fighting each other in their rush to reach him.

The crabkids began eating Rick's face. They snipped his skin off with their pincers and popped the shreds into their mouths, wolfing the bloody strips down, while their siblings pushed them out of the way, trampling over them to also feast on Rick's flesh.

And all the while, Anastasia was sliding him in and out of her vagina. Once, she pulled him almost all the way out, leaving just his head inside her—his skinless body roasting in the heat—then she rammed him in DEEP again.

Deep into the mass of metal child-faced crab-insects.

Many of the crabkids became wedged between Rick and the cunt walls by this penetration. Rather than die, however, they started eating Rick's sides.

Rick shut his eyes. The crabkids snipped off his eyelids, and bolted them down, then they pulled out his eyes and ate them. Then they ate his optic nerves too.

And yet Rick could still see, could still feel horror and the pain, was still terrified with a terror that stubbornly refused to peak and push him over the mental edge into the refuge of insanity.

The crabkids ate Rick's ears.

This is Hell! he accepted as they shattered his skull with their pincers and began eating up his brain. Others rushed into his mouth and feasted on his tongue,

I'm existentially screwed, Rick thought between silent screams that merely permitted the voracious decapod children access to his throat and stomach. *I'm screwed as bad as the damned down there in the lake of fire. There's no difference between us. My body's*

regenerating itself just like theirs' are. Else I'd have died ages ago.

Then in horror he realized the illogic of the thought: *Died? No one dies in Hell, do they? They're already dead.*

Then confusion struck him. *But I'm not dead—I'm not dead!*

And—unbelievably to Rick—Anastasia was still fucking herself with him. She rammed him in harder and faster now, her passion accelerating, ramping up to a rapidly approaching sexual crescendo.

Anastasia Wormwood came.

Rick felt her orgasmic tremors, earthquakes of agony as her vagina contracted tight around his mutilated form, breaking his bones, mangling him like a car in a crusher. The sex tunnel he was imprisoned in jerked and twitched, threatening to rip his broken body to shreds.

Then, suddenly, all the crabkids fled from him. Like they'd been called home by a warning whistle, they departed en-mass from his ravaged shell, streaming out of his fleshless mouth, out of his brainless skull.

Seeing without eyes, Rick watched them scuttle back into the vaginas in Anastasia's vagina walls from which they'd emerged.

He sensed their mindless panic as they fled.

What now? he wondered, the crabkids' fright multiplying his own fear.

Anastasia now had him held deep inside her. She stabbed herself with his destroyed body in short rapid jerks as her climax played itself out.

Rick knew something bad was coming, but what? His dread built up in layers till the anticipation would have killed him if that was possible here.

Then, he saw it. Up ahead.

A bright red/yellow glow trickling down Anastasia's sex tunnel. At the same time a gust of furnace heat seared his head.

The oncoming glow became a liquid river. Incandescent yellow and red, with brown, steaming shit-like chunks floating atop it.

It flowed relentlessly toward Rick. And the intense, terrible heat that preceded it . . .

In almost mindless terror, Rick realized what it was. *Oh, God!* he screamed wordlessly. *God, please NO! It's lava . . . magma! She's coming fucking magma! God, help me!!!*

The molten rock reached Rick and poured through him like he was a sieve. In a torrent of agonies a hundred times worse than everything he'd already experienced, it burnt away Rick's flesh, burnt away his mind, burnt away his life, his essence.

This time Rick died for real.

***

Anastasia grimaced in ecstasy as her lava come spurted from her pussy. She kept masturbating with Rick's skeleton as the burning fluid arched out into the lake of fire like semisolid pee.

It was a long, hard, and *painful* orgasm—utterly fantastic—her best in a long time.

Once her immense tremors subsided, Anastasia pulled Rick's skeleton out of her body.

She sighed languidly at it. "You really should have listened to Soledad, baby."

She flung Rick's stripped bones away. They instantly vanished.

Anastasia Wormwood then lay back and savored her afterglow while watching the damned being tortured.

CHAPTER 36

Soledad

In the morning that never ended, blue light flashed. Soledad Bathory appeared on the rooftop of Anastasia Wormwood's villa.

After a brief look around, the beautiful witch walked briskly over to the white bench where a charred skeleton clutched a brown briefcase tight against its ribcage. Sniffing, she could still smell the fire on its bones.

She groaned aloud on seeing the blackened skeleton's shattered and emptied head. "Fuck, Rick, she ate your brains too? Wow, Anastasia did a bad number on you."

She grimaced, shook her head. *So the pussy trap caught you too? How come guys never seem to learn? I warned you good, didn't I?"*

Imagining she read blame and censure in the skeleton's eye sockets, Soledad Bathory turned away from it and strode to the edge of the windswept rooftop, keeping upwind of the skeleton's oven-burnt smell.

She stood a long moment there, watching the white clouds walk by on their mile-high legs. It had been ages since she'd been down here. She sniffed in the wind, smelt distant flowers. Ah, yes, occasionally The Groad had a delightful ambience. She sighed as the wind whistled in her ears, as it whipped her dress about her like it thought the green garment an autumn leaf scared to leave its tree.

Soledad felt very responsible for Rick's gruesome end. *If only I'd not been so preoccupied with my own Sookie Ling mix-up, I'd have kept a spirit watch on him, warned him about any pitfalls. And . . . damn, what was I thinking setting that creature free anyway? And now, Slave thinks I'm some kind of supernatural hitwoman. But I couldn't have known, could I? It was a cut-and-*

dried, open-and-shut plan, a harmless way to take Lucy Tang out before she murdered more people who, okay, might deserve murdering anyway. I didn't even do it for the bloody money! I'm rich enough already! Shit! Everything seemed so straightforward, how was I supposed to know she'd crash into Malone? I couldn't know that, could I? Slave doesn't really believe me though, I'm certain of it. But she should, after all I practically unzipped Malone's pants for her. This a grade-A mess. Shit, I hope Malone stops Switch in time. If that thing kills Sookie, I'll never forgive myself . . .

Her thoughts really depressed her. She blinked back tears, most of them for Rick.

Finally, she scowled. *I'd better stop putting off the inevitable, face that damned corpse behind me. If nothing else, I'll see that Sookie gets her money. Rick would have wanted that.*

She crossed the roof back to the bench, then attempted to prize the brown briefcase from Rick's dead fingers. It was odd—it felt almost like the skeleton didn't want to let go of the money. Yes, Soledad felt clear resistance from the charred, pitted digits; each time she pulled the case away, the skeleton pulled it back again.

She was certain also now that she saw something proprietorial in the skeleton's toothy grin.

Soledad Bathory didn't scare easy, but a cold chill—like she'd been stabbed with an icicle—ran down her spine. *Damn, he looks like he's just daring me to take some of his money!*

She tried telling herself she was just imagining it, but she couldn't shake the chill off. Cold dread spread through her; she felt it like cold hands groping her breasts.

And the skeleton simply would not let go of the briefcase.

"Dammit, Rick," she finally growled in a mix of fear and frustration, "let go of the damn money—I want to help you pay Sookie off!"

The skeleton let go then. It released its grip abruptly, its arm bones falling limp to its sides. Staggering back with the briefcase, Soledad shivered. She had the explicit knowledge that the burnt frame of bones facing her would haunt her forever if she didn't keep her word and give Sookie the money.

Then Soledad caught a movement out of the corner of her eye. She spun around; a massive black snake was slithering into the hut at the roof's farther side. She watched it go, bemused. Something about the reptile didn't seem quite right.

The black snake disappeared into the hut. Soledad decided to let it be, it wasn't bothering her.

Leaving Rick Roger's skeleton watching the landscape of walking clouds, Soledad Bathory vanished along with the case of money.

CHAPTER 37

Chang Lee

"Okay, sir, he's on your floor now."

Chang Lee—the leader of the eight men Sookie had stationed in Dallas Washington's living room for protection—put away his cellphone and hefted his pump-action shotgun.

He nodded around at his men, "Okay, guys, be ready, Stan's coming." Guns poised, they stood watching the front door with hawk-like eyes.

Chang Lee was a small man with short black hair and an inscrutable face. Dressed in a cream suit. A very deadly man, as proficient with a gun as with a knife, and also well-versed in hand-to-hand combat. Occasionally his mouth twitched, revealing his irritation at the loud female frolicking coming from the bedroom. (Not wanting to scare her guests, Sookie hadn't told them there was an assassination attempt on her in progress. So behind closed doors, the party went on.) Chang found the sound of their lovemaking distracting. He didn't need to be startled by a woman's climactic moans when he needed to shoot straight.

He'd been very startled, however, when Sookie told him he was to possibly kill his superior.

"Stan McCaulkin in cahoots with Lucy Tang? Boss, that's unbelievable."

"Chang, I older than you—live long enough, everything believable." She'd scowled, green eyes flashing bright, then added, "Also, make little noise as possible, many guests sleeping."

Chang had nodded. Sookie departed back into the bedroom. Beyond her he'd glimpsed a woman wearing a strap-on inserting a large vibrator into another's anus, while a third woman gleefully applauded the second's moans. He thought the moaning woman was Sookie's friend TLC. Or maybe she was the one wearing the strap-on.

The door had closed on the scene, leaving Chang musing. Not on the sights of sex, but on Sookie's puzzling last instruction: *Not make noise with guns?* He laughed. *That'll prove just a little difficult, boss.*

Except maybe he could convince Stan to give up without a fight. Talk first, shoot after. Not a bad plan; Chang still wasn't convinced old Stan McCaulkin had turned traitor.

All in all, however, Chang Lee felt he had the situation well in hand. He and his men—three of them in the corner behind the door, two hidden behind the drawn window drapes, and one in each corner behind him (and all of them armed with heavy artillery)—were more than enough match for one man.

He felt a twinge of uncertainty then. This was Boston, a.k.a. Weirdville, and Sookie had said Stan was jacked up on some drug, possibly dragon—

With a loud crash, the apartment door blew inward off its hinges and Stan stood there.

The heavy wood door crashed onto a coffee table, shattering its glass top.

Chang Lee ignored the crashed door, keeping his eyes on the man framed in the doorway. He instantly saw that there was something VERY wrong with Stan McCaulkin.

He raised an arm, signaling that his men not shoot. Not yet anyway.

Chang was puzzled. Stan was completely unarmed. Instead of a weapon, he was carrying a fruit—a white pod the likes of which Chang was certain he'd seen somewhere before. But where?

He put that aside for a moment. Stan—a big old guy already— now looked even bigger, and a whole lot more muscular. In addition, his face was frozen in a grimace like a gargoyle's, his lips curled back and snarling, his eyes bulging and yellow like they'd been injected with piss.

Then there was the strange heat radiating from Stan's body into the room. This was no exaggeration—the air-conditioned living room felt steamy now.

Stan stepped into the room. Chang and all his men stepped towards him, their guns keeping him unwaveringly covered.

"Okay, old man, back up." Chang said coldly. "Boss Sookie's having fun with some friends. She doesn't want any visitors at the moment."

"I need to see her," Stan said, stroking his beard with his right hand. His other arm cradled the white fruit like it was a football. He took another step forward. "I need to update her on a few developments about Lucy Tang's death."

"Man, what the hell happened to all your teeth?" was Chang's confused reply. Around him, he could sense his men all as confused as he by the red and bleeding disaster zone that was Stan's mouth, raw gums with only about ten scattered teeth left, one of which had detached from Stan's upper jaw and fallen onto his tongue while he'd been talking. Stan rolled the tooth about in his mouth like a sweet. "What the . . . ?"

Chang stopped the question because at that moment Stan dropped the white pod he was carrying on the floor, where it cracked and began spurting yellow gas from its fissures.

Elusive memory hit Chang Lee like a fist. "It's a nightmare fruit!" he yelled at his men, "Watch out! Shoot! Shoot!!"

He himself was already firing at Stan, but the big old man was already in motion. He watched in disbelief, as, the room filling with the yellow gas, Stan ran unharmed through a hail of bullets and punched Jacky O, one of Chang's men, in the chest, his hand penetrating into the man's body and reappearing a moment later gripping the man's heart.

Stan flung the still-beating heart away. Blood gushing from the hole in his chest, Jacky O collapsed dead to the ground.

Next moment, the gas-leaking nightmare pod exploded in a burst of light that made Chang shut his eyes.

When he opened them again, he stood ankle-deep in water, in a bog that was at the same time the same living room—the chairs, TV, and three walls and the front door confirmed this, only there was now water and mud on the floor, and fungus growing on the walls.

Yellow mist now swirled everywhere; in parts of the room it seemed an almost solid wall of icteric smoke. The fog cleared for a moment to his left. He gawped in disbelief: through the living room's missing fourth wall he could see a forest, and . . .

A monster—a snake with a hundred legs—rose up from the mud and launched itself at Chang. Reacting on pure instinct, he staggered back, firing his shotgun as he did so. He blew the creature's head off. It slumped down dead, then dissolved into purple goop.

Cocking the shotgun to reload, Chang splashed back through water that swarmed with red snakes.

The yellow thinned. Everything now had the sepia tint of ancient photographs to it. Of dreams gone horribly awry.

Chang now realized that everything around him was complete pandemonium. Shooting and screaming. His men were all being slaughtered by surreal creatures.

His normal iron calm cracked beneath the impossibility of what he witnessed. On his left, a werewolf (His eyes bugged—*a werewolf?*) was dragging the bottom half of someone across the floor—guts and kidneys trailed after the severed waist. The werewolf vanished into the yellow haze, its place instantly taken up by a HUGE speckled owl from the beak of which dripped blood. The bird splashed towards Chang. He let off a shotgun blast at it. The owl limped sideways, vanishing into the yellow.

Chang cocked the firearm again. *Okay,* he pondered, *where the hell has that bastard Stan gotten to?* He looked about, saw no sign of Stan. Then, remembering why he was up here in the first place (if indeed he was still up on the High Tower's fourth floor)—gotta protect the boss lady—he backed carefully away toward where he figured the bedroom door ought to be.

He peered back once; yeah, the bedroom door *was* there—he could hear confused female voices talking loudly behind it. He recognized the loudest confused voice as Sookie Ling's. He was relieved that they didn't sound terrified: that meant Stan hadn't yet gotten inside. Maybe the traitorous son-of-a-bitch had lost his way in the damn haze.

"Mr. Lee!" A gasping face poked out of the swirling yellow. One of his men, Owen Smith. Owen's eyes were wide balls of horror. "Mr. Lee!"

"Calm down, man! Have you seen Stan anywhere?"

Owen shook his head, his knuckles white on his automatic rifle. "Nowhere, sir. These creatures, they're something—"

"That bastard Stan opened a portal to Hell. The monsters—"

A huge gray tentacle whipped out of the yellow mist and wrapped itself around Owen's head. The tentacle wrenched sideways; Owen's head disappeared off his shoulders. Then a metal spike from somewhere in the mist skewered the corpse through from back to front and kept it held upright.

Next, two eyeless heads on a single segmented neck floated out of the haze and began drinking up the blood spurting from Owen's neck.

"Taste good, baby?" the left head asked the right.

"Tastes real good, baby," the right head replied the left.

Chang pissed himself, and didn't even realize he had. And when he did realize why his pants were wet, he didn't care—he was busy gawping at the strangest sight of all: a little boy with an old man's head in his belly and spider legs projecting from both his sides was ripping Jamie Lo to pieces. The kid was pulling Jamie's intestines out like they were spaghetti in bolognese sauce and shoving them in his mouth.

The weird boy looked toward Chang. Grinning, he gave Chang a thumbs up, then returned his attention to his ghoulish meal. Chang thought he heard the kid say: "I always love Chinese, Granddad!"

Chang raised his gun to shoot the little monster, then became aware of movement behind him. Forgetting the weird boy, he spun around. There was no one there, just the bedroom door.

I'm fucking hearing things, Chang realized. *Or am I?*

Then he realized something else. *So far I've been extremely lucky to escape being slaughtered by everything out here. The bedroom seems safe; I've got to get in there.*

He tried the door. It was locked. (Behind him in the living room, loud noises filled the air: growls like metal scraping metal, roars like a wrecking ball smashing concrete; above those and worst of all, the gunshot sound of teeth cracking human bones. There were a few actual gunshots too, but those sounded impossibly distant, like they were happening someplace else.)

Shit! Chang banged on the door. "Boss Sookie, open up the damn door, we're being murdered out here!"

The responding loud gaggle of confused female noises from the other side of the door assured Chang Lee that Sookie and her friends thought he was one of the creatures doing the killing.

This was confirmed a moment later, when, while banging louder, he heard a series of muffled gunshots from the bedroom. Simultaneously, it felt like he was being knifed in the chest and belly.

He stared down at himself in appalled disbelief. Blood was spurting from several holes in his suit, staining the cream fabric red. *They shot me? Those bitches fucking shot me?* He looked at the door, it had four holes in it.

Then, like the sounds were coming through the bullet holes, Chang heard clear conversation from the bedroom:

"Did you get it, Sookie?" a loud nervous voice asked.

"Not sure, I shoot again."

"NO!" Chang groaned, to no avail. *Bang! Bang! Bang!* Three more shots smashed through the door and into him. Howling, he dropped his shotgun, grabbed his belly with both hands. Oh, the fucking agony!

And Sookie's voice through the door: "I think I kill it this time. It scream louder. Chang take care of rest."

Chang staggered back into the mist, already dying. He collapsed to one knee, then a meaty hand grabbed his arm and jerked him upright again.

Chang forced his eyes to focus, the pain in his body was razors ripping out his innards. It was Stan who'd yanked him up. Once again, he was aware of intense heat, like he was standing too close to an open oven.

"Stan? Stan? Why're you doing this, man? We're like brothers . . . and Sookie's always been good to all of us."

Stan laughed his old man laugh, grinned a smile of empty teeth. And at that moment Chang's numbing mind cleared for a second, and he realized that this person wasn't the Stan he knew. There was someone else—something else, a coldblooded ruthless presence—behind his eyes. (He also noticed that Stan's body was covered with gunshot wounds, none of which were bleeding. Most of the wounds seemed filled with a bubbling, black tarlike substance.)

"I told you, Chang," Stan said gruffly. "I've got business to discuss with the boss. Deadly business."

"Don't kill me, man," Chang pleaded.

Stan's piss-yellow eyes peered coldly into Chang's for a moment, then he laughed. "Okay, I won't kill ya. For old time's sake." He dragged Chang Lee through the yellow mist to a slime-soaked chair, and propped him up in it. "You're gonna bleed to death shortly anyway." He pointed across to where the kid with the old-man-face in his belly was still gorging himself on Jamie Lo's innards. "But watch out for the creatures."

Then he walked across to the bedroom door. Too breathless to scream any warnings, Chang watched Stan open the bedroom door with a single kick and walk inside. He noticed that there was a bog inside the bedroom too, and trees growing in there. And were those things crabs? Could crabs get that big?

He heard female screaming.

Next thing, he heard loud splashing behind him. Looking around with the last of his strength, Chang saw Sookie's PI friend Bud Malone gaping in shock at the yellow-obscured carnage everywhere. In one hand, Malone held a pistol, in the other an oddly flickering blue knife.

He waved weakly to Malone, then, once he'd gotten the man's attention, pointed towards the bedroom door.

"Help Sookie!" he croaked. "Stan's gone mad!"

Malone nodded. He ran past Chang into the egg-yolk haze.

Chang slumped back down weakly. *Won't be long now*, he thought. *This sure is one damn fool hell of a way to die—shot by the very woman I'm protecting, but at least I'm dying nice and easy, not like—*

Then he felt something wet and slippery wrap itself around his legs. Then a large blue human-like face—too many pink eyes—lifted up from the mud at his feet. The thing opened its mouth and roared at Chang . . . it had bright steel teeth and a steel tongue.

It licked Chang's chest, then reared back smiling.

"Now Woggle eat you," it said. "You bleeding sweet red blood call Woggle from undermud. Woggle know you going to be scrumptious meal."

Shit! Chang Lee thought in horror, too weak from internal damage and blood loss to even scream as the many-eyed monster climbed up his body and began ripping the flesh from his face and neck with its steel claws.

The yellow mist covered both predator and prey.

CHAPTER 38

Malone / Stan / Sookie

After dashing past the dying man in the chair, Malone paused in the bedroom door. In here, there was little yellow mist. There were trees, however, large leafy boughs with branches that hung down to the mud floor like mangrove prop roots.

His eyes flicked around the room, looking for Sookie.

(On entering the suite, Malone had immediately recognized its warped condition as the work of a nightmare pod and was alert to the additional dangers it presented. 'How the hell?' was a question for later. Now there was work to be done.)

The trees in the bedroom hid most of it from view. The ceiling was higher up than it should have been if there was another floor overhead.

Feet sucking in the mud, Malone walked between two trees to see better.

He didn't immediately notice either Stan or Sookie. The strange wooden knife in his left hand (which had begun flickering blue the moment he'd reached the fourth floor) was hot against his palm and fingers. He felt energy pulsing in it, energy that seemed to strengthen him.

Once through the first line of trees, he had a clearer perspective of affairs in the bedroom.

At the queen-sized room's farther end, about ten naked shrieking women huddled atop a massive bed. An equal number of other women lay motionless on the bed sheets, their rising and falling bosoms showing they'd fainted from the excitement.

The cause of the excitement? A creature—it looked like an octopus though its head was human—that was flinging tentacles at the bed, trying to clamber onto the mattress and reach the women.

So far they were keeping it at bay with stools and handbags. One blonde was beating at the creature's tentacles with a double-dildo.

Malone mused at the sight. Two of the screaming women (and one of the fainted ones) wore strap-on harnesses fitted with large phalluses.

The women noticed Malone. "Help us!" a busty brunette shrieked.

Malone strode quickly over, placed his gun against the monster's head, and pulled the trigger twice. The creature howled as black gore blew out of its head, then, tentacles dragging off the bed, it slumped back into the ooze. Malone winced; the monster's mouth was a ring of needlelike teeth. (He knew its apparent death was only temporary. It was a *nightmare*: except dispatched with weapons from its own home realm, sooner or later it would dissolve then resurrect—possibly even in another form.)

He looked at a blonde wearing a blue strap-on dildo. "Where's Soo—" On seeing sudden terror leap into the blonde's eyes, he spun around. Behind him the women all screamed.

He winced. A monster crab was charging at him, pincers clicking loudly. Feeling his bowels clench with fear, Malone shot it, discharging all the bullets in his gun into the crab. It jerked and thrashed as the slugs ripped it apart, yet kept coming. It only collapsed when it was almost nose-to-nose with Malone.

Shuddering, he turned back to the women, who were huddled together against the wall. Several more had fainted in the interim, their bodies slumped like sacks of meat.

"Where's Sookie?" he asked.

An athletic middle-aged redhead stepped out from the terrified huddle. Even disheveled as she was by fear (sex too—he couldn't help but notice the glistening smears on her thighs) she reeked of class—lots of it.

"I'm Dallas Washington," she said, somehow keeping the hysteria out of her voice. She pointed to a gap between the trees. "Sookie ran off that way. Stan's trying to kill her. He went after her."

"Something's knocked out all the bastard's teeth," another woman added. "He looks like dog shit a cat pissed in."

One of the previously fainted women woke up then. "Dallas baby, why are there trees and a crab and *a man* in our bedroom? Am I still dreaming?"

"Yes, TLC darling, you are," Dallas replied. "Go back to sleep, hon. I'll wake you when the nightmare's over."

TLC dropped off back to sleep.

Wondering what hallucinogens she was on, Malone turned to rush after Sookie and Stan.

"Hey, wait!" Dallas yelped. "What about us? You can't just leave us here like this. Sookie took the only gun we had."

Malone turned back to stare at her. She nodded back. The other women all nodded with her. He thought on it a moment, concluding he really didn't have time to waste explaining why he needed his gun more than they did. He slid out the pistol's empty clip, replaced it with a full one, cocked the gun and handed it grip-first to Dallas.

"Lady, do a Dirty Harry on whatever fucks with you," he said and ran off past the dead crab into the trees, splashing water and pushing a way through dangling wet leaves.

***

Beyond the trees Dallas had indicated was a large hole in the bedroom wall. No—Malone quickly corrected himself—not the 'bedroom' wall. This wall was black stone like volcanic rock.

He stepped into the hole. Into a tunnel. It was dark in there, but now the wooden knife in his hand began glowing like a blue lamp, banishing the darkness like it was an exiled king. Thanking the heavens for its light, he padded quickly forward.

The passageway led down. He paid little attention to its outline or shape, his mind urgent with questions: *Now, where is Sookie? More important, where is Stan? If he's gotten to her—*

A gunshot sounded. Ringing metallic echoes confirmed that it was ahead of him, not behind. Knife held out in front of him, he ran towards the noise.

He turned a corner, and there they were in a spacious cavern:

Sookie Ling—dressed in her standard cheongsam—was covered in blood. Her left arm looked broken, it hung limp by her side. She was perched up on a rocky ledge, with Stan on the

227

ground below, staring up at her and trying to grab her. Sookie (Malone marveled at her survival instinct—how the hell had she gotten up there with a useless arm?) had her gun aimed down at Stan.

Interestingly, this part of the tunnel was brighter, a red glow spilling from beyond Stan and Sookie mingled with the blue light from his knife. Another source of light was Sookie's own fluorescent green eyes. The mingled primary colors—red, green, blue—had summed into the off-white of a dying man's skin.

"Stan, I warn again!" Sookie was yelling while spitting blood. "Keep big prick away from me! Fuck me and I kill you!"

Despite the dire situation, Malone couldn't help laughing at that. Sookie would always be Sookie. ("Sookie, I told you he wants to kill you, not rape you." He imagined her response: "What difference, eh? If put such big prick inside me, fuck kill me!")

"Come down, Boss Lady," Stan said. "I won't hurt you, I promise."

"That what say before, asshole; then break arm. And how come you not die, eh? And why all teeth fall out, and eyes swollen and mouth smelling like Bangkok prostitute asshole? Even prick look like horse wearing pants."

Stan gripped the edge of the ledge with a hairy hand and began climbing up. Sookie knelt and fired, point blank into his face. Stan fell back, the explosive black splatter from the rear of his head hitting the ground before he did.

Stan lay there twitching, then slowly he got back to his feet. He reached for the ledge again.

"Shit, stay fucking dead!" Sookie screamed, a froth of blood spilling from her lips. "Why not dying? And where Malone? He suppose protect me."

"Over here, Sookie."

Startled, she spun toward him. The pain on her face altered into an agonized smile.

Malone walked toward them.

Sookie spat blood down in Stan's face. "Ah yes, asshole. Real macho man here, kick butt good, and then—Yeow!"

In her delight at seeing Malone, Sookie had grown careless and walked too close to the ledge's edge. Stan, who'd been turning to face Malone, had grabbed her leg and yanked her off it.

After flailing in midair, Sookie ended up in an untidy heap on the floor to Stan's right.

Stan walked towards her. Sookie pushed herself up on her unbroken arm, looked up at Stan, pointed a finger—"Fuckin' asshole,"—then fainted out cold. Once her eyes closed, the light in the cavern altered to neon purple.

Before Stan reached the unconscious woman, Malone slipped between both of them. He brandished the glowing blue knife at the big man, whose forehead showed a dotting of gunshot wounds. His shirt was similarly covered with punctures, out of which pumped black goop.

And Malone noted that Sookie had been right about another detail: Stan's crotch now bulged like he'd stuck a melon inside his pants. Yeah, that penis would have killed Sookie Ling dead alright. He winced on recalling what it had done to Mia Wong's anus.

Malone frowned at Stan. "This is between you and me, *Switch*."

Stan laughed, tugged on his beard. "So you know my real name. How 'bout you just keep calling me Stan for the rest of your short life?"

Malone looked at the possessed man's eyes—yellow bags of mucus taped over a sagging, empty mouth—and grimaced. "Yeah, let's do that—it's much less confusing. But it's for the rest of *your* short life, monster, your body-hopping career just ended."

Stan sneered. He shrugged his broad shoulders, flexed his immense biceps, cracked his knuckles one at a time. "Don't tell me what comes next, little man; let me guess: you're going to kill me with that flashlight you're holding? Have a fucking rethink."

Flashlight? Then Malone realized what he meant: *Oh, this creature doesn't know my knife can hurt it!* He pondered that a moment. *Yeah, but can it? Soledad's been really distracted of late. If she gave me the wrong . . .*

Then he thought, *What the fuck ever? You only live once!* and scowling, lunged at Stan, slashing the glowing knife hard across the man's chest.

Stan flung a punch at Malone. Malone, rolling with the punch, nonetheless felt a rib shatter under its impact. As the pain cut in, he understood exactly how Sookie had come by a broken arm. *And the way she was spitting blood? She may have broken ribs too.*

Then he forgot his pain. Stan's bulging eyes were gaping down in horror and pain at the wide rent Malone's knife had opened in his clothes and body.

Malone too, was perplexed. Teeth were spilling out of the hole in Stan's chest. Lots of them. The white enameled nuggets poured from the wound in a steady stream that showed no signs of abating.

Stan looked up from his wound, the expression on his face now one of fear. "Where'd you get that knife?"

"Do you fucking care?" Malone swiped at Stan again. This time the creature was ready, he ducked sideways towards Sookie.

Malone again maneuvered himself between the two of them. He figured that if Stan could kill Sookie, he wouldn't mind dying himself. Disposing of Sookie was after all the Switch creature's mission, its entire reason for entering Stan's body.

He grimaced. *But Sookie won't be dying here and now* (a quick glance at her confirmed she *was* still alive) *as long as I can help it, so . . .*

Stan charged desperately at Malone. Sidestepping the mad rush, Malone slashed the man's back open from shoulder to waist.

This time Stan screamed like he was in mortal agony. He stopped and gaped in disbelief, hands feeling for his back, where more teeth spilled endlessly from the torn flesh. Then, after glaring at Malone like he'd like to kill him, Stan turned and ran off into the red light beyond the ledge.

Malone watched him go. Spilling teeth like he was, the big man would be easy to hunt down and finish the job.

But first he needed to get Sookie some medical attention.

He turned to her just as the purple lighting in the cavern shifted up a grade to off-white again. Which meant three primary colors again—red, blue and . . .

Sookie stared up at Malone, her blazing green eyes both agonized and curious. "Where Stan?"

Malone pointed to the trail off teeth. "Off to see his dentist, I think."

She grinned. "You true hero, Malone. Real John Wayne macho."

He stuck the glowing knife in his belt, gathered her carefully up in his arms, then carried her back through the tunnel to her bedroom.

CHAPTER 39

Switch

Switch ran and ran and ran down the passageway. Now that it had escaped Malone, the bodyhopper's primary emotion wasn't fear of death, but fear of failure. It had almost failed back there. It mustn't fail. Failure wasn't permitted in its makeup. It would not return to limbo without completing its mission.

But, neither could it return to fight against Malone's knife, not with its current wounds.

No, Switch needed another body, a strong fresh one, then it could return and finish the job of killing Sookie Ling.

Its primary worry now was that it still bled teeth, which left a clear trail for Malone to follow. Switch hurried down the reddened tunnel, desperately seeking to elude the strange glowing knife. Its body burnt with agony, but that was the least of its problems—bodies could be changed. What was important was that it not die in Stan's body before it found a replacement host. And—even augmented by Switch's supernatural capabilities—the machine of Stan's flesh was close to giving out. That worried Switch too. If Stan's body died with Switch still in it, the game—this hunt—was over. It would have failed for good. And it must not fail. It must NOT!!!

Then, teeth still spilling from its wounds, Switch turned a corner and the tunnel flared into the mouth of a second, much wider, much brighter cavern than the one it had fled from. And simultaneously, the bodyhopper imagined it heard loud human voices up ahead.

It smiled.

CHAPTER 40

Malone

Once Malone had handed Sookie over to the women in her bedroom (and confirmed that they'd both called Robopol and an ambulance) he reentered the tunnel to hunt down Switch.

Again the wooden knife provided light for him to navigate by. It was still his only weapon: Dallas Washington had refused to give him back his gun. He couldn't exactly blame her: the slimy corpse of some creature—a pungent mixture of tentacles, eye-stalks, and mouths—lay across the foot of the bed. One of the women had sustained a nasty bite when the monster had tried to drag her down into the ooze.

He frowned. Best Dallas hold onto the gun then. Besides, firearms hadn't had much effect against Stan so far.

Malone jogged on. With each step, his broken rib felt like a knife stabbing into his lung. Thankfully, he wasn't spitting blood yet. The pain motivated him, it was an incentive to get this over with quickly.

Running through the cavern where he'd fought Switch, his thoughts went to Josephine 'Slave' Bailey. He smiled as her face swam into his mind, then felt depressed. *Damn, I hope I don't frigging die down here—whips or no, I have to see her again.* Here and now, on this dangerous quest, he suddenly realized that Slave was the single most important person in his life. *But I've only known her two days! And so what? Romantic lightning does strike, you know.*

He followed the trail of spilled teeth out of the cavern. The way the teeth were scattered across the continuing tunnel told Malone that Switch had also been running.

Running to escape me. So it's sure as hell scared. He took little confidence in the thought; it spawned another worry: *Switch has shown itself to be a wily creature. It must know it can't hide while it keeps pouring out teeth, so . . . so it will have to make a stand. And since it can't face my knife, it'll likely try to ambush me.*

The trail of teeth continued unerringly forward, past several dim turnoffs. Gritting his teeth against his pain, Malone followed it in a sphere of purple light, his knife's blue mixed with the tunnel's red glow.

Then, turning an abrupt corner, the light brightened to yellow and the tunnel widened. It began growing hot.

The trail of teeth continued into the heat and light. Malone ran on, till, like he'd slammed into an elephant, he was stopped by a seemingly solid wall of noise.

He stopped, his mind frazzled with white noise. Then, like a door opening to grant him admittance, the sound receded. It was only then that Malone realized what he was hearing were human screams. Like the universe's largest cat's chorus gone mad, like a million—no, a billion—torture chambers had been fused into one.

Switch's trail of teeth continued into the widening space.

Struck by the sudden intuition that at this point discretion was indeed the better part of valor, Malone stuck his knife in his jacket. Then, carefully pressing himself against the wall, he followed the trail of teeth onward.

And suddenly, like he'd walked through a final invisible veil, he was staring down on a scene from a nightmare.

No, this was worse than a mere nightmare, a whole lot worse . .
.

He now realized why it was so damned hot.

He'd arrived in a massive cavern, stood at the top of a low cliff. There was a literal lake of fire below him with a million people (?—they seemed many more than that, if such a number was possible for the naked eye to capture) boiling in its waves. The lake's sulfurous surface churned violently. Occasionally transparent bubbles floated free of the lake. These contained people, or still-living parts of them. The bubbles burst, their human contents fell free back into the raging flames.

The light in the cavern all came from the fiery lake.

Hell, Malone, realized in horror. *I've stumbled down into Hell.*

In the vale below him, towers of flame blew left and right over the lake like burning ghosts.

Even toned down, the screams of the tormented were beyond imagination. Squinting, Malone made out the expressions on several of the nearest faces: In his life he'd never imagined a person could look so terrified. Or seem in so much agony.

And the heat? That was so intense, he was sweating fiercely now.

Demons flew over the burning lake, horned and winged monsters that seemed a mingling of pterodactyl and man (or woman). These beings carried pitchforks with which they stabbed those roasting in the flames. Occasionally, they lifted one of the damned screaming from the lake—impaled through on black metal spikes—and bit chunks from the person's body. Then they dropped the tormented soul back into the blazing yellow expanse, onto the thousands of trembling, burning others.

And there were other creatures (*Demons too?* he wondered) in the lake that defied description. Things that looked like . . . Malone's brain stretched to its outer limits yet failed to come to terms with what his eyes were feeding it. They were simply outside human conception.

He forced his eyes from the dreadfully riveting sights. The sweat poured from him. Heat sweat and the cold sweat of fear. The fear—utter terror—now gripping him was worse than he'd ever experienced before. He felt close to madness, close to gibbering like an imbecile. His mind raged: *I've got to get the fuck out of here right now! Right fucking now!*

He somehow calmed down, plumbed the dregs of his courage, remembered why he was here. His eyes tracked Switch's unwavering trail of teeth down the short valley slope that descended by his cliff vantage point. Right down next to the lake of torment, from where each fresh wave of terrified noise pulsed like radio transmission. *Hell no, son-of-a-bitch! I'm not heading down there for any reason, whatsoever. If I by any mistake slip . . .*

Following the white trail, his eyes found Stan running along beside the lake of fire. And he noticed something else. Or rather, someone else. A giant red-skinned woman lay draped on a crag jutting forty feet out of the lake. She lay at repose, as relaxed as if she was sunbathing.

The red giantess lay facing Malone; he saw her clearly. Her huge body was incredibly shapely, long-legged and full-breasted, voluptuous to a fault.

He looked up to the top of the crag, at her face, a fittingly gorgeous complement to her flawless figure. Despite her bald head being so red it seemed scalped, and the black spiral ram-horns jutting from her forehead, her beauty was unearthly, breathtaking, with cheekbones that seemed sculpted from frozen blood, beautifully curved lips, and a perfect nose.

Her eyes were terrifying, however, deep ovals like wells of flame that blazed with cold ruthless evil.

He realized that the giantess was completely hairless all over. Her bald vagina was a flaming slit between her huge splayed legs. Her arms and legs ended in massive hands and feet with long black nails.

The red woman's fiery eyes were focused downward. Malone saw she was watching Stan, who had now paused his flight around the burning lake and was also staring up at her. Teeth still poured from Stan's body. He was staggering too, like he was on his last legs.

Sweat running off him in little rivers, Malone prayed Stan was close to death. He was still wishing he dared descend into the valley to finish Stan off, when, in a flash, the red demoness grabbed Stan off the floor in one of her massive hands.

Malone gaped at what happened next, when, spreading her incandescent vagina lips with her fingers, she inserted Stan headfirst into her sex and began sliding him in and out of it.

Malone looked up at the demoness' beautiful face. There was no mistaking that she was using Stan as a dildo. Her blazing eyes spoke volumes of intense lust. Around her as she pleasured herself with the man, the screams of those burning up and yet not dying in the lake of fire modulated in degrees, making strangely insane music.

Momentary panic thrilled through Malone: what if Switch could transfer itself into this demoness? That would be an utter disaster. Then he stopped worrying. He doubted a creature like this—one as powerful as this, a supervisor in Hell—could be invaded and taken over by another.

He figured the smart thing to do now was leave, but he wanted to see the end of this, just to be sure. It wouldn't do if after the huge woman was done having her fun, Stan came out whole again. (It seemed a logical worry: no one roasting below was dying.)

So Malone watched the demoness use Stan as a human sex toy, sliding him in and out of her body faster and faster, until, with an almighty shriek of delicious demonic delight, her body squirming and visibly trembling on her rocky perch, the red fingers of her free hand grabbing and squeezing her huge breasts, she climaxed, molten glowing lava squirting out from her volcanic vagina into the lake of fire.

When her tremors subsided, Malone watched her pull Stan— what remained of him—from her cunt.

He sighed with relief on seeing she'd pulled out a charred skeleton. He watched her blow a kiss at the blackened bones, then drop them into the lake of fire, where they floated a moment then sank from sight.

He sighed again. *Thank heavens, that's over. Switch is gone for good. Time I got the hell—*

Then in shock, he realized that the demoness had noticed him watching her, and that, smiling at this second intrusion into her realm of the human damned, she was already stretching out a hand to capture him too.

The massive red fingers flailed toward him.

Malone turned and hightailed it out of there. Behind him, the screams of the tormented were like wind filling out a ship's sails, forcing him farther and faster. At once too, the screams seemed the cheers of spectators rooting for him to win the race for his life.

So great was the adrenalin rush of his dread, he forgot he was injured. His legs pumped and pumped, his heart thumped violently like it would explode.

Malone only stopped running, when on turning a bend a quarter mile later, he almost slammed into a stone wall across the tunnel that hadn't previously been there.

Skidding to a startled halt, he stared panting at the blockage.

Damn, he thought when he realized what had happened, *where's the rest of the goddamn tunnel gone?*

The screams of suffering had now faded to just the merest background impression of sound.

Then something touched his shoulder and he almost leapt out of his skin.

CHAPTER 41

Malone / Anastasia

Malone swung round, dreading to see the red demoness' fingers grabbing for him.

He relaxed a little. It was the naked Junoesque blonde from the elevator in the Freak Dungeon Bookshop's building, the one Rick Rogers had been giving head to. She was way up in the air, however, the heels of her black shoes almost three feet high. Her vagina was practically level with his mouth.

She smiled coolly down at him. "A hellish hello to you, Malone."

He looked around her, saw no sign of a clawed pursuing hand, then paid her proper attention. (He recalled telling her his name while asking her to pass on his message to Rick.) "What are you doing here?"

"I work here. By the way, we're not yet introduced properly. Anastasia Wormwood at your service."

He remembered his manners. "Pleased to meet you, of course." He tapped the wall. "Where's Rick?"

She frowned. "He couldn't stand the heat; he got the hell out of the damned kitchen."

Malone mused over that cryptic reply a moment, then pointed at her shoes. "How'd the hell do you keep from falling over," he asked. "You look like you're on stilts."

"How do you think? Practice." She shrunk her heels so they were normal height again. "This better? You prefer your women shorter than you?"

"Yes. I mean, *no*. I honestly don't care how tall a lady is."

Anastasia asked, "What are you looking for down here, Malone?"

"The way out."

"It's vanished. Shut off."

"I see. How do I get out of here?"

"You can take the hellevator."

"Where is it?"

"Come with me," she replied, then turned and walked off back down the stone corridor.

Having no choice, Malone followed her. Almost unconsciously, she began elevating on her shoes again.

It was an odd trip for him, walking after a naked woman whose buttocks were literally in his face. And her rear view was even more impressive than her frontage. Also, the heat had simmered down with distance, so he had little distraction. Only the pain in his chest countered his possible lust.

Anastasia Wormwood led the way along a side corridor which after a while became rising steps. They climbed.

"Dammit!" Anastasia yelped on bumping her head on the stone staircase roof. She glared down at Malone, who pretended not to notice, then after spitting angrily against the wall, shrunk her shoes back to normal again.

Finally they turned off the corridor, emerging onto a rocky ledge that again overlooked the lake of fire, but from higher up.

Malone was grateful for the distance. Also, someone had thoughtfully constructed a solid metal bannister around the ledge, converting it into a balcony, so there was no chance of him falling down. There were even a few rock-hewn chairs.

At this height the heat was much less; even the screaming made odd music. The winged demons with their tridents crisscrossed the cavern like dragonflies. Then, with a return of his fear, Malone understood: this place was designed to permit others (who had to be demons also) watch and *enjoy* the torment below. Across from he and Anastasia was another sheer rock face. Other, similar viewing galleries were set into that wall too, at different levels descending right down to the burning lake. He suspected there were balconies beneath this one too.

He leaned over the bannister to confirm this, and was instantly struck by an oddity.

"Where's the red demon lady?" he asked Anastasia. "I don't see her down there."

"In bed, sleeping off her last orgasm. That's twice she's come today, I think."

Something about Anastasia's reply made Malone suddenly wary of her, but he shrugged it off. Besides, the pain from his broken rib was now catching up with him. All he wanted was to get out of here and stay out. Here wasn't the place to be, what with the panorama of eternal human suffering below them, flames that raged so fiercely it seemed they hated the dead.

A demon flew up from the lake. A horrid, snake-faced thing. It hovered in front of their balcony, its scaly reptile wings fanning heat at them. It smiled deferentially at Anastasia, then pointed its flaming trident at Malone. He shuddered at the inhumanity in the creature's eyes.

Anastasia shook her head and laughed. "No, Dimael. This one's still living . . . oh, I mean leaving."

With a frown that spoke intense regret, the demon descended again.

Malone's relief was unquantifiable.

Anastasia laid fingers on his arm. "Be good, Malone," she said. "You can see for yourself—you don't want to come here when you die."

"So, am I supposed to go to church or something?"

"That's for me to know and you to work out."

"C'mon, give a guy a pointer. I'm already middle-aged and work in a high-risk profession; how much longer d'you think I've got?"

She grinned. "I work here, Malone. View it this way: why should I tell you how *not* to arrive here? Then there'd be no one to torment, and I'll be unemployed. We need clients . . . business, duh? So, like I say, you work that bit out yourself. Everyone does. All I'm gonna tell you again, Malone, is: be good. Once your lights go out that last time, there's no replay."

And with her words came a sudden blast of heat over the balcony like someone had opened a furnace.

"Shit, now I feel like I'm being roasted."

"I forgot you're normal flesh and blood." She turned, pointed left into the corridor behind the balcony. "The elevator's over there, second door on the right. Tell the operator I sent you, and that you're going up to the ground floor."

"You're remaining here?"

"I feel like watching a little more. Life after death is very educative." She turned her back to him, gripped the balcony railings with both hands, head bent over it so her face glowed orange with reflected fire. Her voice dropped to a rumbling subhuman octave. "Have a good life, Malone. Now go; maybe we'll meet again."

Malone went.

***

The elevator was set in the corridor's black stone walls. The floor indicator read '−666.' Malone winced.

The elevator operator was a stocky black man with flashing red eyes. The name tag on the breast of his blue-satin-and-gold-braid uniform read 'Mr. Chews.'

"Now where would *you* be going, my good sir?" Mr. Chews asked Malone with a toothy grin. "You escaping from our hospitality?"

Malone's eyes set in cold slits. "Ground floor, man. Anastasia sent me."

The negro's grin broadened and he stepped away from the door. "Ah yes, sir. Please come right on in then. I'll see you practically to your front door."

CHAPTER 42

Malone / Slave

The ride up to Boston seemed to last forever. Finally, the elevator shook to a halt. Malone checked the indicator: Floor '0.'

"Here's your stop, sir," Mr. Chews said as the door slid open. The black man had said nothing during their upward trip, he'd simply stood in a corner tapping his feet and humming a bebop melody that gave Malone the creeps.

The door opened fully. Malone realized he was staring into his own kitchen. Shocked, he turned to look at Mr. Chews.

"Sure it ain't your front door, sir," the man said, "But I think it's close enough, right?"

Nodding, Malone stepped out. He turned back to the elevator cage, which had somehow replaced the door into his living room.

"Thanks."

Mr. Chews grinned broadly and bowed. "Well, goodbye, sir, have a nice day and hope to see you around sometime."

"I sincerely hope not," Malone retorted.

The dusky elevator operator took no offence. Instead, he burst out laughing. "Well you never know, sir, do you? One really never knows."

With that parting shot, he stabbed the controls with a finger. In a flash, the elevator vanished and Malone was left staring at a normal, partly open door.

The first thing he did now he was back home was grab a glass, rush to the sink, and drink a lot of water. He'd never felt so dehydrated in his life. Then, he slumped against the kitchen counter and ran his mind over everything he'd just been through.

He felt the thrill of accomplishment, however slight. *Switch is dead, Sookie's saved, and—*

He realized someone was speaking out in his living room, then remembered he no longer lived alone.

Slave! Faced with Hell's cornucopia of infernal wonders, Malone had completely forgotten her. Now, his heart leapt, his pulse quickened. He strode quickly to the door, then paused.

Through the crack he could see her. She was beautiful, a dream in motion. Dressed in shorts and tee shirt, her brown curls caught up in a rubber band, she strode back and forth across the parlor, cellphone pressed to her ear and an extremely worried look on her face.

Unnoticed, Malone listened to her side of the conversation, just as her voice rose in agitated pitch:

"Listen, Soly, I don't care if you're busy returning Rick Rogers's money to Sookie Ling—who the hell's Rick Rogers anyway? . . . Oh, Steelberg's there too? So frigging what if he is? I don't care if the entirety of Robopol is there in the room with you, along with half the doctors in Boston. I need you to find Malone. . . . What the heck do you mean you don't know where Malone's gotten to!? Ask Sookie what she's done with him—he was saving *her*, wasn't he? . . . No, I won't calm down . . . stop *telling* me to calm down! . . . Why not? . . . Because I love him! Don't you get it!? I LOVE MALONE! I LOVE HIM!!! . . . What? Just find him, Soly—this is your damn fault with your goddamned magic. . . . Oh, I shouldn't insult your spells? . . . Or, what? You'll turn me into a pig? Look, witch, find the man I love for me right now, okay, or else . . . What? . . . Okay, I'm listening . . ."

Malone was shocked. *She loves me? It's not all just S and M horniness? She actually loves me?*

"Hey, baby," he said.

She spun around and saw Malone grinning in the kitchen doorway. Her eyes first widened in disbelief, then a smile exploded on her face like a day dawning, like the sun rising over hills. "Hey, Soly," she whispered into the phone, "don't worry, everything's fine now. I'll call you back later."

With no further explanation, Slave flung the phone onto the green sofa and ran into Malone's outstretched arms.

"Soledad said you were missing," she moaned into his chest. "I could only think the worst—I thought you were dead."

"I love you too," was his honest reply. Her squeezing him like this hurt his ribs big time, but for her love he could easily endure the pain. For her love, he'd willing endure just about anything life had to offer.

Slave finally caught the meaning of his words. She looked up. "You love me? For real?"

"For real." He kissed her, and for that moment, the world was perfect, time and space ceased to exist. Her soft lips crushed against his, he held her to him like he'd never let her go.

Finally, however, they separated. Dragging him after her to the sofa, she realized he was grimacing.

"Broken rib," he replied her concerned stare. "I need a doctor. That Switch son-of-a-bitch threw a mean punch."

She nodded worriedly, then asked. "So it's over then? For good?"

"Yeah, it's over." He pulled the wooden knife from his pocket and dropped it on the coffee table. It no longer glowed; it was just an ordinary carving again.

Slave scowled suddenly, her lips framing a question. "Darling, how'd you get into the kitchen without me seeing you? I've been out here for the past twenty minutes."

Malone smiled, glad to be home again. Other than for the hurt in his chest, the past two or so hours might never have happened. "Baby, you'd never believe me if I told you."

AFTERLUDE

The final resolution of things was remarkably anticlimactic.

Malone had broken two ribs during his fight with Switch. Sookie Ling had a shattered rib and two fractured bones in her left arm.

Soledad repaired both Malone and Sookie's bodies with a single spell. One moment both were in agonizing pain, the next the pair were wondering what they'd been agonizing over.

"See?" she said afterward. "Occasionally, magic does have its uses."

Sookie snorted. "Stupid magic not even kill Lucy Tang successfully. Hero like Malone have more use."

Malone winced at that. Would Sookie ever forget about him accidentally wiping out her nemesis?

Dallas Washington, however, grinned broadly. "Yes, they do, Sookie." She winked coyly at Malone, handed him a card, then tapped the glossy red-and-gold rectangle with a fingernail. "My private number; call me *whenever* you feel like. You know, Malone, I think the pair of us need to see *a lot more* of each other. For one thing, you've such lovely hands."

TLC grimaced at that comment. She determined to fist Dallas especially hard as punishment that night. She'd widen her up so much Malone would think his penis was swimming in Lake Michigan if Dallas attempted having sex with him.

***

Fixing the body transfers was more work, but almost as easily resolved. Once all the concerned parties were gathered together in Malone's office, Soledad took care of things.

The main anticipated problem, Mia Wong's body dying, which left four displaced souls (including the Manx cat Bubbles, and Scott Parker who was stuck in a bottle), but only three bodies (including the cat's) to fit them in, never really become a problem. This was because, in the interim, Jenny Yang had gone insane inside Scott Parker's body. From being a logical sensitive woman, she'd turned into a raving babbling lunatic in a strait jacket.

So, in a straightforward sequence of soul transfers, Soledad switched Scott Parker back into his own body and put Jenny Yang into the soul bottle in his place. Similarly simple transfers put the cat Bubbles back into its own body, and Mia Wong into Jenny Yang's body.

(Soledad had told Lt. Steelberg that she'd captured Scott's soul out of 'the ether.' The robot didn't care how or where she'd found him. Its sensors were overloading with supernatural illogic—now Robopol had *another* suite full of nightmares at Sookie's High Tower to somehow pacify. Steelberg just wanted an end to all this madness.)

Everyone was pleased, or, in Mia Wong's case, relieved. "I'm glad I'm a woman again," she said. "But, this is soooo weird."

"You're really pretty," Scott Parker said. The handsome young man had come out of the soul bottle with absolutely no memory at all of being in it. Or seemingly of time passing since he'd been inside it. He flashed a disarming grin at Mia Wong. "How about you and me have dinner together sometime? Say like tonight? Or let's save some time and do lunch. I know this great place just around the corner."

(Malone was impressed: this kid was a smooth operator.)

Mia Wong first looked about to say no, then she nodded a shy 'yes' and quickly picked up her cat. Bubbles initially resisted and hissed (In Jenny's body, Mia didn't smell like she normally did), but she scratched it behind the ears like it liked her to and it settled down to be petted.

Scott and Mia (and Bubbles) left together.

"There goes a happy ending," Slave quipped as they shut the door behind them.

That left Malone, Soledad, Slave, and Lt. Steelberg in the office.

"I'm glad this has ended relatively well," Steelberg said. "This city already has way too many *normal* criminals to hunt down." It pointed to the soul bottle, inside which the tiny gas ghost that was Jenny Yang's soul raved. "I'm not pleased she came out of it so badly, though." Steelberg swiveled its plastic face to regard Soledad. "What will you do with her now?"

"Leave her in the bottle. In her current state she's best where she is."

The robot straightened its battered hat on its head. "And if someday she regains her sanity, what then?"

Malone said, "Hey, Metal Guy, you're thinking way too far ahead. Besides, haven't you got any hoodlums to catch?"

The white robot laughed metal static. "Be seeing you around, Malone. Thanks for helping Boston out again."

It left.

Soledad kissed Malone on the cheek, then, flickering blue, vanished along with the soul bottle.

That left Slave and Malone.

"I really wish I could teleport like she does," Malone said. "That definitely beats having to drive everywhere."

"I'm not sure I'd want to," Slave replied. "Knowing Soly, the spell might require the blood of virgins somewhere in it. Or a pact with the devil."

Malone grimaced. "Seriously?"

"My darling Master, you have no frigging idea of the sort of stuff she gets up to in her basement."

Hand in hand, and extremely happy in one another's company, Slave and Malone ascended the stairs to their apartment.

The End.

ABOUT THE AUTHOR

Wol-vriey is Nigerian, and quite tall.

He currently resides in a state of uneasy stalemate with his threatening-to-thin-beyond-redemption hair, and believes there actually are things that go bump in the night.

Wol-vriey recycles the ridiculous into reasonable reality for the reader.

His WEIRRRD philosophy?

WEIRRRD = Warp/Write Everything into Realistic Ridiculous Readable Distorted Dream Dimension Descriptions.

Wol-vriey blogs at:

http://oddityfarm.wordpress.com

OTHER GREAT TITLES FROM

Burning Bulb

PUBLISHING

WWW.BURNINGBULBPUBLISHING.COM

WOL-VRIEY
BIZARRO AND TRANSGRESSIVE FICTION

BOSTON POSH (BUD MALONE #1)

In 2028 AD, the USA is a nation ravaged by hungry dragons and dinosaurs. In Boston, Massachusetts, private eye Bud Malone is hired to rescue a kidnapped heiress. But nothing is as it seems.

Malone works to unravel a tangled web involving Boston Chinatown, a 200-year-old woman with a 9-year-old body, white robots, a human-liver-eating psychopath, a golem, a porcelain dragon, and a snake goddess with a crush on him. There's also a woman obsessed with chicken sex. Then Malone meets Posh Lane, a gorgeous call girl who's desperate to quit her pimp.

Romantic sparks ignite between Posh and Malone, but Posh's past suddenly catches up with her in a BIG way. To save Posh, Malone agrees to run a quest for Earth's new rulers, the Forks. But, Malone has no idea that agreeing to the Fork's odd request will send him on the weirdest trip he's ever been on in his life.

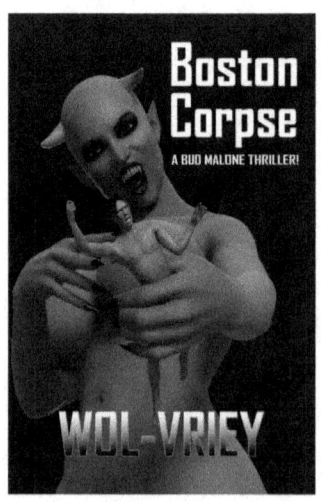

BOSTON CORPSE (BUD MALONE #2)

MAGIC CAN BE MURDER! - Drag queen Lucy Tang is back in Boston, and is hell-bent on settling her vindetta against casino owner Sookie Ling. And suddenly, Bud Malone, PI, has the case of his life to resolve.

When Boston's robot police force are baffled by a mind transfer case, they come to Malone for help. The one person who can likely help Malone out here is the witch Soledad Bathory. But Soledad seems to know a lot more than she's telling him. It's a case not made easier when Malone meets Soledad's beautiful cousin, Josephine 'Slave' Bailey. Slave has her own plans for Malone, most of which involve teaching him BDSM and making him her new Master.

Oh, and Rick Rogers owes Sookie Ling a whole lot of money, a gambling debt that's going to be literally Hell to pay!

BOSTON CORPSE - Not your average detective novel!

Burning Bulb
PUBLISHING

WOL-VRIEY
BIZARRO AND TRANSGRESSIVE FICTION

VAGINA MUNDI

Rachel Risk is a professional thief with super-strong hair that can stretch like tentacles to manipulate objects. Ashley Status has both a digitally augmented brain, and 'muscle-purses' in her arms and legs in which she stores inflatable objects—cars, guns, rocket launchers, etc.

When Raye is framed as the fall girl in a jewel robbery, the pair flee Chicago's vengeful robot gangsters and take refuge in the Hotel Bizarre, where the gorgeous 'vagina singer,' Femina, is performing for a week.

But the Hotel Bizarre is even stranger than its name suggests, and very soon Raye and Ash are involved in an deadly adventure, a struggle for survival the likes of which they'd never imagined possible—with loads of deviant sex, drugs, music, and violence at every turn. And just what is the old woman in the skin desert really doing with all those cats glued to her walls?

VAGINA MUNDI—a Bizarro Hymn in praise of WOMAN!

VEGAN VAMPIRE VAGINAS

The biggest bank heist in US history. And Tom Palmer can't remember pulling it off. And no, this isn't your standard case of amnesia. After a one-night-stand gone horribly wrong, Boston salesman Tom Palmer wakes up with a vagina implanted in his left hand. Then his day gets worse.

Tom is transported across space-time to a nightmare version of Boston, one where the Bizarro virus has transformed half the population into cannibals. Worst of all, Tom discovers that in this new Boston, he's the infamous gangster Pussypalm, wanted for robbing the Federal Reserve Bank of Boston a year ago. He also learns that the vagina in his hand is prophetic, i.e. it talks . . . after sex.

With 130 people left dead during his bank heist and six billion dollars missing, Tom knows he's living on borrowed time. It is in his best interests not to remember anything. Because once he does . . .

Burning Bulb
PUBLISHING

WOL-VRIEY
BIZARRO AND TRANSGRESSIVE FICTION

VEGAN ZOMBIE APOCALYPSE

In the post-apocalypse worlderness, zombies rule the earth. They're allergic to meat, and brains literally make them explode. Zombies now eat blood potatoes, parasitic tubers grown in the flesh of humancows corralled in maximum security farms. Two fugitives meet in the ancient ruins of Texas. The first is Soil 15-f, a womancow who's escaped her farm a week before she's due to be killed and her blood potato crop harvested. The second fugitive is Able Kane, former head necros food technician, now sentenced to death for heresy. But Soil is no ordinary humancow.

Unknown to herself, she's the vegan zombie agricultural revolution, and the zombies desperately want her back. And the necros equally desperately want Able Kane dead. He's fled with a forbidden discovery which will reshape the world for the worse if used. And Able is just hardheaded/misguided enough to use it.

MELANIE NEMESIS CATCHPOLE

In Springfield, Massachusetts, Melanie Catchpole is hired to fetch back a magic teddy bear worth millions of dollars from a warehouse across town. Problem is, the warehouse is down in Springfield's O-Zone-that totally weird sector of the city where Bizarro fell to Earth. The 'O' is a fairytale land, a place where dreams and nightmares literally live and breathe.

Worse still, the gingers—mutant cannibals—prowl the O. The gingers have already eaten everyone else Melanie's employers sent to get back the magic teddy bear.

Accompanied by the handsome but ruthless Doug Fisher (who she finds sexy but doesn't dare entrust her heart to), Melanie enters the O-Zone. Melanie and Doug are instantly caught up in an adventure they'd never have believed credible even if written as fiction . . . and Melanie's used to experiencing the very weird as the norm.

And now, additionally, there's a mystery to unravel: What does the dark, freezing-cold being called The Fixer want with Mary, the barkeep's daughter?

Burning Bulb
PUBLISHING

WOL-VRIEY
BIZARRO AND TRANSGRESSIVE FICTION

BIG TROUBLE IN LITTLE ASS

From Bizarro master storyteller Wol-vriey comes a truly weird western tale that will leave you awe-struck and on the edge of your seat...

In the town named Little Ass, tight-assed prostitute Rosa overhears a gunslinger's plans to assassinate rancher Edison Bennett. Once the badass Bennett learns of the plot, he ensures there'll be hell to pay for any attempt on his life!

Yes, it's going to take all of gunslinger Jude's shooting prowess, his eclectic collection of strange firearms, a trusty horse that requires an owners' manual, and the help of the lovely and invigorating Nell (who's EXTREMELY odd when the going gets weird), to survive the Bizarro hell that Edison Bennett unleashes in order to hold onto the land that he'd stolen from Madam Zizi.

BIZARRO 101 (A BASIC PRIMER)

Welcome to the strange place:

A collection of 37 flash fiction stories designed to introduce one to the Bizarro/New Weird Genre.

Weird, dreamy, nightmarish, absurd, sad, surreal, humorous . . . this collection of tales is all this and more.

***

"This primer is the very essence of any and all styles and types of Bizarro writing. Wol-vriey collects, distills, and bottles up these 37 tiny stories for your sensory enjoyment. This is an absolute must-read for anyone new to the genre, because it demonstrates the scope of what Bizarro is, and what it can be."
                              –Teresa Pollack, Bizarro commentator and blogger

Burning Bulb
PUBLISHING

ANTHOLOGIES
BIZARRO AND TRANSGRESSIVE FICTION

THE BIG BOOK OF BIZARRO

The Big Book of Bizarro brings together the peculiar prose of an international cast of the most grotesquely-gonzo, genre-grinding modern writers who ever put pen to paper (or mouse to pad), including:

NIGHT OF THE LIVING DEAD horror writers John Russo & George Kosana; HUSTLER MAGAZINE erotica contributors Eva Hore, Andrée Lachapelle, & J. Troy Seate and established Bizarro genre authors D. Harlan Wilson, William Pauley III, Wol-vriey, Laird Long, Richard Godwin and so many more!

From Alien abductions to Zombie sex, The Big Book of Bizarro contains OVER FIFTY STORIES of the most outrélandish transgressive fiction that you'll ever lay your capricious and curious hands upon!

WARNING: This book may be one of the most controversial and dangerous books you'll ever read.

WESTWARD HOES

Nine outlaw writers rode into town from obscurity to pen nine tantalizing tales of horror and fantasy, and leaving once they branded their own personal marks on the weird western genre and became living legends of the American Frontier experience.

Like drunken Indian scouts, the writers fervidly tracked down and captured the Western genre, tore off its fashionable veneer and ravished its exposed essence.

So belly up to the bar with your favorite soiled dove and enjoy perusing these thrilling tales of Old West debauchery, danger and desire; compiled by the publisher of The Big Book of Bizarro and featuring the bizarro novella *Big Trouble in Little Ass* by Wol-vriey.

Burning Bulb
PUBLISHING

ANTHOLOGIES
BIZARRO AND TRANSGRESSIVE FICTION

THE BIG BOOK OF BIZARRO SPECIAL KINDLE EDITIONS

OTHER AWESOME COLLECTIONS

Burning Bulb
PUBLISHING

GARY LEE VINCENT'S
DARKENED
THE WEST VIRGINIA VAMPIRE SERIES

DARKENED HILLS

When evil descends on a small West Virginia town, who will survive?

Jonathan did not start out his life to become a rambler, it just worked out that way. William was a troubled youth with something to hide. Both were from Melas, a small town tucked away in the West Virginia hills... a town where disappearances are happening more and more frequently.

After the suicide of a wanted serial killer, the townsfolk thought the nightmare was over. But when a centuries-old vampire is discovered they find out the hard way it's just getting started. Dark secrets can only stay hidden for so long and when the devil comes to collect, there will be hell to pay. Can Jonathan and William find a way to stop the vampire before it's too late? Find out in *Darkened Hills!*

DARKENED HOLLOWS

In the heart-stopping sequel to the award-winning *Darkened Hills*, Jonathan and William must return to West Virginia to face possible criminal charges stemming from their last visit to the damned town of Melas, where both had narrowly escaped the clutches of a vampire seethe.

And as livestock start mysteriously getting murdered with all of their blood drained, worried farmers are searching for answers - leaving the local Sheriff and his deputy racing against time to learn the cause before a more violent crime is committed.

Burning Bulb
PUBLISHING

www.DarkenedHills.com

GARY LEE VINCENT'S
DARKENED
THE WEST VIRGINIA VAMPIRE SERIES

DARKENED WATERS

When the world goes to hell, the chosen must arise!

As Talman Cane orchestrates a flood of epic proportions in this third installment of the *Darkened* series the towns of Melas and Tarklin are caught completely off guard by the deluge. Hell-bent on finishing what they started, the evil brothers return to the lunatic asylum to take care of the witnesses and add to the ever-growing army of the undead.

Aided by Lucifer himself and the insane vampire demon Legion, the stage is set to channel all of the forces of hell to come forth. In an all-out race to survive, Jonathan, William, and Amanda soon discover they are up against impossible odds as Lucifer opens the Gateway to Hell, ushering in the zombie apocalypse and the End Times.

DARKENED SOULS

Melas and the Madison House are about to be rebuilt.
True evil is about to be reborne!

Young ex-priest and vampire-killer William is drawn back to the West Virginian town that almost killed him, where his vampire arch-enemy Victor Rothenstein still stalks the earth.

The town of Melas lies destroyed after the battle of the End of Days. But why is wealthy Jackie Nixon so eager to rebuild it using the bone dust of murdered souls?

Terrible evil has visited before, but the Gateway to Hell is about to be reopened in a horrific climax. And this time – it's personal.

WWW.DARKENEDHILLS.COM

Burning Bulb
PUBLISHING

RISE OF THE DEAD

AN EARTH-SHATTERING ANTHOLOGY OF ZOMBIE TERROR

Featuring Stories By:

John A. Russo   Tyson Blue   E.L. Stice   Nelson W. Pyles

Andy Rausch   Stephen Spignesi   R.D. Riley   Zakary McGaha

David J. Fairhead   Gary Lee Vincent   David C. Hayes   Rachel Montgomery

Paul Victor Wargelin   David F. Walker   William Vitka

Rich Bottles Jr.   Douglas Brode

RISE OF THE DEAD - a collection of seventeen
tales of unspeakable zombie terror. Featuring a foreword and
short story by John A. Russo!

www.TheJohnRusso.com

Burning Bulb
PUBLISHING

"THE BLAZING SADDLES OF SEX SATIRES!" ~ GEORGINA SPELVIN

THE BOOBY HATCH

It's a Zany Love Lab where Looney Professors Measure Pleasure!

From Legendary Horror Writer
JOHN A. RUSSO

THE BOOBY HATCH

With NIGHT OF THE LIVING DEAD, John Russo helped blaze a path in the horror genre that has never been equalled. In this hillarious erotic novel, he blazes a path through the wild, zany Sex Revolution of the 1970s.

Sweet, innocent Cherry Jankowski works for Joyful Novelties, where she tests sex toys ranging from the ridiculous to the sublime. But she can't find love or peace of mind and her efforts are hampered by a Peeping Tom, an exhibitionist, a cross-dressing boyfriend, a quack psychiatrist, and even her own product-testing partner, Marcello Fettucini, who can't get it up anymore and is scared of losing his job!

www.TheJohnRusso.com

Burning Bulb
PUBLISHING

WEST VIRGINIA-THEMED HUMORROROTICA

BY RICH BOTTLES JR.

HELLHOLE WEST VIRGINIA

From the heights of Mothman's perch high atop the Silver Bridge in Point Pleasant to the depths of Hellhole Cavern in Pendleton County, evil lurks within the shadows as the sun sets upon the haunted hills and hollows of West Virginia.

Bizarro author Rich Bottles Jr. blows the coffin lid off horror genre clichés with this tour de force cast of Eco-friendly vampires, beach-yearning zombies and sex-starved she-devils.

LUMBERJACKED

If you are easily offended or do not possess a truly depraved sense of humor, this story may not be the light summer reading fare you desire. As for the four feisty female freshmen stranded on top of West Virginia's third highest mountain, they have no choice but to experience the sick, twisted debauchery and perverted mayhem described deep inside the tight unbroken bindings of this horrific missive.

Lumberjacked takes the reader to a nightmarish world where character development and aesthetic integrity are prematurely cut short by the swinging axes of maniacal lumberjacks, who are hell bent on death and destruction in the remote forests of Appalachia. And at the climax, when paranoia crosses over to the paranormal, Lumberjacked makes Deliverance look like a family raft trip down the Lower Gauley.

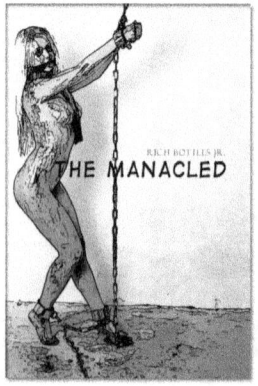

THE MANACLED

What happens when twin brothers lease out the former West Virginia State Penitentiary with the false purpose of filming a documentary on supernatural phenomena, but their true intention is to make a porno-graphic movie?

Chaos ensues as the disturbed spirits of murdered convicts, along with the reanimated dead from the neighboring Indian Burial Mound, take their vengeance on the unwary and undressed trespassers.

Zombies, ghosts, mobsters and porn collide in this bizarro tale from horror author Rich Bottles Jr.

Burning Bulb
PUBLISHING

THE MOST FRIGHTENING MOVIE
EVER MADE IS NOW A NOVEL!

night OF THE LIVING DEAD

JOHN A. RUSSO

NIGHT OF THE LIVING DEAD

Why does **Night of the Living Dead** hit with such chilling impact?
Is it because everyday people in a commonplace house are suddenly the
victims of a monstrous invasion? Or is it because the ghouls who surround
the house with grasping claws were once ordinary people, too?

Decide for yourself as you read, and the horror grips you. All the
cannibalism, suspense and frenzy of the smash-hit move are here in the
novel.

www.TheJohnRusso.com

Burning Bulb
PUBLISHING

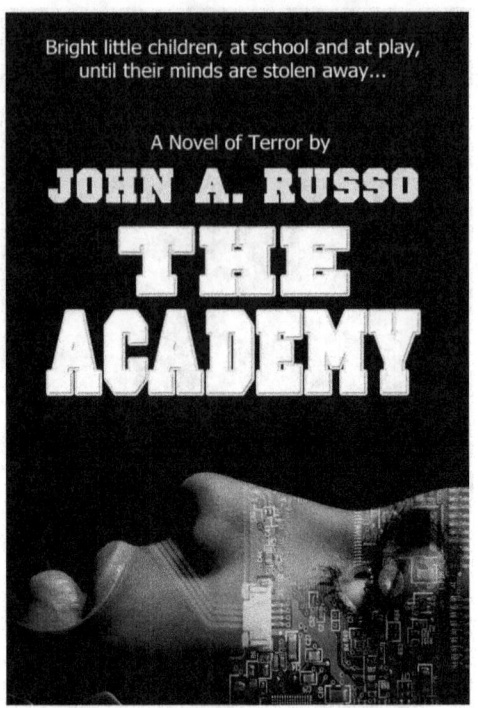

Bright little children, at school and at play, until their minds are stolen away...

A Novel of Terror by

JOHN A. RUSSO

THE ACADEMY

THE ACADEMY

The Academy. It's every parent's dream, turning their little darlings into geniuses, superachievers, perfect little children.

And if there's a problem, the Academy fixes that too. It's a simple operation. Just a little device. Then a teeny pink scar on a tender little skull . . .

One boy knows the secret. Now he wants his mind back. But it's much, much too late. Too late for anything but the ugly feelings. The bad feelings. The messy sexy feelings. The knife-cold hatred, the murderous rage, for total, screaming, blood-drenching revenge . . .

www.TheJohnRusso.com

Burning Bulb
PUBLISHING

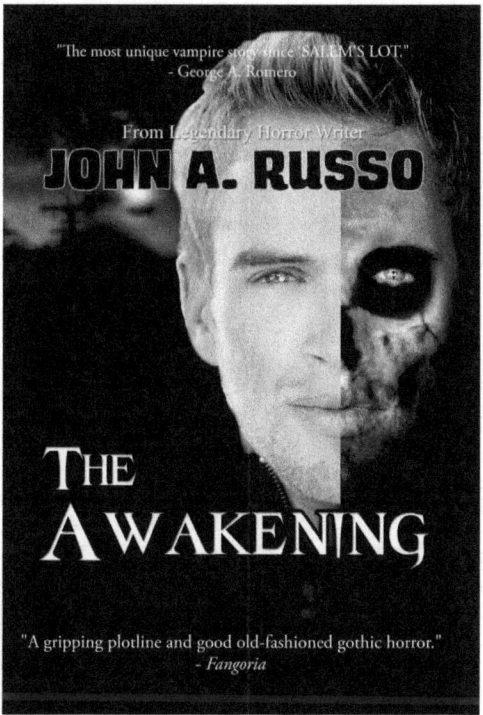

THE AWAKENING

For two hundred years, he has rested. Now he rises. Now he will be satisfied. Nothing can stop him. No one can resist him.

Benjamin Latham is young and handsome, his eighteenth-century mind wakened to a bizarre twentieth-century world. And there is the need deep within . . . an animal need, frightening, murderous, unholy . . . a vital need that must be fed.

And with his need comes a power over men and women to do his bidding, to quiet his dark craving . . .

Until the murders begin. And the inquiries. All suggesting the same hideous truth.

Now Benjamin must find a sanctuary: a lover, a partner, a friend. Someone who can share his darkness. Someone he can lead to . . . The Awakening.

www.TheJohnRusso.com

Burning Bulb
PUBLISHING

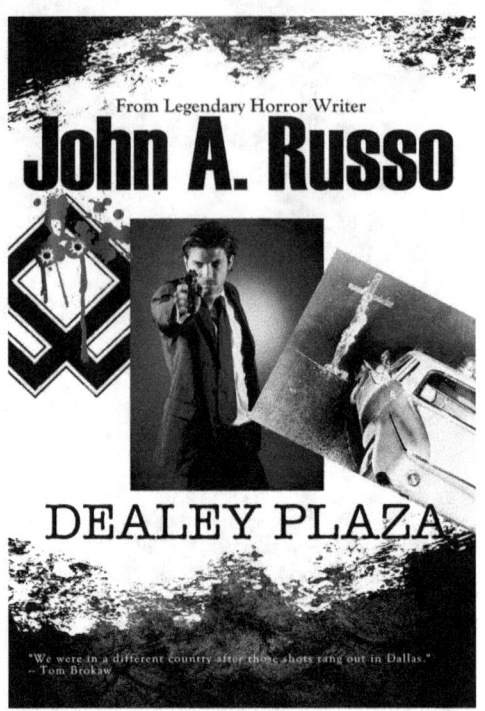

DEALEY PLAZA

From legendary horror and suspense writer JOHN RUSSO comes a harrowing tale where no one is safe!

Dealey Plaza is one of the most notorious places in America, and when youthful conspiracy buffs go there in 1964 to stage their own reenactment of the Kennedy Assassination, four of them are brutally murdered ~ the first victims of a hate-filled legacy that continues for four more decades.

The survivors of that long-ago Dallas trip, each of them now icons of the American way of life, are about to be honored ~ or killed.

Who will live and who will die? Will it be country-western star Lori McCoy? Her loving husband? Her scheming ex-husband? Or the case-hardened FBI agent and longtime friend who risks his life trying to protect them?

www.DealeyPlazaBook.com

Burning Bulb
PUBLISHING

From Legendary Horror Writer
JOHN A. RUSSO
LIMB to LIMB

LIMB TO LIMB

SUCH A PRETTY GIRL . . .
Tiffany Blake was a beautiful long-limbed dancer with a glorious future and the backing of a rich benefactor. Then a monstrous accident severed her leg at the hip.

SUCH A COLD, CRUEL KNIFE . . .
And now her fellow dancers are disappearing without a trace. One by one they fall victim to a dark and deadly pattern of evil – caught by the bloody, brutal logic that would have them pay with their lovely bodies for the cruel fate of another . . .victims of the sadistic madman whose flashing knife will make them writhe a gruesome new dance.

www.TheJohnRusso.com

Burning Bulb
PUBLISHING

"A sense of infectious fun, straight from the author's pen."
— Nightmare Library

From Legendary Horror Writer
JOHN A. RUSSO

LIVING THINGS

"Russo carries his talent for the horrific neatly over into the novel form."
— West Coast Review of Books

LIVING THINGS

Beneath the shimmering Miami sun sprawls one of the Mafia's biggest empires, a glittering world of lavish beachfront mansions, neon-painted nightclubs, beautiful women, expensive cars—and absolute control over the state's billion-dollar drug trade. But, one by one, its ganglords and henchmen are falling prey to a new rival. His powers are fueled by monstrous ancient rituals; his hellish undead legions slaughter mobsters and innocent citizens alike, his unholy lust for power is virtually unstoppable.

Now a burned-out ex-detective and a brilliant anthropologist must enter a gruesome, nightmare world to fight this master of malevolence and illusion. Their time is short, their weapons few, and they face an ultimate, terrifying choice - annihilation or the loss of their souls to the eternal torment of those who never die. . .

www.TheJohnRusso.com

Burning Bulb
PUBLISHING

MAD WORLD BY ANDY RAUSCH

"*Mad World* is dark, twisted, no-holds-barred fun."
—Jason Starr, author of *Bust*, *Slide*, and *The Max*

EVERYONE'S PLAYING AN ANGLE IN THE CITY OF ANGELS

Mad World tells the stories of a black hitman who doubles as a university professor, a Catholic priest who longs to be a gangster, a would-be author from Kansas, a gay phone sex operator who claims he's straight, a group of rich twentysomethings playing a deadly game of life and death, a vicious Mafia boss, and a sleazy Hollywood movie director. As each of their stories intersect, the body count piles up and the action comes nonstop in this tense, white-knuckle thriller by first-time author Andy Rausch.

"A wild ride. If you like it gangster, *Mad World* delivers."
—Daniel Birch, author of *Get Some*

Burning Bulb
PUBLISHING

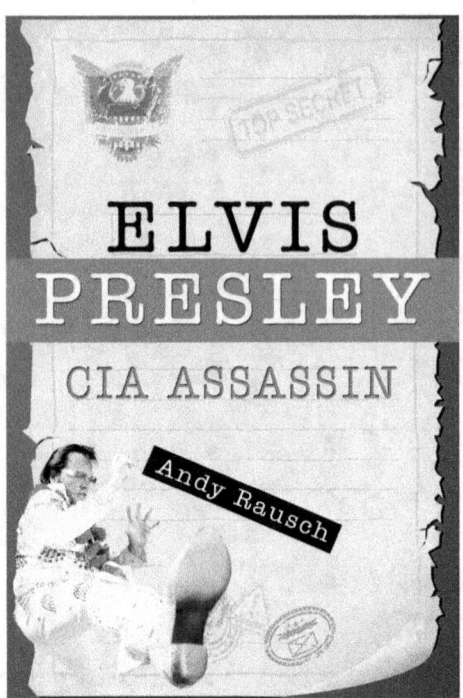

ELVIS PRESLEY, CIA ASSASSIN

"I can guarantee you. Read this book and you'll never look at Elvis the same way again!"
~ Douglas Brode, author of ELVIS CINEMA AND POPULAR CULTURE

SOON TO BE A MAJOR MOTION PICTURE

In 1970, singer Elvis Presley secretly met with President Richard Nixon. This new comedic novel imagines that Presley became a Central Intelligence Agency operative, eventually moving up through the ranks to become a skilled assassin.

Presented in an oral history fashion, the book tells us about Presley's secret transformation by the people who knew him best.

Did he fake his death in 1977? Was Presley involved with the Watergate scandal? The Iran hostage crisis? Communicating with aliens?

Read this book to find out the answers to these and many more questions.

Burning Bulb
PUBLISHING

THE TAILSMAN

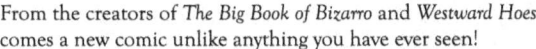

From the creators of *The Big Book of Bizarro* and *Westward Hoes* comes a new comic unlike anything you have ever seen!

He's hot on the trail, looking for some *tail...*

Sly Franko was a man of the West, a forger of the wild frontier. Like the Country Western song that would be written years after he died, the words, "Faster horses, younger women, and more money," seemed to be the anthem of this horn dog cowboy.

Franko would ride into town on a blazing saddle, find the closest saloon to wet the whistle, belly up to a good card game, and find him a hot-loving hussy to get his cowpoke on with.

However, Sly might have met his match when a visit to bathroom leads to terror and death. Can Sly and his poker buddies solve the mystery before more of the townsfolk are murdered? Find out in this exciting premier issue of *The Tailsman!*

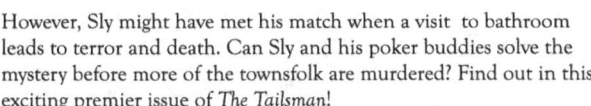

WWW.BURNINGBULBCOMICS.COM

THE HAGS OF BLACK COUNTY

by Michelle Bowser

Ruled by a committee of Hags, and fueled by toothless rivalries, Black County lurks just far enough out of the way to be completely unnoticed by the rest of civilization. Its inhabitants have been mentally warped for generations and the land itself seems to have the power to drive anyone unlucky enough to visit into ridiculous hillbilly madness. When a construction Company needs to bury a pipeline through its ludicrous hills and valleys, a twisted charm goes to work and every aspect of already bizarre Black County life takes a gory turn for the hysterical. Take a preposterous trip along with its citizens, both native and new, through escapades such as the Hag parade, the grand opening of Madame Skunk's House of Ill Repute, the demolition derby riot and the rabid, zombie clown apocalypse.

THE ABANDONED SOUL

by Daniel Sellers

After spending most of his 20s in a drug and alcohol fueled daze, a young man finally hits rock bottom. Having used up his friends and their good graces, he ends up squatting in an abandoned house. Forcibly sobering he begins to realize that he is not alone in this abandoned house. Left with one last friend and a mountain of regrets, he must decide if this presence is a guilty conscience, or a malicious hunter.

WE WISH YOU A HAPPY KILLDAY

by Jason Heroux

"We Wish You a Happy Killday" is the story of an international b eloved holiday called "Killday" where one day a year everyone over the age of fifteen is permitted to register for a license allowing them to kill one other person. But this year Chad Ovenstock doesn't feel like killing anyone. His friends and family urge him to participate in the festivities, but he can't seem to get into the holiday spirit. On the day before Killday Chad comes in contact with Ambrose, an old friend who suffered a nervous breakdown and is now part of The One Ant Army, a mysterious cult dedicated to making the future disappear. When the holiday finally arrives Chad refuses to participate and tries to survive on his own, surrounded by constant gunfire, countless corpses, and the nagging suspicion that Ambrose may have secretly brainwashed him into becoming a member of The One Ant Army cult.

Burning Bulb
PUBLISHING

www.ingramcontent.com/pod-product-compliance
Lightning Source LLC
Chambersburg PA
CBHW071123170626
46809CB00002B/482